The Somali Pirate

-3-

by
Quinn Haber
&
Noor Fayrus

ISBN: 0615669484
ISBN-13: 9780615669489
Library of Congress Control Number: 2012912694
CreateSpace, North Charleston, South Carolina

PhantaSea Books

The Somali Pirate

-3- *White Star Empire*

by
Quinn Haber
&
Noor Fayrus

For Issa

Extinction

Because of a lack of protection for Somali coastal waters, foreign fishing trawlers, using much more sophisticated but environmentally dangerous equipment such as dragnets, have found how lucrative fishing in undefended Somali waters can be. Day and night these foreign "pirate fleets" plunder the marine resources of Somali waters, which includes the Exclusive Economic Zone (EEZ) two hundred nautical miles from the shore; through the use of illegal methods including explosives and gill nets, they damage the coastline and deplete marine resources.

Today, thousands of tons of marine produce are caught illegally by fishing ships from several nations such as Japan, Taiwan, Korea, and Italy, as well as other countries.

To defend their livelihoods and their natural resources from extinction, Somalis have resorted to forceful means such as detaining fishing ships and crews, which is usually reported as Somali piracy.

Mohamed Diriye Abdullahi
Culture and Customs of Somalia (2001)

Contents

Introduction

THE FUNNY THING ABOUT SOMALIS is, while history presents them as a hotheaded people bent on clan warfare, they at the same time exhibit a strong sense of national identity and pride in their collective culture. It is precisely this patriotism, as expressed by the Somalis of today, along with their business acumen, that gives Somalia hope where otherwise there would be only a fathomless black hole.

Noor Fayrus, a young Somali of the Darod clan and pirate of extreme daring, along with his followers, the Dagger Dogs of Zayid, decided to take on the warlords, Islamic radicals, and Western-backed militias who had seized control of their country. Their agenda was bold yet simple: to reinstate a functioning government in Mogadishu and make Somalia a pirate state with a treasury based on oil revenues and ransom payments.

As Noor spearheaded the engagement from the east, leading an argosy of dhows and pirate ships towards the Mogadishu harbor, land-based regiments of the Dagger Dogs of Zayid assaulted the capital from the north, south, and west.

Noor came to fully embrace his role as the *Hoggaamiye* — a spiritual and military leader influenced by voices from *Jannah* ("Heaven"), and he was eager to work out the technical aspects of running a country. At the moment of victory, when even the UN would capitulate to Somalia as a de facto pirate state, he would be awarded a seat on the Council of Emperors, Somalia's new governing body. This much was promised him by Zayid's Assembly of Presidents, AKA the "big fish."

On the eve of the decisive battle, the assembly, which for a long time had been exploiting Noor's talents and resources to fulfill its own agenda, which increasingly suggested global domination, promoted him to commander of Ocean Assault Mogadishu (OAM). Noor's legions of armed followers — who, again, regarded him as a divined leader — provided Zayid with scores of ready-made battalions to drive the putsch on Mogadishu and install the big fish as heads of state.

Somalia, as the world's new pirate empire, would be more than African clan grandstanding that the West could neutralize with a limited military engagement, for by the eve of the *afgembi* [coup d'état], Zayid had an arsenal of nuclear warheads, plus other high-tech weaponry, such as anti-satellite rockets, that would demand Somalia's instant respect around the table of UN heavyweights. But as the chief purpose of empire is to expand and consolidate, it was unlikely Zayid would stop at Somalia's borders, especially given the fact that Somalia's old enemies, Ethiopia and Eretria, were so close at hand.

Noor had gone through intense trials and tribulations before finding his *raison d'être* as a great pirate leader and future Somali statesman. He believed, as did his many followers, that he was masterminding not only his own destiny, but also that of the Motherland. That he had gotten Zayid, AKA "the Organization," serious about taking Mogadishu lent credence to that notion.

But Zayid was an organization with far-reaching tentacles, and Noor was only one of them.

Quinn Robert Haber
Berbera, Somaliland, 2013

Prologue

THE SANDS OF TIME have fallen darkly, and there are few people that I can trust, so I entrust my final logbook to the Oracle. Will she succeed in transmitting it back to my editor? I have my doubts. A vast ocean separates me from my former life. *In sha'a Allah*, my only wish now is for my loved ones to learn of my fate.

This book is the most important of the three because it carries with it many hard-learned truths and, sadly, a message of love.

Noor Haji Fayrus
Socotra Island

J.

AFGEMBİ

War

"NOOR!" CALLED CAPTAIN AXMED from the quarterdeck, holding up a flak jacket. "Take this bulletproof vest!"

"Nay, Captain!" I replied. "I wish for my enemies to see that it is the *Hoggaamiye* who smites them!"

"Aye, Commander!" Axmed cried back, making a strong fist. "He with the white star upon his chest!"

Just then, fountains of water shot up in a line of hellfire, the last blast of ordnance hitting our mothership dead center.

"Incoming!" a pirate cried, but all too late as he was blown to high *Jannah*, his arms and legs separating from his body as he met his maker.

"Release the super-skiffs!" ordered Admiral Cosob from the mothership abreast — a freighter-class galleon called *The Madoobaad*.

The dagger dogs onboard that dark and heavy craft heaved at the capstan bars, their burly upper arms bulging out from their ammunition vests, until at last the hull portals were opened and the hidden progeny released.

Like a swarm of angry wasps, fast-attack crafts, too numerous to assess, shot out from the bilge and raced towards the offender — a navy destroyer nigh a quarter league distant. How the iron sleuth was able to sneak up on us so slyly was anyone's guess, but I reckoned it was because we'd all been so focused on the harbor ahead that we failed to see her as she breached our outer phalanx.

"Steady as she goes, men!" shouted Captain Axmed from the helm of the *Windrose* as our crew recovered from the blow. The *Windrose* was a yare and able craft, so much so that even with a fresh cannon hole in her deck, her captain regarded it as little more than a fly prick on a camel's ass. Alas, many had been murdered by the sudden attack. As we mopped their blood out through the scuppers, the gore seemed to flow without end.

"*Aaargh!*" I cried, scowling over the harrowing scene of death, then over our bow to the gates blocking the Mogadishu harbor. I was as ready as any dagger dog to ram that useless defense and get on with the business of slaughter in the name of revolution and empire. It was Somalia's common people who for all-too-long had borne the brunt of warlord tyranny, foreign imperialism, and Islamic extremism, and it was against that triage of occupiers that we would shortly do battle, banishing them forever from the Land of Punt. Our victory would be a victory for all Somalis who had silently prayed for nationhood as occupiers tore that dream asunder.

Fast-attack crafts race towards the offender

"Captain!" I shouted. "Once we ram the gates, sail for the beachhead! Our enemies will be expecting us to moor along the quay, so we'll fire upon them as we pass!"

"Aye-aye, Commander!" replied he, nudging the wide wheel towards destiny.

I shouted across the beam for *The Madoobaad* to fall back, then told them to moor along the quay once we took out the garrison there. It was crucial the black galleon abeam and its returning super-skiffs help secure the harbor for the derrière guard — that thousand-strong argosy of standard skiffs and badan dhows sailing in the wake of our motherships. This vast secondary force of pirate grunts was going to storm the beach laden with small arms, RPGs, and daggers, and would be little match for a garrison neutralized by our motherships.

When we came within four hundred meters of the gates, I proceeded to the bow and leaned five RPG stingers against the gunnels; then, when the jetty rocks could clearly be differentiated one from another, I straddled the bowsprit, placed my feet upon the lion figurehead, and lifted a loaded RPG launcher to my shoulder.

The harbor was eerily quiet as we approached. Mogadishu was at war, this much was certain by the smoke over the city and by the frequent reports of bombs in the distance. But the harbor garrison had not yet fired.

"Twenty meters... ten meters... five meters..." I counted down the distance to the barrier, then with a great grating of wood against iron, the harbor gates gave way beneath our bow.

I stood upon my ebony perch to unleash my deadly trident. "Come out, come out, wherever you are," I uttered, looking for something to blast at as we ghosted past the jetty rocks.

But naught presented itself as a viable target. Aye, never have I seen the Mogadishu harbor so quiet. The quay, with its shipping containers situated willy-nilly upon the concrete, was as bereft of human life as the garrison behind it.

"Where is everybody?" I whispered.

"Mayhap they went to fight in the city," answered R'akibum in broken Arabic. The Yemeni sailor had suddenly appeared behind me, rubbing his big black beard.

"Aye lad," I replied, "it can only be."

"*Humph!*" he fumed as he shoved his marlinspike back beneath his belt.

"What is she doing here?" I said of my sister Amina Rage. She was standing on the quarterdeck with the captain. "She should be in the sickbay."

"Beats me," R'akibum replied. "Maybe the explosion on deck brought her up."

"Is she shipshape?"

"It looks that way from here."

Pirates stood on the gunwales brandishing automatic weapons while others clung to the ratlines clenching daggers betwixt their teeth; all searched steely-eyed for signs of activity along the docks and beach.

"This'll be a fair point easier than a cargo delivery," the portly Yemeni laughed. "We're going to sail right up to shore and offload the brigades."

The beach was nigh 100 meters afore, while astern, *The Madoobaad* was gliding past the broken gates, and in her shadow sailed the first dhows of the war argosy.

The Madoobaad

"I don't like this," I replied with snarled lip, "I don't like this one bit. It's too easy, too suspicious. Make way, good Yemeni. I'm going to speak with the captain."

R'akibum stepped aside so that I could round his barreled chest.

"Ahoy thar, Cap'n!" I cried aloft, approaching the quarterdeck.

He craned his neck alow, and as he did, a missile flared past where his head had just been; only by looking down to see me was he spared his noggin.

Boom! Boom! Boom! sounded artillery in the ambush, incoming munitions striking our gunnels and blasting men to shreds.

"Irons astarboard!" commanded the hale captain. "Fire upon the containers!"

Astarboard the *Windrose*, forty-five mounted guns and scores of modern muskets manned by black pirates lowered upon the containers lining the quay, then opened fire in a hellacious chorus of retaliation that blasted to hell the tanks and artillery hiding within the steel box structures. As the makeshift pillboxes were reduced to burning shards, wounded infidels crawled from the fiery hovels and splayed out dead upon the pavement.

A bitter engagement played out for a few hours thereafter, the *Windrose* sustaining more devastating blows as tanks and technicals kept rolling out from behind the garrison compound.

It was the assistance of *The Madoobaad* that helped us gain the edge. With Admiral Cosob at the helm, he took her about and freed the sights of her quadruple stern chasers. How those heavy irons made mincemeat of our mechanized opponents! Cosob's cannons unleashed one half-ton shell after the next upon the beleaguered encampment, until at last, bombarded to shit and utterly demoralized, they raised a white turban, surrendering.

"Oh, Captain!" cried Amina, throwing herself upon him. "You've breached the harbor phalanx!"

"That we have, Miss Rage," said he, lifting her off her feet and giving her a kiss. But when he let her back down, she collapsed.

"*Dhakhtar Nasir!*" the captain cried across the beam, then crouched low beside Amina.

The wiry Yemeni physician emerged from a companion ladder moments later. He looked my sister over for bullet wounds, and not finding any, he performed an auscultation.

"Is she breathing?" I asked.

"A heartbeat?" the captain inquired anxiously.

She suddenly awoke, slurring her speech and reaching for the captain. He took her outstretched hand.

She sat up, then tried to stand.

"No, no…" urged the doctor. "You must rest."

"I require that she be taken—" the captain began, but a bullet struck his head midsentence. He hit the floorboards like a tinman that'd been switched off, a brief shot of blood spouting from the side of his head.

"Captain?" Amina said, crawling over to him. Blood pooled around her knees and stained her white corset. She lifted his head into her lap and tried to force open his eyelids. "Axmed?"

The captain wasn't coming back. He was dead.

My sister began breathing heavily. She rocked back and forth with the lifeless captain's head cradled against her breast.

"Come, *harbarwadaag*," I said to my sister from the same mother, gently squeezing her shoulder. "He died a gallant death and is with Allah now. We must get you to safety."

She looked up, wasted and enraged. Tears streaked over her gaunt cheeks while her eyes were bloodshot and red.

"Come, *walaal*," I supplicated. "*Dhakhtar* will take you—"

"Who did this?" she asked calmly, resting Axmed's head gently back down on the floorboards.

"Amina..." I reproached endearingly.

"Who did this!" she shrieked, then rose to her feet and slogged like a blood-soaked zombie to the gunwales. "Who killed my captain!" she cried across the beam.

"He did," said Quartermaster Cabdulqaadir, coming beside her. He pointed to a man hiding behind a pile of food aid stacked upon the quay. The sniper was attempting to reload his rifle over the barrier of stuffed bags.

Amina snatched Cabdulqaadir's dagger from his scabbard, then with a great wail like a screeching cat, she grabbed a block of deadeyes and flung herself over the gap betwixt the ship and dock.

"No, Amina!" I screamed, but she'd already let go of the pulley and was freefalling from some twenty feet up.

When she hit the dock, she went down instantly and appeared to have broken an ankle, for only with great difficulty was she able to get up and walk again. Holding the dagger at her side, she limped forward in her bloodied dress like some crazed, cheated bride hell-bent on revenge.

The man reloading his gun kept a sharp eye on her as she approached. He seemed to have jammed his breech lock. He called in the direction of some barrels stacked nearby.

Two RPG-wielding commandos emerged from behind the petrol drums.

"Amina, get down!" I yelled, raising my RPG and taking aim at the sudden gunmen. The shoulder-mounted cannon kicked hard back against my shoulder as the projectile left its cylinder.

The rocket flew clear over the gunmen, exploding behind the barrels.

I looked over to Umulkheyr, ship's carpenter. He just shook his head.

Alas, the two bastards below let fly their own rocket-propelled grenades, aiming at my sister.

She quickly ducked left twice, evading the missiles as she continued unflinchingly towards the sniper who'd killed her lover.

The two commandos proceeded to reload their shoulder-mounted cannon.

I reached down for my TT-30 pistol, which was held fast to my thigh by means of a black leather holster. When I lifted the pistol before me, a white glow emanated from the breech cracks, for inside was a bullet of *Jannah*, given to me by Captain Shar'ma'arke. Shar'ma'arke was a huge Sudanese man who'd commanded the *Qadan* — the first mothership I'd ever crewed aboard. He'd told me the bullet could stop anything. I took aim at the infidels.

"You should save that, Haji," warned Cabdulqaadir.

I hesitated.

Amina was almost to the sniper, who was still struggling to fix his rifle, while the gunmen behind her were already taking aim.

"Fire, *axmaq*!" I shouted to the pirates along the ratlines and beam, calling them *fools*.

A flurry of machinegun and small arms fire exploded around me.

The quartermaster procured an old pistol, steadied it upon the gunnels, then together with my mates made Swiss cheese of the RPG-wielding infidels.

As for the sniper, he would've been better off running, for Amina was presently skinning him alive with Cabdulqaadir's dagger.

Afore and aft, Wadani Clan skiffs were docking and their pirates were storming the quay, while abeam, fresh commandos were racing forth on technicals to combat them.

In the heat of the fray, four Wadanis hauled the *Windrose* into berth, while *The Madoobaad*, still unblemished, motored into dock afore.

Scores of corsairs spilled from the ships to the quay to make battle with the infidel pigs defending the capital. Resilience increased, but so did our putsch, and we soon drove the enemy back and commandeered some of their mounted-machine-gun trucks.

I glanced aport and saw the argosy of dhows making the beachhead, where like ants in a frenzy, buccaneers by the thousands jumped onto the hot sands and raced on foot towards the city center.

"Amina!" cried Cabdulqaadir.

My sister had fallen over the stack of food aid where she had skinned the captain's killer.

"Qarshe! R'akibum!" I called the trusted cannonmaster and Yemeni deckhand. "Make fast your weapons and follow me!"

We alighted from the *Windrose* carrying machineguns.

"Looks like she's finished," said R'akibum. He was looking back at the *Windrose*, which had sustained heavy damage.

As for Amina, when we finally got to her, she carried a ghostly pallor upon her gaunt cheeks, while the sniper she'd skinned had no face left to speak of, for she had cut it off with her dagger — even his eyes had been plucked from their sockets. "I got the motherfucker," she mumbled deliriously.

"Good job," I told her, pushing her dreadlocks clear of her face.

"Aye me lass," remarked burly gunner Qarshe, her onetime sparring partner. "Ye led the charge to land. No man shall ever forget that."

"Haji was supposed to take point," she said.

"The sea-dogs would've rushed ashore anyway," ruminated R'akibum, rubbing his beard.

"Is she all right?" said Cosob, armed with an AK-47 as he came over from his ship.

"Ahoy, lad!" I replied. "She's done a great thing here, but we must get her back to the sickbay. She's not well."

"Your star, matey!" he said with a start, gawking at the tattoo glinting o'er my heart. "And your hands! *Allahu Akbar*! I knew it was true! The powers of *Jannah* side with us!"

Cosob then bent down and touched my sister's forehead. "Bring her aboard *The Madoobaad*," he instructed. "We've a good physician onboard."

"I, I—" Amina stuttered.

"I'm sorry about Captain Axmed," Cosob consoled, taking her by the hand.

Her tears flowed unchecked. She turned away.

"I'll help you back," Qarshe said.

A technical truck suddenly whipped around a burning container. We took cover behind the stack of food aid and trained our weapons on the vehicle.

"Noor!" called the Wadani pirate Marwo Mohamoud from behind the wheel as he brought the vehicle to a screeching halt, the dagger dogs on the flatbed barely able to hold on. "The fight is on, Commander!"

"*Hoggaamiye*! *Hoggaamiye*!" grunted his Wadani pirate passengers, gesturing for me to hop on back.

"*Haa*!" I affirmed, then turned to Qarshe and said, "See to my sister's care aboard *The Madoobaad*."

"Aye, Commander," said he, lifting her upon his great shoulders and marching towards the ominous black galleon.

"*Haji...*" my sister called tiredly back.

"Don't worry, *walaal*! I'll return for you!"

"Take this," she said, tossing me a woven cloth.

My father's monogrammed initials were woven among the folds. It was his turban.

"Wear it," she urged softly, rallying what energy she had left. "It will protect you."

"*Haa walaal!*" I shot back, tying it around my head.

Cosob, R'akibum, and I rushed over to the technical and joined the pirates on back, then Marwo slung the rig into gear and raced towards the presidential palace, stopping occasionally to pick up more warriors of the allied pirate clans. There must've been a dozen pirates on that flatbed representing four or five different hijacking bands, Cosob and I representing the old Khatar Force 1 expeditionary squadron.

Marwo was blasting Radio Mogadishu from the cab. The newscaster announced a ten-thousand-dollar reward on my head, dead or alive.

"Is that all you're worth?" chuckled Cosob.

"That's probably all they can afford," I laughed. "Obviously, the infidels have taken over the radio station. We'll have to get control of the local media ASAP. The propaganda war is just as important as the military engagement. We must win the support of the public."

"*Haa*, Commander, ASAP," Cosob agreed.

We rounded a corner and into heavy fire that immediately blew out our front tires.

Our technical gunman kept our cover with a flurry of heavy rounds.

"Everyone off!" I ordered. "Split into teams of three and rendezvous at the presidential palace. Comb the streets for infidels. Take no prisoners."

Marwo slipped out of the cab and tore off his shirt, telling me to wear it. "Radio Mogadishu mentioned your white star. As is, you're too much of a target."

"As you wish, *jaalle*," I conceded to my comrade, pulling his faded black T-shirt over my head and turban.

As our technical gunner kept firing off rounds, I shouted for Marwo, Cosob, and R'akibum to follow me, then led them down a street to my left.

"Split up into teams of three!" Noor ordered.

The Somali Pirate 3 – White Star Empire

En route to the Bakara Market, Somali pirates were everywhere battling the infidels — those African Union soldiers and their Western "specialist" counterparts assisting them in the capital's defense. These latter we called "black hearts," and they were no more than white mercenary dogs who kept meddling with Somalia's internal affairs under one shitty Western mandate or another. At one directive they'd supply a tyrannical ruler named Siad Barre with arms so he could massacre northern Somali civilians, and at the next directive they'd march into Mogadishu under Operation Restore Hope to counter warlord General Aidid and turn Mogadishu to Swiss cheese in the process, killing thousands of emaciated Somali combatants before pulling up stakes. No wonder so few Somalis trusted white men in our country. They were either carving us up into colonies and making us slaves, as during the British/Italian/French *ascendo* plantations of the imperial days, or they were sending their deadly navies into our seas, claiming black pirates were a scourge to the world that must be stopped by any means necessary while shrewdly omitting the part about Western and Asian interests dumping toxic wastes and fishing illegally in Somalia's nearshore Exclusive Economic Zone (EEZ) for decades.

If only Western interests would stop meddling! As Western journalist Michael Maren so perspicaciously wrote in his article "Progress in Somalia is Endangered by Foreign Presence," which he penned after spending many years in my homeland: "The progress that has been made in Somalia is substantial. Somalis themselves posses most of the resources they need to rebuild their country. Sometimes this is difficult for Westerners to accept. We want to believe they need us. The truth is that they don't. Without foreign intervention, Somalis will rebuild their economy. Then they will rebuild their political systems."

In our present (December 15, 2011) assault on the capital, al-Shabaab was conspicuously absent, but the black-heart mercenaries were everywhere to be seen. In their usual crafty style, they were sending black AU peacekeepers into the streets to man the frontlines while they stood on rooftops or whizzed by in their V-bottomed tanks, picking pirates off from fortified positions.

I did catch one white dog on ground level, hiding behind a corner and popping off unsuspecting Wadani pirates with a machinegun.

I pointed at my eyes, then into an alleyway, instructing my team of three to watch my back as I went to ambush the infidel pig from behind.

As I moved through the alleyway, sandal-clad Somali fighters dashed by in the opposite direction. I continued cautiously forward, keeping close against the buildings, my unit darting from alcove to alcove behind me. Smoke and the rattle of gunfire filled the way ahead, while a whirlybird could be heard circling above. Whether it was Battery B Hussein was anyone's guess.

Black-heart merc on ground level

Suddenly, there was a great exchange of machine-gun fire punctuated by two explosions: *Fzuui*-Boom! *Fzuui*-Boom!

By the sound of the ordnance, I knew it was incoming airborne artillery either of the RPG variety or fast and furious helo rockets. Whatever the case, the sudden blitzkrieg drew my rifle sight intermittently between the streets and skies in that up-and-down confusion begot by modern urban combat.

A swarm of gunmen took shape in the smoke ahead.

"Take cover!" I ordered my unit under my breath, signaling them back in their alcoves.

I hid behind the doorway of a shell-shocked building as the battalions came forth from the haze, their guns pointing every which way as they limped and crawled through the alleyway.

Alas, it was my pirate brethren who were crawling forth from the dust. "*Allahu jixinjix*," I sighed, my rifle going slack beside me as I watched them collapse one after the next against the buildings, creating a virtual sidewalk of bloodied, mangled bodies. The corsair casualties fell without cease until at last a black pirate reached out a charred, trembling hand, saying with a final death rattle: "Tanks."

Then I heard it, and no sooner than I heard the grinding of gears did I look up to see a panzer division rumbling through the mist. One, two, three mechanized monsters moved along their traction belts and over a wall they'd just blown down, taking out scores of Somali fighters in the process. Black-hearted foot soldiers soon followed. Sporting helmets of steel, they marched like robots beside their iron-monster masters.

"Haji!" Cosob called ahead.

"*Sshh!*" I waved him back, keeping a sharp eye on the panzer division as they crossed the alleyway.

Mangled pirates were still moaning, for not all were dead. Once the mechanized unit cleared, I ordered my unit to attend to the injured, saying, "Take who you can back to *The Madoobaad*."

"Aye," Cosob said, relaying the command to R'akibum and Marwo. "We've a good physician there."

"You too, Cosob," I said.

"But Haji?" He was looking at me in disbelief.

Beside the iron monsters marched black-hearted foot soldiers

"I would do the same for you, if you were down. Take the casualties back to the mothership, then proceed to the presidential palace, and I'll meet you there. This quarter is much too dangerous. We don't stand a chance against the panzer division here."

"What about you?"

"I'm going to take out that sniper."

"Alone?"

"*In sha'a Allah,*" I prayed, "with my bullet of *Jannah.*"

"No, Haji," reproached Cosob, shaking his head. "We—"

"Belay! I have my smart phone. At oh-twelve-hundred we'll touch bases. Now go!"

I hurdled over the bodies in the street before he could respond, then proceeded furtively over the tank tracks.

LESS THAN HUMAN

NAUSEA AND VOMITING GRIPPED ME from the very core. I stumbled against the wall, my machinegun dangling beside me as I puked my guts out into the dirt street. I checked my vomit; it was black.

Seeing Somali pirates die made me sick to my stomach. It's a reaction I'd had, and one that'd been getting stronger, ever since I'd returned to Somalia and saw scores of fellow Darod pirates killed. By birth and heritage, I was of the Darod clan, and a part of me always died alongside them when I saw them gunned down. But the remorse I carried went far beyond that...

Be it Darod, Hawiye, Isaaq, or Dir, in my eyes, when Somali blood spilled, it spilled beyond clan lines. Even though I wasn't as devout a Muslim as some of my Sunni brethren, who comprised ninety percent of my countrymen, I still believed, like them, that humans were equal before Allah. I may have gotten this from my wife Issa, who hailed from the Rahanweyn clan.

I'd married Issa not to strengthen our clan ties, for the Rahanweyn were from a group of people in the south called the Sab who traditionally stood opposed to us Darods of the north, and I certainly didn't marry her because she was a devout Muslim who'd been living at a neighboring mosque in Puntland under the protection of a cleric named Imam Abdullahi — Allah knows I had enough demons to deal with then without needing to invite their pious scrutiny of my libertine ways. Nay, I married Issa because regardless of who she was, whatever her clan, background, beliefs, or wherever she came from, the truth was that I cared about her, plain and simple. I saw her plight in the barren light of day, unfiltered by social mores and clan affiliations. I saw a human being just like me — a Somali, black, troubled, sometimes hungry, never free. I saw it with such immediacy that my thoughts, preconceptions, and personal history that dictated how I was supposed to act and think were never given a mite of headway. *I saw Issa with my heart,* and I sensed that's how she also saw me.

Some people thought that Somalis, and especially Somali pirates, had "nothing to lose," and that's why we behaved the way we did — but nothing could've been further from the truth.

When I'd first met Issa, she was like most Somalis and Somali pirates — she had nothing left but her very life, everything else having been stripped away by hardships and plight. Our layers of creature comforts gone, the world hell-bent on our quick demise, as Somalis we had the ultimate to lose, i.e., life. This was a far cry from "nothing to lose." Life was all we had left — it was everything.

Westerners may have had difficulty understanding this, but that is why Somalis fought. It was survival, we had no choice, not unless you'd expect us to just lie down and die. I know that many Westerners in their callous arrogance wished just that upon Somali pirates, that we would just relinquish the fight, roll over, and die so that their dirty First World deeds in our ancestral fishing grounds could continue unchecked. But if there was one thing about Somali pirates, if to the rest of the world we were nothing more than dagger-wielding dogs, we were dogs that would not die. Throw us a bone in the form of a ship, and we went after it to survive. Remember the old adage: *a dog that refuses a bone is not alive.*

Life is *all* we had left, and when you're backed against the wall, when you're young, hungry, and angry, no matter how skinny from lack of food, you will respond like a trapped lion whose cage momentarily opens. You will run, you will lash out, and you will pounce on the first thing that tries to enslave you again.

In their self-righteousness, the civilized world grew fond of saying things like "those feral Somali pirate gangs are a scourge that should be bombed out of existence," but now you know why we did what we did: the "civilized world" had trapped us in a corner by centuries of their colonial oppression, militaristic meddling, and more recently, by using our shores as their closet prostitute from which to constantly rape our ecosystem, steal our fish sustenance, and leave us and our grandchildren for dead by unloading millions of tons of their toxic wastes on our sands — all for filthy lucre, mateys, *all for filthy lucre.* No Somali, no matter how heartless, could ever have dreamed up such a diabolical story of genocide by contamination and poaching — yet it had been going on in our country, in reality, for a very long time. As Somalis, we were the targets, aye — *we were the victims* that nobody around the great UN table of "human justice polity" ever whispered a word about.

Somalis, living in arid lands, having few material possessions and falling victim to sundry wars and tragic circumstances, knew what it meant to live on the edge. "The horror," I reminded myself time and time again, "the horror."

How many more slaughtered Somali pirates would be pushed into open pits like our starving children were after dying from disease and malnourishment? As depressing as it was, I did what the rest of my countrymen did: I put one foot before the other, kept walking, kept fighting for survival, never giving up until Allah's faceless equerries came to take me unto *Jannah*.

With eyes emitting blinding white light, the majestic saints of Allah would come, riding upon golden winged horses to take me like they took all Somalis departing prison Earth. Wearing glinting silver armor, they rear their immaculate horses before you, then reach down with gleaming steel gloves and take you upon their laps. With a storming of equine wings and a thundering of hooves, the immortal horsemen will carry you into the sky, delivering you unto a great gilded chariot with many empty seats for final transfer up to *Jannah*.

I know such things because during a near-death experience I'd had off the Socotra archipelago, Allah's equerries came for me. In the end, I was released back to Earth to finish my mission, which, *Allahu Akbar!* was finally coming to pass with Zayid's great assault on the capital.

If tomorrow never came, Somalis would fight for today — this much was certain. We would keep going for as long as we could, right to the bitter end. This in essence was the mantra of every Somali, and if there were ever a more life-embracing and death-defying people, I'd yet to meet them.

If Somali pirates were mere dagger-clawed dogs to the rest of the world, to many of my fellow countrymen we were heroes. We embraced life and not death. The international community had forced death upon us by stealing our food and poisoning our land, so we did what any courageous and life-affirming peoples would do: we fought back.

As a Somali pirate, I did what I could and I did it fast. The task before me now, as I darted through the streets of Mog, was *finding that black-hearted sniper and taking him out!*

I rounded the corner to see the panzer division smashing down more barriers on its relentless plow through the old quarter.

In the dusty aftermath of limestone walls grinding beneath heavy tanks, I skirted down the street adjacent the alley where scores of my comrades had met their untimely deaths.

'Twas not long before I spotted the black-hearted sniper hiding behind his corner as he picked off Somali pirates one by one. Realizing he could be firing upon Cosob and the extraction team, I moved fast to neutralize him. Dashing between crumbling doorways and blasted-out walls, I closed in on my target.

The black heart stopped shooting for a moment, retracting back around his corner.

I ducked into an alcove for cover.

He dropped his magazine clip, then reached for another.

"Fucker," I said evenly in English as I stepped out from behind my barrier.

He jammed his clip into his rifle and whipped around, but all-too-late, for I took him out with one clean shot to the chest.

Humans may have been equal in Allah's eyes, but those mercs were less than human. I watched the pig fall, his blood mixing with the dirt street, fertilizing the soil of the coming empire.

CALLING ALL *WARANLE*

I TURNED ON MY SMART PHONE. There were forty-nine voicemails and hundreds of texts. I called Cosob, but there was no answer.

A call came down via Zayid's G-6 direct satellite network reading "blocked."

"*Hayye?*" I answered *hello* in Somali.

"Noor, it's Bashir. What happened?"

"We were ambushed near the Bakara Market by a panzer division and sustained heavy casualties. Some have been taken back to *The Madoobaad*."

"How many *waranle* are with you now?"

"Warriors?"

"*Haa.*"

"None. I'm alone."

"I see you are still three clicks from the presidential palace. *Deg-deg*, Haji! Hurry it up! We have specialists there and many pirates, but the African Union is putting up fierce resistance. We need your backup. Use your bullet of *Jannah* if necessary."

"What about al-Shabaab? I haven't spotted any yet. Are our southern forces holding them back?"

"Al-Shabaab withdrew from Mogadishu on August sixth."

"Are you serious? And we know this only now?"

"We had poor intel, *jaalle*."

"What about the airport? Who controls that?"

"TFG forces, but they're losing ground. They've been using mustard gas, so we've sent in our chemical warfare unit. Our men in masks have already succeeded in breaking their supply train. They've found the enemy's cache of chemical weapons and are burning it as I speak."

Destroying the cache of chemical weapons

Just then, shots rang out through the alleyway behind me. I turned to see a white man being gunned down, followed by a cry of *Allahu Akbar!* from some unknown direction. That black heart had been sneaking up on me fast. Had one of my brethren not been on him, he probably would've taken me out.

"Haji? What's going on out there?"

"This place is crawling with AU mercs, Commander! Proceeding to Villa Somalia now. Out."

"*Deg-deg,* and watch your back."

I started running but got sick again, vomiting into the street. I wiped my lips, and black spew marked the back of my hand. My illness was still with me. *"We'el!"* I cursed, *bastard!*

○~○

Progressing towards Villa Somalia, where the presidential palace was located, I turned off my smart phone because incoming calls and texts were proving too much of a distraction. Even on vibe mode, my concentration was thrown off by the constant buzzing.

The streets were thickening with bands of pirates trying to battle enemy forces positioned on rooftops and defending against commandos who were employing down-and-dirty, hit-and-run tactics. The AU forces had learned the city well, their single fighter mercs proving the most lethal as they crept around corners to blast any number of unsuspecting *waranle*.

But that being said, black-hearted snipers on high were increasingly falling to their deaths — taken out by Somalis, or perhaps by guardian angels watching our backs.

Suddenly, a Black Hawk rose from behind a building and started firing rockets and machineguns down into the street.

I darted along a limestone wall, incoming munitions blasting it to shit behind me. I dashed by a Somali warrior who was getting to a knee and aiming his RPG at the airborne nemesis, only to be strafed with bullets before he could get the shot off.

The helo continued over my head, so I doubled back and wrested the RPG from the dead pirate's hands.

The whirlybird became the target of scores of *waranle* firing Kalashnikovs and AK-47s, so it climbed for safety, but not before I eyed its trajectory with my newly acquired weapon.

I pulled the trigger, and a rocket-propelled grenade launched from my shoulder-mounted cannon, streaking with a straight smoke trail along the line I'd sighted. The unsuspecting whirlybird flew right into its path, the RPG exploding out its tail and fouling its flight systems. As malfunctioning missiles misfired from her undercarriage, she went into an uncontrollable spin, falling towards the south.

The pirates on the ground ballyhooed at my shot, then all went running in the direction the Black Hawk was going down.

Reeling from my near-perfect takedown, I got caught up in the excitement and ran behind the gang of dagger dogs towards the crash site.

The chopper had vaulted into the Hodan Quarter, smashing into the Mogadishu cinema with a thunderous report. The old theatre was decimated, the helo itself becoming a roaring fireball lodged into the roof. A burning black heart forced open the hull door and tumbled from the fiery wreckage with an infernal scream.

A number of young Somali combatants went running to where he'd fallen, saying, "We'll feast on his cooked flesh!"

If cannibalism occurred, it wouldn't have surprised me, given the ferociousness of spirit a sudden victory could beget in a long-oppressed Somali. But I would never find out directly, for I came to my senses then, realizing this was not my quarter to hold. I made my way with all due haste back towards the presidential palace.

THE HEADLESS SAINT

IN THE HEART of the old Italian quarter stood the Mogadishu Cathedral, built in 1960. It was one of the last remaining superstructures from the colonial era still standing in the city, and it was the last edifice between the presidential palace and me.

Suddenly, two Task Force F-35 fighter jets dropped bombs to my left, so I ran towards the cathedral's flying buttresses, seeking shelter within the gutted apse.

Once again, as if a guardian angel had my back, I was spared a sniper's deadly shot, for a black heart hiding atop a flying buttress fell dead beside me. A bullet had entered the back of his head and escaped out the front, blowing his face off.

"*Allahu jixinjix*," I prayed, then proceeded over a pile of rubble and into the nave.

All along the gothic columns demarking the Hall of Miracles, Somali refugees beheld the skies with dread, searching for enemy jets. Islamic tribunals had blown off the cathedral's ceiling in 2006.

I made my way past the transept, coming before a marble saint named François whose head was missing.

The refugees were murmuring about me, so I turned and bore my glowing star, saying, "Be brave, fellow countrymen, and take up arms if you can. Fight the infidel occupiers, for a new empire is at hand."

I leapt into the street and ran towards Villa Somalia, but a Task Force jet swooped down without warning, training its rockets on the cathedral behind me.

"*Maya*," I uttered, "*no!*" Then my heart leapt a beat stronger, for Battery B came swooping down before the church to defend it.

Battery B defends the refugee encampment

As the F-35 unleashed a trident upon the old cathedral, Battery B responded with Gatling cannons, taking out the missile mid-flight before turning his revolving guns on the jet fighter, breaching its cockpit and perhaps killing the pilot, for the $100-million craft immediately spun sideways and crashed into the street, its fiery debris just missing the cathedral.

"*Allahu Akbar!*" I cried, raising high my carbine as Battery B hovered before me.

At the sound of more fighter planes in the vicinity, B flashed two thumbs-up, then took his SuperCobra low through the city.

RED SANDS

THE PUTSCH HAD REACHED the presidential palace. My pirate brethren and I, along with scores of common Mogadishu residents joining the revolution, created a virtual phalanx around the old Italian edifice, with many *waranle* aiming behind us to ward off sporadic attacks from returning enemy forces. Before us, an AU garrison held the building like a medieval fortress, taking potshots at us from behind columns and blast craters in the walls.

We could've unleashed a hail of rocket-propelled grenades upon the compound, doing away with its occupiers in seconds, but the idea was to keep the palace intact, for a convoy of high-ranking Zayid officials was standing by to consummate the coup by summarily moving in. All dagger dogs were instructed not to shoot anything but bullets upon the edifice, and all were obeying their orders.

We were in the process of assembling a team of specialists to storm the compound by force when bad news arrived on our smart phones almost simultaneously. A convoy of Zayid diplomats was under attack on the northern outskirts of the city where they'd parked in waiting. They were hunkered down in their trucks behind the red sand dunes there, protected by a virtual wagon circle of technicals but desperately needing backup. Some dagger dogs assailing the palace also received texts bespeaking a pending mustard gas attack upon the convoy, sharply raising the urgency level. I called Bashir.

"Noor, I've been trying to reach you," said the commander of Cent-com Puntland. "The convoy of political elites is under siege."

"In the red sands, *haa*. What about the chemical attack?"

"The enemy forces have been launching mustard gas into the convoy. The big fish have taken shelter inside the lorries, but won't be able to hold out for much longer. Take a technical and some experienced fighters to the northern checkpoint at once. Our chemical warfare unit is already there, waiting for you to lead the counterattack. This directive is of the upmost urgency. Should the Assembly of Presidents be wiped out, our

Empire will be DOA. Get in and get them out of there now! Do you copy?"

"Aye-aye, Commander. Copy that. I'm on my way."

"And Noor?"

"*Maxaa?*"

"This time I want a prompt update!"

"*Haa.*"

I switched off my phone and gathered the requisite men. Among them were Petty Officer First Class Mohamed Good and Second Mate Jama Qays, whom I'd spotted along the phalanx. Finding a technical was not difficult, for Zayid already had a dozen or more surrounding the presidential palace. As commander of Ocean Assault Mogadishu, and more so as the *Hoggaamiye*, all manner of vehicles, weapons, and men were at my immediate disposal. As we drove off, four or five more *waranle* hopped onto the back of the technical.

At the northern checkpoint, we were briefed on the situation, and eleven of us were issued chemical warfare suits and gas masks, the impermeable fatigues having recently been removed from Zayid troop casualties. Some suits were stained with blood and had bulletholes patched with duct tape. But these were the only suits left on hand. The checkpoint field commander, a certain Omar Aw Mahdi, vowed they would protect us from poisonous gas.

Noor in a chemical warfare suit

"Our cavalcade of technicals has been neutralized," Omar said, "and the enemy has used mustard gas to wipe out the troops protecting the Assembly of Presidents."

"What else do they have?" I asked.

"The infidels have few other defenses aside from small arms and mustard gas, if that's what you're asking. They number about twenty-five and appear to be working under the command of an overlord, who has set up camp in the center of the lorry circle. We tried to free the big fish but were ambushed from behind when the enemy shot at us from the dunes. With our numbers down to six, we had no choice but to retreat to the checkpoint and wait for backup."

"Can the big fish hunkered down in the lorries survive the mustard gas?"

"I think so, *haa*, but you must hurry. Either the chemical overlord will take them prisoner or execute them — if he hasn't already done so. For now, we must assume they're still secure in the back of the trucks. Rumor has it that your uncle's lorry is bulletproof. Is this true?"

"Osman is here?"

"He was part of the convoy."

"Is he alive?"

"*Ma ogi,*" replied Omar Aw Mahdi, *I don't know.*

"*Waranle!*" I gathered my troops. "We're going in on the technical with RPGs and machineguns. Take caution not to hit the lorries! If you accidentally kill any of the assembly locked inside, you'll go before the *Safaarad.* The enemy has mustard gas and small arms.

Driver! Take us over the dunes to the chemical over-lord. I'll take him out with the big gun."

The driver squeezed behind the wheel in his chemi-cal warfare fatigues, another *waranle* sat shotgun, while the rest of us climbed onto the back and assumed our positions. I grabbed the handles of the massive mounted machinegun, which was bolted to the flatbed, then the driver hurtled towards the dunes, a cloud of dust whip-ping up in our tracks.

We zoomed between two dunes, then directly up a tall one, blasting over the top with sand pouring from our wheel wells.

The overlord stood up amid his lorry encampment.

I opened up on him with my burly armament.

The toxic overlord moved not a millimeter, remain-ing stolid in his camouflage fatigues and gas mask. He was a huge figure, but not one of my bullets made con-tact, for the technical was jouncing something fierce down the sand dune, throwing off my aim.

We spun to a halt at the base of the dune, and all the dagger dogs jumped from the truck, firing upon enemy combatants as they fled for cover in the lorry circle.

"Don't hit the trucks!" I reminded my comrades, but shouting from behind a gas mask was like scream-ing into the crack of a camel's ass, and I doubt if anyone heard me.

Mohamed Good got to a knee inside the clearing and lifted his RPG launcher to his shoulder, training it on the toxic overlord.

"Don't shoot!" I cried, for that huge man stood before a much larger lorry.

Alas, the projectile got off.

The overlord simply cocked his head to dodge the missile. It proceeded to stream into the lorry hold behind him, exploding with a blast of thunder.

A cacophony of screams sounded from the hold, and seconds later, the rear door lifted and numerous men in business suits spilled out, some with their backs on fire. As the assembly elites rolled over the sand, trying to extinguish their burning clothes, the overlord emitted a boorish laugh, then reached for a green canister. He yanked a lever from the side of the can before tossing it at the smoldering politicians.

Thick yellow gas began issuing from the can. The assemblymen coughed and wheezed, covering their mouths and shutting their eyes.

I dashed by the lord of chemicals, who moved not an inch as I passed, then dove into the toxic cloud to help the downed assemblymen.

Mohamed Good was already there, along with another dagger dog in a gas mask. We struggled to drag the big fish clear of the toxic cloud. Between the three of us, we saved but four assemblymen, pushing them into the truck's cab and shutting the doors behind them. We didn't have time to save anyone else.

Bullets shattered the sideview mirror over my head, so I led my unit behind the truck to mount another offensive, and soon we were returning fire against the overlord's gas-masked combatants, who kept darting this way and that through the noxious cloud, taking potshots at pirates and assemblymen.

All at once, I grew very ill and had to vomit. I removed my gas mask and retched into the sand, then inhaled mustard gas.

"Keep your mask on!" one of my comrades said, pushing it back over my face and tightening the straps.

I struggled to breathe against the asphyxiation wrought by the mustard gas; it felt as if I were being strangled to death. I dropped my AK-47 and stumbled alongside the truck, then fell to my knees and grasped my neck.

A shadow loomed through the yellow mist before me, becoming the toxic overlord, stepping forth from the noxious cloud with swirls of poison gas lifting off his shoulders and back. He sauntered before me, all calm-like with his hands held snugly in his coat pockets.

I felt for my TT-30 pistol beneath my chemical warfare suit; it was still there, holstered to my thigh.

The toxic overlord

As I gasped for air, the toxic overlord stepped onto my neck and emitted a boorish laugh. He applied more pressure, blocking my windpipe and silencing my breath, his own heavy breathing sounding ever louder through his large gas mask.

On the verge of blacking out, I ripped the nylon fabric away from my thigh and wrested my pistol from beneath the protective garment.

The overlord immediately kicked it out of my hand, which enabled me to breathe as he lifted his foot. As I struggled to get up, he reached down and grabbed the gun, its bullet of *Jannah* gleaming through the breech cracks, then he stepped on my chest and pointed the barrel at my face. "*Uh hu hu!*" laughed the giant as he cocked the trigger back.

I closed my eyes and heard a shot go off.

WAXAAD LEEDAHAY XUMMAD

BRIGHT LIGHT, SHADOWS, then voices.

"*Haji, maxay tahay mushkiladu?*" Bashir asked, *how do you feel?*

"*Dawakhaad baan dareemayaa,*" I responded, *I feel dizzy.* "Where am I?"

"At our Garoowe treatment center."

"What happened?"

"You were exposed to mustard gas and passed out."

"What about the overlord?"

"*Kuma?*" Bashir asked, *who?*

"I took care of him," said Cosob, stepping before the cot upon which I lay.

"You were there?" I inquired.

"Admiral Cosob was with you all along," Bashir replied, "albeit always out of sight. When you decided to go rogue in Mog, I had him follow you for your own protection. I think that Cosob here saved your life on more than one occasion."

Quinn Robert Haber & Noor Haji Fayrus

I thought about it for a minute. "So you're the one who was spotting me in Mog?" I put to my old comrade. "You're the one who was taking out the snipers around me?"

"Yes, Haji," replied not Cosob, but Bashir. "And he also hopped aboard the technical when you zoomed to the northern checkpoint. His face was wrapped in a turban, so you didn't even know it was him when he changed into a gas mask and shadowed you at the lorry corral."

"He killed the overlord, Haji," remarked my uncle Osman, coming to my other side, "and saved our lives."

"Osman!" I said with surprise, then wheezed. My throat felt sore and constricted.

"At ease, Commander," said Admiral Cosob, touching my leg. "You need to rest."

"*Waad mahadsantahay, saaxiib.*" I told him that I was very grateful.

"This belongs to you," Osman said, handing me my TT-30 pistol. The gun was heavy and warm, its breech cracks bleeding with light.

"The bullet of *Jannah*," I remarked. "*Mahadsanid, adeer.*" I thanked Osman, calling him uncle.

"Six big fish died in the siege on the caravan," Bashir put in, "but if it wasn't for you guys, we would've lost the whole assembly. *Mahadsanid* for a job well done."

"What about—" I had to pause to cough, "w-what about the *afgembi?*"

"The coup d'état is losing momentum," Bashir lamented, rubbing a hand over his close-shaven head. "The AU has called in reinforcements from Ethiopia. Their numbers are great, while our troops grow weary."

"Take me—" I coughed again, "take me to the front!"

"Lie still, Haji," Osman pleaded. "I've prepared some milk and mutton. Surely you must be hungry."

I nodded in the affirmative.

"I'll bring it now," he said.

"H-how did—" I wheezed, "how did I get here?" I asked Commander Bashir.

"Battery B airlifted you from the red sands."

"Can he take me back?"

"To the lorries?"

I cleared my throat. "To the front."

"Relax, Haji. *Waxaad leedahay xummad.*" The commander said I had a temperature.

"The *dawo* is ready, Commander," spoke a man wearing a doctor's smock as he stepped forth with a mighty syringe.

"*Mahadsanid*, Sooraan. Noor, we're going to administer some medication," Bashir said. "You've been exposed to toxic chemicals, and this will help you. It's best you take it before you eat. It will have a stronger effect."

The doctor approached with the needle, its tip dripping a neon green liquid. "Your *gacan*, sir," he said, asking for my arm.

"*Dawadani waa noocee?*" I asked what kind of medication it was.

"*Antibaayootig.*" He called it an antibiotic.

"*Waa hagaag,*" I conceded, *okay*.

He located a vein and slid the needle in. The injection burned like fire through my bloodstream, and even before the syringe was empty, I felt a wild kick of energy. As soon as he removed the needle from my arm, I sat up.

"Haji, you must rest!" Bashir ordered.

"The sudden animation is a side effect of the medication," Nasir put in. "It will pass."

"I want to fight!" I insisted, standing up and pushing away my cot.

"The war can wait, Haji," Bashir reproached. "Please rest. We've milk and mutton. Osman!"

"Here we are, gentlemen." My uncle approached with a cart of lamb, rice, and a large plastic bottle filled with milk.

I grabbed a shank and tore into the meat. "But I must fight," I mumbled with a mouthful. "I am the *Hoggaamiye*."

The commander just shook his head.

"If Noor is still in the fight, so am I," remarked someone just coming into the room.

I took a swig of milk, then wiped my mouth and asked, "Battery B?"

"I shall take you there," said the portly Somali helicopter pilot as he stepped between the others. The ex-USMC marine had deserted the U.S. military during Operation Restore Hope.

"You have your orders, B," warned Bashir at close quarters.

"I wish to assist the *Hoggaamiye*," rejoined the pilot.

"He's not well, gentlemen," Bashir struck a diplomatic tone. "The pirates on the ground will determine the course of battle."

"But I'm fine," I said, wiping my hands on a sheet before pulling on my fatigues. "I can fight."

"It's the medicine talking," Bashir replied, "giving you crazy energy, but really, you need to rest."

I pushed the cart aside and asked him, "Do you really want this?"

"*Maxaa?*" he said, *what?*

"The *afgembi.*"

"Of course."

"Then you'll let me fight!" I pulled on my boots.

Cosob and Osman joined Battery B and I on the tarmac. My uncle was determined to reclaim his big-rig from the red sands.

Jama Qays opted out of the fight, saying he was feeling ill from the gas attack. "Understandable," I said. His gas mask tube had been shot clean through. Given how much mustard gas he must've inhaled, I was amazed he was still standing. I could only surmise that he, like me, had been administered the *antibaayootig*.

Bashir approached the helicopter door and handed me a satchel called a *qandi*, made from acacia fibers. "This contains more medicine," he said. "Take it when you need an energy boost."

I took the pouch and replied, "See you in Mog."

"Be careful of air bubbles in the medicine," he warned. "Squirt a little out before you inject."

"*Wa hagaag.*" I told him *okay* as Battery B fired up the rotary blades.

"*Haddii Eebbe yidhaahdo.*" Bashir wished us luck, then headed back to the compound with Jama Qays. We lifted into the dusk and headed south.

THE LIGHT OF DEATH

"*MAXAY TAHAY MUSHKILADU?*" Osman asked me how I was feeling, speaking very loudly. He and Cosob were sitting opposite each other in the SuperCobra's jumpseats behind Battery B and myself, who were seated shotgun.

"*Waan ka sii darayaa!*" I yelled back that I was feeling better.

"Look there!" B said, pointing up at the skies.

"*Xaggee?*" I asked, *where?*

"A shooting star. Did you see it?"

"*Maya.*"

"What's up with Bashir, anyway?" B asked.

"You tell me!" I shouted over the roar of rotary blades. "Sometimes he's got his head up his *footo!*"

"He's just looking out for you, *walalo!*" remarked Osman, calling me *brother.*

"How far to Mog?" I asked B.

"ETA ninety minutes."

౭౨

About an hour into the flight, we entered a massive cobalt thunderhead. Rain pelted the windshield, and the going became increasingly turbulent, with lightning cracking everywhere through the darkly churning cloud.

"Should we fly lower?" Cosob inquired.

"Too dangerous," B said.

A particular violent lightning event began flaring up to the west.

"*Holac faalladho.*" Cosob uttered cravenly. He was referring to the mysterious "flame rays" sometimes witnessed by Somali sailors during monsoons — magnetic lightning that, when striking ships, caused them to effervesce with a strange blue light. Westerners had their own name for the phenomenon: Saint Elmo's fire.

A rolling chain of thunderbolts formed a lightning ball, which bounced beneath the clouds before zooming headlong at us. Battery B barely had time to react before it smashed into the SuperCobra. The entire cockpit flared with blue electrons, jolting us like we were in electric chairs. Our hair stood on end, and our skeletons flashed visibly through our flesh, then I watched in horror as lighting shot from my stigmata. The helo began to spin and a toolbox flew into my head, knocking me unconscious.

෨

I awoke in a wadi — a desert riverbed — facing the burning wreckage that was the chopper. I'd been thrown clear of the crash, but others weren't so lucky. Battery B lay halfway through the smashed windshield, one arm twisted behind his head, his other arm missing, while his neck was turned well past ninety degrees.

I rose to my feet and shambled through the disaster. Flames danced in the rain, reflecting off a streamlet gathering in the wadi, then an arm rose up from the debris.

"Osman!" I cried, smoke escaping from my mouth.

"Haji, my leg," he groaned, "I think it's broken."

His left leg was bent awkwardly below the knee.

"Haji, your star," he remarked, reaching up and tearing away what was left of my shredded shirt. The marking on my chest was effervescing with currents of energy.

"Your hands," he added.

Indeed, the stigmata on my hands were glowing brightly, too.

A dark figure stumbled forth from the wreckage, smoke emanating off his body.

"Cosob!"

"B didn't make it," he murmured, then came over and felt the top of my head, revealing fresh blood on his fingertips. "You've hit your head pretty good there, lad."

"*Fadlan ma i caawin kartaa?*" Osman asked us to help him.

"Let's get him up," Cosob suggested.

We lifted Osman from the wadi. His left leg was crooked and unmoving, and he was moaning loudly.

As we hobbled away from the wreckage, my *qandi* pouch bounced off my knees in the rising torrent. "Cosob, the *antibaayootig*!" I exclaimed as it floated past me. He reached down and snatched it from the water.

We slogged out of the wadi and up a sand dune, where we laid Osman down as gently as we could.

"*Allahu, jixinjix!*" he screamed for Allah's mercy.

Cosob and I sat down on either side of him and watched the burning SuperCobra get carried away in the flashflood.

"*Dawakhaad baan dareemayaa. Fadlan i toosi aroor sub-axnimo.*" I said I was feeling dizzy and was going to fall asleep, and that they should wake me in the morning.

Cosob came over and felt my forehead. "*Maya,*" he said, meaning *no*. "Don't sleep. You've hit your head and have a temperature."

"*Cudur seexiye xanuun baan leeyahay.*" I insisted that I had a sleeping sickness and must sleep.

"*Joogso!*" he said, *stop!* "You must stay awake or you will die!"

I fought to keep my eyes open. "Prepare me a syringe of *antibaayootig*," I mumbled. "It'll keep me awake."

Cosob began fumbling through the *qandi* pouch.

"*Deg-deg...*" I asked him to hurry.

I was slowly losing consciousness when he placed a syringe in my hand. "Sh-shoot it— sh-shoot it into my vein," I stuttered, then passed out.

❧

When I came again to myself, Cosob and Osman's faces were illumined by a strange halogen glow.

"The *Hoggaamiye*," Cosob stated.

My star was effervescing with phosphorescent energy. I went to touch it, and a ball of energy took shape in my hand. Terrified, I threw the lightning ball aside. It exploded into the sand behind Osman.

"Easy there, Haji," he said, temporarily ignoring his badly broken leg.

I got up and slowly moved my other hand towards my heart, and from about five inches away, an energy ball was already forming. I cupped my palm beneath the ball and lifted it before me. While I could behold the phenomenon directly, the others had to shield their eyes. But when I realized I had control over this thing, this power, my eyes only widened.

I spun halfway around, throwing the ball lightning at the wadi. It submerged beneath the surface and exploded silently underwater.

"*Allahu Akbar!*" Cosob howled as I sharpened my learning curve, shooting lightning balls in rapid fire. Somehow the serum was animating the electromagnetic field within me — a power that seemed to have been supercharged the moment the ball of lightning struck our chopper and shocked me deeply. For some reason, the star given to me by the Oracle and the stigmata inflicted upon me by the ghost of Captain Shar'ma'arke were especially affected by the supercharged energy, enabling me to mold balls from their collective bioluminescent power.

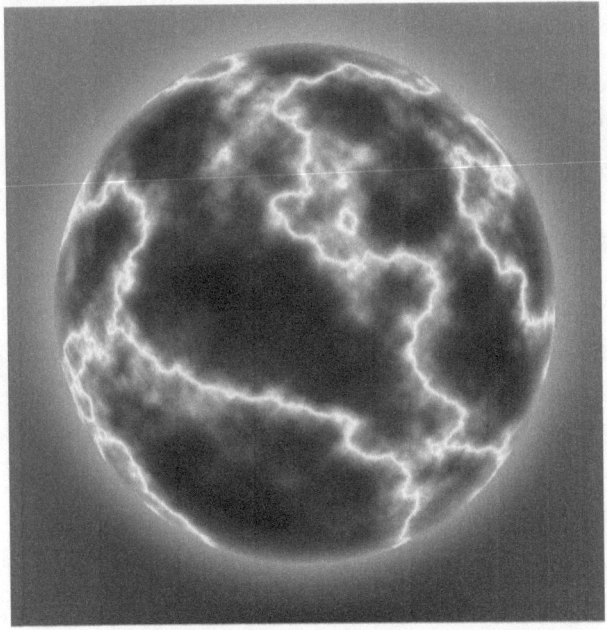

Ball Lightning

I stood upon a nearby dune so as not to endanger my mates with stray fire as I proceeded to play drums upon my chest, throwing ball lightning with each slap to my breast. Like the conductor of some strange cosmic orchestra, I carried the soundtrack of the storm with the thumping of my flesh, shooting ball lightning far and wide through the smashing heavens.

The Somali Pirate 3 – White Star Empire

In the strobe of electric flashes, I caught sight of men on camelback watching from the opposite ridge, so I stopped my impromptu lightshow. Whistling and applause sounded back from them.

"*Assalaamu calaykum!*" I shouted out in greeting.

"*Calaykum assalaam!*" they cried back together.

Before I could call out again, I collapsed onto the sand, exhausted from practicing my new powers.

∾

I awoke in an *aqal* — the nomadic home of the Somali pastoralists. A middle pillar called the *udub-dhehaad* supported a roof of branches and roots, called the *dhigo*. Woven mats were draped over the *dhigo* for insulation, while a tarpaulin was spread over the exterior to hold back the rain.

My head throbbed painfully. I reached between a cleft in my hair and ran my fingers along a row of thick, fibrous stitches that tracked across a bump there, but in investigating my fingers afterwards, I saw no signs of blood. The pastoralists had sealed my wound sufficiently enough. As for the white star over my heart, it was no longer glowing, nor did the stigmata on my hands emit any light, although a throbbing sensation pulsed from these areas in addition to my head.

I was lying upon a *darmo*, a sleeping mat woven from palm leaves, and was naked beneath the cotton *maraykaani* blanket that had been placed over me. Nearby, a small wooden and leather stool known as a *gambar* carried a neatly folded change of men's clothing of the traditional pastoralist type. My dagger rested atop the folded offering, snug in its leather sheath, while my TT-30 pistol hung off to the side, slung safely in its holster. As I was alone in the *aqal*, I could only assume the clothes were meant for me.

I stood and wrapped the first white sheet around my waist; it reached to slightly above my ankles. The second sheet I shaped into a loop and draped over my left shoulder.

I lifted my *ma'awis* — my sarong — over my right thigh and holstered my handgun there. There was no need to open the breech to check if the bullet of *Jannah* was still there, for it shone white-hot through the end of the barrel and through every crack in the hardware, however minute.

I lifted my dagger — Abbo's dagger — by its rhino tusk pommel and tied its leather sheath around my waist. My attire was completed with a sleeveless cotton shirt.

I went outside and shielded my eyes from the sun, which was shining brightly over the *guri* — the nomadic homestead I'd been lodged in. Children were playing about with rocks and sticks, women were milking camels and ewes, while a group of men sat together in the *ardaa*, drinking tea. The *ardaa* was an open area within the settlement covered with floor mats and protected from the wind by a thorn bush fence.

"*Subax wanaagsan!*" I said, approaching the pastoralists. They were dressed like me, in nomadic Somali garb.

"*Subax wanaagsan!*" one replied as he got up from his *gambar.*

"*Iska warran?*" another asked me how I was doing.

"*Maxay tahay mushkiladu?*" a third asked, more in the medical sense. This last was Cosob.

"*Cosob! Waan ka soo raynayaa,*" I lied, telling him I felt better, but truth be told, I felt like shit.

"*Waa xaggee Osman?*" I inquired of Osman's whereabouts.

"Resting in an *aqal,*" he replied. "The *wadaad* straightened his leg."

"They did?" I was shocked that traveling nomads had the capacity to fix a broken leg.

"*Haa,*" Cosob affirmed. "It's only temporary, but they were able to straighten it and apply a splint. They've given him some ginger tea and a bit of the *habad albara-kah* black seed to ease the pain."

"*Marti!*" a nomad said, calling me *visitor* as he handed me a small glass cup. "*Shah xawaash?*" He was offering me spiced cinnamon tea.

"*Alhamdu Lilaahi,*" I thanked him kindly, saying *Gratitude to Allah.*

Another pastoralist came with a metal kettle called a *kildhi* and filled my glass with steaming fragrant *shah xawaash.* Even though the day was quickly heating up, a Somali loved his hot tea no matter how oppressive the sun.

"*Mahadsanid,*" I thanked them again, then asked who was in charge, saying, "*Halkan yaa xukuma?*"

"*Aniga. Magacaygu waa Ankomah. Magacaa?*"

"So you're in charge, Ankomah. *Assalaamu calaykum!* My name is Noor Fayrus of the Darod clan."

"*Calaykum assalaam!*" Ankomah returned my formal greeting. "I am Warsangali."

"That's my mother's clan!"

"*Haddii Eebbe yidhaahdo!*"

"Allah be with you, too, good Ankomah. *Mahadsanid* for rescuing us from the flood. Our helicopter crashed in a thunderstorm, but I see the rain has stopped."

"*Xaggeed ka timi?*" he asked where I was from.

"*Waxaan ka imi Puntland. Waxaan ku dhashay Dante.*"

After I told him the name of my province and the village where I was born, he asked about my profession: "*Maxaad ka shaqaysaa?*"

"*Waxa aan ahay waranle.*"

"*Waranle?*"

"*Haa,* I'm a warrior."

Ankomah asked about my "magic powers."

"We're warriors," I repeated. "There's a revolution going on in Mogadishu, and we must get back. *Ma ku taagannahay waddadii saxa ahayd ee Mogadishu?*"

He replied that Mogadishu was not far off, then offered to take Cosob and I on a recon mission. We agreed, so he called for some camels.

We left the *guri* compound and trotted through the desert behind Ankomah. He guided us through a maze of sand dunes, then up the spine of a particularly large one, and sure enow, Mogadishu appeared in plain sight nigh four leagues distant. A thick haze lingered over the city, evincing the battle still raged.

"*Allahu Akbar!*" Cosob exclaimed, saying *God be praised!*

"*Mahadsanid,*" I thanked our host, then added, "The hospitality among your kind is legendary. When the empire is won, I'll see to it that you are more than compensated."

"*Dhib ma laha!*" he answered, *no problem!*

Cosob and I shared a chuckle. This nomadic *wadaad* seemed to have little idea what was transpiring in his country and the changes that were coming to everyone.

The decentralized nature of Somalia was most glaringly evident in respect to our nomads. If there was any stronger argument for the case of an anarchist society, it was in the Somali pastoralist who had no need for centralized government. I made a mental note to do my best to see they were left in peace once the empire succeeded, but if they came to us seeking special entitlements, they — the nomads, pastoralists, and hunter-gatherers — deserved it after so many centuries of total self-sufficiency.

"What about Osman?" Cosob inquired as we trotted back to the *guri*.

"You've a good physician aboard *The Madoobaad*, do you not?" I asked.

"*Haa.*"

"Can he mend broken bones?"

"He's a surgeon, so it stands to reason."

"How about your sickbay? Is it shipshape?"

"Assuming *The Madoobaad* is still yare, *haa* — it's the best sickbay I've ever clapped eyes upon."

"Then we shall take Osman there."

"*Sidee?*" he asked, *how?*

I looked down at my camel, then back at Cosob.

He nodded, and we trotted on ahead.

TURNING THE TIDE

BACK AT THE *GURI*, we saddled up two camels, thanked our hosts, and moved out. I led the way and Cosob followed, with Osman riding piggyback on Cosob's camel. We'd affixed a makeshift gurney to the animal's side, allowing Osman to lean back against the rear hump with his leg held straight in front.

As we neared the city, an exodus of retreating pirates and refugees moved in the opposite direction.

Coming upon one band of dispirited *waranle*, I stopped to inquire about the conflict. African Union forces had broken Zayid's phalanx around the presidential palace and were pushing back hard against the revolutionaries, they said. Even the *Hoggaamiye* had abandoned the cause, they complained, so all hope was lost.

I removed my turban from around my face.

Still the warriors did not recognize me, so I procured my bullet of *Jannah* for all to see. The light it cast was so great that each man had to shield his eyes from it.

"I am the *Hoggaamiye*," I said, "and the war is not yet over."

Some of the fighters dropped to their knees, but was it in deference or exhaustion?

I passed around gourds of water and stores of *muqumad*, which was jerked meat, packed for us by Ankomah. "Stow your doubts and rest a moment, good *waranle*," I said. "I shall go ahead into the city, but I want you to tell every retreating fighter you see that the *Hoggaamiye* is back with his bullet of *Jannah* to smite the enemy."

A weary, halfhearted battle cry sounded up: "*Haddii Eebbe yidhaahdo!*"

Cosob and I returned their call of Godspeed, then galloped forth towards the city of reckoning.

THE PIRATES' JUG OF DEATH

CLOAKED IN ROBES AND TURBANS, we rode into the war-torn metropolis, the pirates' bitter defeat everywhere in evidence. African Union soldiers, many bearing Kenyan badges, had set up checkpoints every few hundred meters. Refugees they were letting pass, but Somali pirate fighters they were executing outright.

No haste was lost on my part to improve upon my costume by wrapping my stigmata with cloth and making sure my white star "tattoo" was well hidden, but still, being surrounded by so many well-armed and well-trained African Union brigades did not rid the sweat from our brows as we passed. Cloaked in the sheets and turbans of the nomads, time and time again we claimed non-combatant status, saying we only sought to get our injured relative to the hospital in the Medina district.

The AU troops manning the checkpoints would say the hospital was full and the route was too dangerous; but nevertheless, we'd push on ahead, and they never stopped us as we passed. After all, what were they going to do? Shoot unarmed natives in the back? It was Somali pirate fighters they were fishing for in the flood of fleeing refugees, not tribesmen on camelback; but had they been just a mite more vigilant of those moving against the throngs, a simple pat-down would've revealed pirate enemy #1 right beneath their noses. "*Alhamdu Lilaahi,*" I whispered in a prayer of gratitude, for our moving *towards* the conflict kept us hidden in plain sight.

Any thought I'd been entertaining about rushing the presidential palace to save the day with my bullet of *Jannah* was beat into submission by a pounding migraine that very well tempted me to cut out that portion of my brain with my dagger. Furthermore, I knew a revolution would be hard to sustain without the support of the multitudes (who for all intents and purposes were presently in retreat); and last but not least, I was genuinely concerned about my uncle Osman's leg, for even though it had been set by the nomads, it was probably still pretty bad. Getting him aboard *The Madoobaad* had always been our first priority.

Unfortunately, our mission of mercy met a grinding impasse at the road leading to the harbor. Pirates were waging a strong defense of the quay, only we found ourselves on the other side of the conflict, behind enemy lines.

The road was a bottleneck, and may as well have been called the pirates' jug of death, for as it narrowed towards the harbor, where the gallant masts of our motherships were even now beckoning us, that final hundred meters was rendered vacant by crossfire. Like the border betwixt Israel and Lebanon, or the one dividing the two Koreas, along that road to our ships, nobody gained an inch. The pirates were fiercely defending the way to the harbor, waging a last stand against the African Union soldiers.

With a rumble of technicals and tanks behind us, we drew our camels aside to let them pass. Our pirate brethren wouldn't be able to hold the dock for much longer, not with the counteroffensive we were seeing, while our own position hiding amongst the enemy was becoming equally as tenuous. Mechanized troops looked up at us with increasing skepticism as we moved about them on our camels.

I drew close beside Cosob and said, "*Waxaan doonayaa inaan tago xeebta badda,*" meaning the beach route was our only chance.

"*Kumaad tahay?*" a soldier called up, *who are you?*

In hearing this, several hostiles trained their rifles on us, keeping us in check as they awaited our response.

"*Adhi-jire,*" Osman replied that we were shepherds, then pointed to his leg and asked for directions to the hospital. "*Waa xaggee cusbitaalku?*"

"Medina!" a merc shot back, pointing adamantly in the opposite direction. He was referring to the Medina district, where the hospital was located.

I removed my turban and raised it on a stick, saying, "*Waa yahay, waad mahadsantay!*"

The ruse worked. As I held up my flag of neutrality and thanked the soldiers informally, they lowered their weapons and let us pass.

We doubled back a few blocks and took an alternate route to the beach, keeping my turban raised all the while. Skirmishes on the streets between AU forces and pirates were no longer in evidence, but there were enough testy mercs around to warrant our white flag precaution. I kept the turban raised high as we galloped onto the beach.

A line of AU soldiers was marching through the sand ahead of us, so I took us into the breakers to get around them, our flag of neutrality never going down. I prayed to Allah, expecting at any moment to get shot in the back.

But Allah was watching over us that day, for not only did the mercs not fire, but the pirates defending the docks let us pass through their phalanx. I told my besieged brethren the number of hostiles coming up the beach and what they were packing, then removed my shirt and sash so all could behold my white star and recognize my authority.

"Your cell phone," I told a pirate. "I need to use it."

"Have you surrendered?" he said, stuffing his phone back into his pocket.

"*Maya*," I replied, *no*, then galloped on ahead. I had no time for his insubordination. The motherships were close at hand, with communications, provisions, and pirates who would fully recognize my command.

WILL TO POWER

ARRIVING BESIDE *THE MADOOBAAD*, I hollered for the crew to come down and help carry Osman over the gangplank. As I removed the *qandi* pouch from my camel's travel pack, a davit hoist was lowered to bring aboard the camels as well. It was the animals' meat,

I was told, that would come in handy if the ship was forced to weigh anchor.

As we made our way towards the sickbay, I held the *qandi* pouch fast under my arm. My own health was deteriorating rapidly, so I was keen to shoot up more serum. It was crucial I stay in the game. The coup d'état was unraveling, but for me the war was still winnable.

"I need a cell phone," I said to the pirates flanking me as we marched down the passageway. "I need status updates, weapon and troop estimates, intel on enemy positions."

"There's been a surge of new AU fighters from Kenya," Qarshe revealed. "They drove us back from the palace on the eve of our success."

"How many?" I inquired.

"Many hundreds," he gravely relayed, "perhaps thousands."

While the surgeon aboard *The Madoobaad* attended to Osman in the sickbay, I was taken to Amina Rage. At first I was angered by what looked like her subpar treatment as she lay amongst scores of injured pirates, but in seeing an IV bag hanging over her with its tube feeding into her arm, and in beholding the fresh sheets upon which she lay, I realized that, under the circumstances, she had been attended to in a sensible enough manner. I knelt beside her cot and held her hand.

"Haji," she whispered, her eyes barely opening as she turned to see me. "I heard you were gone."

"No, Amina, I'm right here."

"So you haven't deserted us?"

"*Maya, walaal.* We were ambushed in the red sands, and I was injured in the gas attack. I was airlifted to Garoowe for treatment, but upon my return to the front, our helicopter was struck by lightning and crashed. Battery B didn't make it, and Osman is hurt bad."

"Uncle Osman?" she murmured.

"*Haa*, but he'll pull through. We've brought him aboard. He's somewhere in here with you."

"So you didn't defect?"

"Who told you I defected?"

"Pirates I hear," she said, "injured pirates returning from the front. They say you fled the battle."

At this, I was overcome with rage. I glanced across the sickbay and saw Cabdulqaadir coming down a companion ladder with a radiophone. I made haste to him and radioed Bashir.

I told the commander about our crash and my subsequent delay back to the capital, then asked about the state of the *afgembi*.

"It's beyond my control, Haji. The troops are pulling back. They've lost the will; there've been too many casualties, while the African Union keep sending in reinforcements."

"*Haa*," I confirmed, "from Kenya."

"The coup will not succeed, Haji. The people are fleeing the city. A revolution backed by a popular uprising is not coming to pass."

"But, Bashir," I refuted, "all they need is courage."

"The war is all but lost, comrade. Save your lives while you still can. Weigh anchor and fall back."

"But, Commander! We can still—"

"Do not see this as a defeat, *saaxiib*," he cut me short. "Tomorrow, Khalidah Malak will be attending the December 18 United Nations Convention in New York. She will send a clear message to the world that Somali pirates are still a force to be reckoned with. The engagement we put on show in Mog will give us far more bargaining power in future hijacking missions, you can count on that."

"The engagement we put on show, *phht*!" I echoed him in disgust. "I should've expected as much from you, Bashir. Well, let me tell you something, Commander, I'm not going to make the Immortal Angel the laughing stock of the UN Convention, announcing we're a force to be reckoned with while at the same time announcing our defeat. This war may be over for you, Commander, but it's not over for me!"

I switched off the radiophone and gave it forcefully back to Cabdulqaadir. I could not believe that everyone, all the way up to Commander Bashir, was giving up so easily. Tomorrow our double agent, the Immortal Angel, AKA Khalidah Malak AKA Alexis Briggs, was slated to make an announcement before the world assembly. Would twenty-four hours allow me enough time to change her message from one of capitulation to one of victory?

The Immortal Angel at Heathrow International Airport

"Can you get me in touch with *Madaxweyne* Tahliil?" I asked the quartermaster, referring to one of Zayid's top big fish.

"Nay, *saaxiib*," Cabdulqaadir denied me tactfully, calling me *friend*. "The commander forbids your direct contact with President Tahliil."

I was infuriated. "Does the commander know I have the ability to shoot lightning from my hands?!" I snapped.

Cabdulqaadir regarded me with raised brows. I bore my palms, but the stigmata had grown pale, and I, too, felt a terrible lapse of energy. The quartermaster did not answer.

"The assembly knows I've been given a bullet from *Jannah*," I continued, removing my pistol from its holster, "and you also know my holy projectile can change everything."

"I'm sorry, Noor," Cabdulqaadir sighed, "but it's not for me to decide."

"*Baqayya*," I said, calling him *coward*, "it is for each of us alone to decide our fate."

He went over to an injured pirate, ignoring me.

WAR'S UNDYING DREAM

"THE SUN NOW SETS, dear sister," I told Amina Rage, "and the harbor will fall come nightfall. The ships will soon weigh anchor, so I must leave. I cannot be party to this."

She reached beneath the folds of her sheet and handed me a United States passport. I opened it, and it was mine.

"I took it from you in Boosaaso," she whispered.

I lowered my head to hear.

"Before stealing aboard the *Windrose*," she continued. "My dearest *harbarwadaag*, my life shall soon escape me. Please, return to your good wife Issa, go back to your children and *Hooyo*. They need you."

"Noor," said *Dhakhtar* Nasir, approaching from behind me, "I've transferred from the *Windrose* to check up on you. Cosob, the men, they say you've grown weak."

"I've had a long journey, Doctor. It's taken a lot out of me."

"Allow me to perform an auscultation."

Amina moved over enough for me to lay down beside her, at which point the doctor did things like take our pulses, monitor our breathing, and check our eyes with a little flashlight. He then procured a small electronic instrument from his leather handbag and guided it over our bodies. It crackled with radio static when it came to within inches of our skin. He inspected my white star and stigmata, which were faded and grey as if they were losing power, but when his gadget passed over those areas, its static became particularly active.

"What is that?" I inquired.

"A dosimeter."

"*Maxaa?*" I was perplexed.

"Please sit up, Haji, and I will explain. I wish to be frank with you — both of you. Through a process of elimination, and also from inspecting some of the other crewmen who took part in the Selection Ministry freighter hijacking, I have determined beyond a question of a doubt that you are both suffering from acute radiation poisoning."

"What is our prognosis, exactly?" I asked, thinking of my younger sister Ayan Rage, who, once falling victim to radiation poisoning, died in a matter of weeks.

"That depends on your level of exposure. It appears as if both of you have had at least a moderate amount, and Noor, these odd markings on your chest and hands are particularly infected."

"How long do we have, Doctor?"

"Radiation poisoning has no known cure, but there are things we can do to slow its advance. I have some salt tablets, and also you must keep very hydrated — drink lots of liquids. There's no sense quarantining you because many of the others here are also infected — and some far more severely than you two. What you need now, Haji, is rest. Once we set sail, I'll check on your condition again."

"I have a serum," I replied, "obtained from the medical facility in Garoowe. It greatly alleviates my symptoms, but it does have some side effects."

"Serum?" asked *Dhakhtar* Nasir. "Do you have it with you?"

"Aye."

I procured my *qandi* pouch and pulled out an injection tube. Its contents glowed green in the dim light of the sickbay, garnering the attention of other patients laid up around us.

"Who gave this to you?" he asked, holding the tube before his eyes.

"A doctor named Sooraan," I replied, then heard the sound of static again.

"*Saxro!*" he cursed, *shit!* He tossed the tube onto my lap and jumped back. "Did you hear that?"

"Hear what?"

"The millisievert counter in my coat pocket. It picked up a strong reading from that stuff from more than a foot away! Please, Noor, you must dispose of this medicine. Toss it overboard. It is highly radioactive."

"Toss it overboard, *Dhakhtar*?" I replied with a black look, stuffing the tube back into my bag. "I don't think so. This stuff may be radioactive, but it makes me feel a whole lot better, at least temporarily."

"But you must, Noor! It will only worsen your condition."

"It gives me special powers, *Dhakhtar* — powers you would not believe."

"What do you mean?"

"I can harness lightning, Nasir. Electromagnetic waves like the *holac faalladho*."

"Flame rays? I'm not sure I'm following you."

"This serum, combined with my white star and stigmata, enable me to create ball lightning from my chest. I can control it with my hands, throw it."

Nasir's brows curled in skepticism. "If what you are saying is true, I would like to see a demonstration."

"I only have three tubes left," I countered. "One I shall give to my sister, for I'm convinced it will improve her condition, and the other two shots I must keep for the war."

"The *afgembi?* But the ships will soon weigh anchor. We are in retreat."

The Madoobaad at dock

"Haji!" a man cried from across the chamber. It was Cosob. I waved him over. "Haji," he said, "the ships are moving out soon. Zayid has capitulated."

"How is Osman?" I asked, ignoring what I already knew about the war.

"He's been given a heavy dose of morphine and isn't particularly coherent, but his leg has been fitted with pins and he shall walk again. The nomads who took us in set it right the first time."

"Never underestimate our traveling *wadaad*," I replied, referring to the pastoralist priests who had brought us to their itinerant encampment — their *guri*. "Where is Uncle Osman, anyway?"

"In the corner astarboard aft."

"Please go there and wait for me, Cosob. I'll be but a few more minutes. *Dhakhtar?*"

"Aye, Noor?"

"You must continue to watch over my sister in my absence. I require that you inject her with small doses of the serum every so often. It will keep her cognizant until I return with more medicine."

"Where will you be going?"

"Just watch over Amina, *Dhakhtar;* and now, both of you, please allow us some moments in private."

"I'll be with Osman," Cosob affirmed, then made his way willy-nilly towards the far corner of the sickbay, for many pirates were laid up in cots, blocking his way.

"If you are leaving her a tube of the serum," the *Dhakhtar* said, "I wish to study it in your absence."

"If you must," I replied, "but I required you inject her as instructed."

"Aye, Noor, I shall."

With that, the good *Dhakhtar* Nasir walked away, leaving Amina and I alone.

"*Walaal*," I told my *sister*, gently squeezing her hand, "I have some medicine for you." I placed the tube of serum beneath her sheets. "*Dhakhtar* Nasir will administer it to you. This *antibaayootig* is powerful. It will give you energy."

"Will you return to America, then?" she asked, her voice barely audible as she held my hand.

"*Imminkaan tegeyaa.*" I told her that I was leaving, then placed her hand on her chest and kissed her on the forehead.

"*Bashbash iyo barwaaqo,*" she whispered, wishing me future prosperity.

"*Waa kuwan antibaayootig.*" I reminded her about the serum, and to reassure her, told her that I took it, also, saying, "*Dawadan waan qaataa.*"

The boom of artillery sounded through the hull. The enemy was on the advance.

"*Bashbash iyo barwaaqo.*" Amina wished me prosperity again, then turned her head and went silent.

I felt her jugular; her heart was still pumping. She had merely fallen asleep, but it goes without saying her condition was grave. I feared for her survival and also my own, for bouts of dizziness and nausea had become frequent for me, and I generally felt enervated and weak. I clung to my pouch of medicine, then called *Dhakhtar*

Nasir back over and informed him that a tube reserved for Amina was hidden within her sheet. I asked him to resume vigil over her, and he tacitly agreed.

I took one last look at my beloved sister, who in her short time as a pirate had displayed remarkable feats of valor, and I vowed to return to her as soon as I was able.

As I made my way over to Osman, some pirates in the sickbay who were well enough to sit up and converse regarded me with black looks. It was only when I reached my uncle and Cosob that this latter revealed the reason for the general antagonism I'd been receiving. According to Cosob, there was an ongoing rumor that I'd been fearful of the battle and went AWOL, only to return under the white flag of surrender.

Again, I was incensed at this report, and in no subtle way made my anger known by calling anyone who believed I had fled the battle *axmaq*! or *fools*!

Pirates, some injured, others sweaty and short on camaraderie, regarded me skeptically.

"Nephew," Osman muttered, grabbing my arm frailly.

"Uncle, you must rest," I advised, kneeling beside him.

"I can hear it everywhere in the hull," he whispered with a rattle, "and see it in the eyes of the casualties who stumble past me: the sun has set upon your great war, *Hoggaamiye*, and the *waranle* are no longer united."

"The fighters may have lost hope," I replied, "but this can be restored."

"I've seen your powers, *walalo*," Osman continued, "the powers given to you by *Jannah* and your power to influence men. But let this war be finished, Haji." Then, grabbing me by the sleeve and pulling me close in warning, he said, "For the pirates have lost faith in you, and you are no longer safe amongst them."

I stood and, together with Cosob, scanned the sickbay. Indeed, furtive glances from battle-worn pirates revealed scowls of distrust. Cosob placed a hand atop his dagger and remained silent.

I knelt back down to Osman and said in private, "The retreating pirates do not represent common Somalis. Most onboard this ship are little more than self-serving desperados who would prefer thievery and thuggery to nationhood. I knew this from the start, but didn't think they'd defect so easily. So you are right, dear Uncle — it's time for me to leave. I'll ask Cosob to look out for you and take you to a better place as soon as one presents itself. For now, this ship is sailing on."

After confirming that Cosob would stay onboard and keep an eye on my uncle, I asked him if any super-skiffs were available. He left to inquire, returning moments later, saying he had consulted Cabdulqaadir on the matter and no, none of the super-skiffs had returned to *The Madoobaad* — and they'd all gone to the front.

"However," Cosob relayed, "your super-skiff has been repaired onboard the *Windrose*; only the *Windrose* has been seriously compromised and will soon be scuttled."

The lights began to flicker in the sickbay and the sound of warfare neared. I confirmed that Cosob would remain with Osman as *The Madoobaad* got underway, then took leave with my *qandi* pouch, passport, TT-30 pistol, and my father's dagger.

I arrived on deck as *The Madoobaad* was shoving off, so unhooked a line attached to some deadeyes aloft and swung out onto the quay.

As *The Madoobaad* made sail beyond the harbor gates, a hull portal opened on the *Windrose*.

Just before that latter craft was scuttled in an explosion of gunpowder and dynamite, I raced out of her hull in my refurbished super-skiff.

Those *Madoobaad* pirates sailing before the mast shouted "*Baqayya!*" as I passed, but the only *cowards* I reckoned in the vicinity were they for throwing in the towel so early.

"*Was* them," I grumbled as I engaged auxiliary power, rocketing off into the sunset, and anybody familiar with Somali expletives would know just what I meant.

MUCAARAD

THUNDER SHOOK THE NIGHT, a thunder so heavy that the very walls of Mogadishu rattled and the ground vibrated like a great Somali drum. I could only imagine the eyes of the AU battalions widening in wonderment at where the tempest might be coming from, only imagine their infidel black-heart overlords sitting up on their cots and listening in fear as the storm of the century drew upon them.

We struck from the thunderheads of hatred at the hand we'd been delivered, my posse of 30,000 *waranle* on camelback freshly recruited from Dadaab refugee camp in Kenya. Bashir did not suspect I had a million dollars to spare, easily wired from my U.S. account to a reputable bank in Kenya, thanks to my sister having returned my passport to me for valid identification. Zayid was not expecting me to purchase so many weapons and camels from the border markets from which to provision my own militia — a junta wrought from a massive legion of Somalis, hungry beyond all measure.

Aye, the Dadaab refugee camp with its 440,000 inhabitants was the largest in the world, and was a fertile ground from which to recruit an army of so many desperate and willing young new fighters. The drought Somalia had recently suffered, in October 2011, had greatly increased Dadaab's numbers, and as we stormed the capital to turn the tide of battle, many more common

Somalis joined the popular uprising. Al-Shabaab many hated, and to pirates many landlubbers could not relate, but an army of refugees formed from their own desperate kin presented a new kind of force that struck a deep chord in many and drummed the ground like thunder as our advance swelled in ranks.

Pockets of al-Shabaab militants still camped out in the hinterlands after their August 6 retreat from the capital proved hopeless against our numbers. Those who tried to stop us were trampled beneath our camels, and their blood mixed with the dust.

I stood upon my stirrups, my star glowing electric from the serum, then pointed my father's dagger heavenwards and screamed, "*Bashbash iyo barwaaqo!*"— repeating the words of my sister when she said I'd soon be splashing joyfully through God's raindrops towards prosperity.

A hearty roar from the troops behind evinced they surely concurred, when suddenly, a jet fighter streaked by overhead, putting a damper on our rejoicing. A single jet fighter could do us relatively little collateral damage, but was this only the first of a flock, perchance from Ethiopia? All Somalis remembered the terrible wars of the Ogaden — of a foreign-backed Ethiopian airforce; of Siad Barre and his scorched-earth tactics. It goes without saying, the single shriek of a MiG rocketing by sent an involuntary shiver through the spine of the entire phalanx.

By the glory of Allah almighty, that forward-flying plane began bombarding enemy positions in the city. Return fire streaking up from howitzers — dedicated AU hardware — attempted to down the aircraft but failed.

"*Allahu Akbar!*" and "*Haddii Eebbe yidhaahdo!*" sounded everywhere behind me as my refugee militia reveled in the sky combat.

Many camels I'd purchased, but a MiG fighter I did not buy — this was either a *Cir Consort 1* aircraft or divine intervention leading the charge from on high.

ৎৄ

How many brittle limestone walls fell before our advance as we thundered into Villa Somalia, the seat of the presidential palace? And how many mercenary pigs drank their own blood as we chopped our way through them with spear, sword, and dagger? Those shooting at us from a distance were answered with Kalashnikovs, AK-47s, RPGs and hand grenades, all purchased from the Kenyan border markets. The panzer division surrounding the presidential palace was all that remained to oust.

As my comrades valiantly fought, I sat my camel down in an alcove, procured my pouch of *antibaayootig*, then rolled back the sleeve of my djellabah and gave myself the last shot of serum. It spread electric blue through my veins, and soon white light shone from my heart and stigmata.

"And now," I chucked, turning my camel about, "now my enemies shall taste true punishment."

THE FIRST STARFIGHTER

I PRANCED CASUALLY through the palace standoff, explosions going off all around me as I neared the front. Disguised as I was beneath my black djellabah robe, nobody knew who I was, and nobody seemed to care, so embroiled was each *waranle* in intense fighting. It was only when a line of refugee warriors got blown up by tank-shot that I stood upon my stirrups and threw off my blood-splattered cloak. Light shot from my star and cast in stark isolation the tank that'd just killed my brethren.

With intense love and anger circulating through my heart, stirring the electromagnetic serum to a point of non-containment, I removed a mass of raw energy from my chest and formed it into ball lightning, the glowing stigmata in my palms helping to shape it.

The sounds of warfare settled as combatants paused to behold my strange science, and in an impossible moment of silence, I threw the lightning ball at the tank with terrible precision.

When my supercharged projectile connected with the tank, an electric blue current raced along every edge of its frame. Then, with a blinding white light, the vehicle imploded into a heap of liquid iron. Enemy fighters who'd taken positions behind the tank screamed as molten pools of melted hardware spilled over their feet.

In the midst of the confusion, I reared my camel before the next tank and unleashed a lightning ball on it, as well. Its frame effervesced blue, then melted no different than the first one had.

An effective tactic now established, I continued briskly along the panzer division, taking out one tank after the next. The melted iron wrought by my attack formed a virtual moat of lava around the palace. The Africa Union forces protecting the building fled inside in terror.

Meanwhile, my militia of refugees was busy weeding out mercenaries hiding along the streets, and soon they cleared the way to the harbor.

It seemed the MiG fighter pilot had been cognizant of our strategy, for his bombardments had not been indiscriminate. He or she had cleared a smoldering path from the airport to the palace, and from the palace to the docks. Reports bespoke of napalm, with casualties in the drop zone displaying severe burns and open blisters.

As for the cowards who'd fled within the palace, their new positions at alcoves and window spaces served them little better. Easily discernable in the night as they fired off live rounds, they were little match for my army of rifle-toting refugees. What my young militia lacked in aim was compensated for by abundant ammunition, for I had virtually cleared out the black markets along the Kenyan-Somali border, often paying a high premium for whatever munitions were available. Now my militia acted as if Mogadishu was their private shooting gallery, making bets on targets, then cheering as mercs fell dead from doorways and window spaces.

A number of hostiles laid down into sniper positions atop the palace, and these were a real threat because they were hard to hit. So, working in conjunction with my camelback militia, I sent some decoys around the back, revealing the snipers' positions as they shot at the moving targets. In the meantime, I proceeded to the third floor of an adjacent building, and in the relative privacy of a bombed-out room, I worked to create a massive lightning ball.

Holding the great orb in my arms, I shuffled up to the window space, then spun around once, hard like an Olympic shot putter, and flung it towards the roof of the palace.

Again my aim was sure (it seemed I could will the object to fly), for the fireball flew up to the corner of the palace and rolled along the edge of the rooftop, zapping an entire row of snipers out of existence. The tactic proved so efficacious that I wasted no time in lobbing another one towards the roof's other side; again, the ball rolled along the top edge, eliminating perhaps twenty mercenary snipers, their skeletons flashing electric blue before turning to ash. *Poof!*

Back with my militia, we rushed the building in a final putsch to oust the enemy from the anemic halls of the government edifice. But the presidential palace was far more than symbolic — to take it was to control a key defensive position in the city centre.

Proven warriors in my charge escorted me into the building, but it soon became apparent the added security was no longer needed, for the presidential palace was filled only with dead hostiles and the ribald faces of our victorious comrades.

I proceeded to the rooftop to better gauge the war's progress. Satisfied the enemy was on the run and not coming back anytime soon, I returned to the prime minister's chamber and set out to establish a command center there. In my eyes, and in all likelihood, the war was truly won — we only had to bring in the media and Zayid's retinue of big fish.

WAABERI

"DAWN HAS COME," said Qaasim, a young refugee who'd excelled in battle. He was peering out an open window space towards the east. "*Waa waaberi,*" he repeated.

"*Haa,*" I affirmed, checking the clock on the laptop before me. "Our broadcast starts in an hour."

I was reviewing the footage of Khalidah Malak making her address to the United Nations thirty-six hours prior. It had sent shockwaves through the political world and was everywhere online, as was the news of "the war in Somalia." I had to laugh.

"*Maxaa?*" inquired Qaasim, *what?*

"The world will soon learn that this war is already won."

He smiled and nodded, then resumed his vigil over the city.

As I watched Khalidah speak, I turned up the volume on my satellite-capable computer.

"Somali pirates will continue to fight for freedom," she said, "until the world body fesses up to the crimes they've committed against them. For twenty years, and ending only recently, thanks to Somali pirates, member nations of this very assembly aggressively engaged in fish poaching and toxic waste dumping within Somalia's Exclusive Economic Zone, our EEZ. Your very own 'fish pirates' brought in half a billion dollars yearly while engaging in their illegal and environmentally destructive activity, costing many thousands of coastal Somalis their livelihoods while the dumping of toxic waste practiced by certain members of this assembly poisoned my people and our ecosystem for generations to come. These crimes should be viewed as reprehensible by the international community, and the Somali fishermen who were forced to become pirates to feed their families and protect their seas must be awarded a full financial recompense for having to abandon their former livelihoods. And finally, there must be full recognition of Somalia's sovereignty and Exclusive Economic Zone. Until these demands are adequately met or addressed, revolutions like we're seeing now in my country will spread throughout the greater region, and with the growing power of the pirate militias, will eventually succeed."

How shocked will the world be, I thought, when they shortly learn that a pirate militia has already succeeded in taking control of Somalia. Although technically we were a militia of refugees, Zayid pirates were rapidly returning, and with Zayid's retinue of dignitaries primed for their duties, the original model of a pirate empire would proceed without further ado. In a serendipitous moment for our junta, most of Zayid's big fish had taken shelter in nearby Hotel Sahafi when the war began to sour, and had remained battened down there amid the recent conflict. It was this retinue of pirate clan owners, managers, and businessmen, along with a contingent of traditional leaders — *akil* — from the affected coastal areas, which would make up the new Mogadishu *guurti*, the body of decision-making representatives. I may have had the ability to stoke public sentiment and fund my own army, but the brainpower and *guurti* needed to run the country under *xeer*, or common law, could only be found in the powerful and pluralistic assembly already set up by Zayid. Some of the dignitaries were already arriving.

BAARLAMAAN

WAHEED, ZAYID'S INFORMATION Technology Manager, was busying himself about the Chamber of Parliament, clearing a stage for the address and setting up his webcam equipment. The putsch on Mogadishu had been so decisive that it had almost ended before it began. The chief reason for this was manpower. As my refugee army advanced towards the city, many thousands more common Somalis took up what weapons they had or could fashion to join the fight, and perhaps ten thousand more Somali pirate *waranle* who had recently been ousted by the AU mercs returned to the theatre of combat. Additionally, and it will forever be argued that perhaps most significantly, the mysterious MiG with its napalm attacks and my displays of deathly ball lightning scared the enemy shitless. Whatever the case, the final putsch had a synergistic effect that affected the very morale of the opposing parties in opposite ways — those fighting for the coup d'état felt sure and invincible, while those put in place to ward off the *afgembi* had too little of their own convictions vested to stand up against a massive front of *waranle* on camelback led by a "lightning-throwing magician," so they either defected or fled.

I recognized few of the white-collared men gathered in the parliamentary chamber, except for Lieutenant-Commander Xeed, who was wearing a black overcoat, and assembly President Tahliil, along with his attachés Prime-Minister Madoobeh and Guardsman Basbaas.

President Tahliil congratulated me on my success. I expressed concern that few representatives of the northern provinces were present, and especially the *Boqor* — the clan-head of the Puntland region.

He told me to stow my worries, saying, "There's still some fighting in the streets. This *guurti* is very young. In time, when it is safer, more *akil* will be brought in to discuss important matters, and we will consult with the *qadi* on points of law."

Although a Somali, Tahliil spoke with an Italian accent, and although he appeared smart, there was just something about him that I did not trust, especially when he told me, continuing with our conversation, "Unfortunately, many northerners will be less willing to join the new empire under Zayid. And Somalilanders, you know how strongly they hold to their secession."

Unfazed, I replied, "I will continue to work towards universal democracy."

"*Maxaa?*" he asked as if he didn't understand. Or perhaps in the crowded room he hadn't heard me.

"*Xeer,*" I said more forcefully, "and *guurti*. Law and assembly."

"Of course," he chuckled. "I would expect nothing less from you. Come, the men are lining up now. Let us take our places before the cameras."

Indeed, in addition to Waheed's webcam, Somali TV network ETN, Horn Cable TV, and sub-Saharan pay-per-view channel GTV were also setting up cameras before the line of dignitaries. There was even a lanky Somali commoner holding out a cheap microphone with the letters RM (for Radio Mogadishu) scribbled on it with a felt pen.

"Who is to speak?" I asked.

"Perhaps it should be you," Tahliil said, "but points of policy need to be outlined to the press, so we have assigned a dedicated spokesperson for that."

We fell in line with the big fish, with Tahliil standing behind me because he was taller. "How is your sister?" he asked as the seconds counted down to the address, and I knew he was referring to Amina Rage and not Fatuma Abdul, for he had not yet met the latter.

"Not well," I said. "She's fallen ill with radiation sickness."

He remained silent for some time after that, at last replying, "So sorry to hear that, lad."

Truth be told, the wars, the crashes, the deaths, stress, and injections of the past few days were starting to catch up with me in a serious way. I could feel the last shot of serum wearing off, for with it came the onset of nausea and a terrible headache. My hands began to shake and my knees felt like they were going to buckle at any second.

"Stand firm," said President Tahliil, placing a hand on my shoulder, "and confident. This is your golden hour."

His encouragement gave me the will to keep steady as the bright portable lights went on and the cameras started rolling. It was hard not to flinch in the face of such light. I hadn't slept for a few days, and if I looked anything like I felt, I must've looked like *saxro* [shit]. I only hoped my wife Issa would be watching, and that she would recognize me along the line of dignitaries by my neon yellow windbreaker, which everyone at home knew was my uniform of choice while on assignment for just about anything.

Alas, I'd once hoped to reveal my white star tattoo and stigmata to the world in this historic address, but as the *antibaayootig* was waning, my hopes were dashed. Indeed, I was lucky enow to be wearing the windbreaker, for the loss of antigen energy caused my white star to turn grey and wrinkly, while the holes in my hands had become equally as unsightly.

A bald Somali in a suit resembling Abdullahi Yusuf Ahmed, the onetime president of the TFG, began speaking for the cameras. "Ladies and gentlemen, today I announce the end of war in Somalia and the establishment of a new government. Behind me stands the National Assembly, a parliament formed of Somali statesmen, clan leaders, and businessmen from the far corners of the country. This governing body shall chart the future of the Somalia Empire.

"Take heed, world powers such as the United Nations, African Union, European Union, Arab League, Russian Federation, United States of America, APEC, and IMF: Somalia is now one-hundred-percent sovereign and will no longer tolerate your meddling and military presence in our airspace, land, or seas. This revolution has been brought about by popular consent, and furthermore, you should note by the brevity in which the war was won that our firepower is not to be trifled with. Our ground troops and hardware assets have very quickly repelled the combined forces of the African Union, and we already have a massive, permanent military in place; our vast pirate fleets now form a de facto navy, and we have air power that you have only just begun to see. So I warn you sternly: any outside meddling, including from the Task Forces such as Operation Ocean Shield operating in our waters without our explicit consent, will be met with overwhelming punishment.

"Our empire is a consensual democracy that mirrors our traditional values — values best summed up in the Somali proverb, *'Balad aan boqor lahayn laguma galo,'* meaning, 'no one can live in a country or city without a ruler or government.' For too long Mogadishu has been bereft of fair and just leadership under *xeer*, which is the contract of common law, and a *guurti*, a national assembly or parliament. The *guurti* you see behind me will act as a tribunal; we will make political decisions and hand down verdicts based upon *xeer* — Somali traditional law — and *Shari'a*, the Islamic law of the Qur'an. These two pillars of governance are not new to Somalia, but are thousands-years-old traditions that have only recently been interrupted by foreign colonialism and meddling.

"Somali common law, *xeer*, shall act in the sphere of our political and secular matters, while *Shari'a* will act in our religious and spiritual domains, and in matters of family. In this way, our empire will have a built-in system of checks and balances, ensuring fair, clear, and equitable guidelines in regards to policymaking and our justice system. Our long tradition of *xeer* and *guurti* coexisting within the secular and religious spheres had once earned Somalia the distinction of the Land of the Gods. Clans and neighboring clans agreed to respect common law, and for over one thousand years, the Land of Punt existed as a caliphate based upon consensual decree and inter-clan democracy.

White Star Empire — An Alignment of Clans

"Colonialist intervention and internal dictators backed by Western powers all but destroyed our time-honored traditions, while the assault on our oceans, first by foreign pirates pillaging and polluting our seas, and now by the Task Forces who prevent us from fighting back against these outrageous assaults on our national sovereignty, all but snuffed out the hope of a brighter future for Somalia.

"Somalia's warlords, by themselves, are nothing compared to the arrogant warlord countries, who, as I speak, seek to extinguish the hope of a new Arab spring in the Middle East, and who, as I speak, combine their militaries to assault the lands and seas of sovereign peoples.

"Somali warlords, working together under our new empire, will fight for the inalienable rights given to us by *guurti*, bestowed on us by *Shari'a* law, and allowed to us by consensual decree, and we will fight to protect the people from continued foreign exploitation of the people's heritage, land, and seas."

The speaker went on to mention something about the pirate courts, the *Safaarad*, then talked about Somalia's newfound stability, even as sporadic gunfire still sounded in the distance. He mentioned that the armies of the empire would not tolerate extremist groups such as al-Shabaab. He pointed out that Somalis were Sunnis, and Sunnis believed in electing their rulers, and he sternly promised that the assembly standing behind him represented a broad-based collation of selected representatives [*guurti*], recently arrived from the far reaches of the country and from every major clan. How much of what he said was true I could not ascertain, but as Tahliil pointed out, it was good to have a dedicated speaker because I could not remark on political matters so fluently.

The cameras panned along the line of new ministers and deputies, and after some closing words by the MC, the address was adjourned, at which point I collapsed.

VEINS OF COMMERCE

I CAME AGAIN TO MYSELF lying on a small mattress and covered with a sheet. I was looking at a ceiling with its plaster peeling off and could hear men conversing. One of them sounded like Xeed.

"Al-Shabaab," said he, "is now aligned with Ansar al Sharia. They are sifting in through the Kenyan border and using the Port of Kismayo as a supply route."

"And this is where the suicide bombers are entering?"

"The Americans and Swedes are coming in from Kenya," Xeed said, "while others are recruited from within our own borders. A chief priority will be to expel al-Shabaab from Kismayo and set up check-points around the capital and especially along the Kenyan border. There are upwards of seven hundred and fifty of these foreign fighters already in our country, plotting to overthrow the empire. We must inform the world press that foreign terrorists from Western nations have aligned themselves with AQAP in Yemen and are trying to destabilize our fledgling democracy."

In my groggy disposition, I lacked the will to concentrate on the rest of their conversation. My entire body felt sore and stiff. I emitted a lengthy yawn and stretched like a cat beneath my bed sheet.

"He's awake," said a man in a doctor's smock. I recognized him as Dr. Sooraan.

Xeed entered the room, followed by Prime-Minister Hassan Madoobeh — a big fish with Tahliil's retinue — and Qaasim, the young refugee *waranle* I'd befriended earlier. Others who looked vaguely familiar spilled in behind them and stood around me. Once it was clear I was okay, Dr. Sooraan ordered these latter away, calling for more privacy and space.

The doctor asked how I felt. I complained of overall fatigue and pain. He chuckled and said he was not surprised, given all I'd been through.

"You've been asleep for two days, Haji," Xeed added. "But you did it — the *afgembi* has succeeded."

I smiled and attempted to speak, but my throat was too dry. I tried to swallow, then coughed and said, "*Biyo*," meaning water.

Dr. Sooraan sent Qaasim to fetch some tea, then asked me if I was hungry for cooked meat.

"*Haa*," I affirmed. "I haven't eaten."

Somalis usually didn't eat cooked foods in the morning, but on account of the war and the trials it had delivered me, I was hungry as a shark.

We started with *shah xawaash* tea, which contained milk, sugar, cinnamon, cloves, cardamom, and black pepper, and as we sipped, Xeed brought me up to speed on the *afgembi*. He said the capital was more or less secured, but mercenary forces continued to occupy numerous border towns to the west, and some key port towns such as Kismayo remained under the control of the Islamists. Somaliland thus far was playing neutral, and heavy politicking was underway to bring in more of their leaders in support of our central government. Three seats on Somalia's new governing body, the Council of Emperors, were already occupied by Somalilanders, which Xeed said was promising. However, he warned, the *Boqor's* continued aloofness to our cause was worrisome. If the clan head of the northerners chose to pit himself against our new government, his sheer popularity and influence could wean away the northern provinces towards more secessionist positions.

As I hailed from Puntland and knew the strong sense of independence shared by the northern clans, I could not discount the veracity of Xeed's analysis. Again, I asked if I could speak to the *Boqor* directly, and again I was met with denial, this time in Hassan Madoobeh's remark, "The assembly forbids it, at least at this stage."

"But am I not part of the assembly now, as promised by President Tahliil in the event the *afgembi* succeeded, which it has?"

"*Haa, saaxiib,*" Hassan replied, "you've earned a rightful seat on the Council of Emperors, and soon will take congress with Somalia's new governing body. But these are very sensitive matters that are currently being dealt with by those already in contact with the *Boqor*. Negotiations may take time."

"Let us eat in the name of God, shall we?" said the doctor as trays of food were placed on the cot beside me.

"*Bismillaah!*" replied Xeed, toasting the meal in Allah's name.

The rest of us responded in like manner, and soon were digging into *wan iyo bariis*, which was lamb with rice, and *soor*, a porridge, which in this instance was made of wheat and peas.

"We've raided the mercs' storehouses," Hassan said, "and soon the capital will reopen to trade. Meddling by warlords and mercenaries will no longer be tolerated on any level. Once free enterprise is established, the empire will be unstoppable."

"*Bashbash iyo barwaaqo*," I affirmed, wishing for much prosperity.

As I sat on my bed eating, I asked about recent events, such as some technicalities concerning the war and the fate of *The Madoobaad*, which carried my sister, Osman, and Cosob, among others.

Xeed relayed a startling piece of information. He said Bashir had expressly scrambled the MiG fighter that had paved the way for my militia to succeed. I found this startling because, for all intents and purposes, Bashir's commitment to the *afgembi* — and, moreover, to me — I'd found to be extremely dubious over the course of the engagement. But now, Xeed was telling me that Bashir had done something of an about-face in support of the battle, and ostensibly in support of me. I could only assume he'd learned of my advance from Kenya, and understanding my new force to be virtually overwhelming, he probably capitulated in his own way to our success by throwing in the MiG. If there was one thing I knew about Bashir, he was very Machiavellian in that he knew how to manipulate situations so that he always came out on the winning side. That being said, I knew Bashir had some substance and wasn't entirely a man of conniving, thus I couldn't help but feel a spark of gratitude for what he'd done. His napalm-dropping MiG may not have been a decisive asset, but I or anyone in my camelback army would have to had agreed, it made the fight that much easier.

"As for *The Madoobaad*," Xeed continued more sullenly, "we've lost all trace of her."

"*Maxaa?*" I asked in disbelief. "Even with the Maritime Automated Pictograph? Even after consulting Waheed?"

"*Haa*," he conceded. "It may be the ship's radar- and satellite-jamming capabilities, but once she left the harbor, it's like she vanished into thin air."

My heart weighed heavily then, believing the ship may have sunk. Perhaps Xeed already knew this, but in my weary disposition was withholding the information. I reproached him, but he just shook his head and said that he and everyone else really had no idea what had befallen *The Madoobaad* and her crew.

"But," he added in consolation, "it's only been five days. Maybe she headed to open water and is reticent to compromise her position just yet. As soon as communication is established, we'll order her to return to port."

I appreciated Xeed's best-case scenario, but still the issue troubled me deeply. "By the way, Xeed," I inquired, "how do you feel? It looks like you've finally been able to put on some weight."

"*Haa*, the malaria almost took the life out of me."

"I'm glad you pulled through so quickly, *saaxiib*. Hard to believe you contracted it in Dante. I lived there for half my life and never heard of anyone contracting cerebral malaria there."

He just shrugged his shoulders and said, "Beats me, but that's where I got it, according to Nasir."

"I remember when they thought you had radiation poisoning. Thank Allah they were wrong."

"*Waan ogahay*," he said, *I know*. "That seems to be the scourge of Somalia these days. But hang in there, matey — you're in good hands now. You'll pull through."

෨

After we had finished eating, we praised Allah for the meal, saying, "*Alhamdu Lilaahi.*"

"Noor," the doctor said, "now that you have some of your strength back, we must administer more medicine."

"The *antibaayootig?*"

"*Haa,*" he replied, then placed a briefcase beside me on my cot.

"Can we save it for later, Doc? I feel pretty good right now."

"*Maya.* I'm under direct orders from Zayid. It's your health one has in mind, Commander."

I was pleased he had called me commander, for I had, in fact, recently been promoted to Commander of OAM — the Ocean Assault Mogadishu naval component of the *afgembi.* That he knew my true rank when so many others did not gave me reason enough to trust him.

He asked the others to leave for a few moments while he administered my medication. He pulled on a surgeon's mask and rubber gloves before opening the briefcase. Five or six serum tubes cast a green glow upon his face. He removed one and carefully loaded it into a syringe, then, after finding a large vein in my arm, he injected me with the *antibaayootig.*

The serum burned as it coursed through my bloodstream, but it cured my aches and pains almost instantly. And then I felt an incredible surge of energy. My stigmata were glowing strong again, and the star upon my heart, which had recently become dull, was now glossy and effusing with light.

"Remarkable," countered the doctor as he took an auscultation. "Your heartbeat is very strong."

"*Haa*," I agreed, studying my stigmata. "Where does Zayid get this stuff, anyway?"

"He has his own laboratory."

"He?"

"*Maxaa?*"

"You just called Zayid a person, Doctor. It's an organization."

"Yes, of course," Sooraan replied. "Zayid, the pirate organization, has its own laboratory, just like they have their own medical facility in Garoowe. The lab was originally set up to develop weaponry, but its scope has been expanding."

"Where is this lab you speak of?"

"That, Commander, is classified. Don't concern yourself with these matters. That's my department, and the realm of science. Just be happy the *antibaayootig* is working. It's the only thing we've found that can counter radiation poisoning."

"But for how long, Doctor? How long will it sustain me? My condition worsens greatly without it."

"We have however much it may take, Commander. Just don't go running off anywhere. Without the serum, you'll be at the mercy of your sickness."

"Can it cure me indefinitely?"

"I don't know." The doctor was frank. He placed the spent syringe in a plastic bag and returned it to the suitcase, which he shut and locked before removing his gloves and mask.

"But you're a doctor," I reproached. "How can you not know? Who can tell me?"

"Nobody knows, Haji," he addressed me informally as he wrapped a bandage over my injection pricks, for now there were many. "You're a test subject, *saaxiib*."

"What do you mean?"

"Stow your worries, *jaalle*. Let's just keep up the injections so you stay well, eh? You'll soon be running an empire. Leave the medicine to me."

"*Mahadsanid*, Doctor. I do feel like my old self again. I suddenly feel one-hundred-percent better."

"Excellent. That's the spirit. I'll leave you with a little *qandi* pouch of antigen, should you need it in an emergency. But rest assured that I or another dedicated physician shall always be close at hand to continue your injections. You do look better already, comrade. You'll be fine, Noor, just fine."

"What about my sister? Can she get the injections too? She's much sicker than me."

"Amina?"

"*Haa*, Amina Rage. She has radiation poisoning."

"I'll consult with Zayid," he replied, eyeing me curiously. He went to leave, then stopped suddenly and asked almost reluctantly, "Haji, did you not hear? *The Madoobaad* is still lost at sea?"

"*Haa*, I've heard. But when she is found, you must help my sister, as well."

"*Haddii Eebbe yidhaahdo, saaxiib* — God willing, my friend."

৵

Obsessing over the fate of my sister, I threw on my yellow windbreaker and made a hasty retreat from the palace. I went down to the harbor, whereupon I met a longshoreman mooring a dhow to the bollards. He said his name was Uways Mumin, and he hadn't seen *The Madoobaad*. The merchant ship alongside, he relayed, was the second of the morning, and the second large craft to come into port since the *afgembi*.

"Who's your employer?" I inquired.

"I work as a stevedore," he said, "and get paid by the merchant mariners. I used to do this as a boy, when great dhows would sail in on the monsoons to unload wheat flour, sorghum, and building materials, then leave filled with sheep, camels, and goats sold right here on the docks by pastoralist families. I can't tell you how happy I am that trade is now resuming and I'm working again. In its heyday, this harbor linked a great trading network between Africa, Arabia, India, and the Indonesian littoral. Even during the Barre regime, there was much work for longshoremen. In the mid to late eighties, the Americans delivered many weapons to the Barre government, and aid was flowing in from the USA, Saudi Arabia, and Italy to help keep him in power.

"The ships you see arriving now hold much promise for the future of this city. The merchant mariners say they've been lured back by the announcement of Somalia's new empire, with the Mogadishu harbor being its principal seaport. They're eager to form new business alliances and are paying me well to help them."

Stevedore Uways Mumin ties a dhow off to a bollard

"How is the army treating you?"

"Zayid's militia? As equitably as I've seen in this port since I was a younker. Ships coming in to trade are allowed to moor, and as of yet, no taxes are being levied. The soldiers manning the checkpoints take a look at the goods entering the city, but generally are allowing the harbor to operate as a free-trade area. They even have two PT boats serving as harbormasters to make sure there's no funny business. If there's one thing about this Zayid organization, they sure know how to run a harbor. I can only hope that things continue in this manner."

"But you haven't seen any of their motherships?"

"The *Windrose* was scuttled, everybody knows that. But *The Madoobaad*, well, some say she was lost at sea, but I really have no idea. I only returned to work just yesterday. I wish *The Madoobaad* would return. I want to see the *zaar*."

"The *zaar*?"

"There's a *haweenay* onboard who does a dance of spirit possession. All the seamen are talking about her."

"Amina Rage?"

"*Haa*, that was her name."

"Well, if you see her return in any way, shape, or form, come down to the presidential palace at once and ask for me directly. I'll notify the guards to let you pass."

I held out a small wad of U.S. dollars, which the longshoreman received merrily, saying, "*Mahadsanid, mahadsanid.*"

"*Waad mahadsantahay.*" I told him that it was I who was grateful, then turned to leave.

"*Magacaa?*" he asked my name.

"*Magacaygu waa Haji,*" I said, "Noor Haji Fayrus."

"*Dhib ma laha!*" he replied, whooping with glee at discovering my true identity. *No problem!* is what he'd said.

HEADS OF STATE

ON MY WAY BACK to the palace, I saw some kids playing *kubadda cagta* in an intersection. The Italians called the game *futbal*, while the Americans called it soccer. There was very little vehicle traffic in Mogadishu, but it's not the *where* that surprised me about their game. As I walked past, I kept asking myself *what* kind of *kubbad* was that — referring to the ball itself, which, while being kicked hither and thither, continued to elude my focus. It bounced in a strange manner and appeared quite heavy. I was thinking that perhaps they were using a melon that had just come off one of the trading ships, when all of a sudden a younker kicked it against the wall next to me, staining the façade red as the ball hit it. It was not a ball at all, but the head of a mercenary, cleanly severed beneath the chin.

The shock of the discovery now passed, I wedged my foot beneath the soldier's helmet and kicked the "ball" back towards the children. The younkers were dirt poor, and it did not particularly disturb me that they were using the head of a vanquished mercenary for sport. I did make a mental note, however, to order a shipload of real *futbals* to distribute amongst them, in care of the new empire, and I had a fleeting notion to promote the inclusion of a Somali soccer team in the world Olympics. After all, Somalis were avid *kubadda cagta* players who could probably take the gold with their sprightly footwork and competitive drive.

Arriving back at the presidential palace, I informed the guards about longshoreman Uways Mumin, then made my way up to my makeshift command center in the prime minister's chamber. I fully expected it to be taken over by an actual dignitary or perhaps by Zayid security personnel, for both types of occupants were now ubiquitous throughout the palace, but what I found instead was Xeed at the top of the stairwell, training a pistol on me.

"Hey there, Xeed, it's me," I said.

"Sure, come on up," he replied. "Security, you know the game."

When I reached the top of the stairs, he asked me how I felt. I showed him my palms and my stigmata were gleaming. "Pretty darn good," I laughed. "At least while the medicine holds up."

Within the command center, the young *waranle* Qaasim had fallen asleep on a tattered old couch. Nobody else was there, but I noticed some upgrades in equipment. There were now some radiophones at our disposal, more computers, wires running up through the roof presumably to an extended antenna or other networking services, while yet more electronic equipment lay clumped on the floor.

"*Mahadsanid* for setting all this stuff up, *walalo*," I thanked Xeed like a brother.

"Don't mention it, Noor. *Waa muhiim*."

"I agree — it's important to carve out our space here. Allah only knows how many prime ministers are roaming the halls out there, and soon they'll be looking for their own office to set up shop in."

"There should be enough room for everybody," Xeed countered. "But it's important we have a secure room from which to operate. I for one have a lot of business transactions that must be conducted in private."

"Understood."

"But Noor," said he, stuffing his pistol back in his suspenders' holster, "look at you, man! You're practically on fire! Look at your hands, and the white star — I can see it even now through your windbreaker. It's glowing like an electric bulb."

"It's the injections, *walalo*," I laughed. "They have a sure-fire way of lighting me up!"

"Can you make ball lightning? I want to see."

Qaasim, apparently having overheard, woke up all at once and sat up on the couch. "Hey, Haj, wus up?"

"Hey there, Qaasim. I'm good — just getting back into the swing of things."

Xeed was still looking at me excitedly. "Will you show me?"

"Ball lightning is very dangerous," I replied. "I don't want to accidentally hurt you or fuck up any of this nice equipment. Maybe later, outside. It's crazy energy, and I have to be careful with its application."

With the sound of boots clunking up the stairs, he unbridled his pistol and said, "We need to get a camera on that stairwell. Excuse me for a moment." He dashed over to the stairs and called down, "Is that who I think it is?"

"Stow your weapon," a *haweenay* said.

"Khalidah?" Xeed asked.

"Where's Noor?" she replied, and a strikingly beautiful woman arrived at the top of the stairwell. She wore a tight, one-piece, black leather suit and held her pistol up against her lips. When she saw me, she returned her gun to her hip holster and said, "Commander Fayrus, I am Khalidah Malak. It's a pleasure to finally make your acquaintance."

"Immortal Angel," I replied with a glint in my eye. She was flawless.

"Some do call me that," she said.

"What a transformation," remarked Xeed, walking around her in study.

"You didn't like me before?" she quipped.

"Of course I did," he was quick to reply. "But the extra volume, more flesh in the cheeks, the facial make-over — it's truly amazing."

Khalidah Malak

She just laughed and said, "They do this kind of stuff in New York every day, but thanks, Xeed, for taking notice."

"I saw your United Nations address," I told her a little nervously — she was that pretty. "Very well spoken, especially considering how little you had to go on at the time."

"*Mahadsanid,* Commander. Had I known you singlehandedly raised a refugee army to consummate the *afgembi,* my speech would've been worded much, much differently. Now look, you've really done it! You've established Somalia's first empire! Congratulations, Commander."

"You too, Khalidah! And please, just call me Haji."

A nearby radiophone started beeping loudly. Xeed answered the call, saying, "*Nabad!*"

"It's Bashir," replied the Puntland commander. "Has Khalidah arrived yet?"

"*Haa,* she's here with Noor and me."

"Noor is there?"

"*Haa.*"

"Good, put him on."

Bashir asked me about the state of affairs in the presidential palace, so I told him what I knew: there was ample security inside, and the new *guurti* — or parliamentary assembly — had been holding meetings in the main auditorium.

He told me to be on watch for suicide bombers masquerading as dignitaries, and for car bombers in the streets. He said there was credible intel that al-Shabaab was planning such attacks, and that all security forces operating under the empire had been placed on high alert. He then asked about my health.

I told him I'd passed out for two days, and that I suffered from intense migraines and nausea if I stopped taking the *antibaayootig*.

"That's the radiation sickness trying to take over," he told me. "Rest assured the antigen is working, but to be on the safe side, I've arranged to fly you out to Djibouti for some tests."

"Djibouti?"

"*Haa*, we have access to a facility there with high-tech equipment. It's important we run a CT scan."

"A what?"

"A way to accurately x-ray your head. The experts want to scan your brain for any signs of trauma that may have been caused by your exposure to radiation."

"My brain?"

"Don't be alarmed, Haji. By gathering this information, your outlook will become clearer, and we'll be able to provide you with a higher level of care."

"When do I leave?"

"A plane has just landed, and I'm arranging an escort now. With the threat of car bombs posed by al-Shabaab, from now on you'll need to move fast when driving through the capital."

෴

As it turned out, the Immortal Angel was part of my escort. She sat beside me in the backseat of a black SUV, and we sped between two technicals towards the Mogadishu airport. She asked me about the Oracle, inquiring if I saw her trying to interpret the future through geometric designs worked into fine sand, in the curves of cowry shells, or in the smoke patterns cast off by burning incense. She said these were the mediums most used by the *faaliso*, or traditional female diviners.

"*Maya*," I told her, "I did not witness her doing any of that. Her source of information was always a mystery to me, and in fact for a long time I was convinced the Oracle was you, or your Wadani-clan lookalike, whom I'm sure you've heard of."

"*Haa*, but unfortunately for the Wadani, since my transformative surgery in New York, she won't be able to masquerade as me so easily. But why'd you think the Oracle was me? Was there really that much resemblance before my surgery?"

"At times she did appear as beautiful."

Khalidah blushed. "At times? So she didn't look like me all the time?"

"She may have drugged me, causing me to see things funny. In quite a few instances, she became as green and scaly as a reptile — really quite frightening, actually. Nothing even remotely resembling you."

"The *Aasho Badhi*? Is that what you were dealing with?" she asked in all seriousness, referring to a desert lizard believed to exist in the realm of the devil.

"*Allahu jixinjix,* I should hope not."

"You're familiar with the case of Mohamed Abdulle Hassan?" she inquired.

"The Mad Mullah?"

"*Haa,* and how, abandoned by the seaward clans, he sold his soul to *Aasho Badhi* in return for invincibility?"

"I'm not sure what to make of that, Khalidah. But I'll tell you something, I'm no Mad Mullah, and I hate it when people compare me to him. He may have fought off the foreign invaders, but he was also a camel rustler, not to mention he massacred thousands of innocent Somalis."

Suddenly, a beat-up old sedan tracked across the intersection in front of our motorcade. Our lead technical did not have time to stop, but swerved in what looked like an effort to smash the car out of the way by hitting its front corner. The vehicles connected, and there was a loud explosion and bright flash.

The driver of our SUV swerved radically around the carnage. Once past the accident, he let off on the gas just long enough for the technical behind us to take the lead, then sped swiftly behind it.

"That was a close one," Khalidah remarked, aiming her pistol at the rear window, scanning for more suicide bombers through the tinted glass.

"They were after us?" I asked, snatching my TT-30 pistol from my thigh holster.

"That was no accident, Haji," she replied coolly.

"Mogadishu is not safe," the driver said, eyeing us through his rearview mirror.

"I hate this city," Khalidah replied evenly.

"We've reached the airport," the driver announced, then tore past a checkpoint and onto the tarmac, where a Cessna was waiting with idling engines.

COMPOUND 6

WE LANDED IN DJIBOUTI and were transferred by another black, dark-tinted SUV to the gates of a French military base, which made me very nervous. Khalidah flashed the guards some identification, and we were summarily waved through the checkpoint.

"What's going on here?" I asked, wondering if I was being escorted directly into the hands of the authorities, perhaps by someone who was not the Immortal Angel at all, but a double agent working for the enemy. After all, her "cosmetic surgery" had transmogrified her into another person entirely. Could plastic surgery do that so quickly? I was starting to have my doubts. The French wouldn't have forgotten my kidnapping of two of their navy pilots three years prior, or the two who were killed when my team shot down their SuperCobra in that same engagement. "Is this some sort of trap?"

"Relax, Noor," Khalidah said, touching my arm, "you're in good hands."

"Who are you, exactly, and where are you taking me?"

"Need I remind you I'm Zayid's top double agent, masquerading as a Lloyd's of London shipping insurance agent and anti-piracy liaison? I have access to just about anyplace on both sides of this dirty business."

"And who am I supposed to be, rolling onto this military base? A pirate under your auspices?"

"Nobody's going to ask you, and if they do, they don't speak Somali, and you don't speak French, so just relax and follow my lead. Zayid didn't task me with this assignment without good reason. You're about to get the best medical care in the Horn of Africa."

"Here?"

"There." She pointed to a non-descript, grey, windowless building. "Compound six."

We stopped before a steel garage door, and it opened a second later. Then the driver cruised us into Compound 6, and the door lowered behind us. Two white men wearing surgical scrubs appeared out of the shadows.

I held my pistol in my windbreaker pocket, remembering the words of Captain Shar'ma'arke when he said its bullet would stop anything. If this was a trap, that theory would soon be put to the test.

"Alex Briggs," one of the surgeons said with a strange accent.

"*Arrivederci*," she replied, then continued in what sounded like Italian as the other surgeon approached me and extended his hand.

I kept a firm grip on my pistol with one hand as he firmly shook my other hand. Whatever was going on, I resolved not to say a word in any language, so kept a shit-eating grin through thick and thin.

The surgeons led us through an open doorway and down a long, cement corridor. The whole place was built like a perfect concrete bunker, with immaculate, unpainted walls. We turned into a room fitted with nice carpeting and couches, whereupon sat Commander Bashir, reading a newspaper.

"You've arrived!" he said, getting up and folding his paper. The two surgeons continued into an adjacent room. "How was your flight? Pretty quick, I'd imagine."

"We lost our point getting out of Mog," Khalidah relayed. "Car bomb."

"*Haa*, very unfortunate," Bashir replied with a tinge of dread. "I think this will be our greatest threat until we can better secure the borders. But I'm glad you two made it. Haji, how do you feel?"

I looked at him skeptically. He always acted glib, but I sensed something odd and secretive about his behavior and this whole visit. "I'm okay," I replied, "as long as I get the injections. I understand I'll be under-going some tests."

"*Haa, saaxiib,*" he addressed me as *friend.* "Come, I have a surprise for you." He offered me an upturned hand, almost in a gesture of reconciliation.

I followed him down another long hallway, then left into a room where I was half-expecting to be waylaid by French commandos and taken into custody or worse. I'd never fully trusted Bashir, and here, on a French military base, my fears had seemingly come full circle.

The room was empty. He went and stood before another door, then grabbed the knob and glanced back at me. I gripped my pistol beneath my jacket and pointed it at him.

"Noor!" said Cosob, jumping up from a leather chair in the next room.

"Haji!" cried Amina Rage from a bed adjacent the chair.

"Nephew!" remarked Uncle Osman, sitting up on a leather couch.

"Hello, Haji," said *Dhakhtar* Nasir, standing behind them.

"Oh, my god, you're all here!" I replied exultantly.

"And so are you!" Bashir addressed me, beaming.

As it turned out, *The Madoobaad* had not been lost or sunk, but had sheltered in a secret cave at Two Brothers isles, from where the injured were airlifted off the island to Zayid's medical center in Garoowe. As for

Amina, Osman, Admiral Cosob, and *Dhakhtar* Nasir, they had been taken by Zayid's transport helicopter to this secret compound to receive a maximum level of care and protection.

"Transport chopper?" I was bamboozled.

"I told you we had another chopper," Bashir said.

I just smiled and shook my head.

"Your surprise at our sea-and-air capabilities never ceases to amaze me," he continued. "You seem to forget just how powerful Zayid has become since you left to America. We now have numerous aircraft, including MiG-35s at our disposal, with expert Somali pilots who've defected from various foreign airforces."

I took the opportunity during that conversation to thank Bashir for the MiG assistance during the final putsch on the capital.

"At the time, it was all I could scramble," he revealed. "Otherwise, I'd have sent more."

"How many MiGs does Zayid have, anyway?" I asked.

"Now that's classified," he replied with a wink directed at Khalidah.

Amina and Osman had been receiving top treatment by European physicians, all under the close scrutiny of *Dhakhtar* Nasir. Osman's leg had been properly reset, while Amina had regained much of her health and energy thanks to steady injections of the *antibaay-ootig*. She'd already undergone several CT scans, and everybody was being well fed with Somali foods and pastas, thanks to Cosob's culinary preparations (which, he admitted, wouldn't have turned out so sumptuous without additional tips from Private Rage, as everyone now called her).

As for me, I remained at the compound for five or six more days, eating, watching TV, calling back home to talk to my wife Issa, mother Warsame, and two kids, Mohamed and Jeilani, and quality time was had with Amina, Cosob, and Osman. The Immortal Angel and Bashir left the day after I'd arrived, having more pressing matters to attend to regarding the establishment of the empire. But for most of the rest of us, recovery was the top priority. I was given a CT scan every day, and serum injections three times daily, albeit in smaller doses than I usually took. The two French doctors continued to study me, as did *Dhakhtar* Nasir, and all appeared pleased at my progress. The medical treatment was officially sanctioned by Zayid, Bashir had said, who placed my recovery and that of my sister at the highest priority. Many sailors who'd been involved in the seizure of the Selection Ministry freighter nigh one month prior were falling ill with radiation sickness, and Zayid had a mind to help them with serum injections, but the medicine was costly and needed to be perfected first on my sister and me before it could be applied to our wider pirate population. Some *budhcad-badeed* would probably die in the interim, Bashir had admitted, but the drug was being rolled out as quickly as possible.

I was never actually shown the CT scans of my brain, but the doctors appeared very pleased with the results. To my surprise, my stigmata and star "tattoo" — as Bashir called it — received little observation by the doctors. I was eager to show them the electromagnetic energy that emerged in those areas after a strong injection, but they preferred to administer the antigen at a level just below the threshold of what energized my electromagnetic field to that extent. They said, according to Nasir, the bioluminescence was an undesirable side effect to be avoided, and seemed to have been precipitated by my brush with lightning during the helicopter crash. My bullet of *Jannah* was enough of a "special weapon," Bashir relayed in an email, and my health need not be put at further risk by spurring on the freakish phenomenon that occurred within me during "an overdose," as he termed it. My sister did not display any electromagnetic disturbance within her, he pointed out, because her electromagnetic field had not been thrown out of whack by ball lightning, and furthermore, she'd been receiving an amount of serum more commensurate with her body weight and its ability to heal her radiation sickness.

That it was now openly spoken that we could, in fact, heal with proper care was enough for me to trust in the process and put to rest my rather juvenile desire to make ball lightning.

Sometimes questions were posed about the nature of the medical facility, being on a French military base, but our inquiries were never fully answered by Bashir; and while *Dhakhtar* Nasir could communicate somewhat with the other physicians, he said he wasn't fluent enough in French to get hard answers about the facility.

In checking up with us via a cell phone call, I put the question to Khalidah, and she was similarly cagey, telling me not to worry about it, it was a secure Zayid facility, and once the doctors gave the word, we'd be released to fly back to Mog or wherever else we desired. She asked me, as did Bashir, if I intended to return to Mogadishu, for there was still a seat reserved for me on the *guurti*. I told them that to sit amongst the Council of Emperors, running a new, sovereign Somalia, was the culmination of my greatest dream, and I'd be there as soon as the doctors released me.

For Amina's part, she said she'd like to return with me to the capital, should our recovery times allow it. Her health had deteriorated far quicker than mine, and more severely before she received her first injection, so in all appearances, her recovery time would take longer. But thus far, she'd made a decisive comeback from the pallor of death that hung over her when I'd last seen her in the sickbay of *The Madoobaad*.

The only real shocker that occurred during my stay at Compound 6 was when I spotted a Selection Ministry label on one of the serum boxes.

"What the fuck is that?" I asked in Somali.

The French, or maybe they were Italians, didn't understand me, so I pointed at the label on the container. They just shrugged their shoulders and went about their business like it didn't mean anything.

I called Bashir by radiophone about it, and this is what he said: "Those containers — the blue, nylon ones — were recovered from the Selection Ministry freighter, along with a bunch of other stuff we stripped from the ship. We used them to offload some cargo, and kept them because they were of good construction and useful for us. As you can see, they can be locked and sealed, and require a PIN to open again. Very useful, very high-tech."

I didn't dwell on it further at the time, but perhaps I should have. After all, the Selection Ministry ship was highly radioactive. It stood to reason those boxes were a hazard to keep in such close quarters. Then again, the serum itself was radioactive, so I guess it just made the whole issue moot. The fact was, under regimented treatment, my insufferable nausea and migraines were going away, and Amina and I were healing. That's all that seemed to matter at the time.

DANGER GAMES

ON MY LAST NIGHT in the compound, Cosob cooked a hearty dinner of Somali salmagundi made from beef, goat meat, pasta, and spices. It was served with rice, and we ate everything out of bowls or with our hands.

After the meal, we washed our fingers in a container Cosob had provided for us, then wiped them on a towel, saying "*Alhamdu Lilaahi*" in an expression of *Gratitude to Allah*, and then we said, "*Mahadsanid, contadu way macaanayd*," telling Cosob that the meal was excellent. Exhibiting classic Somali hospitality, he brought Osman and me some *qaat* to chew on afterwards.

While we were mulling *qaat* leaves and spitting into cups, enjoying the pleasant *mirqaan*, the *high* the plant bestowed on us, Cosob asked me about a previous hijacking we'd undertaken. "Remember that swaggy we jumped in November? The inside job with the Norwegian tanker?"

"Off Socotra? Yeah, too easy—"

"Do you remember the *Faranji* onboard with the beard?"

"They were all Europeans, weren't they?"

"*Haa*, but there was a bearded guy who wanted to join Khatar Force One, remember?"

"I can't really recall..."

"Anyway, after the ransoms were paid, the black heart contacted Zayid directly and said he'd devised a way to upgrade KF-One in a way that would revolution-ize hijackings. Zayid was highly suspicious at first, but the guy was very persistent, so the big fish agreed to meet with him."

"What was his name?" Osman inquired.

"Thor."

"Thor what?"

"Just Thor. So he made a formal presentation before the Assembly of Presidents, and they unani-mously agreed; his plan was the future of Somali piracy. They've since hired him to test his strategy in the field, and soon we begin training with him."

"Are you serious?" I remarked.

"Absolutely," Cosob replied. "Khatar Force Two, matey. I've already talked with Bashir and he said, so long as you feel up to it, you can join the team."

"Will you be using super-skiffs?"

"*Maya.*"

"Then what is this white man's new strategy?"

"It's top secret — they haven't even told me."

I raised my brows in a smug expression. "But we've already been through that," I countered. "Join Zayid's elite strike force, take the top-secret missions, and if you survive, which we somehow did, then get pro-moted to command positions. The empire awaits our counsel, *saaxiib* — we no longer need to play those dangerous games. It's time to reap the fruits of our accomplishments."

Cosob offered me more *qaat* leaves, saying, "I know how strong your desire must be to sit amongst the Council of Emperors, but in all honesty, *walalo*, I think you'll quickly grow bored with it. You're too young to be a stodgy old *guurti* member. You're a *waranle*, Haji — a warrior, not some wrinkled old *wadaad*."

I just stared back at Cosob, not knowing what to think. I chewed my cud and ruminated. Why was he calling me a wrinkled old priest?

"Join me, Haji," he pleaded, "join KF-Two. There'll be only five of us, including the white guy. This is super-elite shit. Thor specifically asked for those of us from the original team with experience with ejection seats. That makes you, me, and Istar Abyad — if he's up to it, and one more."

"But we won't be using the super-skiffs."

"*Maya*. We train in the hinterlands of Yemen, far from *bad-weyn*."

I regarded him wide-eyed, now totally *mirqaan*, my left cheek ballooning with *qaat*. He was a real slice of *muqumad* — a real son-of-a-bitch. He knew I loved adventures. He knew I was a slave to secret missions. I smiled, then laughed. Cosob knew me well, too well. *The bastard!*

INAN-LA-YAAL

AFTER SIX NIGHTS in the compound, Cosob and I bid farewell to Osman, Amina, and Nasir, then boarded a twin-prop Fokker aircraft on base, piloted by a black Djiboutian who spoke only French.

We flew south to Mogadishu, where Cosob and I deplaned. We watched the pilot head north again, his old flying ship buzzing loudly as it lifted off the tarmac.

Moments later, a motorcade of shiny black SUVs pulled up. Probably government vehicles, but we were still a little jittery. A window rolled down, and the Immortal Angel appeared, offering us a lift.

"You knew we were coming," Cosob laughed.

∾

Less than a week later, I'd find myself flying out again, departing for my first training mission with Thor, the Norwegian. We met him at Zayid's camp in Yemen. He never came to Somalia, probably because he was a white man, and also the privacy and geography afforded by the Yemeni backcountry was more suitable to our training. In fact, the most advanced tactics of Khatar Force 2 required specific terrain — none of which had anything to do with the ocean. It was extremely exciting training, to put it mildly, and it didn't take long for me to concur with Zayid: this would revolutionize piracy. And I couldn't deny that Cosob had also been right: I was hopelessly addicted to danger.

When not in Yemen, I was back in Mog, getting more injections and helping run the empire, or I was visiting Amina in Boosaaso, who was there with Osman, Nasir, and my middle sister, Fatuma Abdul.

While steady shots of the antigen had restored my usual vigor, Amina seemed to be getting worse. By March of 2012, three months after she'd initially fallen ill, she was altogether *'alaantiisiiba 'adaatay*, which is what Somalis say about someone who is very sick. The literal translation is their "leaf has become pale," and for a lady whose skintone was usually a beautiful, cinnamon brown, it pained everyone who knew her to see her becoming so ghostly fair — her husband, especially.

Jamal Abdallah Awaad had taken leave of his job in the UAE, entrusting his two children to the care of his housekeeper in order for him to be with his infirm wife. Fatuma Abdul had phoned him almost as soon as Amina wound up on her doorstep, figuratively speaking, care of Osman, who could not take care of her himself because of his injured leg. But *Dhakhtar* Nasir, under no clear directive save for a personal interest in Amina's welfare and a curiosity about the antigen he was administering her, was offered a room by Fatuma. Thus he remained in the house as Amina's personal doctor, providing round-the-clock care.

Amina was sleeping most of the time, and when she was awake, she was most commonly dizzy and nauseous, with bouts of vomiting and high fever. All of this deeply troubled the good doctor, but more so Jamal, who, as the months crawled by, increasingly blamed me for Amina's condition. As March became April, and April waxed into another hot and cloudless May, I found myself at the receiving end of sundry insults from Amina's conservative husband. Jamal used to work at the Las Qoray tuna factory — a business that became a cover for one of Zayid's clandestine pirate bases. Jamal was even more stodgy than Osman used to be, and now that his wife — my sister — was dying, he in no uncertain terms told me what he thought of me and my occupation.

"You've been a terrible influence on Amina," he grumbled. "Look at the promises you've made her, and see how much you've hurt her with your reckless adventurism. It wasn't enough to ditch your own family in pursuit of piracy. You had to take Amina away from me and our children, as well."

"Shut your mouth, *qorqode*," I told him, calling him a bad husband who overly concerned himself with running household affairs. "Quiet down, lest you wake her. Amina became a pirate on her own volition. In fact, I made a point to tell her it was not possible to enter the sweet trade as a *haweenay*."

"Exactly," countered Jamal, his once jovial smile now a permanently bitter frown, "you told her she couldn't become a pirate while you yourself practically celebrated the activity. You know Amina is a proud but restless woman, and you knew that if you told her she couldn't do something, she'd take that as a challenge."

"If Amina was a restless wife, then you're to blame for that. You should have satisfied her more."

He took a swing at me, which I narrowly deflected. I fired back at his jaw.

Fatuma came storming into the living room, trying to break up the skirmish. "Both of you!" she cried as she forced her way between us. "This is *my* house, so cut it out or get out!"

"Where's Said?" Jamal asked her, wiping a bloodied lip.

"He'll be home very soon."

"Well," Jamal quipped, "tell him to throw this *labo-shaadle* out."

"*Footo weine!*" I shot back. He really was a *fat-ass*.

"That's enough!" Fatuma scolded us both.

Two of her children came rumbling down the stairs to see what all the commotion was about, but I was long done arguing with an ass.

"*Labo-shaadle,*" I muttered under my breath, shaking my head. Jamal had called me a totally destitute man; a man with no job, land, or livestock; a man that connives his way through life. What a load of crap! I was the king of the jungle, and he knew it. What I wanted to say, but didn't, was that he was jealous. I had socked him pretty good, though, so that was enough homestead regulation for now.

"What's up, Haji?" inquired Gin, Fatuma's son.

"*Bilaa micne*," I told him, *nonsense*. "Your father will be home soon. *Du'o, inan, du'o.*" I said he should look to his father, and not us, for guidance and blessings.

I promptly left the house and walked briskly to Osman's place, trying to blow off steam. My uncle lodged me until I caught a flight to Mog.

WHITE STAR RISING

"*TAALLADII WAA MAXAY, AWOOWE?*" a younker put to his grandfather, inquiring about a new monument that'd been erected in the city centre.

"*Badmaax Sulub,*" the elder replied, calling it *The Steel Sailor.*

"*The Steel Sail,*" Bashir corrected him with a chuckle and a wink.

"*Mahadsanid,*" said the old man, then remarked it was "*quruxsan*" — beautiful.

"*Barwaaqo,*" Bashir chuckled, saying simply "prosperity," then resumed strolling alongside Khalidah and me.

"*Hoggaamiye! Hoggaamiye!*" two Somalis exclaimed as we passed, effecting a little bow while holding their hands in prayer.

I nodded in return and thanked them.

"You're very popular in the city," commented Khalidah.

"Perhaps they're refugees," I replied, downplaying her assessment.

"Even more reason for them to thank you," Bashir put in. "The majority of refugees you brought back from Dadaab now have stable employment with the Empire, which in turn has given us the manpower we need to supply the capital's security forces, police, construction workers, and longshoremen."

"And there they have reason to thank you and Zayid, Bashir," I rejoined. "The capital invested to hire them and rebuild this city would not have been possible without the Organization."

"Perhaps in the beginning, Noor. But now, as you know, many wealthy Somalis have returned from overseas to invest their own money in local enterprises."

"Ah, and this is where foreigners fail time and time again in their interventions into foreign lands," Khalidah remarked. "If you don't give people food and jobs right away, they'll fight back. But if you do, they'll just as soon join your cause instead."

"Especially when it's a national cause," Bashir put in.

"Precisely," replied Khalidah.

The Steel Sail

We strolled towards the Bakara Market, passing many homes with men sitting in their courtyards drinking tea. Those who noticed us, and almost all of the security personnel who we passed, gave us a nod or wave, and many were smiling no different than the children playing *kubadda cagta* in the streets. After Zayid's first shipment of soccer balls to keep the younkers occupied, entrepreneurial businessmen and Somali philanthropists shipped in many more. Somalia's first Olympic *futbal* team was already in training.

"How is your sister?" Bashir inquired.

"Amina?" I exhaled heavily. " '*Alaantiisiiba 'adaatay*, but we're all hoping she'll pull through."

"Why does she remain in Boosaaso?" Khalidah asked. "Better treatment could be had in Europe or Dubai."

"She doesn't want to leave," I replied.

"Nasir is with her," Bashir put in, "giving her the *antibaayootig* that has been working so well for Haji."

"If only it showed the same results for her," I sighed.

"Khalidah is right, Haji. We can send Amina overseas anytime."

"She prefers to stay at home in Boosaaso. Believe me, it drives her husband crazy. He's torn between staying by her side and returning to their children and his job in Dubai."

"Well, if she's happy in Somalia, let her stay," Khalidah suggested.

"I agree," added Bashir. "If she's that sick, it's important for her to be happy now, and to allow her to make her own decisions."

"Aye, Commander," I put in. "Her radiation poisoning is much worse than mine. I understand there is no known cure, short of the antigen. It won't make a difference where she stays now, I think, so long as she's in peace."

"Allah bless *Dhakhtar* Nasir," Khalidah said.

"And the antigen," added Bashir. "I've been working closely with the doctors on its trials."

"How about you, Noor?" asked Khalidah. "How are you holding up with the *antibaayootig?*"

"For me, it's worked wonders. It saved me from the brink of death. So long as I keep taking it, I feel fine. Actually, it gives me a lot of energy."

"And what if you stop?"

"Then I get bad headaches, and my vision becomes blurry."

"That, and the nausea," Bashir remarked, "is the reason we've yet to prescribe it to others with radiation poisoning. We're still working out the kinks. Haji is our A-class model. The brain research he's allowing us to perform will go a long way in helping us reduce the side-effects for others."

"I know that pirates are still dying of radiation sickness," Khalidah put to him. "Perhaps you should administer them the serum now? At least it will give them a fighting chance."

"For many sleepless nights, I and certain physicians have pondered this. But we've come to the conclusion that the antigen must first be perfected before it is administered on a wider application. It may be helping

Haji, but it's not having the same effect on Amina, and there are the side effects. Haji's body is slowly changing, adapting to the serum. We need to find out how this occurs. The toxicology is still being perfected, but we believe we are close to a breakthrough."

"Your body is changing, Noor?" Khalidah asked.

"A little bit," I conceded. "Look here." I pointed at the tip of my left ear, then my right. "My ears were never this elongated. They've become more angular and pointed."

"They look normal to me," she remarked.

"They're my ears, and I know."

"It may be due to his migraines," Bashir posited. "His body may be showing a physiological reaction. This is what I meant by adaptation."

"And my teeth," I said, showing Khalidah my canines. "I think they're sharper than before."

"I can't tell," she replied. "Everyone has pronounced fangs."

"Remember what we talked about, Haji," Bashir continued. "Your teeth may look like they're getting longer because your gums are receding in reaction to the serum. But they are not getting sharper, not unless you're filing them at night."

Khalidah and I chuckled.

"I suppose so, Bashir. Fortunately, that's all the physical changes I'm experiencing from the serum, aside from my blurry vision and headaches when I stop taking it, or my sensitive hearing when I take too much. Not a bad swap to save my life, Commander. Once you perfect the medicine, I'd like to see all the sick pirates offered my same level of treatment. The *antibaayootig* can help them, I know it."

"In time, Haji," he said, "in time."

TRACKING WITH MOHAMED

THE TARGET SHIPS WERE VISIBLE with the naked eye. They'd set their course close to Socotra Isle, probably believing Ocean Shield's new base there would all but guarantee safe passage. OS had opened the base with much hoopla, saying merchant mariners would no longer have to sail hundreds of miles offshore.

Somalia's various pirate bands had all joined the Zayid Organization for the war, but recently, Zayid had all but dissolved the pirate navy. What Ocean Shield didn't know, and what the two ships in convoy would soon be shocked to learn, is that Zayid's piracy operations had not ceased at all, but had merely been in the process of a major upgrade, thanks to sophisticated new tactics and equipment, all of which were about to be "rolled out" from a mountaintop in the middle of the island, far from ports or anything maritime whatsoever.

The target ships huddled close together...

It was late September, and now that the summer monsoon was over, Khatar Force 2 was eager to get its new program off the ground. That the task force navies were based right beneath our noses and that it was broad daylight didn't make an ounce of difference in the effectiveness of our plan. Success or failure came down only to our training and equipment, and after six months of intensive drills in the Yemeni backcountry, we were as ready as ever to take it to the field. As for our equipment, it was all custom-made, top-notch stuff, and came at just a fraction of the cost of the gear we'd been using for KF-1.

KF-2's team of five was led by Thor the Norwegian and complemented by, in no particular order,

Admiral Cosob, Qaasim (the young *waranle* who'd helped me during the war), a Yemeni "tracker" named Mohamed who'd defected from the Yemeni army during the Arab spring unrest there, and me. As for Istar Abyad of KF-1, he'd been too sick to join the new strike force, and died of radiation exposure shortly after our training began, may his soul rest with Allah.

Thor was the first to leap off the Dawkam, the highest peak on Socotra Island at over 5,000 feet. Mohamed jumped immediately after, then Cosob, Qaasim, and I followed in quick succession. Even at sub-terminal velocity, our wingsuits enabled us to track rapidly away from the spire, and soon we were flocking together, our angle of attack well practiced from months of training along Yemen's big cliffs.

My wingsuit had been custom tailored to fit the exact dimensions of my frame, and its wing design scientifically modeled to enable the maximum amount of lift. As the updraft caught my wing panels and the span of fabric betwixt my legs, I kept my chin tucked in to allow air to flow smoothly over my back. I soared my neon yellow wingsuit around the majestic Socotra peaks in perfect formation with my team, whose "flying squirrel suits" had also been custom designed and color coded according to their measurements and whims.

The Haggier Steppes of Socotra, with Dawkam Peak at top

To reach the open ocean, it was mandatory to track around a technical stretch of mountainous terrain, proximity flying close to the walls of the lofty Haggier steppes. But with many months of intensive training behind us, we soared as confidently as the Egyptian vultures that plied the island, our knuckles just skimming the cliff faces and our knees dangling mere inches over the taluses as we passed.

Egyptian Vulture soaring o'er Socotra Island

We rocketed at terminal velocity over the high plateau, then swooped down along a big wall spanning the
southern coast. A final carve around a lofty cape found
us gliding out to sea with plenty of altitude and speed.
Hellfire was coming for the target ships, this much was
certain.

The wind whistled o'er my back as I sharpened my
angle of attack (AoA) to keep up with my mates. Qaasim
and I were the lightest in the flock, giving us more lift
but less speed, and with Thor and Mohamed tracking far
ahead but lower in altitude, and with Cosob flying somewhere in between, we made haste to increase our AoA.

But be it the grenades strapped to my chest or the
pistol affixed to my helmet where the video camera
usually went, I felt increased drag on that long glide
out to sea, no matter what my angle of attack. Thor had

taught us a lot about wind and ground rush, but nothing about air density, and as the thick salty air blasted against my face, it occurred to me that perhaps I was being slowed by a sea-level climate very different than the high desert air where we usually practiced.

Allahu Akbar! Mohamed was already deploying over the target ships, with the rest of us preparing to pull in like manner.

My airspeed was approximately 90 knots when I decided to pull. I reached for my pilot chute, then gave it a firm yank, throwing it clean behind me. I tucked in my arms and waited for my canopy to inflate, but nothing happened as I continued falling fast. I rolled to one side and glanced behind me, but saw only sky. That's when I realized I'd inadvertently grabbed my wing and not my PC.

The groundrush below was fast and furious, with the roof of the target ship expanding exponentially. Approximately three seconds to impact, I felt my pilot chute still stowed beneath my container, so gave it a firm throw back.

I drew my arms in tightly once more to minimize the burble, or slipstream trailing off my back, and prayed to holy Allah there'd be no PC hesitation.

I achieved line stretch one second before impact, and canopy inflation just before I hit the roof deck. I pressed my knees and ankles tightly together, bracing for a parachute-landing fall.

I touched down sideways, rolling along my leg, thigh, and buttocks. While hard, the PLF touchdown had worked, preventing me from breaking a limb. However, to the chagrin of my team, my parachute-landing fall caused me to hit the bridge too loudly, jeopardizing our surprise attack.

Paratrooper Mohamed swoops in for landing

Thor wasted no time in stage two of our plan. While the rest of us were still unhooking our canopies, he removed a pair of grenades from his vest and pulled their pins simultaneously with his teeth before setting them on the roof and yelling for us to get back.

There was no place to go on the roof except for further away, so we all made haste to the furthest corner and dove to our stomachs just as the grenades exploded.

A shockwave jolted through my limbs and showered me with metal debris. Fortunately, my canopy container proved an effective shield against one particularly unwieldy piece.

"*Tag*! *Tag*! *Soco*!" Thor barked in Somali, telling us to *move our asses*!

"*Deg-deg*!" echoed Cosob, telling us to *hurry* as he helped me to the blast crater.

Mohamed let down a rope, and the five of us quickly descended. No sooner did our boots hit the control room floor than we had our pistols in our hands, except for Thor, who was carrying an uzi. Being an expert skydiver and BASE jumper, he'd been able to keep the gun affixed to his thigh without allowing its weight to throw off his balance in flight. The rest of us were using pistols that had been attached to the top of our helmets in place of sports cameras; and as I held my own TT-30 pistol firmly in my clutches, I gained renewed confidence after my botched landing.

We stormed onto the command deck. Two sailors fled while the others quickly surrendered.

Not long after we locked our prisoners in a cabin, the oil tanker sailing abreast came abeam, and the two sailors who'd escaped jumped over the gap, then the tanker started clawing off.

Thor, quick in mind and action, drove our containership fast against the tanker, then handed the wheel over to Mohamed and told him to keep us wedged at the gunnels. There was a horrendous creaking of iron as the two vessels converged, and while the rest of us were struggling to keep our balance, Thor was already scaling the deck's crane.

To the amazement of the Somali pirates manning the cargo ship, and undoubtedly to the horror of our enemies sailing abeam, Thor lifted a shipping container high over the tanker's deck before letting it drop from the crane. It smashed clear into the enemy's hold, as could be ascertained by the massive splash of crude oil that appeared upon impact. But Thor in his genius did not release the cables, and shortly after he abandoned the tower, he radioed us by walkie-talkie to drop anchor.

I found the release lever and did as instructed, causing us to clubhaul even sharper against the bow of the ship abeam. In the mayhem that ensued, the cable lines connecting the crane to the container, now stuck within the hold of the tanker abeam, drew taut, causing the crane to collapse and become wedged up against our gunwales. With both ships now securely and irrefutably entangled together, the enemy vessel had no choice but to kill her engines and spare further disaster.

By the time the task forces had come to the attention of the distressed vessels, both ships were at anchor with their crews rounded up and held hostage together in a shipping container. We shot holes in the roof so they could breathe, and threatened to drop the container into the sea if the task forces tried anything funny.

Ocean Shield jets and all manner of radio chatter riddled the air with urgency, but the fact was they were all too late. Now only ransom payments would ensure the safe release of the hostages and dangerously compromised oil ship.

To avoid an all-out massacre and avert an environmental disaster in the fragile Socotran ecosystem, full payment came within days, marking the double hijacking a smashing success.

"Thirty million for the empire!" I exclaimed as I tossed duffel bags full of cash onto the deck of a waiting submarine.

"And thirty million for us," quipped Cosob, hefting his canopy container higher over his back.

"Aye, gentlemen," added Thor in English. "Expensive parachutes we're carrying, eh?"

I translated to the others, and we all had a laugh as we hopped onto the deck of the submarine and escaped down her hatch. No sooner was her portal sealed did she slip beneath the black water, ne'er a glimmer to be seen from the new moon on high, nor a glint of light from Zayid's top-secret craft. In reality, KF-2 had a crushing start-up cost. It was easy to wingsuit in, but extraction was another story. The secret sub, not unlike the one Istar Abyad had described on Selection Ministry Island, used an underwater dock and employed "sonar invisible" technology. I was sworn by penalty of death to keep her classified — a penalty which now, as I write this, is irrelevant.

GLASS HOUSES

BY OCTOBER 2012, ten months after the *afgembi*, Somalia's new empire and the world's first pirate state were on firm footing. In that time, Zayid had invested in four Russian MiG-23 multi-role fighters, eight helicopters, three anti-satellite rockets, various speedboats and submarines, and had developed a standing army of over 100,000 *waranle*. Mogadishu had an effective police force, the city's infrastructure was being rebuilt, and the occasional suicide bombing notwithstanding, there was stability within the country not seen for thirty years. What enabled this were two things: cash flow and a new nationalist sentiment.

The initial injection of cash had been provided by Zayid shortly after the *afgembi*, immediately creating jobs for hundreds of thousands of Somalis, employing them as security personnel, shipbuilders,

street sweepers, manual laborers, masons, paint-
ers, and in all manner of reconstruction projects,
while a significant number of citizens were con-
scripted into the new military. This early investment in manpower served not only to quickly secure
and upgrade the capital and other major cities, but
more importantly, it provided people with occupa-
tions and income streams that kept them busy doing
constructive things while giving them a new national
identity rooted in the Empire. That's precisely what
had been missing during America's occupation of
Iraq (begun in 2003) and what U.S. generals fought
so hard to implement in Afghanistan. Zayid had
paid attention to world events and knew that only
by implementing a robust counterinsurgency plan
early on would Somalia stand a chance at overcoming the growing pains expected during its initial
transformation.

Additional capital flowed in from entrepreneurial
businessmen and women from the Muslim world and
beyond who sought to capitalize off Somalia's emerging markets. While the search for oil-rich deposits
believed to lie beneath the sands of Puntland continued, markets in commodities, telecommunications,
media syndicates, military assets, livestock, stone and
mineral quarries had boomed so quickly that hundreds
of Somalia-based stocks were soon being traded on the
world market.

Meanwhile, the country's security had largely been attained by investment initiatives into projects that engendered a nationalist sentiment among it citizens, for the Assembly of Presidents knew from the beginning that they would not be able to control Somalia for long without the support of its inhabitants.

In conjunction with the revival of Somalia's national institutions, its leaders reached out to other "rogue" nations for trade and solidarity. While the Western world was shocked by Somalia's meteoric rise into a pirate empire, our allies in Iran, North Korea, and other blacklisted countries were happy to covertly do business with us in defensive ballistic missiles, while many Muslim countries were pleased we had stabilized our own affairs so quickly and thus made it publicly clear they would come to our defense if America or any other arrogant western power should attack. In this way, Somalia capitalized off the Arab spring that had been in full swing in places like Libya and Yemen by claiming its right of self-determination in a world that increasingly encouraged just that in regards to foreign policy.

However, Somalia's use of long-range rockets to knock western spy satellites out of space did lead to a Security Council Resolution [SC-1232] authorizing military force to topple the empire, but Europe, America, and Russia, facing severe debt crises, dragged their heels on the resolution's implementation. Half the countries who sat on the Security Council were heavily investing in Somalia's new "white star" economy, anyway, and given their own precarious fiscal health, they knew that to topple the empire would be a death knell to world markets as well. An outright veto of SC-1232 would make the Western world look bad, so approval, and then inaction, was the easiest way out. The end result was a slightly increased Ocean Shield presence and endless threats of stronger actions, which, as with Syria, Iran, and North Korea, never came to pass.

A further contributor to Somalia's impunity regarding its anti-satellite program was a world sentiment turning sharply against the proliferation of satellites circling overhead, for recently a number of them had been falling out of orbit and crashing into populous cities, killing hundreds of people. Our blowing military spy satellites to smithereens before they could "decommission" themselves "naturally" by crashing down to Earth gave a fair amount of satisfaction to concerned citizens worldwide.

SOMALIA, A SUCCESS STORY

THE UNRELENTING SUCCESS STORY of the Somali Peninsula was becoming a thing of both jealousy and admiration by even the world's most developed nations. While they were wallowing in their own crises of confidence, class warfare, debt, and corruption, Somalia was blazing ahead with a skyrocketing economy and strong central system of governance that boosted national pride and gave confidence to Somali businesspeople to invest across communal divides.

America was particularly frustrated, for Somalia had achieved in less than a year what they had not been able to do in Iraq in ten. We'd established the foundations of universal democracy through *xeer*, our common laws. These laws, while seldom written, were respected by members of varying factions and clans. Our parliament, the *guurti*, was entrusted to hand down verdicts to *xeer* infractions through our tribunal, the *Safaarad*.

Xeer, co-exited with Somali Islamic law, *Shari'a*. What America for a decade had tried to achieve in the Middle East by proxy — to divide the spheres of church and state — Somalia had already attained in the division of our secular and religious domains via *xeer* and *Shari'a*. Had any of the Anglo countries bothered to study Somali history, they would've discovered that we were merely reviving an age-old Somali tradition of governance that spanned back 1,000 years. Any true empire keeps its secular, political matters distinct from its religious, spiritual matters, otherwise it risks having its hands hogtied by anachronistic systems of governance or misguided by religious extremists. We were no exception.

Concerning secular matters of our new government, district and regional governors consulted with their traditional leaders — clan chiefs known as *akil* — to discuss import points of law. Local judges called *qadis*, who were on the payroll of the Department of Justice, handed down verdicts in the provincial courts. Federal law itself was decided by the *guurti* — parliament — consisting of a premier, the Council of Emperors (formerly the Assembly of Presidents), and a powerful bloc of businessmen, with Zayid's former pirate court, the *Safaarad*, serving as chief justice administrator. Thus, the White Star Empire resembled Iran in centralization of power and "trickle-down justice" on the provincial level, but unlike Iran, religious authority took a secondary seat to secular law, and furthermore, we had massive public approval, not based on fear, but consent of the genuine article. The number-one enemy within our borders continued to be al-Shabaab.

Al-Shabaab was much more than a sect of religious extremists — they were outright terrorists whose ranks of suicide bombers were mostly foreigners from America. Their goal to destabilize the empire was, at heart, no different than that of the West: there were desperate measures by a diminished group (al-Shabaab) and failing world (the West) to destabilize the empire and once again make Somalia a subservient ward to their own greedy agendas. It was like 500 years prior, in 1499, when Vasco de Gama, in full retreat, lobbed cannonballs at Mogadishu in a spate of jealously that he couldn't take it for himself. Vasco de Gama ghosted over the horizon to a malarial death, while Somalia carried proudly forth in Somali hands. Centuries more of attempted takeovers by the colonial West and more recent efforts by warlords and Islamic extremists to divide and conquer the motherland would all be met with failure, for Somalis as a whole were a "fierce and turbulent race of Republicans," as English explorer Richard Burton so succinctly stated. We were a people who valued self-determination above all else.

Freedom to Live: What Somalis Value Most

THE OIL FIELDS OF PUNTLAND

THE COUNCIL OF EMPERORS held a session I was sure not to miss. For the first time since the establishment of the Empire, the *Boqor* had agreed to come down and sit with us in *guurti* to discuss *xeer*.

The Şomạli Pirẳtẻ 3 - Whịtẻ Şt̃ảr Empirẻ

Being a Darod myself, and hailing from Puntland, I was very concerned about the inclusion of the northern provinces in the new government. Ten months had passed, and still Somaliland insisted on its independence, while Puntland, with its seat of government in Garoowe, held fast to its 1998 claim of regional statehood. With the *Boqor*'s continued denial to sit with parliament, the north would forever feel aloof from our dictates, and thus the empire would meet a major impasse within its own national borders. It was of extreme importance the council avoid this embarrassment and get the *Boqor* to at least tacitly agree to permit our rule to extend into his territories, for any major resistance on his part nurtured the seed of civil war. Such a regression would put a major hole in our domestic map and severely tarnish the empire's reputation, for a civil war with the north would end in a pogrom, with the government of Mogadishu emerging as the sure victor.

It was a delicate matter that sat before us, to appease the *Boqor*. The leader of the entire race of Puntlanders had gotten the job for a reason — he not only hailed from the direct lineage of Abdirahman bin Isma'il al-Jabarti, the *Cusmaan Maxamuud* clan father, but he was a man of great learning.

The speaker of the house blew his buffalo horn, commanding silence within the parliamentary chamber. An acacia tree worked in frieze across the domed ceiling spread its branches over the forty-two men and three women who composed the Council of Emperors. These new leaders of Somalia, my own head counted amongst them, were seated around the chamber periphery in towering, black velvet chairs, while before us on a polished blue floor with a white marble star in its center stood the Assembly Premier, Rashiid Cassanelli.

"Ladies and gentlemen," he addressed the *guurti*, his eyes moving along the line of council members, at last settling upon the *Boqor*, who sat at a table with two of his attachés, "we must protect the homeland from Ansar al Sharia, but to do that, *Boqor*, we need your assistance. If you would permit our military into your territory, we can ensure the safety of your cities, ports, and markets."

"*Haa*," uttered many assemblymen and women. What everybody knew, but nobody dared to publicly relay, was that Zayid needed the *Boqor's* dominions most of all for their abundant seaports, which held strategic locations to build major pirate bases and which promised the free flow of goods via the Red Sea and Arabian Peninsula. But I was surprised the premier would try to play the *Boqor's* intelligence, making the case that the threat of al-Qaeda in the Arabian Peninsula, based just across the way in Yemen, was the real reason the empire needed his cooperation.

The *Boqor*, for his part, had every reason not to trust the council of politicians, businessmen, ex-pirates, and ex-warlords surrounding him. Their agenda was as palpable as it was visual. While he was dressed in traditional provincial fashion, wearing a white *ma'awis* sarong and sleeveless cotton shirt, a Somali *tooray* dagger replete with cattle horn pommel proudly displayed in its leather sheath, Premier Cassanelli and most of those seated around him sported business suits and ties. The empire's aggressive oil-exploration efforts behind the *Boqor*'s regional lines were well known, as were certain assemblymen's attempts to seed lobbyists into the *Boqor*'s northern *guurti* to forge business alliances. Only I, with my yellow windbreaker and father's dagger, and a few representatives from the Abgal and Habir Gedir clans, were dressed more traditionally.

"And what need do I have of your protection?" the *Boqor* reproached, his steady, sandy voice as timeworn as his hoary features. "Ansar al Sharia and al-Shabaab have always made the government of Mogadishu their main target, not Somaliland. To align the home of the *Cusmaan Maxamuud* with your empire would make us more vulnerable, not less."

"But geographically," continued Premier Cassanelli, a Somali educated in Italy, "you already are vulnerable. Puntland will be AQAP's first beachhead."

"Geographically?" replied the *Boqor*, rubbing his orange goatee with a bony hand, his other hand grasping a gnarled wooden staff. "We're on top of the nation geographically. At the nexus of three major seaways, we have long enjoyed a measure of independence from Mogadishu. This independence has been borne of our own historical circumstances and sustained by the steady economic activity afforded by our shores. We are a well-loved and well-guarded dominion, and always have been. As home to the clans of the Darod, the Dhulbahante, the Majeerteen, and the Warsangali, The Land of the Gods is best protected by the head of the *Cusmaan Maxamuud* people, not by a *guurti* in Mogadishu. So do not worry about our protection. We have an army of our own, ships, and aircraft. In fact, *you need us* to keep Ethiopia, Eritrea, and Djibouti in check."

"So you will allow, then," continued Premier Cassanelli in his crafty manner, "the coordination of our militaries in matters of national security? Surely you've seen our capabilities, heard of our pact with other nations that would come to our defense at the first footprint of foreign invasion?"

"Ah, but you are merely asking the same favor but in a different manner. Puntlanders know what it would mean to join your empire, and you should know them better than that. We are very resilient to outside interference, even if that 'outside' interference comes from Mogadishu. Perhaps a short review of our history will best illustrate why we see ourselves as distinct from you and refuse to be controlled by your central government.

"In times predating Islam, Puntland hosted the fabled Port of Zeilah, whose early Barbaroi tribes of the northern Somali coasts were trading with the inhabitants of Arabia and Egypt, which was then under Roman rule. Zeilah *was* Somalia's center of trade and power, and for centuries was the focus of the country's culture and economy, until Negus Yeshaq, the 'King of the Christians,' sacked it in fourteen fifteen.

"But the downfall of Zeilah at the hands of infidels was but one minor setback among many, and none could keep the Land of Punt down for long before it emerged again as a stronghold of Somali commerce, politics, and culture. Century after century of digging in to defend ourselves against outsiders and solidifying our rule along ancient clan lines has equated to real independence that we will not so easily relinquish. And you talk of security…" He giggled quietly. "Somaliland has enjoyed a level of peace and security for decades, and as mentioned previously, your empire can only undermine that."

"Not necessarily, *Boqor*," put in President Tahliil, who, like Premier Cassanelli, spoke with an Italian accent. "It seems as if you are gravely misunderstanding the will of Zayid. The empire, along with each and every member of this assembly, wishes only to further our beneficence into your dominion. As you are here now, discussing common law with us, you and the elders of the Puntland/Harti sub-clans will be granted a permanent seat on the council to make sure the securities we provide, the spoils we share, and laws we make will be allocated justly by way of political representation, according to the specific needs of each region. Your inclusion in the empire is of great benefit to you, for we share in your same love of a Somalia that is self-determining and independent. There must be some common ground we can find to strengthen our alliance in this great moment for our country."

"Perhaps," replied the *Boqor* after a long pause. "I shall depart now and consult with my *akil* on these matters. If we wish to engage in further talks with this council, I shall let you know."

The *Boqor* turned to leave, and the room filled with chatter, for he was leaving too much at stake, too much in question to appease the wishes of the *guurti*. I was of the same mind of many seated around me. We wanted to stop him and discuss specific points of *xeer*, but Somalis, if their common law was to have any merit, never forced a man to remain in council against his wishes.

Thus, the *Boqor* continued to the door, stopping there to warn, "*Nabad gelyo, baarlamaan.* I have a great deal to gain by remaining free of your dictates. Somaliland has long since seceded, and thus we are the rightful owners of the oil fields in Puntland."

The crowd went berserk, some going so far as to shout profanities down at him. The house speaker tried to silence the assembly with his polished horn, but was unable. But it didn't matter — the debate was already over because the wise old *wadaad* had fled, but not before hitting the nail right on the head: too many in my cabinet cared only of greed, and the rich oil fields rumored to lie under the *Boqor's* feet proved too great a temptation for them to leave him be.

I remembered then, that not long ago I'd been the chief proponent of oil exploration in my homeland, but now that I was on the other side of the fence from my clan head, who would neither join the empire nor relinquish the rights to his oil deposits, I became deeply confused regarding my own allegiances.

A splitting headache tore through my brain. I buried my face in my hands. My greatest fear — that my clan head would reject the empire I'd fought so hard to establish — was coming to pass. I turned around in my lofty chair and began to climb down, planting my face into the immaculate black velvet as I passed out.

IN THE CARE OF SCIENCE

"WHERE AM I?" I mumbled, waking up in a room surrounded by medical apparatuses. An IV tube was stuck in my arm.

"*Ha dhaqaaqin*," spoke Bashir as he appeared over me, telling me to be still. He said there'd been an accident. "*Shil baa dhacay.*"

"*Maxaa?*" I asked deliriously, my body feeling sore and numb at the same time.

"You passed out, Haji," he relayed, "at the *guurti*. Do you remember?"

"Vaguely."

"Well, *saaxiib*, now you're safe and sound. Thank Allah you didn't fall from your chair. Had you hit your head, it would've been far worse."

"Where am I?"

"Compound six."

"In Djibouti?"

"*Haa*."

"How long was I out?"

"A fortnight."

"Two weeks! Are you serious?"

"You went into a coma, Haji. We weren't sure if you'd pull through."

"A coma? Are you kidding me? Bashir, what is wrong with me?"

"That's what we're here to find out. I've been with you the whole time, *jaalle*."

"The antigen," I muttered.

"*Maxaa?*"

"Maybe it's the antigen," I said.

"Maybe it's the radiation," he somberly replied.

"I need more antigen!" I exclaimed in a panic, trying to sit up.

"Just take it easy, *saaxiib*," he called me *friend* again, coaxing me back down. "You may be right about that. We've been giving you the serum via an IV drip, and it seems to have brought you back. Doctor Sooraan is here. We'll get more serum in you and run some more tests. And let's get some food into you, okay?"

"*Waa hagaag,*" I replied in the affirmative. "*Waxaan u baahannahay dawada madax.*"

"You have a headache?"

"*Haa.*"

"I'll bring some *asbiriin.*"

"*Mahadsanid, saaxiib.*"

He went to leave.

"And Bashir?"

He half turned to hear.

"*Mahadsanid,* for staying with me."

"*Dhib ma laha,*" he said, *no problem.*

He returned a few minutes later and placed a tray of food on my bedside "Sit up, matey," he said. "Let's put some meat back on those bones." He handed me a cold glass of milk, saying, "*Caano geel,*" meaning *camel milk.*

"*Mahadsanid.*"

"*Sanuunad,*" he replied, pointing to a stew made of mutton. "*Iyo bariis,*" he added, showing me a bowl of rice. He asked if I minded leftovers, as the food had been served for lunch and just reheated in a microwave.

"*Bismillaah!*" I said, meaning *in the name of God!* Somalis often say this before eating.

He prepared for me a plate of rice and stew, then pointed to two aspirin tablets on the tray, advising I take them after the meal.

"*Waa dhantahay mahadsanid,*" I thanked him kindly for the provisions.

After lunch, Bashir helped me down a long hallway and into another room where Doctor Sooraan, wearing his lab coat, stood before a CT scanner. They laid me down on a rolling table and guided my head into the machine's portal, then a bright florescent light moved back and forth before my eyes. Eventually, I was extracted from the machine, unharmed but still feeling weak from my coma.

As Bashir was helping me out of the room, I overhead Dr. Sooraan remark, "*Sidee?*" I turned to see him placing x-rays of my skull upon a lighted easel. He was asking *how?*

"Is there something the matter, Doctor?" I asked.

"Ahh… no Haji," he said unconvincingly "These are standard tests." He signaled for Bashir to continue assisting me out.

"What's going on, Bashir?" I asked as we shuffled down the hallway.

"You heard the doctor," he replied staidly. "Just running some tests is all."

"*Haa*, but he seemed to be concerned about the results."

Bashir remained silent for a time, then replied, "*Wallaah?* Really? I didn't notice."

"*Haa*, when he—"

"Look, *walalo*, you've been through a lot," he cut me off. "Just get some rest and leave the medical science to the experts."

We arrived back in the infirmary, and he helped me into bed.

"I would like to know the results of the test, Commander," I said politely.

He gently forced me to lie down, saying, "Just get some rest, *walalo*, and don't worry about it for now. I'll find out the results and tell you later, when you're more cognizant."

"Cognizant? But I'm fully awake."

"*Maya*," he claimed the negative, "you're still muzzy. Now stop worrying so much and be thankful we brought you here for treatment. You're in good hands, Haj — trust us."

As soon as he left, I tiptoed silently through the hallways behind him. He returned to the CT scan room, so I stopped by the door and listened.

"Remarkable," commented the doctor. "You see here? His brain is undergoing significant changes."

"In size, Doctor?" inquired Bashir. "Is it getting bigger? Is that why he's having such terrible headaches?"

"No, Commander, in shape. See here?"

I peered around the doorway and saw them studying my x-rays.

"The very tissue of his brain seems to be rearranging itself inside his cranium."

"Rearranging itself into what?"

"*Ma ogi*," replied Dr. Sooraan, saying he didn't know. "I've never seen anything like it, but I can tell you it does not appear to be random. Rather, his brain is reshaping itself into something specific — something that is not human."

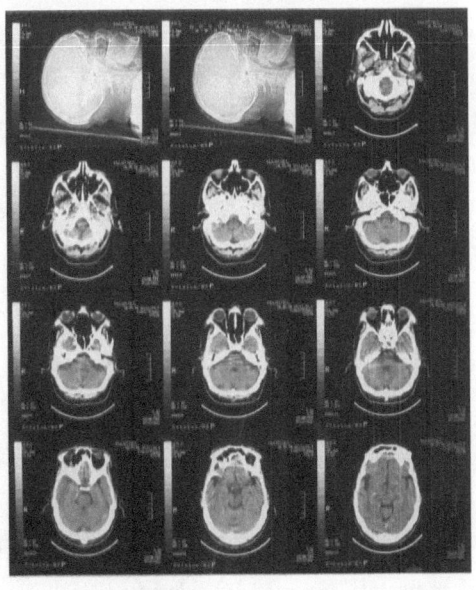

'His brain is reshaping itself into something… not human'

"*Maan fahmin*," Bashir replied, saying he didn't understand, "but inform Zayid."

"Of course," the doctor said.

"What about Noor?" asked the commander. "What shall we tell him?"

"*Waxba.*"

"Nothing?"

"*Waxba*. Those are Zayid's explicit instructions. Besides that, it won't do him any good to concern himself at this point — these are very complex matters."

"Please clarify, Doctor."

"The serum appears to be both the cause and the cure of his brain's transformation. In order to protect healthy tissue from tissue that has been damaged by radiation, the antigen has created a sort of moat around the infected areas, quarantining them from the rest of his brain, and this appears to be why the structural changes are occurring, at least in part. But see his ears and canines? They appear to be changing, as well, sharpening in symmetry with his brain's overall transformation."

Bashir dragged a palm over his closeshaven head and emitted a weighty exhale. He was clearly perplexed, but mostly he appeared very concerned.

"Gentlemen," I said, entering the room. "Please enlighten me about the test results."

Dr. Sooraan hurriedly switched off the viewing platform and insisted I should be resting.

"Show me the x-rays, Doctor."

"You won't understand them, Noor."

"Then you can explain to me what you were just explaining to Bashir."

"Commander," he said, "please see Noor back to his room. He needs to rest."

Bashir's eyes smarted on him, but Sooraan's expression remained firm.

Alas, without so much as making eye contact with me, Bashir grabbed my arm and proceeded to tussle me out.

"Get your hands off me!" I pushed him away, causing me to go unstable.

"Just look at you, Haji," he said. "You can barely stand on your own two feet. I'm just trying to help out. We must do as the doctor says."

"What's all this about my brain changing?" I insisted.

"Return to your room," Sooraan replied bluntly.

"*Maya.* It's *my* health that's at stake here. I deserve to know."

"He's right, Doctor," Bashir at last came to my defense.

"But he won't understand the data."

"Try me, Doctor," I countered.

"*Maya,*" he held firm.

"But you must," I insisted.

"Zayid forbids it."

"*Maxaa, Dhakhtar?* Zayid *forbids* it? Is this true, Bashir?"

The commander was slow to answer.

"What the hell's going on here?!" I was infuriated.

"Get him out!" the doctor ordered.

"Not until I get some answers!" I shot back.

"Commander?" The doctor signaled for my removal again.

"Don't even try," I warned Bashir.

"The serum is having an effect," Bashir revealed, turning from me to the doctor.

"What kind of effect?" I inquired.

"*Joogso!*" The doctor told him to *stop*!

"But his life may be at stake!"

"You don't know what you're talking about!"

"Then explain it to him!"

The back-and-forth between Bashir and the doctor continued like this, until at last Sooraan held up his hands and said, "If you must, Commander, I will tell him what I told you, but if Zayid finds out what he knows, it will be your head and not mine."

Dr. Sooraan reluctantly switched the x-ray panel back on and proceeded to describe how my brain was rearranging itself. He said the main part of the human brain, the cerebral cortex, was divided into four sections called lobes. He showed me how the lobes had changed positions within my skull, and how another part of my brain, a much smaller organ called the cerebellum, had been "quarantined" within a "moat of antigen" because it had been infected by radiation. When I asked him what this meant for my overall brain functioning, he said he didn't know and that further studies would need to be conducted. He mentioned some medical gibberish about the cerebellum being "older, evolutionarily," and said that might have something to do with the physical changes observable on my external body. I asked him to clarify again, and he threw up his hands, saying that's all he could tell me, that it was beyond my level of education, and that most of it was just speculation on his part, anyway. But he reassured me that the serum was helping to offset the large doses of radiation I'd sustained prior to the *afgembi*, and said that in order for me to stay healthy and avoid more blackouts, he'd be increasing my intake three-fold.

I asked him a question that had been plaguing me, haunting me for a long time: "*Goormaan joojin doonaa?*"

"When can you stop taking the antigen?" he echoed my inquiry. "There is no known cure for radiation sickness, you know that, Noor. *Waxaad leedahay caabuq kaah.*"

"*Haa,* I know I have radiation infection, but can you answer my question, Doctor? The *antibaayootig* is starting to harm me."

"Harm? No, Noor, it's saving your life."

"But it's rearranging his brain," Bashir interjected.

"Perhaps for the better," the doctor replied. "Look again at the x-rays. Observe how the serum is rearranging his brain in such a way that quarantines the infected tissue."

"But it's isolated an entire organ, Doctor!" Bashir shot back. "This cerebellum or whatever you call it."

"Precisely," replied Sooraan, pointing at that small "brain within a brain." "Fascinating, isn't it?"

"So I'll be taking the serum forever is basically what you're saying," I remarked.

"In all honesty, Noor, I don't know, but I will say you're very fortunate to receive the wonder drug. The selection me—" He coughed and covered his mouth.

"The what, Doctor?"

"The selection methodology in the development of the *antibaayootig* was no more efficacious than its application on you, the perfect subject."

"I have no idea what you're talking about," I lamented.

"Like I said, *jaalle*, such things are beyond your level of education. Don't be insulted by that — few people in the world, let alone in Somalia, have the medical schooling necessary to begin to fathom such mysteries."

I raised my brows, at a total loss of what he was saying.

"Please, Noor, you really do need to rest. I promise that should we discover anything new regarding your condition, I'll be the first to let you know."

"Just like you let me know about this," I reproached, pointing at the x-rays.

"Be reasonable, Noor. I've barely had time to study them, myself. Now please, I'll come by your room in about an hour to administer more *antibaayootig*. Don't worry, comrade, you're now in the care of modern science."

I grew nervous, and Bashir noticed. "And Allah," he said as he accompanied me out.

HOME

ON THE ADVICE OF DOCTOR SOORAAN, I was soon transferred to my old house in Boosaaso to recover under Nasir's care. As my sister Amina was there, it seemed like a good idea. It'd been a while since I'd spent any time with her, and unlike me, her condition was worsening regardless of her antigen intake.

On the morning after my arrival, Amina was helped to her seat at the dining table, but even before the *canjeeros* were served, she complained of nausea and requested to be taken back to bed.

So we ate Somali pancakes by her bedside, Fatuma helping to feed her, and I giving her sips of hot *shaah hawash*, a tea spiced with cardamom, cloves, and ginger. Amina was pleased, saying Fatuma's *canjeeros* were unbeatable, while the tea she claimed warmed her from the inside out.

While Fatuma tended to the dishes, I remained at Amina's bedside along with her husband Jamal and *Dhakhtar* Nasir.

"Your voice sounds different," Amina said.

"In what way?" I asked.

"It's raspy, and higher. You don't notice?"

"I've had a bit of a sore throat."

"I'll have a look later," put in Nasir.

"I'll be okay, *Dhakhtar*," I replied. "I've been spending a lot of time in Yemen this year. The desert is very dry and windy. The climate must've affected my voice."

"What have you been doing in Yemen?" Jamal probed.

"That's classified."

"Really? Even with Amina here? Zayid hasn't dumped her already, has he?"

Amina shot Jamal an expression of disapproval. He really could be a *footo delo* at times — a real *asshole*.

"First of all, Zayid is an organization, not a man," I countered. "Secondly, my secrecy is for your own protection."

"Maybe he's with Ansar al Sharia," he told the others. "You know, al-Qaeda in the Arabian Peninsula?"

"Get real, Jamal."

"Don't tell me to get real, Haji! What's real is the mess you've caused my family. My wife's now confined to a wheelchair and refuses to return to Dubai!"

"Don't shout over her!" I warned.

"Don't tell me how to talk over my wife! I'm the one who stays with her night and day, dealing with the fallout you've left behind!"

"It was my choice…" Amina strained to say.

"Hush, *walaal*, just relax," I said, gently touching the side of her face.

"You've been brainwashed by the great *Hoggaamiye*, my *maranti*," Jamal mocked me before his *wife*. "His Empire Riyals, his star power, his cockiness have made you bored with me. We had a good life back in Dubai. You had your beauty business; there was safety, security, our children."

"Stop insulting her," I said.

"*Haa*," concurred Nasir. "She needs to rest."

"I'm not insulting her."

"But you are. This isn't about me, Jamal — this is about Amina and the great feats she's accomplished for Zayid; the high merits she has earned."

Amina reached up a frail, shaking hand. I squeezed it gently. "Please stop fighting," she said.

"Please, Amina," continued Jamal, taking her other hand, "please come back to Dubai with me. We'll get the care you need."

Amina looked from him to me, as if seeking my advice.

"Nobody's keeping you here," I said.

"I wish to remain in Somalia," she spoke clearly.

"In Somalia," echoed her husband in disbelief.

"*Haa*," she replied. "This is my home."

Jamal threw up his hands and said, "You people are crazy, you know that? *Waad walantahay!*" He headed for the door.

"Where are you going, Jamal?" I demanded.

"To blow off steam, oh great *Hoggaamiye!*"

"He doesn't understand me," Amina muttered, squeezing my hand more firmly.

"Nor me, *walaal*. He's just upset is all."

"*Haa*, he's just a little concerned," put in *Dhakhtar* Nasir.

"How have the injections been going?" I inquired.

Nasir broke eye contact with me, not answering. I looked at my sister. She smiled back sheepishly, shaking her head in the negative.

It was a stupid question. It was plainly evident the injections were failing her; Fatuma had told me as much upon my arrival.

"Look," I said, aiming to clear the air, "I'm going to go and see if I can help Fatuma with anything. Would you like to watch TV, Amina?"

She smiled and nodded, holding out a hand.

Nasir placed a remote in her palm but asked me to turn the TV on manually, which I did.

"*Mahadsanid*," Amina wheezed. She began flipping through the channels, settling on a Somali talk show on Horn Cable TV.

I stood behind her, giving her a gentle shoulder massage, eventually saying, "I'll be back."

৶

While researching about radiation on one of Fatuma's computers, I heard Jamal shouting, so ran into

Amina's room where he stood over her with a smart phone.

"What's going on here? Why are you yelling, Jamal?"

"You!" he looked at me with bloodshot eyes. "You and your stupid pirate books! You see this?" He held the phone before me. "This is the electronic version of your second book, *Dagger Dogs of Zayid*. Is all this crap true?"

"I narrated it to my editor in America, but didn't actually write it."

"But is it true?!"

"Most of it."

"About Amina?"

"All of her parts are true, *haa*. The only part still open to debate is the sighting of Captain Shar'ma'arke on the Selection Ministry ship. Some who were there said it was merely an optical illusion created by the white man."

"So you did fuck the captain!" Jamal scathed at my sister, throwing the phone hard at her bed. It bounced over her, just missing her face.

"Jamal…" she said, barley able to speak as she raised a hand towards him, "*Jamal…*"

Jamal got all up in my face, saying, "Are you happy now, *Hoggaamiye?* Are you happy what you've done to my marriage?"

"Jamal, please," Amina fought to say. "Captain Axmed is dead."

"Does that makes an ounce of difference?!" he scathed. "You think that takes away what you've done, or your feelings for him?"

"Leave her be, Jamal," I warned. "She's sick."

"Sick in the head is what she is!" He shouted at her, "How could you do this to me?! You have shamed me and the names of our children!"

"Jamal, wait," I reproached, grabbing his arm.

"*Was* you!" he cursed, spinning around and socking me in the mouth. "*Was* both of you!"

After telling us to fuck off, Jamal stormed out of the house, slamming the door as he left.

"I'm sorry, Haji," my sister mumbled. She was crying.

As I wiped my smashed lips with the back of my hand, blood dripped through my stigmata. "No, *walaal*, don't blame yourself," I said. "It's my fault."

"What happened?" asked Fatuma, rushing into the downstairs bedroom.

"Jamal's upset," I relayed. My lips were swelling, and it hurt to speak. "He hates the sweet trade."

"He hit you?" Fatuma remarked, taking a closer look.

"I'm fine," I said.

"No, you're not, *harbarwadaag*. Your lip is cut pretty bad." She had called me *brother from the same mother*. "Oh, no, your tooth is loose."

"Stay with *walaal*," I said. "I'm going to the bathroom to check it out."

I went upstairs to my old bedroom, then into the adjoining bathroom. I rinsed my mouth out with water and felt my upper left canine falling out. I pulled it, and to my shock beheld a sharper one already growing in behind it. Beyond that, Jamal's blow had driven both my canines into my lower lip, puncturing it deeply. The two holes bled steadily, and I had to wedge a piece of towel betwixt my teeth and lower lip to help arrest the flow.

Upon closer inspection, my physiology was indeed changing. My ears were becoming elongated, and even my forehead appeared more angulated towards the front. I attributed this to my brain's rearranging itself within my skull to ward off radiation, and the stretching of the bone structure was undoubtedly the cause of my terrible headaches. The antigen was a powerful drug, that much was certain. But the antibiotic was combating my illness, and only when I stopped taking it did the pain of my transformation return.

I procured my *qandi* pouch and gave myself three shots of serum, as instructed by Dr. Sooraan.

SNEKOR TOGGLE

THE OLD FAYRUS RESIDENCE in Boosaaso had always been a good place for family gatherings. The three-bedroom house, bequeathed to my middle sister Fatuma Abdul, her husband Said, and their three children, had a spacious living room and dining area, while Boosaaso

International Airport allowed easy access for those flying in by way of greater Africa and the Middle East. Uncle Osman lived close by, and the bustling port town was full of fine teashops and places to stroll, such as the beach, which was so close that the sounds of the surf lolled one to sleep at night.

As it were, Amina Rage was home, but very ill, while her husband Jamal had left in a temper and not returned. Said was on business in Oman, leaving Fatuma at home with the kids and her computers, while Uncle Osman was presently talking to my wife Issa over Skype. Our family gathering, then, was less than ideal, but was the best we could do under the circumstances.

I had already spoken with my mother and wife over Skype. They wanted to see my safe return to them in America, but they both understood the importance of my remaining in Somalia for the time being. The coup d'état and workings of the parliament had been making headlines all the year long, and apparently I was in the news from time to time as the *Hoggaamiye wadaad* — a spiritual leader who'd guided countless displaced refugees home to a better life. The world was divided over if I was a philanthropist or a terrorist, and while the FBI had interviewed my mother, wife, and publisher on several occasions, my bank accounts had not been frozen, and so in all likelihood I'd still be allowed to return to America as a conditional permanent resident. Fortunately, Issa had applied for an extension of my green card's travel allowance shortly after my departure, extending the time I could legally leave the USA from one year to two on something DHS termed "early parole." Still, it remained a mystery to me why America had not outright exiled me from their society. When I left that land of black-hearted infidels, I did not care about it in the least; my only goal was to return to Somalia to wage a war of retribution upon the high seas, taking revenge at the world for their abundant sins committed clandestinely in my country. Such were the thoughts that plagued me as I prepared myself in the downstairs bathroom to speak with my son Mohamed and daughter Jeilani.

"How does he look?" I called over to Osman, who was talking with Mohamed over webcam.

"He looks sick," he called back. "His face is all green, and he has an ugly scar across his forehead. It looks like they've screwed a bolt into your son's ear to secure his brain."

"OMG!" I exclaimed, stumbling forth from the bathroom. "I have got to see this!"

"*Hayye aabbe!*" Mohamed said hello in Somali. "Are you a vampire?"

"*Dhiig!*" I growled, brandishing my fangs and extending my birdsuit's wings. "I vant to suck yer blood!"

"*Aieeee!*" Mohamed and Jeilani screamed. My daughter was dressed as a princess.

"Vhat happened to you, Mohamed?!" I gave my best Dracula impression. "You're all green!"

"I'm Frankenstein!" he giggled.

"Frankenstein's monster, sweetie," I heard Issa say off screen.

"Happy Halloween!" I sang operatically, raising my wings high.

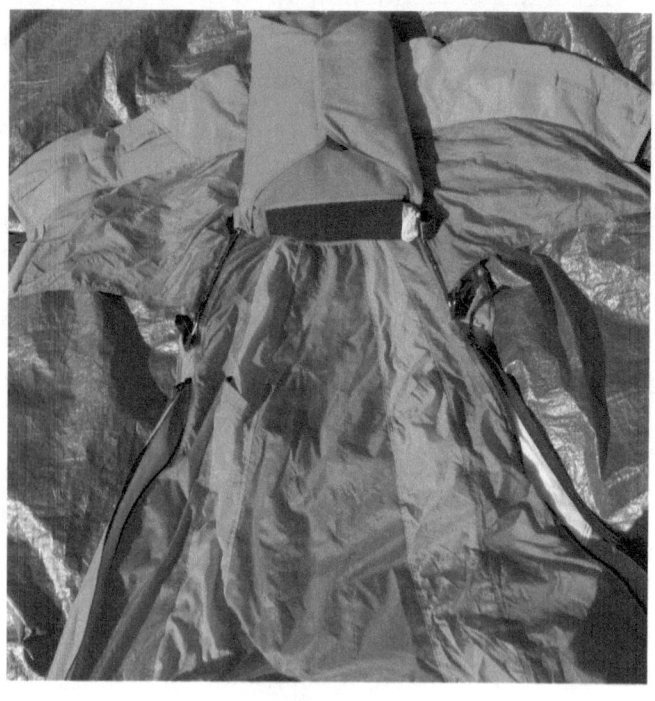

Haji's Wingsuit

"Where'd you get that costume?" Issa asked, squeezing in behind our kids. She was dressed like a wicked witch. "It's really cool looking."

"This, my lovely," I warbled like the dark count of lore, "comes from Transylvania, tailor-made to fit the exact veight and vesurements of my frame."

Osman just shook his head and said, "What has America done to you people?"

"It's Halloween, Igor!" I shot back. "The only blackheart holiday we celebrate! Did you not read my first book?"

He laughed.

"I see you are ready to haunt ze streets of St. Paul," I told my kids, "and go trick-or-treating for lots of bloody candy!"

"Yeah!" they screamed.

"I like the bright yellow, daddy," said Jeilani, "and the white star."

"Just like my windbreaker, sweetie, only I can really fly in this thing."

Issa laughed.

"It's true," Osman said. "He really can."

"Then tell him to fly home to me," Issa remarked. "Tell him to fly back and sink his fangs deep into my neck. Those are really great teeth, *nin* — very realistic."

"These are my real teeth."

"*Ha ha ha!*"

Fatuma came behind me and said into the camera, "Guess what, Issa? I know it sounds crazy, but Haji is telling the truth about his wingsuit. It's for skydiving and BASE jumping."

"BASE jumping?"

"Jumping off buildings, antennas, bridges, and cliffs, or spans and earth, as they call the latter. He flies for a while, doing something called tracking, then deploys a parachute and lands safely on the ground. With a wingsuit like his, you can jump off a tall cliff and fly for many minutes totally unassisted."

"He does this?"

"I have pictures of people doing it in Europe. I've posted them on my Facebook page for you to look at."

"That's the sporting side of it, ladies," Osman added. "But Haji does it on the job."

I eyed my uncle askance. That information was classified. Was he going to reveal more operational secrets? Alas, for some reason I knew I wasn't going to try to stop him. I had already told him, Fatuma, and others, and anyway, Khatar Force 2 had been doing some super-cool shit that I'd been itching to tell my friends and family about.

"*Wallaah!*" Issa asked, *really*! "On the job?"

WSBASE jumping in Norway, from Fatuma's FB page

A moment of silence passed. At last, I turned towards the camera and said, "*Haa*. We either jumps off seacliffs or are flown by plane over the vicinity of a target vessel, then we jump and track — "fly" — over the ship wearing these wingsuits, completely undetected by radar. We deploy our parachutes and land onboard, seizing the vessel before the crew has any idea what's happening. It's totally revolutionary. No more heavy RPGs, rope ladders, super-skiffs, or any maritime equipment whatsoever. If we attack at night, we can land onboard a vessel without them having any idea we're there until we storm the bridge. We're the ultimate silent predators, attacking from the skies." I jumped up from my seat and emitted a terrifying bat shriek.

The younkers screamed, and even I was frightened by the strange voice that came out of me.

"Where are the seacliffs?" Warsame asked, scrunching in behind the others. She was dressed in traditional Somali garb, as usual.

"We've established exits on Socotra."

"Exits to where?"

"Jumping points from which to attack passing ships without necessitating an airplane. With a wingsuit like this, you can jump from a high cliff and track for many leagues in a matter of minutes, easily evading the enemy's air and sea defenses."

"But, *inanka*," she asked, calling me *son*, "I thought you were afraid of heights?"

"Running ABE's out at sea helped me get over it. But aerial boarding ejects were different. In ABE's we launched from sea level and flew a hundred meters into the sky, then deployed our parachutes and descended under canopy. In wingsuit base jumping, however, we jump from sheer cliffs then fly along the wall in what is called proximity or proxy flying."

"Why do you do that?" Issa inquired.

"To remain stealthy until we fly out over the water, and also the updraft along the cliff gives us more hang time. Anyway, ninety percent of my flight occurs with this wingsuit. Only at the very end do I deploy my PC and canopy."

Flying under canopy on a full moon boogie

"My wingsuit has special Snekor Toggles," I added, "enabling me to reach my brake toggles without unzipping my arm wings — a major benefit if we're coming in hot."

Issa drew a blank. "So what happens once you're onboard the ship?"

"I drink the black hearts' blood!" I crooned like Count Dracula, curling my fingers before the camera.

The children screeched.

"But seriously," she reproached.

"But seriously," Warsame interjected, pointing at her watch, "we'd better get going while there's still candy to be had."

"Bye, *aabbe*," and, "*Ciao, Haji*," my little ones sounded back as they slipped away from their seats, deserting the screen. Only Issa remained, but the rugrats quickly dragged her away.

"*Ha-ji!*" she growled, apparently upset at not getting an answer about the hijacking specifics.

"The devil's in the details," I replied wryly. "Happy Halloween, *macaan!*" I called her sweetheart. "*Waan jacaylaa.*"

"I love you too, Haj. Send our love to Amina."

With that, she was gone, then Warsame waved goodbye and switched off their screen. The monitor before me went black, and in the darkly reflecting glass, my own fanged image terrified me utterly.

DEATH IS ALLAH'S LAW

NOVEMBER 3, 2012, was a day of infamy for Somalia and my family, especially. At Amina's request, I took her down to the seashore to watch the sunrise. She wanted to get closer, so I pushed her wheelchair over the sandbars, then carried her in my arms over the low tide floodplain.

As the glistening star of day broke the back of *badweyn*, illuminating our faces, she told me to be neither sad nor afraid, for she had accomplished all she had wanted, and this was Allah's way.

My eyes welled with tears as she trembled in my embrace. She reached out for the sun, saying, "In Allah there is peace."

Thus, Amina passed away.

∾

The death rites were performed according to Somali tradition and Amina's wish that she remain in Somalia. We chose the Boosaaso cemetery because Dante was impractical. A white shroud, or *kafan*, was wrapped around her torso and extremities, then she was placed in a casket we called a *nahash*, which doesn't have a lid and is used only to transport the body.

An Imam met the men at the gravesite to say a prayer, calling out the name of Amina followed by Warsame Abdul and Asha Abdi — the names of her mother and grandmother. The women and children stood a few meters away.

Osman and I helped remove Amina's body from the casket and lower it into the grave. Two *wadaad* — men of God — already inside the pit carefully set her down, then removed enough of the shroud from the sides of her body so that her body touched the earth. We helped the *wadaad* out of the grave.

While filling the pit with soil, everyone chanted, "*Al-mowtu xaqu Laahi*," Arabic for *Death is Allah's law.*

Women came forward and sprinkled water on the grave as a symbol of perpetuity, then everyone departed shortly thereafter, doing their best not to linger or wail.

XANUUN

THE DAYS THAT FOLLOWED Amina's passing were extremely difficult for me. Not only was I acutely aware of the loss of yet another sibling due to radiation poisoning, but also my own condition filled me with an equally harsh but very physical *xanuun*, or *pain*.

Fainting spells bookended by strange dreams of a quicksilver face were followed by hours of lying awake with nausea and migraines. I attributed the symptoms to my grief over Amina's sudden passing and fears about my own fate, but when my gums started to bleed and my hearing became so sensitive that the sound of someone talking caused me to recoil in pain, I sought out *Dhakhtar* Nasir for proper administration of more antigen, and any other help he might be able to render.

"*Ilaahay samir iyo iimaan ha inaga siiyo,*" he said as he met me in the upstairs bedroom where I lay, my sheets matted with cold sweat. He was first and foremost expressing his condolences about Amina, saying, *May Allah, by this incident, fortify our faith and patience.*

"*Aamiin,*" I replied, *may it be so.*

I asked for help with my serum injections, but he said he first wanted to perform an auscultation. After checking my eyes and ears, pulse and breathing, he snapped on a rubber glove and closely inspected my teeth, gums, and tongue.

"How do your teeth feel?" he asked, pulling his now bloodstained glove from my mouth.

"They hurt like hell, *Dhakhtar*," I replied, but in a Somali manner of saying. "Why is my mouth bleeding? Why do my ears hurt? Why the bad headaches? Please, can you help me, *Dhakhtar*?"

He remained silent, looking very distraught, then fumbled through his medical bag and removed a silver flask. "This might hurt for a minute," he warned as he untwisted the lid, "but it will do your mouth some good. Here, take a swig."

"Rum?" I could smell it from a league away.

"*Haa.*"

"Durst you make light of my situation at a time like this?" I reproached.

The old *dhakhtar* exhaled a lengthy sigh, took a swig himself, then said with burning breath, "*Maya, saaxiib*, I do not. You weren't the only one who stayed with your gracious sister until the bitter end, and it doesn't get any heavier than that. Please, just take a sip."

As he went to hand me the bottle, his left eye started to tear, then a streak raced down over his right cheek. He tried to wipe his eyes with one hand, but it was useless — his face was soon as wet as mine, only his was sodden with sorrow, not cold sweat.

I drank of the rum, and it stung my gums like a strong mouthwash, but unlike a strong mouthwash, I didn't spit it out. The taste of rum overpowered the stench of blood in my mouth, and this was enow for me to swallow the old pirate drink.

We exchanged the bottle a few times, and the mild, nagging headache I'd been carrying all morning finally started to ease. "Now about the antigen, *Dhakhtar*," I pressed my chief concern. "I need more guidance on how much to take and when."

"The *antibaayootig*?" he asked with a quavering voice.

"*Haa*, the serum. I know it couldn't save my sister, but it's helping me. I just need to know more about it."

"*Waan ka xumahay, saaxiib*," he apologized, snapping shut his doctor's bag, "but I can't help you with that."

"*Maxaa*?!" I was shocked. "*Waayo?*" I asked, *why?*

He stood and replied, "Zayid tasked me to administer the *antibaayootig* to Amina, not you." He started to wipe his eyes again, for fresh tears were streaking down. He turned to leave.

"But *Dhakhtar*!" I insisted.

"You have your own stockpile, do you not?"

"*Haa*, but I need your help with the injections."

"That is all." He headed towards the door.

"But I'll die if I do it incorrectly!"

He stopped at the door and remained there with his back turned to me, then started to audibly weep.

"*Dhakhtar?*"

"I can't do this anymore," said he, grabbing the doorknob and closing the door. He set his bag down on the dresser, then opened it and procured a hand-kerchief, with which he dried his eyes before turning to me and saying, "Haji, I'm going to come clean."

"What's this all about?"

He came to my bedside and said with painful sincerity, "I came to the conclusion months ago that the injections were bad, so I stopped administering them to your sister. This is why she died prematurely — from the withdrawals, and her initial radiation exposure. I'm so, so sorry, Noor, but you should know that Amina was in full agreement with my findings. The antigen is very dangerous. It alters brain tissue and kills slowly. I've seen the x-ray results, seen the CT-scans. Even with more and more antigen, like the star on your chest that struggles to survive, you will eventually run out of energy and die."

I was confused. My head was numb with booze. I cradled my skull in my hands, trying to cover my ears, trying not to hear, only my stigmata would not allow this. I rolled over in my bed, covering my head with a pillow.

"How do you know this?" I eventually asked, letting the pillow go.

"Haji, you know I come from the old school of medicine. I still view traditional remedies as superior to synthetic ones. But I do know enough about modern medicine to know you can't fight fire with fire. By injecting more of a radioactive substance into your system, I just can't see how that will help you in the long term. It isn't cancer you're fighting, Haji, but radiation poisoning. This *antibaayootig* that Zayid is harvesting is experimental in the extreme."

"That may be so, but without it, I'd already be dead like my sister, correct?"

"No, Haji, I'm afraid you don't understand." He rubbed his forehead as he shook his head remorsefully.

"What don't I get? What's the big secret?"

He reached down and massaged my shoulder a bit. "*Saaxiib*," said he with dire sincerity, "there are some fates worse than death. When I found out the truth behind the serum, I could not in clear conscience continue administering it to your sister, even if that meant she would die by taking her off it. I've grown too close to your family, and furthermore, I've come to believe in you as the *Hoggaamiye*, even if I am a Yemeni. I have too much respect for you to allow you to remain Zayid's guinea pig."

He appeared very concerned. His voice warbled uneasily, and his expression was both caring and fearful. "Zayid has been using you," he uttered quietly, "in a bioweapons experiment."

"Biological warfare?"

"No, something entirely different. The antigen stays the onset of acute radiological death as it reverts the human physiology into its primordial structure. The experiment's main impasse was that the antigen — what they misleadingly call *antibaayootig* — kills the subject before the physical transformation is complete. You are the longest living subject thus far, and many have been tested."

"Really? Where are they, then? I've never seen them."

"In underground laboratories." He shook his head in chagrin. "Haj, it's a crime to all humanity what Zayid is doing. But you are lucky: you have thus far outlived your cohorts in the experiment. The scientists attribute your longevity to your brush with lightning in the helicopter crash, which they believe has provided you with the missing link needed to bypass the point of catastrophic radiation overdose. Somehow, the powerful jolt of electricity has caused your body's electromagnetic field to aid in the biosynthesis of the radioactive serum. Experiments on mice show that once the cerebellum takes precedence in the brain's functions, the 'moat of radiation' can be safely extracted from the cranium."

"You mean that pool of serum in my brain can be removed?"

"*Haa.* What the serum does is concentrate the radiation around the cerebellum. Once the transformation of the physical organism is complete, the poison can be extracted almost fully from the body. This is why you've been having headaches and nightmares, and this is why your head has been changing shape. Your cranium is adapting to the restructuring of your brain and is elongating to make room for the serum's concentration around your cerebellum. If you live long enough to survive the transformation, you can, in fact, be healed of radiation poisoning, but I regret you will no longer be yourself."

"What do you mean? In what way? And why can't the radiation be extracted now?"

"To extract the serum prematurely, that is, before the cerebellum has grown its own protective bone cavity, causes massive hemorrhaging, the end result being brain death — something akin to a full lobotomy."

"If what you're saying is true, what will I be like if I stay the course? What exactly will become of me when my transformation is complete?"

"This is hardly an exact science, *saaxiib*, but the end result will be something akin to a bird-man."

"A what?"

"A bat."

"You've got to be fucking kidding!"

"The lab results have been positive. Mice have grown fangs and wings."

"Fuck off," I laughed. "That's preposterous."

"I only wish it were, Haj. But look at the way in which your body is changing. It's only a matter of time before—"

"Before what? Before I grow wings? Hey, *Dhakhtar*, I got news for you: my head may be doing fucked-up things, but there's not an ounce of wing tissue beneath my arms."

"Another shortfall with the serum's application on humans," he somberly conceded. "The head transforms, while the rest of the body remains the same. It may be the way the heads of mice are more directly adjoined to their bodies, allowing for expanded restructuring of the greater physique."

"So, in keeping with your theory, who the hell would want to create a bat without wings?"

"Your wingsuit training wasn't as innocent as you were led to believe. Its ultimate goal was not to reconstitute Khatar Force One, but to prepare you for the eventuality that you would need wings of your own to fill in the gaps in your transformation. You will soon have the arm power and speed to flap your wings and gain lift, while traits like night vision, an acute sense of hearing, and an elongated skeletal frame will complete the specimen."

"Specimen for what?" I asked, now quite frightened by what I first thought had been something akin to psychobabble.

"Zayid's ultimate fighting machine. Colonies of weaponized bat-men hiding in the dark recesses of the world, ready to swarm out of buildings, ships, and caves to attack like a terrible stormcloud."

"Weaponized?"

"Your ability to harness electricity, Haji — to create and throw ball lightning. This is what Zayid has in mind for his army of bat-men."

"Bat-men," I laughed. "Give me a break, Nasir."

"Once your physical transformation is complete, they'll subjugate you to all manner of experiments to try to crack the code of your electromagnetic abilities."

"And how is that a worse fate than death? Supposing what you're saying is true, my head will be a little elongated, but I'll have the ability to fly and will be free of radiation poisoning."

"Look, *walalo*, I know how strong your desire is to live and get through this, but the experiments on mice were enough for Amina to opt out of such a fate, and if I knew any other way to help you, I would. But for now, the truth is all I have for you, so that you can make an informed decision. I can no longer tow the line. Experiments on humans to this end, and especially on my friends, should not be allowed to happen."

"What happened to the mice?"

"It was their cerebellums — that primordial appendix of the brain. Once the cerebellum took precedence in their mental functioning, the mice, usually timid and docile creatures, became rabid in behavior, violently attacking any living thing — including their own species — to feed upon."

"That doesn't sound to me like an easy army to organize."

"Zayid's hope is that man's larger and more evolved brain, his higher reasoning, and the relative separation of the brain from the rest of the body via a longer neck will help to offset the cerebellum's urges. But I'm not so convinced, and at any rate, it's not worth the risk. Frankly, *saaxiib*, and I say this with as much compassion as I said it to your older sister, it would be better to accept one's fate with Allah in high *Jannah*."

"So let me get this straight. You told Amina to stop taking the serum on some crazy hunch that Zayid was using it to create an army of rabid bat-people?"

"Not a hunch, Haji. I know for certain. Zayid is working in conjunction with a foreign biotech company in the development of the serum and orchestration of the experiments. The only reason they let you walk free is because, as their number-one subject, they need your continued trust and training. But soon they'll break the news to you, probably with a dagger held behind their back should you choose to defect."

"I don't know, Nasir," I replied, smirking and shaking my head. "That sounds like some crazy science-fiction shit to me."

"Worse, I'm afraid, because Zayid is doing it less for science and more for money. Once the drug is perfected, once they crack the code and create a human bat, they plan on selling the science to the highest bidder, foreign militaries included — and possibly to one of our most hated enemies. Then Zayid will turn its back on the empire and let come what may in a brave new world of biotech warfare, most likely aligning the

Organization with the highest bidder and taking sanctuary in their dominance."

"Bat-men, biotech warfare, the treason of Zayid. I don't know, Nasir, I'm finding this all very hard to believe. If Zayid got wind of what you were saying about them, I can tell you they would not be pleased, to put it lightly."

"Much more than that, Noor. If you so much as breathe a word of what I've told you and they find out about it, you may as well hand me the black spot now. I've taken an oath under penalty of death not to tell you, Amina, or anyone close to you about this, but again, I could not live with myself seeing you being subjected to such horrors, and neither could Amina Rage accept such a fate. So please, not a word, eh? If you stop taking the antigen, you must not tell Zayid, or they will send me, Sooraan, or another doctor to force it back into your system. If you do stop taking it, I must be completely honest with you: yours will be a painful death. But if you do keep taking it, your future will be as horrific as I've described it, and your chances of a positive ending down that road are slim at best."

"Very well, then; whether your story is true or not, for the sake of your helping me in the past, I shall return the favor and keep mute about it. But tell me, *Dhakhtar*, if I stop taking the serum, how long do you think I'll live?"

"If you stop taking the antigen, or even cut down, your time will be numbered to mere days is all I can say. Perhaps you can survive a week before going into cardiac arrest. Zayid knows the serum alleviates pain. They know you rely on it to survive. That's why they keep your supply full and know you'll take it on your own volition. But rest assured, they have people watching to make sure."

"They do?"

"I am one of them."

"They asked you to spy on me?"

"*Haa.* But now that I've told you the truth, I'll tell them you're still taking the antigen even if you stop. Don't rock the boat on this, Haji. Try to continue on normally, and if you must die, do so nobly, like your sister. If they suspect trickery, I will disappear and they will reassign another physician in my shoes."

"I'll just leave Boosaaso."

"Then you must pretend to be taking the antigen, for someone will be watching wherever you go in the world. Of this I can assure you."

"And what if I decide to die?"

"To be honest, *walalo*," he said soberly, shooting me furtive glances, "use that silver bullet of yours. Don't wait it out."

"The bullet of *Jannah*," I remarked in sudden realization. "Captain Shar'ma'arke said it could stop anything. Maybe it can stop my sickness?"

"I don't think so, *walalo*."

"*Maya?*"

"I don't believe in fairy tales."

I gave myself three shots of serum, then walked down to the local teashop and ordered some *shaah filfil* — black pepper tea. Men were gathered inside, and if before my arrival they'd been discussing news or reciting poetry, by the time I sat down they were gossiping about me. I'd grown accustomed to this sort of thing, being something of a celebrity in Somalia. Wherever I went, people were always coming up to me, saying, "*Hoggaamiye! Hoggaamiye!*"

Today, however, men got up from their tables to offer their condolences. "*Ilaahay samir iyo iimaan ha inaga siyo,*" they said, to which I always replied, "*Aamiin.*"

Amina's passing still lingered in the news and continued to haunt me for a variety of reasons. To the general public she'd been many things: a bond between the Reer Salaax and Warsangali sub-clans via her marriage with Jamal Abdallah Awaad; others regarded her as a mystical priestess called an '*alanqad*, who could be visited by *zaar* — a powerful spirit that, when visiting her, caused her to do her ritual dance of spirit possession; while yet others saw her as a *waranle* — a classic Somali fighter, pure and simple.

For me, Amina Rage had been the black sheep of the family, but of course branding her as merely a rebel could never do her justice. She was by far the most creative amongst us, her skill at *xenna* painting sought far and wide. She'd been a skilled entrepreneur, enabling her to maintain a successful business in the United Arab Emirates. She was a caring family member, especially in times of crisis. But most of all she'd been the most daring pirate I'd ever come across, and while her escapades were nothing short of reckless, she managed to carve her way into the history books as Somalia's first female *budhcad-badeed.*

Thus, it was with appreciation that I accepted the condolences of the strangers at tea. Their saying, "May Allah, by this incident, fortify your faith and patience," not only reflected Amina's popularity in Boosaaso, but it reinforced my own faith in my decision to continue taking the antigen. For me, certain death was never an option.

The tea was poured from a metal kettle called a *kildhi* into a small glass, then the server asked for my opinion.

"More sugar and a bit of goat's milk, please," I replied after tasting it, puckering my lips a bit in reaction to the black pepper. That my gums weren't bleeding as much and my mouth could handle a bit of spice gave further evidence that the antigen injections were working to combat my illness.

After the server left, I asked the patrons for some privacy, and once they were back to their gossiping and poetry, I procured my cell phone and called Bashir.

I asked the commander innocent questions about the antigen, like where it came from and when I'd be healed.

It was being manufactured by a group of pharmaceutical experts, he replied vaguely, who were working in conjunction with Zayid's top physicians, such as Dr. Sooraan. My best chance at recovery, it was reiterated, was to continue on an aggressive injection regimen while the science was being perfected.

"But it killed my sister," I told him, probing his reaction.

A moment of silence, words of condolences, and then his carefully measured response: "It may be she wasn't taking enough. Has *Dhakhtar* Nasir told you anything?"

"About what?"

"About how she died."

"He believes her body may have already been too compromised by radiation exposure," I lied.

"Well, there you go, then. I regret that, for Amina, we may have done too little, too late. My apology is deeper than the deepest sea."

"She's with Allah now."

"How do you feel, Haji, I mean physically?"

"Better."

"Excellent. I'll be flying you back to Djibouti for more testing, but first I need you to fly another KF-Two mission."

"*Goorma?*" I asked, *when?*

"Next Tuesday, the thirteenth."

"A hijacking?"

"*Haa*, a big one. A super-target."

"Details."

"It's too sensitive. You'll be briefed on the load."

"This is a skydive?"

"*Haa*, a terminal velocity hit. This is a very important mission for Zayid."

"Why?"

"Patience, Haji. You'll find out soon enough. Just be at the Boosaaso airport next Tuesday at nine o'clock in the morning and have your canopy packed, slider-up. Xeed will meet you in the parking lot and escort you to the plane, where the rest of your team will be waiting."

SKY PIRATES

"MAY IT BE SO," was my response to Xeed's expression of condolence as we walked over the tarmac. I don't recall him ever having met Amina, not that it mattered.

Xeed wore his usual black-tie attire, replete with a briefcase handcuffed to his wrist and undoubtedly filled with cash, while I wore my yellow windbreaker and canopy rig, opting to carry my wingsuit in a duffel bag. A tracking suit would've been easier, but knowing nothing about the mission ahead, I erred on the side of flight time and distance as opposed to outright speed.

"Have you taken your injections?" Xeed asked.

"*Maya.*"

He stopped in his tracks and regarded me with an air of surprise.

"I have some in my bag. I'm going to shoot up on the load."

"Thank Allah for that," he said.

"Why the concern?"

"You need it to survive, *walalo.*"

"Yeah, well the side effects can be really bad."

"So I've heard. I feel for you, Haji, really, I do. Didn't Nasir tell you? Your body's going through changes — that's part of the process."

"Yeah, I know."

"I can see your ears and teeth have changed. Does it hurt?"

"Only if I stop the injections."

"Then keep shooting up. It's better you turn into a bat than wind up dead. Didn't Nasir brief you on that?"

"*Haa.*"

"He did?"

"Er…"

"I was just kidding, Noor."

"So was I."

"Well, it's a shitty subject to joke about, *jaalle.* Just keep taking the *antibaayootig* and you'll be fine. The side effects will pass."

"How do you know?"

He stopped before the cargo door and said, "I wasn't born yesterday."

Before I could ask him what he meant by that, the door of the aircraft slid open and Cosob held out his hand. "Welcome aboard, Haj," the admiral said. "We've got some catching up to do."

I took his hand and climbed into the back, taking a jumpseat beside the rest of my team, except for Thor, who sat in a standard seat directly behind the pilot.

"*Hayye, Noor,*" said Khalidah Malak, sitting shotgun. "Did you get my package?" She'd sent me a decorative *heedho* container filled with fresh dates and *muqumad* (Somali jerked meat) during my recovery in Boosaaso.

"*Haa, waad mahadsantahay.*" I replied I was grateful.

"*Waan tacsiyadeynayaa.*" She expressed her condolences less religiously than others had, which I appreciated.

"Let's get this show on the road," Xeed said, taking the seat beside Thor. "Noor, put these on."

He tossed back a pair of military-grade earplugs.

The pilot engaged the throttle lever, and we began to roll, so I quickly stuffed the rubber plugs into my over-sensitive ears.

"Are you part of this mission, Khalidah?" I shouted over the roar of engines.

"We're just dropping you off!" she shouted back, eliciting laughter from the others. "Xeed and I will proceed to Dubai on business!"

"Noor!" Xeed hollered. "You have about twenty minutes to gear up! Cosob will brief you on the mission! If there's anything you want to leave behind, place it in the larboard stow. The pilot will deliver it to Mogadishu, and you can pick it up at the palace when you get back!"

"How long is this mission supposed to last?"

"Cosob! That's your cue!" he said as our wheels lifted off the tarmac.

෴

Twenty-five minutes later, we were entering the DZ — the drop zone. I'd taken five shots of antigen and put my wingsuit on. It was a modified version, with Snekor Toggles and a legpouch deployment system with shrivel flap. The cargo door opened, and KF-2 prepared to jump.

The target vessel, a massive containership loaded with luxury cars from Europe, was clearly visible from ten thousand feet up, as was the warship shadowing it. The delivery of high-end vehicles to the UAE was said to be worth half a billion dollars, while the destroyer sailing port quarter was part of Ocean Shield's new VEP mandate. The Vigilance Escort Program was the UN Security Council's naval response to the establishment of the White Star Empire. All non-military vessels sailing near Somalia now required a military escort, or faced steep fines. Fines be naught, it would be a suicide mission sailing cargo of that value through the Gulf of Aden unassisted.

"They're coming!" Cosob shouted, craning his neck out the door to see behind the plane. But my acute sense of hearing picked up the rumble of approaching fighter craft well before I laid eyes on them, even with my earplugs in.

"Now!" Cosob cried, leaping from the load. We scrambled to exit the aircraft after him.

My jump began badly. I exited sideways, and the pistol attached to the top of my helmet clipped the top of the cargo door, causing me to go immediately unstable. While the rest of my team, who were all wearing tracking suits, flocked towards the ships at terminal velocity, I was floundering far behind, caught in an uncontrollable spin.

Cosob and Mohamed tracking towards the ships

The faster I spun, the dizzier I became. What's worse, I could feel myself "potato chipping" in a highly varying angle of attack. I stretched my arm and leg spans to their maximum and held them there with a will of iron, hoping this would slow my spin and help regain stabilization. It only made things worse.

I thought I'd pass out from whirling around at three revolutions per second. I was in a world of unintelligible blue, having lost all sense of groundrush. I knew that to deploy under such circumstances would most certainly lead to multiple line twists and perhaps even catastrophic line-over malfunctions, while the BASE rig I was flying under had no backup parachute.

Faintly recalling something I'd learned in practice about correcting pitch instability and wobbling, I took an opposite approach to my predicament: I relaxed my arms and slightly increased the arch of my back. My potato chipping eased, but I was still spinning fast. It seemed the wing-loading ratio on my modified suit might've been miscalculated, causing a tug-of-war between my body weight and the wingsuit's stable glide ratio.

With my sink rate hard to adjudge and my terrain reference shot, I couldn't tell if I was two minutes to impact or four seconds — but I took the risk anyway, tightly drawing in my arm and leg spans.

My body continued to whip around like a stick caught in a whirlpool. I knew that unless I stopped the rotations, my death would come via ocean impact.

I steepened my AoA to the maximum, and as my speed ratcheted up to 120 mph, I was finally able to control my spin. But now I was losing well over 200 feet per second through a low-level cloud that completely blinded my altitudinal awareness.

I slowly opened my arm wings in the freefall until I attained an even glide, then carefully stretched out my leg span. Feeling myself beginning to wobble again, I kept my head down and my center of gravity forward. My wings stretched taut, and the airstream flew smoothly over my back, greatly improving my glide ratio, and when I dropped out from beneath the cloud, the turbulation that had plagued me since exit suddenly vanished.

I kept my chin tucked in and flared my nostrils back, sucking in a deep breath of relief. I still had about 3,000 feet of altitude, and while I could see the rest of my team already deploying over the target ship far in the distance, I knew that with my lift-to-drag ratio of 3.0, I stood a fair shot at closing the gap; this was the magic of my wingsuit's efficiency — with every foot I dropped, three were gained going forward. (At the time, the lift-to-drag average for wingsuiting was 2.5).

Suddenly, two MiG-35 fighter jets tore through the sky below me and blasted rockets at the destroyer shadowing the containership, blowing apart its bridge.

Cir Consort 1, reloaded

I screamed out victoriously, which sounded more like the screech of a pterodactyl because my throat was so dry. That's when I realized that the white star design sewn over the chest of my yellow wingsuit was glowing, for beneath it, my star tattoo had somehow energized. Perhaps it was from an unprecedented dose of serum and the effect of the spin, but whatever the cause, my electromagnetic force had been animated to the point of electron overflow. Ball lightning was already starting to form at my chest.

I increased my AoA to gain speed on the target vessel, for now that the rest of KF-2 was onboard and *Cir Consort 1*'s new multi-role fighters had made quick work of her military escort, the assault on deck would not wait for me.

The containership was as long as ten city blocks, and motoring steadfastly ahead as I swooped down along her larboard side, where containers of cars were stacked to 800 feet high. I caught the updraft of the headwind and flew proxy along the wall of boxcars, aiming to land on the vessel's gunnels.

Suddenly, a shooter appeared from a crevice in the wall and trained his weapon on me. At the sound of gunfire, I tucked in my wings and went into a barrel roll, and while I was pivoting around, I formed ball lighting at my chest.

At the end of my rotation, I spread my wings and emitted a terrible bat shriek, flinging the effervescent ball at the enemy.

The shooter froze in terror as the ball lightning connected with his chest, vaporizing him in an instant, his rifle bouncing off the containers as it fell towards the deck.

"*SHRIEEK!*" I screeched like some horrible prehistoric bird at numerous shooters who appeared along the wall before me. As their carbines flashed, I cut sharply between a canyon of boxcars amidships, and as I did, bullets ricocheted off the containers behind me.

More and more black hearts popped out from the faux canyon walls, but with the swiftness and dexterity of the Egyptian falcon, I carved strategically through the terrain, shrieking like a flying demon as I vaporized them with lightning balls.

As I neared the far corner of the containership canyon, I spotted a black heart positioned along the promontory fiddling with his weapon. Not wanting to spoil my line, I held my wings steady and kept a close eye on him.

Two seconds later, I bore my bloody fangs and emitted an unholy *SHRIEEEK*! The infidel looked at me with an expression of mortal terror as I tore my talons across his face.

Drops of blood flew back from my fingers as I swooped along the wall aport. The time was nigh to deploy. I reached over my wing to release my pilot chute, but felt only my canopy container.

I reached again but could not find my PC. Then I remembered — and just in time — that I'd been fitted with a leg deployment system. As I yanked the PC from my thigh and heard the shrivel flap rip back, I tucked my arms in tightly to decrease the burble off my back. Impact was but seconds away. I knew this was my only chance.

I prayed to Allah as my bridle stretched far back, at last yanking the 7-cell canopy from my container. But my worries had just begun...

Having gone unstable while fumbling for my pilot chute, I opened off-heading, heading straight towards the wall. If I knew anything about BASE jumping, it was that an off-heading opening and wall strike was the number-one cause of fatalities.

Fortunately, I was flying with Snekor Toggles, and that split second spared by not having to unzip my wings before grabbing my brakes bought me a crucial second of time. Alas, as I looked up into a mess of line twists, I knew that pulling on my rear risers would be almost useless. I gave 'em a hard flare, anyway, running out of options.

I felt a slight jerk backwards, but it wouldn't be enough to prevent wall strike.

Big steel containers loomed ever closer before me, forming a merciless face of death that was eager to crush my skull. My helmet served primarily to hold my pistol, and like a camera helmet, it provided very little if any real protection.

With my demise now imminent, I reacted primordially. I closed my eyes and screeched like some mythical bird as I flapped my wings hard back. I could feel my wings moving with blinding speed and dexterity.

When impact didn't come, I opened my eyes to see that I'd gained not only distance from the wall, but also altitude. I stretched my rear risers far apart and kicked my feet with all my might, and *Allahu Akbar*! I succeeded in freeing the line twists!

Finally in control, I set my eyes on a landing site in front of the bridge, then swooped down and flared at just the right moment, touching down from heel to toe on deck.

Cosob appeared at the command deck window seconds later, holding his pistol to a white sailor's head, then Thor announced over the loudspeakers for the crew to surrender lest they wanted to see their black-heart captain shot dead.

One by one, the Euro pigs came out from their hiding places. We threw them all into a makeshift brig. Zayid knew that others would hole up and hold out to play hero, so sent *Cir Consort 1* back with a cargo plane full of mustard gas, which was summarily dropped over the deck.

Thus, the empire's new piracy stratagem came to pass, and so, too, did *Dhakhtar* Nasir's dire warning that I was turning into a bird-man.

RECONSTRUCTION

THE *BOQOR* HAD RETURNED to Mogadishu along with Ahmed Mahamoud Silanyo, the president of Somaliland, and Abdirahman Mohamed Abdilahi, the Somaliland Parliament speaker of the house. Even before I could figure out how to best approach Bashir on the subject of the *antibaayootig*, I found myself sitting beside him in the parliamentary chamber along with the rest of the *guurti*, fielding grievances of the Somalilanders.

The main problem we were facing was, as mentioned previously, that Somaliland had seceded from the rest of the country in 1991 and had since enjoyed total independence, a relatively high level of prosperity, and, most significantly, a state of peace that would've put to shame all those who, for decades, had claimed Somalia was naught but a cesspool of chaos and violence.

"But beyond our right to sovereignty," Somaliland President Silanyo spoke from the immaculate, blue and white marble floor, "we have a right to opt out of this *guurti* altogether."

A murmur of disapproval rumbled around the chamber.

"That would be very unwise," spoke our own speaker of the house, Ibrahim Osman Daar. "The day may come when you need our protection."

"I think you are missing the point," countered the Somaliland president. "To put it plainly, we do not believe in your empire. It is not the Somali way for a central government to demand allegiance of all the regions and clans, and you know that. The white man introduced this concept of centralized power. The model of democracy you espouse is false because it supplants the regional *guurtis*. In essence, you are making a joke of traditional Somali customs and jurisprudence by saying that government is permitted to interfere with customary law."

"Just a moment," said President Tahliil, who held a permanent seat on the Council of Emperors. "You are doing a great disservice to the representatives of the clans here, who have by their own volition chosen to be part of this *guurti*. And how can you talk of local administrative autonomy when the fourteen regions under your own republic are held accountable to your executive and legislative authority?"

"That is incorrect," countered President Silanyo. "Our regions hold their own local elections and run their own courts. The Somaliland Supreme Court deals only with issues between courts, governmental matters, and constitutional law. Our executive authority does not infract upon the *qabil* system of local clan governance. Perhaps you are forgetting that for ten years now, we've been a multi-party democracy, with each district council holding its own elections — elections in which six different parties are allowed to compete in their own provinces.

"But what I see here," continued the Somaliland president pointedly, "is the classic result of an African *afgembi*. The leaders of the coup create their own government, and there is no opting out of their rule unless another *afgembi* comes along to supplant them, ad infinitum. You are destroying the model of clan autonomy that has for centuries given Somalia its unique system of local courts and politics. What you are doing in Mogadishu is a repeat of the centralization of power experiment forced on Somalia in recent times by the West, and it inevitably leads to a government of brute force and megalomaniacal warlords of the ilk of Siad Barre. Do not forget that the people of *Jamhuuriyadda Soomaalil-and* rejected centralized government long ago in favor of the traditional model of customary law. We are wary of your empire because it impugns our time-honored belief in each Somali's right to life, liberty, property, and self-determination, as expressed through our custom-ary laws. You are continuing the legacy of your colonial predecessors by forcing all Somalis to consent to your authority and legal structure. However, we will never bow down to you or any other government, for we give allegiance to no law but *xeer tolnimo* and to no higher authority other than God. Thus our motto, *There is no god but Allah, and Muhammad is the Messenger of God.*"

President Silanyo's attachés praised Allah aloud.

"*Oh là là,*" our own President Tahliil drawled in Italian.

Suddenly, a younker ran into the chamber with three security guards chasing after him. He threw him-self at the feet of Somaliland President Silanyo and clutched his legs. "Please don't let them take me!" he pleaded. He was bereft of shirt and sandals and covered with his own blood, which seeped out from thousands of little pricks all over his body.

"*Daryo!*" shouted one of the pursuing guards, then seized the boy and started dragging him away.

The child had ostensibly been disowned by his family and committed a crime, which meant he had no protection under local law. All at once, he looked up at me and called out, "*Hoggaamiye*! Please! Don't let them take me!"

He must've recognized me by my yellow windbreaker, for it was well known I wore it at *guurti*. There'd been photographs enow for any Somali, even a child, to recognize me here.

"Please help me, *Hoggaamiye*!" he cried.

I didn't know what to do or say.

"*Joogso*!" ordered Assembly Premier Rashiid Cassanelli, telling the guards to stop.

The sentries, who were not palace security but appeared to be the regional police we sometimes referred to as *waranle* (same word for *warriors*), halted, but they kept a firm grip on the younker's arms.

Premier Rashiid climbed down from his seat and stood before the child. "*Magacaa?*" He asked his name.

"*Magacaygu waa Ali Sinimoo.*"

"*Xaggeed ka time?*" Cassanelli asked Ali Sinimoo where he was from.

"*Waxaan ka imi Benadir.*"

"*Wagosha?*"

"*Haa.*" He affirmed he was from the Benadir region, south of Mogadishu.

Cassanelli then asked him what the trouble was: "*Maxay tahay dhibaatadu?*"

"I was hungry," the child said, trying to refrain from crying. "I stole some dates from a market stall, but the clansmen caught me and issued my *garr*. They tied me to a tree and covered me with honey. Soon the ants came, the big ones of the marsh trees. They were eating me alive. I screamed for help, but the *guurti* just watched. Then *Haddi Eebbe yidhaahdo*! It started raining and the old men left. I escaped from the tree and sought shelter back in my village, but was chased out by the *waranle*. I have no *oday* — my clan didn't like the judge appointed to me at birth. The *waranle* kept coming after me, so I came here. Please, tell the officers to let me go!"

A councilwoman, a representative of the Abgal clan region, reproached the *waranle* thus: "Stealing some dates warrants such a severe punishment?"

"The *inan* tells only half truths," replied one of the provincial officers, a tall and skinny man wearing a dirt-stained, long-sleeved collared shirt and *ma'wais* — a sarong. "He didn't tell about his rustling a camel from the clan chief."

"I didn't know it was his!" protested the child.

"Four times in three weeks this *inan* has committed crimes," another *waranle* said. "By way of our *xeer tolnimo*, the *guurti* was just. This is a local matter. We have no business in your supreme court."

"This is parliament," put in the speaker of the house.

"No matter," replied the guard, brusquely pulling the younker's arm, "he is *dayro* — an outlaw. He has no family to insure him. He must be returned to the village for the *guurti* to determine how he will pay the blood price."

"Blood price?" reproached the speaker. "His crime is not related to blood. It is *garr.*"

"That is for our *guurti* to decide," insisted the *waranle.*

Premier Cassanelli came before the provincial guards and said, "If the *inan* has no family to surrender the required payment to your elders, I shall help him." He pulled a wallet from his coat and withdrew a handful of Empire Riyals. "Will five hundred suffice?"

The *waranle* looked at each other with raised brows, then one replied, "Give us six hundred to compensate our journey, and we shall present your offering before the chief. If he rejects it, we shall be returning with his counter price."

"Good enough," said the premier, handing them more cash.

They turned to leave with the boy. He screamed *no!* and tried to sit, but the guards just lifted him by his arms and kept walking.

"The *inan* stays here!" I demanded, vaulting down from my high seat and blocking the path to the door. "He needs urgent medical attention."

"This was not part of the arrangement," the guards complained.

Two women on the council came to my defense, demanding the child's release.

The *waranle* scoffed, for in the traditional *guurti* system, women were never allowed in court unless they were being tried for a crime.

I procured from my windbreaker a wad of Riyals probably totaling 2,000. I offered it to the guards, saying, "We shall chastise him here. Our own court, the *Safaarad*, practices strict *xeer*. But first the *inan* needs medical attention. By the looks of him, he won't make it back to Benadir."

The guards took the money and pushed the younker into me, then left without another word.

"*Mahadsanid, Hoggaamiye*," the child said, clutching my jacket while looking up at me tearfully.

"*Waa hagaag, inan*," I replied, saying *it's okay, boy*, then hunched down and told him more quietly, "Ali, you must learn to stay out of trouble. The *dumar* will take you someplace to recover. Be strong."

The *dumar* — the women —— agreed to see him to Medina Hospital. They escorted him out of the chamber, bloody footsteps marking his path. Like so many other displaced Somali kids, Ali would most likely have to fend for himself. But thanks to the empire, Mogadishu was a much different place than it was before. Now there were abundant schools, job recruitment centers, and more social services overall. Vast amounts of displaced persons lived together in squat houses and shanties further on the periphery as they worked towards upward mobility. Somehow, I knew Ali Sinimoo would make it. My action was met with loud applause that hit my ears like thunder.

The *Boqor* took the floor and said, "And who did you pay off to orchestrate that little piece of theatre?"

"Excuse me?"

"How very coincidental, *Hoggaamiye*, how very convenient such a drama should transpire while discussing *xeer* and the provincial courts."

"What are you insinuating, *Boqor?*"

"I'm saying that you and this assembly are a sham."

A great clamor became the chamber, with many pointing a finger sharply down at the *Boqor* as they spat recriminations.

The speaker of the house blew his buffalo horn, silencing the hubbub.

The *Boqor* waved his gnarled wood staff up at the ceiling, saying, "You paint an acacia tree over your heads and call yourselves the *guurti* of the land, forgetting that the clans are politically independent. Even my good friends from the north," he pointed his staff at his attachés, "even they have made this mistake, seating twenty-five elders in their upper house of parliament, believing that in doing so, Somalilanders would take the bait. But in fact, the establishment of the Somaliland parliament has done little to convince many northern citizens of the legitimacy of the Somaliland government. You will not fool the people into swapping their local judges for government judges, nor into swapping the laws specific to their communities — their *xeer tol-nimo* laws — with the dictates of a big government, be it their own government or any other, and especially the dictates of an empire."

"Respectfully, *Boqor*," I countered, "the Council of Emperors does not sit as judges, but as lawmakers. Our judges are the *Safaarad*, whose court is as legitimate as any *guurti*."

"Bah!" he scoffed. "Your so-called judges are politically appointed, for I have not heard of any province sending their *oday* here. *Xeer* is the only Somali justice, while every Somali knows that government laws and courts are a sham."

"Not the Somalis in this city," President Tahliil came to my defense, "who are flocking here from all corners of the country like the boy Ali, seeking our protection. Regardless of your insistence to the contrary, the citizens of Somalia are validating our legitimacy with their allegiance to our laws and in their investing in the empire, and in return we provide them with services, with a friendly business environment, and with a clear system of justice."

"A friendly business environment, you say?" the *Boqor* quipped. "More crafty words from knaves who levy a business tax, but all Somalis know that under traditional *xeer*, taxation is illegal. Like the Europeans of the late nineteenth century, you are trying to supplant the old system of trust with a new system of greed, and the freedoms of the communities with a forced democracy. Ali Sinimoo should have been sent back to his clan — you shouldn't have inter-vened."

I went to reproach the elder, but President Tahliil cut me off with a rejoinder of his own: "I reject your harsh prejudgment of the Empire, *Boqor*, because it doesn't reflect the truth of our history. It was the Barre regime, and not us, that destroyed Somalia's humani-tarian values and the republican values left over from the colonial regimes before him."

"*Haa*, ladies and gentlemen," I put in, address-ing the assembly as a whole. "Ali should not be forced to return to the *xeer tolnimo* of his *guurti* because, as we've just seen, the local laws invented by the provin-cial judges allow them to act with impunity. There is no oversight of their *guurtis*, no higher law to regulate their activities, and thus there's no objective way to prevent abuses against those whom they may unfairly judge and punish inordinately."

A subdued murmur darted around the assembly, followed by sporadic applause.

"This is not so," countered the *Boqor*. "The *odays* in the provinces are held accountable by the communities they serve, and the communities can fire those judges if they don't perform according to expectations."

"According to expectations," I huffed. "That's what worries me and those of us who take seriously the standardization of law in the empire. We do not feel that individual rights and liberties should be suspended for the sake of communal stability. As it is now, *xeer* is interpreted in various ways according to the whims of a particular village — villages where women are not allowed to speak at hearings, where their abusers can find protections behind the male-dominated *guurtis*, and where kids such as Ali, who may not have insurance monies or an effective *oday*, face an uphill battle to prove their innocence."

The council applauded firmly.

"The provinces," rejoined the *Boqor* loudly, quieting the assembly, "the provinces reject nationalized laws in favor of local laws and courts that conduct their own hearings and pass their own verdicts. This has always been the customary law of Somalia — a law agreed on for centuries by all clans in all dominions. And so I ask you, *Hoggaamiye*, who gave you the authority to change that? You say *Jannah* sent you? Are we simply to take your word for it? You talk about abiding by a universal justice, so I take it upon myself to ask you a fair question on behalf of all Somalis: Why should we supplant hundreds of years of our unique, clan-based legal tradition in favor of a one-size-fits-all system whose center of authority lies with a group of revolutionaries who have taken the capital by force and whose leader has not been appointed by consensus or referendum, but by an executive decision within the revolutionary party itself? Frankly, Mr. Fayrus, not all of us buy that you are a heaven-sent leader, and while I do not doubt you've inspired many with your spirit and daring, due to your young age and lack of experience in matters of justice and politics, I do not see any reason either I or any Somali should trust your decisions or the dictates of this revolutionary assembly."

The northern delegates seated at his table clapped vigorously, although there were only five of them — hardly enough to counter the chorus of boos that came down from the council on high.

After commanding silence in the chamber, I reproached the elder thus: "Very well, then, *Boqor*. What do you suggest we do? Shall we lay down our laws, our secular traditions, our very lives before extremists like al-Shabaab, or before power-hungry warlords and foreign governments who wish to control us and our resources?

"I have a great deal of respect for you, *Boqor*," I continued, "Allah be witness to that. And as a fellow Darod, I understand the love of independence shared by you and the northerners, but I warn you, the world is a different place now, and unless Somalia stands together, the dangers that can present themselves to an isolated, seceded province are far more serious than any risk posed by some pretended dictatorial empire. The old Somali model won't work anymore because the extremist groups know they can overpower provincial *guurtis* and replace our secular, customary law with their strict *Shari'a* law, supplanting your courts with their own.

"Most of all, a country of disparate pastoralist political systems can do little to fight the scourge of imperialism such as foreign piracy and toxic dumping, which I've seen firsthand, which has killed two of my sisters, has ultimately killed my father, and which is slowly killing me."

The *Boqor* was taken aback. He softened his glower, lowering his eyes to the floor.

"So let it be known far and wide," I addressed the assembly and all the clans with a robust call, "the *guurti* can only be protected on a national level by consolidating it under one roof, and the people can only be protected by standardizing its laws! The blood that stains the floor of this parliament was not shed by our courts, but yours. Innocence or guilt is not the domain of clans to decide, but the dominion of universal law. We offer an empire that champions equal rights for all, including women and children, and a council that is good and just before the eyes of Allah."

The chamber resounded with widespread applause. The two women still present stood as they clapped, followed by all the men — all save for the *Boqor* and his retinue, who fled in a temper. I covered my ears against the noise, for it assaulted my sensitive hearing like a lion's roar.

In seeing my dilemma, the speaker of the house blew his horn, but to no avail — the chamber continued to boom like thunder.

I fell to my knees in pain, then crumpled to the floor.

VOYAGE INTO THE UNKNOWN

LATER THAT EVENING, in the quiet of my office as I responded to emails and snacked on jerked beef, Bashir came in and told me the CEO wanted to meet me in Zeilah.

"*Maxaa?*"

"*Haa,*" replied the commander. "His ship will be in port tomorrow morning."

"The CEO of what?"

"The Organization."

"Zayid has a CEO?"

"Of course. Every large company does. The boat leaves at nine o'clock, so be onboard by then. It's a large tri-hull catamaran — you can't miss it." He turned to leave.

"Wait! Where will I be going exactly?"

"Zeilah!" He shot back from the doorway. "Oh, yeah, it's an overnighter, so bring a bag."

"Zeilah really exists?"

He looked at me as if I was a dumbshit. "Are you serious?"

I drew a blank.

"Salal region? In Somaliland?"

"Really?"

"We ought to have your head checked again, matey. Anyway, just be there, Haj, and have a good trip. Most guys never get a chance to meet the CEO. We'll chat when you get back. I gotta run."

❧

Bashir was right — there was no way I could've missed the CEO's ship, even if I did wake up bleary-eyed. It looked as if a spaceship had landed in the middle of Mogadishu harbor, so modern and sleek were its lines.

I was tendered by skiff out to the wonder of nautical engineering. It was so large that we drove directly beneath the hull, from where I alighted astern and climbed aboard.

If there were any security guards onboard, they didn't make themselves known. Instead, a lovely East African woman wearing a blue scarf neatly tucked into a white, button-down jacket greeted me and led me inside. She walked with an erect and stately elegance, undoubtedly well practiced in her high-heeled shoes and knee-length skirt. I was intrigued.

She took me to a lounge area and offered me a seat before a coffee table, upon which stood a tall metal kettle of tea called a *kildhi*, and crusty breakfast pastries that I thought were Somali *sambusas*, but when I bit into one, my face puckered up at the taste of sweet cream. The hostess laughed, calling them *il pasticiotto*.

"*Hilib miyuu ku jiraa?*" I asked if there was meat in it, and the sound of my own voice startled me. It was higher than usual, and very scratchy. I found no reason for this — I was relaxed and my throat wasn't dry.

"*Maya,*" she answered in Somali, "there's no meat in *il pasticiotto*. It's an Italian specialty, made expressly for you by our onboard chef."

"Is he Italian?"

"*Haa*, she is. Would you like something else?"

I raised my brows and shook my head. I wasn't used to cream fillings or being served like a king; furthermore, I was feeling a little queasy. I asked where the bathroom was, saying, "*Mee baytalmaygu?*"

"*Saani u soco iyo bidix u leexo.*" She pointed the way, having said *straight ahead and to the left.*

I was soon standing before a mirror, staring into the eyes of a deeply worried man. My head appeared more elongated and chiseled, my face was yellowish and jaundiced, my gums were bleeding again, while my upper canines had grown out fully. What's worse, a layer of skin had grown over one of my stigmata, and on both my hands the lower portion of my fingers were growing together, becoming webbed. I tried to peel the skin away, but it hurt too much. Unlike a scab, the elastic growth appeared a permanent new appendage of my hands.

I stretched my left eyelids far back and looked deep into my eyeball. It was slightly bloodshot, but that's not what concerned me. The irises around both my pupils were turning red and my vision was becoming foggy.

I lifted up my windbreaker and shirt to find my chest star turning black. I'd missed my morning injections.

I rifled through my *qandi* pouch and prepared five tubes of *antibaayootig* by shaking them and removing their plastic seals, then shot up all five in quick succession. I felt a surge of energy and my vision began to clear; however, the rest of my physical aberrations remained, including my queasiness. *Seasickness*, I muttered, but the trick didn't work — I could no longer lie to myself. The trimaran was stable and I rarely got seasick. I was changing in a fundamental way, and my illness was becoming harder to combat with the serum, even with five injections three times daily.

I staggered out of the restroom, repacking my *qandi* pouch and trying to gather my wits, when suddenly, the hostess touched my arm, scaring me half to death. She asked if I was okay.

"*Madax xanuun baan leeyahay.*" I told her I had a headache, then asked her how long we'd be at sea. "*Socdaalkanu intee ayuu qaadan doonaa?*"

"Three hours to Zeilah."

"To Zeilah," I replied, probing her eyes for signs of insincerity. Zeilah as I knew it had ceased to exist hundreds of years ago.

"*Haa*," she said matter-of-factly, "in Somaliland. This ship is very fast."

"I can see that," I remarked as the craft gained speed, its very hull stepping up over the water as we rocketed forth with impressive celerity.

The Somali Pirate 3 - White Star Empire

"Can I offer you a tour of the ship?" she asked. "It's one of Zayid's favorite acquisitions."

"*Haa*, anything to get my mind off things."

"You sound very stressed, Mr. Fayrus."

I nodded sullenly.

"Well, don't be," she replied, grabbing my arm with her lovely long fingers. "You're safe here. You're in good hands."

"What's your name, by the way?"

"Amaranta."

"Ama—?" I began. Her name was in no way Somali.

"Amaranta. It means unfading flower."

"Indeed," I replied, becoming lost in her alluring lips, her beautiful eyes and face.

"Come," she offered, breaking a long silence. "Let's take that tour."

Quinn Robert Haber & Noor Haji Fayrus

THE *FARANJI*

OUR SUDDEN ARRIVAL at Zeilah came to me as somewhat of a surprise, for as I'd been resting on a couch, I hadn't been paying much attention to the world outside.

The landscape of Zeilah appeared to be part of the Somali peninsula and not an island, for vast, low-lying savannah stretched from the coast far inland, gradually slanting up into a mountainous horizon.

We tendered to shore, making landfall in the lee of a cobblestone point. To the east and west, for as far as the eye could see, the coastline was similarly contoured, with breakers striking the windward sides of endless little points before wrapping in and dissipating over rocks and reef.

Zeilah

A handful of crewmen and I were transported by jeep along a dirt road that followed the coast. We traversed two short bridges spanning wadi flows before arriving at the entranceway of a large ranch or plantation, or so I assumed by wire fencing that ran far off into the distance from either side of a rustic, overhanging sign that read, *'Ascendo Zayid.'*

We continued on for another five minutes before stopping in front of an extensive mansion built in the colonial style, with wide, open patios splaying out beneath decorative Byzantine verandas. I recognized the style of architecture from old Italian structures in my hometown of Dante and from the remnants of colonial-era edifices in Mogadishu. At first, I was surprised that Zayid would choose a style evoking such a period of our history, but in glimpsing the minaret of a mosque rising up behind the mansion, my apprehension was put at ease. Whoever the CEO was, he wasn't an infidel.

An older Somali dressed in a nice, collared shirt came down to greet me, while the jeep and its crewmen put in at a nearby barn.

The majordomo guided me to an expansive patio and announced, "This is the *ardaa*. Please wait here. Your host shall be with you shortly."

He was referring to something known as the men's fire corner, which is a place just on the perimeter of a

Somali dwelling where the grown male children and father sleep, except for when it rains.

"*Ma rabtaa spremuta?*" the Somali butler said, offering me an orange juice.

"*Haa, waan harraadsanahay,*" I told him, *yes, I'm thirsty.*

While waiting for him to return with the juice, I noticed some movement at eye level in the shade of a nearby alcove, so went to investigate. A cage was tucked into the ingress, and inside it, a yellow bat hung upside down by its feet, and by the looks of it, was quite asleep. To the right of the cage, leaning up against the wall of the alcove, were two long, fiberglass wings that could only have been things called "surfboards," which I'd once seen people using for sport on a TV documentary. I shook my head, perplexed by the strange accoutrements the CEO collected.

"Sir?"

I turned to find the majordomo holding my drink. "Your *spremuta,*" he said.

"*Mahadsanid,*" I replied, taking a few sips. It was good and sweet. "What's this stuff for?" I asked, gesturing towards the alcove.

"Those belong to the host's son," he said, pointing at the surfboards. "When he visits, he uses them to ride upon the waves, just for amusement. I tell him it's too dangerous — too many sharks — but he goes anyway."

A tall white man wearing a business suit and eye patch emerged from the shadows of the residence.

"Your host has arrived," announced the major-domo.

The "host" was a tough-looking guy with a cleanshaven head and intense, weathered expression. He didn't bother putting out his cigarette as he extended his other hand and introduced himself with a thick Italian accent. "*Galab wanaagsan, Noor, magacaygu waa Zayid.*"

I was startled, not only to be greeted by a *Faranji* — a European — but that he called himself Zayid

"*Iga raalli ahow?*" I asked, *excuse me?*

"Your surprise is not unexpected," said he, still holding out his hand. "*Assalaamu calaykum,*" he greeted me in the Islamic fashion instead, saying *peace be with you,* then he added, also in Somali, "*soo dhowow, jaalle,*" which meant *welcome, comrade.*

My mouth was agog at the strange turn of events. White people were never seen in Somalia, let alone living there, and I still couldn't ascertain why he referred to himself as "Zayid." Nevertheless, he'd offered me a formal Islamic greeting, and with a fellow Somali smiling on as if to reassure my safety in the white man's palace, I extended my hand to that of the *Faranji*, saying, "*Calaykum assalaam,*" meaning, *and peace be with you.*

Zayid

"Admiring Sheba, are you?" he asked.

"*Maxaa?*"

"Sheba," he replied with a wry grin, "our yellow-winged bat." He poked a finger into the cage, almost touching the little mammal through the little golden bars, but a large ring on his finger denied him contact. "Beautiful creature, isn't she? I found her in the savannah when she was very young. She couldn't even feed herself, let alone fly. He mother must've fallen ill or been taken by a predator, so I took her in and nurtured her myself, using a cloth soaked in milk from which she could suckle with her fangs, and groomed her with cotton swabs doused in warm water."

As I listened to the *Faranji* speak, I became transfixed by the exotic yellow bat.

"Her scientific name is *lavia frons*," he said, putting his cigarette out in a nearby ashtray. "Yellow-winged bats are all over this scrubland. Have you ever seen one before?"

I shook my head.

"Not surprised. Their blue-gray bodies and reddish-yellow wings camouflage them to a high degree. To most people — and predators — they look like dead leaves. They feed at night, moving from perch to perch as they attack approaching insects. What is most interesting, yellow-winged bats are monogamous. They live with a single mate their entire lives, protecting one another, grooming one another, hunting together, and raising their offspring together."

"Does she—" I began, then stopped myself, suddenly ashamed for being drawn in so quickly by the *Faranji*. Too many questions yet remained of him, not the bat.

"Does she have a mate?" asked he, having correctly read my curiosity. "It doesn't appear so," he chuckled dryly, "or maybe it's me. The back of her cage is open, see? She leaves at night to feed, but always comes back to me. I'm inspired by her independence and loyalty, much as you inspire me, Haji. I know you've been ill, *jaalle*, but look at Sheba here and take heart. She was once very sick as well, but with the help of Zayid, she pulled through, and like many of her species, she has a high tolerance to withstand pathogens and can be deeply infected with something but not develop a disease from it."

I did not relish being compared to a bat in a golden cage owned by a white man, but some of what he said did resonate with me. He seemed to be saying that I stood a fair chance at healing because the animal kingdom showed by example that it was possible for a species to adapt to extreme hardships, given the proper genetic disposition and set of environmental circumstances. It could not be denied that something about me, or the *antibaayootig* provided by Zayid, had enabled me to survive when others in my same straits had long since died. Perhaps the serum was changing me for the better, making me stronger.

"Nice *tooray*," the *Faranji* said.

I looked down at the dagger sheathed at my waist. "It's my father's."

"*Haa, waan ogahay* — Abdullah Haji Fayrus." He said he knew the dagger was Abbo's, and recited his full name.

My brows curled in skepticism. "Have you read my books?"

"Come," he said, touching my shoulder and offering the way back to the veranda. "We have much to discuss."

THE LAND OF THE GODS

"TO KNOW WHO I AM," began the *Faranji*, "let us start from the beginning. This will be important to you, so *mahadsanid* for coming. In learning about my history, you shall also learn a great deal about yours."

We were sitting at a small café table situated alongside the patio railing, which commanded a view of the adjacent mosque and a glimpse of ocean to the north.

"The beginning came before me," he said, lighting another cigarette "I know you don't usually smoke, that's why I don't offer one."

I eyed him curiously. How did he know so much about me?

"The Land of Punt," he continued, pausing to exhale his drag. "The Egyptians were right to call your ancestral home the Land of the Gods. The ancient Romans called it Cape Aromatica, due to its abundance of aromatic botanicals such as frankincense and myrrh. The geographical position of this region commands a superior trade advantage, but also creates a zone of isolation from which your people have developed their highly distinctive culture.

"Unfortunately, Somalia would not be spared the sins of the colonial era, when the superpowers of Europe sought to cut up Africa into their own monopolies and fiefdoms. Great Britain and Italy once controlled this area, while France seized the French Somali Coast, now called Djibouti.

"In eighteen ninety-nine, the Italians established a northern protectorate under the sultan of the Majeerteen clan — your father's clan — and in this time my family made great gains in the sugarcane rum trade, settling on this very *ascendo*. My family's dynasty in Puntland was further solidified by alliances we forged with local sultans and clan elders.

"In nineteen twenty-seven, when the Italian administration was established in all the regions of Somalia, Italian influence extended to the very heart of the capital, with Italian becoming the official language of government. To further protect my family's legacy in your country, my grandfather became involved in the colonial judicial system.

"The Italians, including my personal forefathers, wished to leave our mark here for centuries to come, so they implemented a national, codified law in the secular Western manner for significant criminal matters, but allowed customary law, *xeer*, to continue on the clan level. For the ease of maintaining social order, we allowed

Shari'a law to remain for family and minor civil matters. In this way, the Italians maintained formal governance of Somalia in a way that did not fully displace the distinct practices of your customary justice, and enabled Italian rule without upsetting the complex fabric of clan society.

"When fascist Italy occupied Ethiopia in nineteen thirty-five, it created Italian East Africa, consisting of Ethiopia, Somalia, and Eritrea. Then in nineteen forty-one, the Italians lost the 'Battle of the Horn' to Great Britain, ceding all but Italian Somaliland to the English. My father, who was born on this *ascendo*, stayed here for the next thirty-two years.

"I was born in Naples in nineteen fifty. My mother, a nurse whom my father had met during World War II, did not wish to remain with him on the plantation. Like the French who'd immigrated to Algeria at around that same time, the natives' increasing unrest here made it too trying for her to remain.

"I was nineteen years of age when my father and the *boqor* at that time arranged my marriage with Amaranta, who was then only two. It was purely a symbolic arrangement, or so I thought when I heard about it back in Naples.

"My father died in nineteen seventy-three, and the *ascendo* was bequeathed to me, but I remained in Italy. As time went on, I'd forgotten all about the *ascendo* and had tried to forget about him, as well, until I ran into trouble with the *Cosa Nostra* some fifteen years later."

"*Kuma?*" I asked, *who?*

"The Mafia."

I raised a brow.

"A gang of killers; think Siad Barre. I had to hide for a while, lie low someplace they'd never look, so on a whim I came here. The *boqor* had lodged his daughter in the *ascendo* care of my father's vast holdings from the colonial era. People were hired to take care of the grounds and watch over her until I came to retrieve her.

"She was then twenty-one years of age, and what started out as my purely carnal interest in her soon became deep love and affection. You've met her on the ship?"

"*Haa.*"

"Even now," he remarked, looking towards the ocean, "she is as beautiful to me as when I first met her, while inside she is indeed the undying flower of her namesake — so full of sweetness and grace."

"For what purpose was the marriage arranged?" I inquired. "It is not customary for a Somali to marry a *kufaar.*"

"You are right. At the time, I was an infidel. But since then I have converted. Amaranta has taught me many things about God and myself. To her and Allah I owe my happiness. Regarding the reason for our arranged marriage, the previous *boqor* was quite fond of my father, and was a business partner of sorts in my family's sugarcane rum and botanicals trade. The *boqor* had many daughters, so gave Amaranta as a gift. He thought it novel to align his Warsangeli sub-clan with the dynasty of an Italian Somalilander."

"Wild story, indeed, but why am I here? What does any of this have to do with me? And what do you mean by 'Zayid dynasty'?"

"I called you here because of your recent exchange with the *Boqor* on the council floor. I was watching a live video feed and was in total agreement with what you said. The *Boqor* was wrong to blame Somalia's problems on the old colonial regimes. Italy, for one, allowed *xeer* to continue. But you are right in saying it's time for *xeer* and the *guurtis* to end, because without centralized rule, Islamic extremists will continue to be a thorn in our side.

"I'm a devout Muslim, Noor, but a moderate one," he stated. "The only way the empire can avoid fractioning into a chessboard of seceded territories is to centralize power and ban customary law in the provinces, or otherwise standardize its code. And the same goes for *Shari'a* law. If we wish to keep it around for family matters and minor civil infractions, it, too, must be codified to ensure that equal justice is levied under the aegis of the government. Without such centralized authority, groups like al-Shabaab and Ansar al Sharia will continue to plague us like a diseased appendage. I've been watching you for a long time, *saaxiib*, and many have been involved in your mentoring. You've finally become the man we all knew you could be. This is why I've invited you to my *ascendo* — to congratulate you, and help provide you with assurances during your time of transformation."

"Transformation? Who are you?"

"I told you, Haji. I am Zayid, the owner of the Organization."

"*You* are Zayid?"

"*Haa*, Zayid Cecchi of Naples, Italy, CEO of Somali's pirate empire. You've fought well in my *askaris*, and now that you've graduated from the ranks of my greatest recruits, I would like for you to join me in running the empire, from the top."

My eyes smarted on his one eye, my forehead pruning in doubt. "But Zayid is the name of the command center in Eyl," I asserted. "It's where I was first recruited, as a matter of fact — the Zayid Mohamed Tower Command Centre."

The *Faranji* chuckled, remarking, "My father purchased that tower during the Battle of the Horn as a place to continue his business operations when it became too difficult to operate on the *ascendo*. When I was born, long after the war, he renamed it after me as a way to continue the mark of our dynasty in Puntland. The gift could not have been more serendipitous.

Being in Eyl, it proved the perfect base from which to launch my pirate business."

"I don't believe you."

"I didn't expect you would. I know it comes as an affront to you that a white man runs the Organization, but I assure you, you are in safe and able hands. You'll be staying the night, won't you?"

I shrugged my shoulders.

"I see you've brought an overnight bag. Abdul will show you to your room — I'm sure you'll find it very well appointed. I regret that some important business has come up that requires my immediate attention, but I look forward to continuing our conversation over dinner. I've some important things yet to tell you, which undoubtedly will help to resolve the many questions you still must have."

The majordomo emerged from the portico and stood over my bag.

"It's good to have you, Noor," Zayid said, getting up from his chair. "Amaranta will be joining us for dinner tonight, and I know you're fond of lamb." With that, he disappeared inside the mansion.

Abdul took my bag and said, "*Waddadan hay,*" requesting that I follow him.

The plantation building was rustic but clean. The doors were of thick construction of the Arabian Peninsula style, decorated with geometric patterns and sporting large golden rings for handles, while here and there in the hallways, Somali artifacts were on display.

My room itself evoked the colonial era, with a framed mirror, velvet furniture, and an antique escritoire. I found an electrical outlet, so plugged in my laptop and powered it up. To my surprise, I had Wi-Fi access.

Email notifications chimed one after the next. Some messages were from friends and one was from Fatuma, but none were from Bashir or anyone on the council. I shut the lid, opting to read through them later.

I went into the restroom, which was as large as most Somalis' houses. A thickly carpeted floor was resplendent with Islamic geometric patterns, while an abundant bathtub with flowery crimson patterns worked into the porcelain stood in a sunlit corner.

I looked myself in the mirror — a habit that was becoming more frequent as I monitored the changes occurring in my physiology. I appeared only slightly better than I did on the morning's boat ride, but at least my headache was gone.

I went over to the bathtub and filled it with hot water, then checked my voicemails until it was cool enough to enter. I kept my *qandi* pouch at arm's length at all times. At last, I took a long, sublime bath.

SOMALINIMO

"ARE YOU MARRIED?" asked Amaranta from the head of the table.

"*Haa.* My wife's name is Issa. She's back in America with our two children and my mother."

"Don't you miss her?"

"Of course. I haven't been home in a year, but we Skype from time to time."

"When will you be returning home?"

"*Macaan,*" Zayid interjected, speaking a word of endearment to his wife, "our guest may not wish to discuss such things at present."

"*Waa hagaag,*" I said, *it's okay.* "Maybe I'll return in the spring, but I'd prefer she move back here. We have a nice house in Boosaaso."

"Haji has a lot of business matters here," Zayid explained.

"*Haa,* and also, I'm not too fond of America. Their customs are not like ours."

"In what way?" Amaranta inquired.

"People often say one thing but mean something else. It's hard to know when people are telling the truth or what they're really thinking. They're a very complicated people who don't trust each other, and especially not Somalis."

"That does sound unpleasant," she said as she scooped basmati rice from a bowl with the first three fingers of her right hand. This was a rural Somali custom, also practiced by Muslims, for the left hand, used in washing the body, was considered unclean.

"Actually, Italians are quite the same," commented Zayid. "I prefer it here for much the same reason. Once I got to know my Somali neighbors, I was really taken by how genuine they are. Somalia may be a land of bards, but when it comes to interpersonal matters, you can count on straight talk."

We shared a laugh.

A house servant brought out a platter topped with a steaming camel's hump. The first slice of fatty meat was offered to me.

"I have not enjoyed this delicacy since growing up in Dante," I said, smelling the sweet meat on my plate, "when we celebrated my father's newfound fortune in *qaat. Mahadsanid.*"

"If only I could harvest *qaat* in Somalia," Zayid replied. "Now that's what I call a cash crop."

To my surprise, another course came, this one just as sumptuous as the first. It was lamb fried in ghee and spiced with cumin, coriander, turmeric, and curry.

"Perhaps you thought we'd be serving pasta with marinara sauce," Zayid joked.

"The lamb is good," I remarked. "What is that photo there?" I asked, pointing my half-eaten shank towards the wall behind him.

Somali waranle

"Somali *waranle* — Darods like yourself. That picture is almost a hundred years old. Those were the original natives of this savannah. They'd come down to the *ascendo* to display their sparring feats and traditional dances. They were true *Somalinimo*."

Amaranta giggled.

"Well, they were," he asserted.

"My husband loves everything Somali, and knows more about my people than me," she said. "You'd think he was the *Boqor*."

"Is that so?"

"Don't listen to her," Zayid quipped. "It is right for a man to know about his surroundings and those who came before."

"Look behind you," Amaranta said. "He has other pictures. See the *dhanto*? And the one of the *'odka*?"

I craned my neck to see. "The dancers, and the singer, *haa*. Those look like some really old photos."

"Zayid collects them."

"Does he?"

"I'm a connoisseur of peninsular art, if you will," he admitted. "I admire the tenacity of your people and how it manifests itself in *Somalinimo*."

"*Somalinimo*," I soliloquized. "The ways of the Somali."

"Precisely. I'm from Naples. I know the meaning of survival of the toughest. Here in Somalia, for all of your history, you've been enduring extreme hardships, and from that you've become stronger. I admire that in a culture."

"The Somali story is hardly a romantic one," I remarked. "It's been a very rocky road for us."

"As it's been for me," he replied. "From my time on the mean streets of southern Italy to my move here essentially in the blind, I've had to fight hard to make it."

Amaranta reached across the table and took her husband's hand. "In the early days, he almost lost his life more times than I can remember," she said.

"How?" I asked.

"From our common diseases, from fighting off brigands, from accidents sustained on the ranch. Tell Haji how you lost your eye, *macaan*."

"Not over dinner, sweetie."

"I don't mind," I said.

"I'm finished anyway," he conceded, placing his napkin on the table. "Do you mind if I smoke?"

"It's your house."

"*Mahadsanid.* Ah, my eye," he continued, lighting a cigarette and taking a deep drag. "I was diving about one hundred meters offshore. This was at a time when many large species of fish regularly inhabited these waters. Somalis didn't care much for fish then, but what can I say — I'm Italian. It was a big part of my diet, and still is, if I can help it. Anyway, I was going after a sailfish. It zipped by me, then dove. I looked down and saw it about fifteen meters beneath me, just floating there.

"I turned turtle and went after it, and just as I was about to sling my spear, a massive shark with its mouth wide agape lurched up from the depths. I don't know what happened to the sailfish, but I was already stroking hard for the surface. My god, it would've been impossible to out-swim that beastie. Its head was as big as a car, its body perhaps twenty meters in length. It was the type of monster only found off Djibouti or in the Red Sea. The thing rushed up and sideswiped me, its jaws catching my left bootie as it rocketed towards the surface. The sudden acceleration put extreme pressure in my head and mask, popping out my right eyeball just as we breached. Its jaws opened wider as it attempted to eat something on the surface, releasing my foot and sending me twirling through the sky. I splashed down with my eyeball dangling in my mask, which was quickly filling with blood, so I tore off the mask to get a better breath, losing my eyeball at sea.

"By the grace of Allah, I made the swim back to shore, the beastie circling all the while. I can only assume it had succeeded in swallowing some other prey such as the sailfish, and was waiting to better digest it before consuming me."

"If Amaranta hadn't been at the *ascendo* then, I would've died from blood loss. She covered my eye socket with her palm as Abdul drove us to the hospital in Djibouti."

"How far is that?"

"It took thirty minutes, and we were travelling very fast."

"Now this story I believe," I said with a wry grin. "I used to go shark hunting with my father around here, and on occasion we'd see a giant fin or massive shadow underwater, patterned like a tiger."

"There's still some biggies out there," Zayid affirmed. "The fish stocks are coming back, and with them, the return of the monster sharks."

"Abdul said that you have a son whom you permit to ride a surfboard in these waters. That cannot be safe."

Zayid's brush with the monster from the deep

"I've tried to warn Salvatore, but he insists he knows what he's doing and has a watchful eye. He lives in South Africa, and says he's used to dealing with big sharks."

"*Phew!*" I blew out my breath, shaking my head. "Well, I'm glad you survived. I've seen people get taken and it's not a pretty sight."

Amaranta squeezed her husband's hand more firmly.

He soon withdrew his grasp and leaned back in his chair, savoring his cigarette. "Noor," he said in time, "since we're on the subject of survival of the fittest, may I ask if you know anything of genetics?"

"What's that?"

"The science of evolution, more broadly, but more specifically it's the study of the human body's inner code and how it adapts over time. Genetics is why you look like your father, and why I'm white like the Italians. It's what gets passed down through the generations."

"I think I understand."

"Although it's a fairly new discipline, the subject has fascinated me for a long time. I'm interested most in natural selection, especially in regards to human adaptation in extreme environments over time. This is also why I've become so interested in the Somali race. In my research, I've found your genetic makeup to be the toughest on the planet regarding its adaptability to harsh circumstances. In the event of a global disaster, such as a nuclear war, for example, most likely it's the Somalis who'd be selected to survive."

"Selected?"

"Genetically, that is. I believe your people would be best suited to adapt."

"Does this have anything to do with my condition, or the antigen?" My brows scrunched down deep in interest.

"*Macaan,*" he asked his *sweetie,* "would you be so kind as to prepare some of your *mirra kahwa?*"

"*Haa,*" she replied, getting up from her chair.

As soon as she left, Zayid leaned over the table and spoke more quietly. "From botanicals, I got into pharmaceuticals, and have been working with some of the best biochemists in the world on your case. Your condition is putting my theory of genetic adaptability to the ultimate test, but I assure you, progress is being made, and we are perfecting the antigen."

"What are you saying? What are my chances? I'm taking more than fifteen doses a day and need more and more just to remain stable. In the meantime, my body is changing in frightening ways."

"I know, I know," he consoled, gently patting the table before me as if to reassure me. "We just need a little more time. A breakthrough may be near."

"A breakthrough for what?" I was becoming louder, going on edge. "What the hell is this stuff?"

He eyed the direction of the kitchen, then continued with a very serious tone. "The *antibaayootig* is a radio-pharmaceutical, Haji, but more than that, it's a delivery system. You're injecting radioisotopes to help confirm the presence of pheochromocytoma and neuroblastoma, which are tumors of specific types of nervous tissue. But the serum is also a delivery system of hormonal and genetic attributes of the bat mammalian. I have told you about bats' high tolerance to withstand pathogens. The changes occurring to your body mark the success of the delivery system, which is good news, for you are gaining the bats' ability to beat an infection. The serum has concentrated the buildup of radioactive material around your cerebellum. The caesium-one-thirty-seven element of that material is water-soluble, so your body should be able to process it naturally by way of something called pharmacokinetics. It's the iodine-one-thirty-one component of the radioactive waste that has proven injurious to you and is battling the resistance capabilities of the bat genomes. Our recent modifications to the antigen have been successful in isolating iodine-one-thirty-one from your thyroid gland. Once that process is complete, we can surgically extract the nuclear waste from your brain, and you'll be healed."

"How long will that take? At what point will I be healed?"

"Soon, *saaxiib*," he said endearingly, sliding his hand over the table to me, "soon."

Amaranta returned carrying a silver tray topped with steaming cups of coffee. "What are you guys talking about?" she asked as she placed a cup before me.

"*Mahadsanid*," I thanked her. "The *mirra kahwa* smells good."

"Nuclear medicine," her husband replied candidly.

"One of his hobbies," she quipped, slightly rolling her eyes without his noticing. She sat down to drink with us and Zayid quickly changed the subject, talking about her outfit.

"By the way, *macaan*," he said, "that's a lovely coantino. Did you pick it out yourself?"

"*Haa*," she answered coyly. Her coantino was a colorfully patterned, four-yard-long cloth tied over her shoulder and wrapped around her waist. I had glimpsed her slender legs on the boat ride, and now I got to behold one of her supple shoulders, as well.

"*Quruxley.*" I told her the outfit was beautiful.

"*Mahadsanid,*" she replied with a blush.

Zayid shot us a wry smile, then changed the subject again, asking what I knew of Samaal.

"I know that he's the father of the Somali people," I said, "from where we get our looks and language."

"Precisely. Samaal is the archetype of your people, representing the strongest, most pure breed of man. The human race was borne from Africa, did you know that?"

I shook my head in the negative.

"If we could only copy Samaal's genes," he continued, "and get back to that original source, men could return to the proverbial Garden of Eden, being free of weakness and disease."

I lost track of what he was saying. Ever since Amaranta had gone off to make coffee, his explanations had been too difficult for me to follow. I just held up my cup and replied, "*Alhamdu Lilaahi,*" meaning *Gratitude to Allah.*

Zayid and Amaranta echoed that sentiment.

⁓

After coffee, Amaranta took the cups back to the kitchen while Zayid and I gravitated towards the veranda. We sauntered before the balustrade overlooking *bad-weyn*, whose broad back slithered ethereally in the moonlight.

Zayid procured a bottle and two small, stemmed glasses from a nearby cupboard. He handed me a glass and said, "I've some lovely cognac from Milan."

I squinted at the bottle through the half-light.

"I know it is *haram,*" he said, meaning it was prohibited by Islam, "but I also know that you enjoy some strong waters now and then. Come, Haji, hold up your glass. On my *ascendo* we can enjoy ourselves."

I raised my glass, and he poured in the syrupy alcohol. I waited for him to drink before taking a sip myself. It was strong but sweet. Truth be told, I'd been trying to process a lot lately, both mentally and physically, so was happy to partake. I thanked him for developing the *antibaayootig* and trying to help me, then in a spate of sullenness, pointed out that two of my family members had already died from radiation poisoning.

"I know, *jaalle*," he consoled, gently squeezing my shoulder. "They're resting with Allah now."

I held out my glass for another serving.

Zayid obliged, saying, "Don't worry, Noor. You'll be all right. Have faith in what we're doing. I do, and I've been in this business for a long time."

"What business?"

"Radiopharmaceuticals."

I rubbed my forehead, still not understanding.

"Medicine," he tried to reassure me.

"About the piracy business," I inquired, "about Zayid, the Organization, what made you decide to buy it?"

"To control the sealanes." He stared out over the glimmering waters. "That was it at first," he conceded, "to command the flow of commerce through this region, which, as you know, was heavily used by Europe. The import/export trade was like an unsecured bank account, easy to physically hack, and better yet, it was insured, and those securities provided the greatest source of cashflow. But eventually, like you, I wanted something more. Few men are content to merely grow their own estate—they want to extend their power and influence to the world at large. For me, that meant turning Somalia into a secular caliphate. And why, you might ask, would a man born in Italy concern himself with this? Well," he chuckled, then took another drink, "through my wife I've learned a lot of things; I've opened my eyes to Allah, and learned the power and grace of the Somali way. She's given me compassion where before there was just another black heart, a *Faranji* who considered his ways superior to those of others, and especially to Africans. But through Somalis like your very own father and Amina Rage, I've learned that protections must be put in place to safeguard the innocent against the crimes of foreign aggressors. I've come to realize how the archetypical Samaal is being assaulted by the archetypical black heart — the colonial European vampire who wishes to suck all that is good and worthy from their hosts, then move on once their victim's lifeblood has been drained. I could not bear to see Amaranta become a victim of exploitation by infidels any more than you could bear to see it happen to your own family and peoples. In my prearranged marriage to an innocent Somali babe, little did I know I would one day find my union, my spiritual union, Haji — my *raison d'être* — with the most destitute and downtrodden people in the world. Thus, with the money and resources at my disposal via the Organization, I knew a new caliphate was more than possible — it was necessary. And that's when you came into the picture."

"Me?"

"*Haa, saaxiib,* the *Hoggaamiye* — the one sent by the Oracle to lead the country to freedom is the one being directed by the divine. You are the spiritual fulcrum by which I knew this nation could progress."

"What do you know about the Oracle?" I intensely searched his eyes for answers.

"I believe she is a messenger of *Jannah*," he said unflinchingly.

"Of Heaven."

"*Haa.*"

"Sent by whom?"

He just shrugged his shoulders and said, "By Allah, perhaps. Where I'm from, comrade, we take seriously things like Holy Spirits, angels, and avatars of God, such as Jesus Christ. Markings like yours — stigmata markings — we hold as true signs of ineffable powers. In Rome, we've built a country within a country called the Vatican, answerable to no person or government, only God, the sole purpose of the church being to protect the faith. These things were part of my heritage of myths and beliefs, but beyond that, they were like imprints upon my soul and psyche. Not only did I believe them to be possible, but I knew them to be true — until I converted. Through Amaranta and the *boqor*, through my experience here in Somalia, I've come to realize Allah is the one and true God, and all the allowances and possibilities I'd once ascribed to Roman Catholicism, I now extend to Islam. It would be ethnocentric to do anything other — to assume that the realm of the white man's God is more legitimate than that of the God of the Arabs. *Saaxiib*, I'm through with Christianity and Jesus Christ. By becoming subservient to the Roman church, entire cultures abandon their long histories of cultural and political independence. I am united with the *Cusmaan Maxamuud* now, and Somalia, with its unique traditions and Islamic faith."

"I appreciate what you say about my people, Zayid. Perhaps we should spill our drinks."

He smirked smugly, answering, "That's not to say that, like the European ships we hijack, I remain aloof of their spoils. Islam is my faith now, *haa*, but I still enjoy a little bit of cultural plunder now and then. Look, Noor, it's not cognac that's fucking us over — it's the Western imperialists at the UN roundtable and their knights templar, the Security Council, who want to stop the empire's progression. And I'm a bit concerned about this new *Boqor* and his refusal to join our *guurti*. We cannot expand outwardly unless our house is in order."

"This new *Boqor* is not the same as Amaranta's father?"

"*Maya*, it's his successor. He was born around the same time as your father."

"Do you know about Abbo through my books?"

"Actually, *walalo*, I knew your father as a trading partner. When he came down to Eyl with Ismael and Rashid, I thought he was going to sign on with the Organization. But unlike you, he decided to go his own way in the sweet trade."

"So you're the reason he went to Eyl," I ruminated aloud.

"You father was very headstrong, Haji. I think he felt uncomfortable with the idea of working under such a large umbrella company as ours. I knew him well enough to honestly say that his decision to go Lone Ranger didn't surprise me in the least. So when you came down, we made an extra effort to recruit you, giving you the grand tour, as it were — which we didn't do for just anybody."

"But why me?"

"The Fayrus bloodline, Noor. Ever since your days in Dante, your family has had a unique place in my portfolio."

"Your what?"

"My little black book — like an extended family tree." He set his glass down, now empty, then yawned and glanced at his wristwatch. "It's getting late. I very much look forward to continuing this conversation on the morrow, perchance over breakfast?"

"*Waan fiicanahay,*" I told him, *fine, that would be okay.* "Did you know Bile Qabowsade?" I inquired, trying to catch him offguard.

He regarded me sleepily and repeated the name as if trying to remember, "Bile, Bile…"

"How about Hirsi Xaarato?"

He flinched. "The name does sound familiar. Ah, I recall now — he was the double-crosser in your first book. I'm glad you finally caught up with him, in a manner of speaking."

He encouraged me back inside, saying, "Let us turn in now, *jaalle*. We're on the verge of great things. After Somalia, we can look at annexing some of our long-detested neighbors. But first, we must secure our own borders. We'll keep working on this *Boqor*. Perhaps we'll soon catch up with him, as well." He winked. "*Habeen wanaagsan, Haji, waa inoo berrito.*"

I told him goodnight also, and that I'd see him on the morrow.

I retired to my room a little drunk, trying to make sense of what he'd said about the *Boqor*. It sounded like he'd insinuated he'd like to dispatch him. I suddenly felt very uneasy about Zayid and where I was staying.

I removed my boots, my TT-30 pistol, and father's dagger, placing these latter on the bedside table. I switched off the light and laid back in bed.

Suddenly, someone entered the room with a candle, moving very quietly.

"Amaranta?"

"*Hayye, Haji,*" she said with a soft giggle. "I've just come to wish you *habeen wanaagsan.*"

"Well, goodnight to you, too, Amaranta. I'd thought you'd already turned in."

"I had," she said, "but Zayid woke me up when he came to bed. I'm a light sleeper."

My laptop, sitting on the bedside table opposite, kept chiming with incoming emails. "They never give me a break," I huffed, then reached over and closed the lid.

She sat down beside me on my bed and said, "Of course, not, Haji. You're the *Hoggaamiye*." She wore a pliable smile, and in the glim of the candlelight, I saw her pink gown fall open over her supple breasts.

I did a double take. Was Zayid's wife coming on to me?

"Can I see it, Haji?" she asked, rubbing a slender hand over my chest. "Can I see the white star?"

I glanced towards the door, caught between the terror of our being discovered and the temptation of a stunning nubile, or so she appeared to me, lit I was with cognac. She opened her mouth slightly and slid her tongue seductively over her lower lip.

I grabbed her hand and pushed it between my shirt buttons while drawing her close with my other arm, then rolled over on top of her.

"Amaranta?" her husband called from the hallway.

We froze in place, and I practically had a heart attack.

She quickly but calmly got up from the bed and pulled her robe over her chest, then blew out her candle and left as silently as she'd come.

Qüïnn Rȯbërt Hȧbër & Nȯȯr Hȧjï Fȧyrüṣ

BREAKFAST WITH THE HUNTER

I AWOKE with a pounding headache, which had become an all-too-familiar occurrence. It would've been preferable to pin it on too much strong waters, but I knew, with great foreboding, that the white man's drink was only partially to blame. The lion's share of my malaise sat squarely with the antigen. That being said, without the *antibaayootig*, I'd most likely already be dead. Strange dreams of white, hairless beings did little to lift my spirits.

I sauntered before the mirror and unbuttoned my shirt. My white star was black and blue like a massive bruise, and wrinkled like a prune. The sight of it almost made me vomit.

I loaded five tubes of serum into my injector in a sequence now well practiced, and only after the last shot could I feel the energy boost, but it was growing progressively weaker. I shot up a sixth tube and that seemed to do the trick. My head stopped pounding so hard, and the star on my chest stabilized, returning to its standard, faded-white color. I shook my head in disappointment. While the serum was helping, I was tiring of the whole Haji-as-lab-rat scenario. The breakthrough in the medicine Zayid had spoken about could not come soon enough. If the toxic substance that was making me sick was now well sequestered within an appendage of my brain, I took his word that soon it could be extracted and I could get on with my life.

Remembering that emails had been spilling in the night before, I opened my laptop. A slew of messages had come in from Fatuma, the last few flagged as urgent. A cursory skim relayed matters of "extreme importance" and "imminent threats" to my safety, with each communiqué imploring me to call her at once.

I found my sat phone and switched it on. There were about ten voicemails from Fatuma and a smattering of others from Mogadishu friends and fellow operatives. I called Fatuma right off.

"*Hayye, Fatuma! Maxaad rabtaa?*" I said *hello, what's up?*

"Haji — thank Allah it's you. I've been trying to reach you all night. Did you get my messages?"

"You wanted me to call. What's going on?"

"Is this line secure?"

"*Haa*, it's my satellite phone, direct uplink."

"Are you with anyone?"

"Not at present. I'm in Somaliland, staying with a *Faranji* named Zayid. He apparently owns the Organization."

"*Waan ogahay.*" She said she knew. "Haji, listen to me and listen closely. You're not safe there. Zayid Cecchi is not who he says he is. He's a top dog in an Italian pharmaceutical company with links to the military."

"Which military?"

"The Italian military, but it goes much deeper. He's involved in a top-secret military initiative involving Italy, France, Great Britain, Saudi Arabia, Qatar, and some Asian countries, including Japan, South Korea, and Taiwan."

"Top secret military initiative? How do you know all this?"

"*Ssshh*! Quiet Haji! You mustn't be overheard! Nasir is dead, shot execution style near our house. Before he left, he said he was going to Mogadishu to meet with you in person."

"Was he robbed?"

"The police report stated nothing was stolen from him; in fact, he had a wad of Riyals in his pocket that wasn't even touched. But when he left here, he was carrying his doctor's bag containing the serum and some papers, none of which were found on his person."

"Papers?"

"He'd been doing intensive research in my computer lab. He said it was medical research, but once I found out he was dead, I reviewed his Internet trail and it led me in an increasingly worrisome direction. He could only get so far with his investigation, but I was able to hack through encryptions on Zayid's database."

"The expellee tracking system?"

"No, this is different."

"Interpol?"

"*Maya*. Zayid, that black heart, in whose house you're currently staying, is working in conjunction with the aforementioned militaries on something called Project Samale. Selection Ministry Isle is where they make and test the serum for military purposes. It's his business, Haji, and you're the experiment."

I froze in shock. Fatuma would not lie about such things. But— "But how did you know I was here with him?"

"I couldn't get through on your cell, so I went to Osman's, and we called your radiophone. Qaasim picked up and said you'd gone to meet the CEO. We thought he meant Bashir, so Osman called him and found out about this man 'Zayid' in Zeilah. We finally found your coordinates via your sat phone."

"Does Bashir know about Project Samale?"

"We didn't tell him."

"Why not?"

"What if he's involved? He knew about Zayid, so maybe he's in on it, too. We had to warn you in secret. Osman is on the way to extract you now. Pack your bags, *walalo*, he'll be there any moment."

"Wait, Fatuma! I need to know more. What else do you know about Selection Ministry Island?"

"The coordinates are hidden by weather."

"*Macneheedu waa maxay?*" I asked her to explain.

"They control the weather over the island so that it's always hidden by fog or storms. The coordinated country initiative involves weather-altering technology from Dubai."

"What exactly is going on out there?"

"They're creating some sort of nuclear medicine, but it's not a medicine at all. It's a drug that causes genetic modification."

"For what?"

"Either to create a superior warrior or to modify people in such a way that they can survive a nuclear attack, or both."

"I, I don't know what to say."

"Just get the hell out of there, Haj. Get out now. Osman is on the way."

"I need to do some investigating."

"Well, don't do it there. It's too dangerous. Don't breathe a word of this to Zayid. Osman is coming to pick you up under an innocent pretext — not with guns blazing. I hope you can get out without a fight, but if necessary, your uncle is prepared to extract you by any means necessary."

"Do you have the GPS coordinates of Selection Ministry Island?"

"*Haa.*"

"Email them to me."

"I already have."

"You're golden, *walaal.* I'm packing my bags."

"Be careful."

"*Haa. Nabad gelyo!*"

"*Jaaw!*"

I yanked on my boots and strapped on my weapons, then threw my laptop into my duffelbag along with my other belongings. I listened carefully for the sound of Osman's truck or for voices in the house. Not hearing anything, I gingerly but quickly made my way down the hallway leading to the front door.

The entrance veranda was already in sight when my eye caught something in a room to my right. It appeared to be an office — probably Zayid's. Framed pictures hung on the walls and were propped up on a desk before a black leather chair, which was empty and turned askance. Again I listened closely, and again silence reigned, so I set my bag just inside the office doorway and went in to investigate.

The photos on the desk were of Zayid and Amaranta, and of Zayid with businessmen both Caucasian and Negroid, while the pictures on the walls were antiques depicting Somali nomads, dancers, and spearmen, some of whom were posing before the mansion, and there appeared to be a photo of the previous *boqor* standing beside Amaranta when she was just a child.

I opened the desk and found a leather file containing several documents written in Italian, some marked *Informazione Riservata* in red. I removed a paper clip from one of these and began flipping through the pages. I saw the words *Progetto Samale* in several places, and I also glimpsed the word *antibi-otico*, which was unmistakable.

"Can I help you find something, Noor?" Zayid stood by the door with pistol in hand.

I shoved the file back into the desk. It took me three tries to close the drawer. "*Hayye*, Zayid. I was looking for a pen."

"There's one on the desk."

Indeed, a pen in a stand pointed right at my nose. I grabbed it and asked hurriedly, "Do you have some paper? I have a phone number in my head I need to jot down."

"It's right there on the desk, too."

"*Mahadsanid*," I said, baring my open stigmata. "I'd write on my hand but, you know, the hole kind of gets in the way."

"Naturally," said he, sauntering forward while polishing his handgun with a rag.

"Nice piece," I remarked, trying to remain cool as I surreptitiously reached for the TT-30 strapped to my thigh.

"Oh, this?" He looked at his weapon. "Forgive my bad habit. I often forget what a strong signal a gun can send when it's in someone's hand." He pointed it straight at me.

I undid the Velcro of my holster. I could hear it tearing, but could he? I was still fumbling for my gun when he turned his on me — handle first.

"Check it out," he said. "It's a Magnum 45, American made."

It was so heavy that I almost dropped it.

"Easy there, *jaalle*. If there's one thing about the Yanks, they know how to make firearms."

"*Haa*," I agreed as I studied the hefty black piece.

"I'll take it off your hands now, Noor. You were going to write a number down?"

"*Haa*." I hesitated. *Was I returning my executioner his weapon?* It occurred to me it probably wasn't loaded, or perhaps he didn't suspect enough foul play to dispatch me at present. But I was certain he'd begin an inquiry, so I handed back his weapon and tried to keep the conversation on him. "Are guns your hobby?"

"You could say so, yes. I use them for hunting, primarily."

I moved away from his desk. "Hunting? With a pistol?" I inquired nervously, trying to gravitate around him, towards the door.

"Believe it or not, I like to shoot at insects," he snickered. "They're the least heartbreaking to kill. Ever shoot at butterflies, *saaxiib*? It's pretty challenging, actually, but you have to wait for them to start flying away or it's no fun, no fun at all, Haji. I see you have your pistol there. Would you like to go out shooting before breakfast?"

"Actually, Zayid, my apologies, but I was just leaving. Something came up with my family."

"Really? I hope it's nothing serious." He loaded a bullet into his pistol.

"Probably not." I placed my hand over my thigh holster and nonchalantly undid the Velcro again. "But I need to go back to Boosaaso and check."

"You can't get there on foot, *saaxiib*. Allow me to arrange a ride. I'll take you myself, as a matter of fact. I always enjoy a drive through the desert. I can pick up some supplies while in town, and we'll have a chance to chat some more. We still have some neat things to discuss."

"*Mahadsanid*, Zayid, but my uncle's already on the way. He'll be here any minute." I grabbed my bag.

Zayid's genial expression turned glum. He emitted a weighty exhale, then said, "In that case, we'll have to arrange to meet again, sooner than later would be best."

"*Waa hagaag!*" I told him *okay!* as I hustled towards the front door.

"Noor?" he called forth.

I stopped and turned. I was now holding my pistol in my hand, but I refrained from pointing it at him. "*Maxaa?*"

"Did you take your injections?"

"*Haa*, several."

"I have a new strain coming in today. It's stronger, so you won't have to take so much."

"*Waan ka xumahay, Zayid*," I told him I was sorry, "but I just can't stay."

"No matter — I'll get it out to you."

"When can I extract the poison from my head?"

"Soon, *saaxiib*."

"*Goorma?*" I asked, *when?*

"*Ma ogi*," he replied in Somali that he didn't know. "But I can test you here, in my lab. Please stay."

I slapped my pistol against my thigh a few times, unsure about what to do. "How long will it take?"

"Not long." He approached me in the foyer, his gun now stowed somewhere on his body.

Osman's horn blasted in the distance.

"He's here," I said.

"Excellent. Your uncle can stay for lunch."

I knew that wouldn't work out. Osman had come to extract me, and a lunch with Zayid would be too strained. If my investigation was to succeed, it was better Zayid didn't suspect me any more than he probably already did. Osman could only compromise what little chance that remained for me to get out clean.

I stowed my pistol, walked up to the *Faranji*, patted him brusquely on the shoulder, and gave him a firm handshake. "*Mahadsanid* for everything," I said with a smile that bordered on the genuine. "You've been more than hospitable. I look forward to our next meeting. I'll call you."

"*Waa hagaag*, Noor. You do that. Can I at least give you some *spremuta* for the road?"

"*Waan ka xumahay!*" I said no thanks, then skipped out. "Tell Amaranta sorry I had to run!" I called back. "Her spiced coffee was the best!"

I was already marching across the dirt road with my bag slung over my back, and none too soon, for Osman came barreling onto the *ascendo* moments later. He blasted his horn, and I flagged him down. He was driving his new big-rig engine, having left the trailer in Boosaaso. He opened the passenger door, and Somali rap boomed out. I tossed my bag up, then climbed aboard the high-rolling cab. He looped the truck around, and we laid some heavy tracks.

Osman in Somaliland

SOMALI *HEESO*

"THANK ALLAH YOU ESCAPED in one piece," Osman said, frequently glancing into his rearview mirrors. "Just don't make me pull over and go running out on me again!"

"Eh! Zayid wanted you to stay for breakfast, can you believe that?" I rocked my head to the heavy music as I checked my TT-30's breech.

"I see you didn't need your magic bullet."

"*Maya*. He drew his gun, but get this! He said it was for hunting butterflies."

"Hunting butterflies?" Osman laughed with a shit-eating grin. "Sick fuck."

"Just target practice, he told me. But he was really quite hospitable."

"Serious?"

"*Haa*, and so was his trophy wife. Would you believe she came on to me?"

"Oh, yeah? Did you get any?"

"Only heartache."

"Good. You wouldn't want to get her stoned."

"Zayid's not *Shari'a*, is he?"

"Did you get Fatuma's intel?" Osman grumbled as he threw his big-rig into high gear. He had a bad right hand and leg.

"Why'd you switch to manual drive, Uncle?"

"After my rig was sabotaged in the red sands, I decided to switch it up. I missed the kick of gears. Did Fatuma give you the intel?"

"*Haa*. Hard to believe this guy owns Zayid. He *is* fucking Zayid, for Allah's sake! We need to launch an investigation."

"That's a mean business, Haj. Did you hear what happened to *Dhakhtar* Nasir?"

"He was shot, and the antigen had been lifted from him."

"Do you know who killed him?"

"Who?"

"The *Safaarad*."

"The *Safaarad* killed Nasir?"

"Their hit men. They sentenced him to death in Mog behind closed doors. I'd prefer a real *guurti* to this crap — at least they're answerable to the public."

"They sentenced him for what?"

"For telling you about the serum — what it really is."

"How do you know this?"

"There's a mole on the inside."

"Who?"

"The court stenographer. He works on bribes to the highest bidder, selling court secrets to foreign governments. Only this time, the *Boqor* was buying.

The only reason I found out was because the *Boqor* sent some guys to question Fatuma and me, trying to verify if the court transcripts matched what we knew about Nasir on the day he was killed. The *Boqor*, convinced the execution was government sponsored, called Fatuma personally to ask about Zayid, you, Bashir, and others, trying to find out who was behind the *Safaarad* and their sentencing. That's when her investigation into the Organization began in earnest. How much does Zayid know about what you know about him?"

"I'm not sure. He caught me snooping around his desk, but I think I played it off pretty good. Have you heard about Project Samale? There's something dark going on at Selection Ministry Island."

"I know, Fatuma told me."

"I have the GPS coordinates."

"They can alter the weather."

"I say we check it out."

Osman gave me a long glance before settling his eyes again on the road ahead. "I don't know, Haj, I'm getting too old for this shit."

"But this can make or break the empire. We need to do this, Osman, like old times."

"Where's the island?" he grumbled reluctantly.

"Six hundred nautical miles southeast of Mog."

"So we fly."

"Too conspicuous. Plus, we can't skydive without an extraction assist. But I have an idea. We'll take the old skiff."

"The rocket-skiff?"

"*Haa*, I understand it was returned to you refurbished. Do you still have it?"

"In my garage, *haa*."

"Is it still a double engine?"

"*Haa*."

"How about the nitrous?"

"All four tanks have been refitted."

"Then we can make it there and back in forty-eight hours. What do you say, Uncle? We do this for Amina and Nasir. If the Organization is secretly involved with the Selection Ministry, we must avenge its victims and bring those complicit to justice."

"I'm in," Osman mumbled, "but only for my brother."

"For Abbo," I affirmed, and we knocked our fists together.

He boosted the stereo and put the pedal to the metal.

CECCHI TENTACLES

THE NEXT MORNING, while preparing the rocket-skiff in Osman's garage, I zipped open my duffelbag to retrieve my *qandi* pouch, but found it missing. Fortunately, a few tubes of antigen had gotten loose and mixed in with the rest of my stuff, which would tide me over until I could get more. I told Osman we'd need to replenish my medicine supply before setting sail.

"From whom?" he inquired.

I was hit with the stark reality that Nasir, my only Boosaaso supplier, was dead. I had no choice but to phone Bashir, who said Dr. Sooraan could bring some up from Garoowe the next day, the only other alternative being to return to Mog or the *ascendo*, where Zayid had a stash. I told Bashir I'd call him back about it. Before hanging up, he inquired what I was doing in Boosaaso. I told him I was visiting family. He asked about how things went with Zayid. "Cool," I replied evenly. "I'll be seeing him again soon." Truth be told, I wasn't sure where Bashir stood in relation to the man, and what he knew or didn't know about Project Samale and Selection Ministry Isle. For the time being, playing it cool seemed the best modus operandi, at least until I could glean more from our investigation.

When I told Osman my shitty options for getting more antigen, he was livid, saying, "It's high time you wean yourself off the shit. That crap is poison, anyway — why do you let yourself be a lab experiment?"

I told him he didn't understand, that I needed it to survive. He asked if I had enough to make it to the island. I told him two tubes was iffy. He said good, that would force me to ration and start breaking the addiction. Besides that, he said, all indications pointed to Selection Ministry Island as the place where the stuff was made, so once we were there, it stood to reason there'd be *antibaayootig* aplenty, just in case.

I'd taken a massive dose the previous day, and it seemed to be tiding me over. Osman was right — it was better we not delay. I could get by on two tubes.

In addition to victuals, fuel, and heavy weaponry, we packed camouflage fatigues and back knit masks, based upon Istar Abyad's report of how the men guarding the island were dressed. We covered the anti-tank launcher with fishing net so as not to arouse suspicion, then hitched the boat trailer to Osman's rig and took the craft down to a launch point in Las Qoray to avoid busy Boosaaso harbor. Another good thing about Las Qoray was Osman had a safe place to park his rig. The tuna factory went back a long way in our family's business activities.

We launched at five after ten in the morning and were soon cruising east on one engine, enjoying some *canjeeros* and a thermos of *Shaah Xawaash* tea Osman had packed. We talked about Zayid, the Italian. Although he was a black heart — a white man — I was still unsure about him. He had treated me well and seemed like a decent guy, but neither was I a fool. I knew he was something of a Mad Mullah or Machiavelli. I just couldn't determine if his treatment of me, in a medical sense, was a genuine attempt to heal me, and if his design to expand the empire was really *Somalinimo* — Somali at heart — or the plan of just another neo-colonialist imposter. Osman had a bad feeling about the *Faranji*, but had few hard facts to go on.

According to Fatuma, Zayid's long history in our country wasn't a hoax. The Cecchi family had been in Somalia as early as 1895, when a certain Captain Cecchi set out to conquer a portion of the interior. Somali Biyomaal warriors in "the valley of the bones" killed him, his platoon of 13 Italians, and his locally recruited troops called *askaris*, but his dynasty lived on in Soomaal lands. As recently as 1985, when President Siad Barre's fascist regime was terrorizing his northern constituents with scorched-earth tactics, Zayid Cecchi invested in Mogadishu's first television station to try to counter Barre's propaganda machine. After the collapse of the Barre regime in 1991, Zayid turned to the telecommunications sector, where investments in that soon-to-boom market proved very lucrative for him, according to anecdotal references from the Somali *hawala* network. From there, he did in fact go into pharmaceuticals, based upon documents Fatuma hacked into online. And now this *Faranji* — this European — was purportedly the owner of the Zayid Organization. Without even going into Project Samale and the Selection Ministry, that a black heart owned the armies of the empire disturbed Osman and me beyond all else, but given the historical reach of the Cecchi tentacles in our country, it was entirely possible. If his ultimate designs were nefarious or not is what we were presently setting out to discover, Selection Ministry Island being the most obvious first place to look given what I'd discovered in the *ascendo.*

After breakfast, we said *Alhamdu Lilaahi*! in gratitude to Allah, then fired up the second engine and ran like cheetahs towards the great Horn.

MIRAGES WELL FORTIFIED

IT TOOK ALL DAY and most of the night to reach the island's vicinity, with Osman and I driving in shifts. Growing impatient with the sheer distance, and to allow the engines a chance to cool, on two occasions we engaged the Maritime Operational Nitrous Oxide Thrusters, aka MONOX, letting the NOS run dry both times. Each shot gave us fifteen minutes plus of blistering speed, cutting a few hours off our journey.

Twice I had to shoot up serum, using one-half tube per dose. I'd been suffering hot flashes and spells of nausea. The rationing kept me as stable as could be expected, given the low doses.

At dawn, with the real-time coordinates of Selection Ministry Island flickering on GPS nigh six leagues ahead, we entered a thick fog. Osman scaled down to one engine to minimize our sound, while I kept watch from the bow.

"Holy shit," I gasped as an entire cityscape loomed up through the mist. "Cut the engine!" I shouted back, but not on account of the otherworldly urbanity so far out at sea. What had got my attention with greater immediacy was a ring of pill-shaped mines surrounding the floating city, two of which floated directly in our path.

Pillbox Mines

Osman stood at the rudder and guided us between them. There had been too little time to do anything but. As we passed, I noticed slots in them like the gun placements on WWII-era pillbox bunkers. I trained my uzi on the openings, just in case. Another concern, besides shooters in the mines, was the possibility of cameras on them alerting them of our arrival — the buoys looked that high-tech.

"What is that place?" gawked Osman as he stared at the high-rises ahead.

"*Ma ogi*," I told him I didn't know, "but we better fall back, and fast. Through my binoculars I can see PT boats patrolling the shore."

Osman brought a spring upon her cable, taking us around. Out between the mines we departed, training our uzis on the gun portals all the while.

"Then where is Selection Ministry Isle?" Osman said, taking up speed away from the city.

I showed him on GPS. "Here, on the other side of the floating city. We'll have to go around, wide around."

"Are you sure about that?" He peered at me with a round eye and bent brow. "Maybe that was it."

"*Maya*," I told him, *no*. "Istar reported seeing that city from the island, so we're close. It's just on the other side, see?"

Osman glanced at the GPS again, then raised his brows in resignation and angled further south.

We stayed well around the floating city, not only to avoid mines but, more importantly, its patrolling security. Once on the far side of its perimeter, I was relieved to keep it squarely in our wake, even though the destination dead ahead, marked by a faint, flickering red dot on my GPS, I knew without question was certifiably dangerous.

The Floating City

DAY OF RECKONING

SQUINTING INTO THE BRUME, I started feeling sick again. I could no longer differentiate between the fog on the sea and the cloudiness in my mind. I was dizzy, nauseated, and forgetful, while my vision was becoming blurred. Dark shadows closed upon my peripheries like omens of death descending in black cloaks. Suffice it to say I was sufficiently terrified for my health, so with SM Isle now a sure bet, I injected my last tube of antigen, determined I'd find more on the island.

No sooner did the *antibaayootig* began circulating through my veins, stimulating my cells with radiological energy, than a lighthouse appeared in the mist.

"Take her down, Osman," I called back.

"I see it," he replied as an oblong beam moved over the water before us. He reversed the outboard until we were stationary, then alerted for me to hold on.

I grabbed the bow.

He dropped the second engine and brought it to idle beside the first, then gripped both throttle bars while looking intensely afore.

When the beam crossed before us again, Osman throttled both engines to the max, racing us at sixty knots towards the lighthouse.

But the probing light was already swinging 'round again, cutting through the fog as it warned sailors of an impending hazard and sentries of oncoming visitors. This latter likelihood is what spurred Osman to flank our speed, for no navigator would knowingly race towards a rocky headland or reef without a darned good reason — and Osman was a navigator of the first degree by both land and sea.

"Duck!" he cried as the tocsin flashed our way. We dove for the floorboards just as the beam passed overhead.

"We're through," Osman drawled in terms that may as well have described our doom had he not taken us beneath the beacon's reach with the acceleration he did. He cut the second engine and lifted it out of the water, slowing us down to practically a ghost as we neared the base of the lighthouse. Small breakers were slinging along a shallow reef, around which I guided Osman from the bow. We passed beneath a raised pipeline or walkway some ten feet overhead, then turned astarboard and followed it.

We reached the base of the lighthouse, which was white but showing rust. The structure was of a strange design, flaring out overhead like an octagonal spindle or top. As we continued around it, red markings appeared along its lower panels. Drawing closer through the fog, a biohazard sign became evident, while above in bold black letters was written in ominous contrast: *XULASHO WASAARAD.*

Selection Ministry Spindle Tower

"We're here," I uttered cravenly.

"*Xaggee?*" Osman asked, *where?*

"Selection Ministry Island."

"Look at the water."

The surface around the skiff was slick and oily, with slightly glowing streaks of orange. "It smells bad," I said.

"*Khatar!*" Osman warned under his breath, flashing me the *be quiet!* sign. He pointed up at the causeway to our right, where an indistinct figure moved towards the tower.

"We can't dock here," I whispered. "There's no way up, and besides that, we'll be spotted if we try. Continue to shore."

"Aye-aye, Haji," replied the helmsman, then brought a spring upon her cable and took us quietly around, continuing directly beneath the causeway. The shadow afforded by the span hid our advance from the flashing tower overhead.

We moored along the shore directly beneath the bridge, then pulled on our black knit masks and geared up with our guns and ammo.

Osman's lorry keys jangled as we jumped over the side. I told him to *stow it!* and none too soon, for as he paused to tuck them away, the sound of heavy footsteps echoed above. We gawked up at the bridge's rusted underbelly as we listened through the thick fog. Suddenly, the footsteps stopped.

We trained our uzis on high, preparing to shoot off the guy's balls, but fortunately for everyone concerned, he moved on.

All at once, an excruciating pain seized my chest like a shot of poison injecting into my heart. I assumed it was my white star acting up with a vengeance, but then I heard Osman groan behind me. He was trying to remove something from his torso.

I pulled up my camouflage jacket to behold three large leeches burrowing into my chest, the pain being more than commensurate. I tried to wrest them free, but they were giant, slippery mutants. It occurred to me in a flash of agony that Istar Abyad had encountered a mutant shark in these same waters. I realized then that the biohazard sign wasn't fooling; whatever the Selection Ministry was dumping into the sea, it had the power to seriously alter creatures genetically.

I admonished Osman to be quiet as we splashed towards shore.

Once on the beach beneath the bridge, we used our daggers to remove the mutant leeches from one another. We had to wedge the tips of our blades clear beneath their heads, and when we ripped their mouths from our flesh, their bodies continued to grab, tearing off large swathes of our skin in the extraction.

More mutant leeches slithered out of the water, making haste towards us over the wet sand.

We hustled along the shoreline until we came to a patch of trees, from where we made our move inland. I frequently stopped to vomit, and Osman appeared similarly cast out. The leeches must've been venomous.

We came to a downed log, so stopped to rest, quaffing our thirst with water and tending to our wounds with rags. The sound of something large, walking through the forest in our direction, spurred us to immediately resume our recon.

At last, we found an asphalt road that had to lead someplace important, so followed it. It made the going much easier. We kept on the shoulder and deigned to dive for cover at the first sign of an approaching vehicle, but to our good fortune, none passed. The further inland we traveled, the more the fog cleared, until at last we came to something worth investigating, for there, next to a tall antenna set in a clearing, a large shipping container appeared. But this was no ordinary container, for it looked very high tech, with sleek steel sides and a red door that must've been solid steel. This could only have been the "radioactive container" as described by Istar Abyad.

As Osman kept watch, I placed my hand over a green arrow high up on the door. I had no idea what I was doing, but my action proved serendipitous, for a sequence of numbers suddenly lit up red on the door's lower left, going from 0 to 10.

"What's the combination?" Osman asked.

"I have no idea."

"Give me your cell," he said, holding out a hand as he scanned the surroundings warily.

"*Maxaa?*"

"Your cell phone, just give it to me."

I reached into my pants pocket and pulled it out. Water dripped from its every jack. "Sorry, Osman, it's shot. I'd wager you wouldn't get a signal out here, anyway."

"Just give me the damn phone!" he snapped.

I handed it to him, and he studied its keys. "Try this," he said. "Nine, two, nine, four, three."

"What's that?"

"It's the numbers on the keys for 'Zayid.' Just try it. *Sagaal, laba, sagaal, afar, saddex,*" he repeated the digits in Somali.

I punched the sequence into the door pad. The numbers flashed from red to yellow, then went back to solid red.

"*Was,*" Osman cursed. "Just let me think…"

There was movement in the forest nearby. Something large was approaching the perimeter.

"*Was! Was!*" Osman scathed under his breath. "What's the bloody combo?"

"I have an idea. Try the numbers for *Samale.*"

"For what?"

"For *Samale,* the mythical father. Here, let me see that." I wrested the phone back and studied the letters on the keys, typing the corresponding numbers into the door: 7-2-6-2-5-3.

The door pad flashed yellow again, but the barrier didn't open.

The thing came out from the trees. It was a giant, armed sentry. He raised a hefty weapon in our direction.

"*Allahu, jixinjix,*" I pleaded for God's mercy, while Osman told the hostile to fuck his mother. "*Hooyaa da was!*" he cried as he let loose his uzi.

The sentry got shot in the shoulder, twisted sideways, and fired off his machinegun — but it was no machinegun at all. Weighty red munitions blasted from his weapon like mortar rounds streaking through the night, tearing past the container and exploding into the tree line behind.

"Go and milk!" Osman cried, continuing to shoot. "Go and milk, Haji!"

"*Maxaa?*"

"The Somali spelling for Samale! Go and milk! *Soo maal! Soo maal!* Just enter it."

I struggled with the keypads as an incoming projectile struck the top corner of the container, exploding like a fireworks flower. I dropped the cell phone.

"*Deg deg!*" Osman cried. "I can't hold him off much longer!"

I looked back at the approaching nemesis. He appeared half man, half machine, with his gun feeding to his facemask by way of intestine-like tubes.

The cyborg closes in…

"*Soomaal!*" Osman shouted. "*Soomaal!*"

"Right! *Soomaal, Soomaal...*" I held my phone beside the keypad and struggled to enter 7-6-6-6-2-2-5 amid the incoming munitions and my failing health.

The red digits rolled green, and the door opened with a pneumatic blast.

"*Tag! Tag! Soco!*" Osman shouted for me to get the fuck inside, and together we pulled the heavy barrier out further. With the sound of a flaring rocket behind, he shoved me into the crack and squeezed through after me, just as the projectile struck the outside. The door reverberated with a deafeningly low *Truuung!* as it absorbed the explosion, the very power of which caused the barrier to close behind us and lock with another sharp pneumatic blast.

We were in, but where?

"*Qofna wax ma ku noqday?*" Osman asked if I was hurt.

"*Dawakhaad baan dareemayaa.*" I told him I felt dizzy.

"It's the antigen," he said. "I don't see any holes in you."

Bright white light emitted from a compartment adjacent, revealing the outline of a man dressed from head to toe in white and carrying a black briefcase. He fled in the opposite direction.

"*Joogso!*" Osman ordered for him to stop, but the suspect kept going.

"*Waddadan hay, Haji!*" *Follow me!* Osman said, helping me to me feet. "We've got him trapped!" I could barely follow as he dashed ahead.

The next compartment housed shiny new barrels marked with radiation warnings, and had a stairwell, down which our suspect fled. Osman rumbled awkwardly down the stairs after him (for his leg was bad), but I stayed to remove a manifest from one of the drums. The sheet was labeled 'Selection Ministry,' the barrel bound for Dante.

My heart sunk at the implications — a sudden grief cut short by the rattle of gunfire downstairs.

I made a dash for the stairwell, my legs all but failing me as I reached the railing. I half slid down the white bar with my knees bouncing off the stairs. I needed an injection, and fast. Suddenly, gunfire rico-cheted off the stairs.

"Haji, take cover!" Osman warned as he engaged the enemy from a nearby doorway.

I stumbled towards my uncle, collapsing at his heels.

He let loose a few more rounds from his uzi before dragging me into better cover around the corner. "What's wrong, nephew?" he asked, worriedly slapping my cheeks.

My head twirled about deliriously. "Antigen," I gasped. "I need more antigen."

"*Waa hagaag*!" he reassured. "We'll find some, but for now I'm going to take care of that black heart! Stay here and don't move. I'll come back for you!"

He jumped to his feet and peered around the corner. Believing the coast was clear, he disappeared into the next room holding his machinegun stiffly before him.

After a minute or two, I got a second wind and was able to stand. Not hearing any gunfire, I followed the direction Osman had gone, coming to yet another stairwell going down, and another corridor to my left. Uncertain if I could negotiate more stairs, I hastened down the corridor instead.

"Osman!" I whispered loudly down the hall, for there was a corner ahead that I was unable to see around. Not getting a response, I continued forward warily, sliding along the wall to prop myself up. If there was one thing about that underground facility, everything was immaculately clean.

I whipped around the corner with my uzi ready to fire, but found only vials of nuclear medicine sitting on a counter.

I had discovered the laboratory where the antigen was made, or so I prayed as I scanned the area. There were bottles of liquids with biohazard and radiation signs, while closer investigation revealed the writing on their labels: *Antibiotico* and *Progetto Samale*.

I reached for a tube of green serum stored in a glass cabinet, but the cabinet was locked, so I smashed the glass with the butt of my gun, then suddenly, the bottles around me were shot to hell, radiological liquids splashing everywhere.

"Get down, Haji!" Osman cried as he fired at the suspect, who was running through the lab clutching a pistol in one hand, a black briefcase in the other, while his face was shielded by a peculiar gas mask.

I fell to the ground.

The enemy trained his gun on me.

I unloaded my uzi into his chest. He staggered back like a man having an epileptic fit, blood running red through his lab coat and splattering out his back.

"*Joogso Haji!*" Osman squirmed for cover behind him.

Pumping the infidel with bullets was the only thing keeping him standing, for once I stopped, he fell back, his head slamming the floor next to Osman with a loud *crack!* The black briefcase flung against the wall and its lid broke off, revealing an eerie glow from within.

"What in *Jannah*...?" Osman said.

I knelt over what looked like a molten hot brick. I lifted up my ski mask to have a better look.

"Haji, get back!" Osman warned. "It's radioactive!"

Indeed, a radiation warning on the lid evinced it to be, in all likelihood, a "live" nuclear fuel rod.

My mask slipped off my head, landing on the rod and immediately catching fire. I flung the burning garment away, alas, at the counter of spilt medicines.

The drugs went up like wildfire, which quickly climbed the walls and spread across the ceiling. The white room became dark with black billows. I endeavored towards the flaming antigens.

"It's too late," Osman warned, grabbing my shoulder. "We've got to get out of here, now!"

I scanned the floor before me for vials, but they were all shattered and on fire.

My uncle slung my arm over his shoulder, helping me to my feet. We reached the stairwell, and there was an explosion behind us. He dragged me up the stairs, and I had to fight to keep from blacking out.

The nuclear "brick of gold"

On the final stairwell before the exit, I believe I did black out momentarily. How my uncle wrested me to the top with his bad leg was beyond me, but most likely, the inferno constantly licking at our backs gave him sufficient impetus.

Smoke filled the room at the exit. Osman gasped for breath as he fumbled with the keypad. "Go and milk, *soo maal...*" he repeated over and over again as he struggled to enter the code. He started coughing severely. "I—I can't breathe!" he choked, and I, too, was dying from asphyxiation. In a final, desperate measure, he got to his feet and slammed his fist high against the door, and *Allahu Akbar!* — a large green arrow lit up where he'd struck and the door opened with a sharp blast of air. He stumbled out of the compound, dragging me by the collar of my camouflage jacket.

Once on the outside, we leaned back against the door to close it behind us, but it quickly became so hot that we had to get away from it.

"The cyborg," I coughed, peering dissolutely around us. "Beware the cyborg."

"*Maxaa?*"

If Osman had forgotten, he now remembered, for that towering robotic militant was already upon us, firing off rounds from some unknown location.

The container flashed over us with the report of incoming munitions. Had I only been lucid enough to remember I was carrying the bullet of *Jannah*, I surely would've used it.

In the struggle to get away, I blacked out. Hairless white beings burned in the fires of my nightmare, clawing through the conflagration and begging for me to save them.

The next thing I knew, I was awake in the forest with Osman standing over me, covered with sweat and glancing frantically around us.

"Haji, thank *Jannah* you're awake! I've lost the way back. I'm going to do some recon. Stay here and stay low."

"But what about—?" I struggled to speak.

"*Sshh!* Just keep it down and try to stay lucid. I was able to shake the cyborg, but I don't know for how long." With that, he was gone.

I lay my head back against the fallen leaves and stared up through the trees, breathing deeply and trying to keep the forest canopy from spinning.

Unfortunately, my respite was short lived, for no sooner had I regained my wits than I heard footsteps approaching. But these were not the footsteps of the cyborg — this much was certain by the slow and shambling manner in which they lumbered through the thickets.

I stayed down and turned my head to see, beholding a figure that filled me with both hope and dread. It was the oracle — the witchy Oracle of Socotra Island who'd inflicted my chest with scars and violated me in other ways even more bizarre. But if it was really she, perhaps she could help me heal and provide me with guidance in the bigger sense. I sat up to get a better look, not having seen her in almost two years.

"Oracle," I said as she shambled towards me in her weathered djellabah robe. I now knew for certain it was her by cowry shells hanging from her rope belt, for she was a *faaliso* of the first degree — a diviner who could foretell the future by deciphering patterns in shells and grains of sand.

She emitted a throaty exhale and continued towards me with her arms slightly outstretched.

I searched the shadow beneath her hood for the reflective eyes she was known to possess, but instead beheld the green eyes of a snake, sinister and somehow dead.

"The Oracle shambled towards me…"

"Oracle," I said again, "thank Allah you're here. My uncle and I are lost. Can you help us get back to the lighthouse pier?"

She drew closer, gargling on phlegm with each heavy breath. It then occurred to me that she was perhaps sick, or maybe she'd narrowly escaped the fire like Osman and I had, and thus was suffering from asphyxiation.

I stood to help her, but she lunged at me, pinning me down on my back and hissing like a snake. I tried to fight her off, but I was too weak, and she was too strong.

"*Joogso!*" I screamed as she tried to bury blood-stained fangs into my neck.

With a final reserve of strength, I pushed her head far back. That's when Osman shot a bullet squarely into her forehead.

I pushed the vile woman off me and scurried to get away like a spider crawling in reverse.

"*Wax waliba sow ma wanaagsana?*" My uncle asked if everything was okay.

I nodded sullenly.

He went over and looked into the woman's face, sparing no epithet of disgust for her appearance, calling her a "fucking zombie."

"I think that's the Oracle," I suggested remorsefully.

"Her?" he said in disbelief. "The *aasho badhi*, more likely."

He was referring to a legend told by the seaward clans about a humanoid lizard of the desert that one could barter one's soul to for invincibility, for the *aasho badhi* was the abode of the devil. The very mention of it made me shudder with terror, for I'd not previously considered the possibility that the Oracle may have been the *aasho badhi*.

"I really don't know who attacked me," I said. "But she wears the Oracle's djellabah, and look at her cowries."

"*Humph!*" Osman couldn't care less. "Whoever she is, she was on top of you, and you screamed, so I shot her."

"*Waan ogahay. Mahadsanid.*" I told him *I know*, then thanked him.

"I found the way back to the boat. Can you walk?"

"I think so."

"Then let's get the fuck out of here."

I put one foot in front of the other and followed him through the forest, dark shadows encroaching around my peripheries. If I could only make it to the boat, I'd have food and tea, and could rest in the hull on the way back to Boosaaso. Once we got a cell phone signal, we could call ahead and order more antigen from Doctor Sooraan.

I could get through this, I kept telling myself as I fought to stay focused on Osman's back, while he kept a sharp lookout for possible threats. I was pretty much useless as a defender. I trained my gun willy-nilly beside me as I walked. I'd barely have the strength to pull the trigger, if necessary.

But we made it to the edge of the beach without further incident. The fog had cleared and we were in plain sight of the boat and lighthouse.

I struggled to lift my feet in the deep sand, so Osman helped me down to the waterline where the beach was hard-packed.

The revolving beacon swung around and stopped on us, then a low foghorn sounded from the lighthouse with deafening bass.

"They've spotted us!" Osman gasped. "*Deg-deg* Haji! We've got to get to the skiff!"

He ran ahead, and I did my best to keep up. He reached the skiff and unmoored it from the pillars. "*Deg-deg!*" he shouted back, turning the craft about.

The lighthouse tocsin continued to blast, its bright beacon trained on me all the while. I stumbled in the glare, then fell.

A dark shadow loomed over me, appearing massive in frame, then descended on me. It was Osman. He helped me up and onwards, his bad leg and my sodden state seemed to get the better of us, but we at last made it to the skiff, and he helped me over the gunnels.

THUMP! THUMP! THUMP! sounded the walkway above, and when it stopped, our fears were confirmed: the reflection of the cyborg appeared in the water, swinging its gun over the causeway railing.

THUMP! THUMP! THUMP! it marched ahead.

I trained my uzi on the floorboards above while Osman dropped an engine. The cyborg must've heard the splash, for it stopped immediately thereafter.

Even before Osman could fire up the outboard, a projectile blasted down *through* the walkway, exploding into the water beside us with incredible force.

"Fire!" Osman cried.

I unloaded my uzi into the pier's floorboards, try-ing to shoot the creature through the barrier. If I were connecting or not soon proved irrelevant, for we were already hightailing out of there.

Another weighty projectile shot down through the pier behind us, detonating massively into the water, then the cyborg lumbered on ahead, launching rockets at us from the causeway.

Osman steered around the spindle tower, blocking the robot's line of fire.

How long until the killing machine would come before the tower windows, lowering its mega-blaster upon *bad-weyn* to take us down?

Osman wasn't waiting around to find out. He dropped the second engine and took up speed.

Alas, an even more formidable nemesis suddenly appeared astern, rising out of the water like a subma-rine. *Allah help us!* It wasn't a submarine, but a flying craft shaped like one. It ascended thirty meters over the water on its forward flight, a vacuum-like portal in its underbelly sucking up all manner of sea life as it advanced. At least two sharks and an entire school of mutant fish were drawn up into the craft, which was gaining on us fast.

"*We'el!*" Osman cried *bastard!* in Somali, then cut both engines. Acting fast, he tore the fishing net from the rocket launcher amidships, then slung the gantry around and aimed it at the airship. He leaned back, took careful aim, then released the deadly trident.

The projectile left the gantry, dropped momentarily, then flared ahead like the great comet of Sultana, narrowly missing the zeppelin. But the shot was not a total loss, for just as the cyborg appeared in the lighthouse window yonder, the missile struck there, blowing the robot to kingdom come along with the spindle tower.

"We're finished." Osman was deflated — he'd missed his primary target. He trained his uzi on the skies, waiting for the devil's airship to arrive.

"*Ceeryaamo*," I struggled to say.

"*Maxaa?*"

I pointed afore.

"Fog," he noticed.

I opened a nitrous feed valve. "Flick the switch," I told him.

"Right, of course," he said, coming to his wits. He engaged the injection starter on the forward control panel, and the nitrous engine began revving up. But soon the horrendous hum of the airship overcame it. Alas, the dark shadow was already upon us, sucking up fish and manta rays astern as we were drawn slowly backwards, soon to be the vacuum ship's next victims.

The blinking red light above the nitrous tank suddenly turned solid, the engage button glowing '*MX.*'

"Now!" I cried.

Osman lunged forward, striking the button dead on.

The skiff shot forward like a bat out of hell, freeing us from the shadow of death.

We raced forward at blistering speed, the airship keeping up the chase and quickly gaining, while far astern in the distance, the aftermath of Selection Ministry tower curled heavenward in a mushroom cloud.

"The fog bank!" Osman hollered over the whistling headwind. "It keeps receding!"

I looked afore and he was right — we were losing ground on the sheltering mist. I reached to my other side and engaged the feed lever on our last nitrous tank. I was suffering from hot, black flashes, about to black out. "Watch for the button," I gasped.

"*Maxaa*⁈" he couldn't hear me.

I flashed him two fingers, then pointed at the *MX* button.

"The second NOS!" he shouted.

I gave him two thumbs'-up, then fell back against the gunwales, barely conscious. The only thing keeping me awake was my chest, which burned like a thousand wasp stings. I lifted my jacket and shirt to see the star over my heart shriveled and black.

On both sides of the skiff, large sea creatures were lifted from the water and wriggled through the air as they fell victim to the dreaded airship.

I felt the skiff slightly lift, then Osman struck the *MX* button and the second shot of NOS had its desired effect. Coupled with the first blast, the second injection of overdrive slung us forward at a truly manic pace.

Alas, the flying sub could not be outrun, and soon drifted over us again. We held onto our benches as the vacuum force kicked in. Just before the skiff left the water, I kicked one of our outboard's throttle bars, causing us to veer.

The spacecraft took us a few meters above *bad-weyn* before the angle I'd set broke us free from its force-field. We dropped into the water and shot into a wall of mist.

Some thirty hours later, as we approached Somalia's shores, a black marabou stork glided overhead.

Osman dropped to his knees and brushed my hair back with his hands, saying endearingly, " *'Alaantiisiiba 'adaatay.*"

He'd spoken something that Somalis say when someone is very sick or in great danger. As for the black stork —the *huur* — Somalis viewed its arrival as a harbinger of death.

I heard him calling over the radiophone, and I believe he got Bashir. He said we were heading to Las Qoray and that I was in a state of shock and needed immediate medical attention and antigen.

⁊

The skiff ground harshly over a rocky beach, awakening me from the brink of death. Osman wrested me over his shoulders and marched up the shore before continuing through tall grass. I was barely lucid as I looked back, but I saw someone in black shadowing us.

We left the sea-grass, coming to a dirt street. The figure tracking us remained behind, hiding at the edge of the thickets.

"Noor Fayrus!" she called out.

Osman whipped around, and I could no longer see her, but this is what she said: "And you, Osman. You must come with me. Your lives are in grave danger." She spoke with an American accent.

"Who are you?" Osman asked.

"Navy SEAL, special ops," she was candid. "There's no time. Please just come with me — I can explain later. I promise you asylum."

"Asylum from whom?" Osman inquired, but no sooner did his words leave his lips than a motorcade of technicals and black SUVs come whipping out from avenues in town, surrounding us like a wagon circle. They came to a stop, and heavily armed men wearing black masks spilled out of them.

The woman in the thickets

Bashir and Dr. Sooraan emerged from a black SUV flanked by private security and approached us hastily.

When Osman turned to face them, I saw the weeds closing where the woman had just been standing.

"Thank Allah you've come," Osman told our fellow operatives. "Haji is very sick."

Bashir and Sooraan took me from Osman while another sentry relieved him of his uzi. I was carried to an SUV and placed in the backseat between the doctor and Bashir.

"Where are you taking him?" Osman asked.

"Don't worry," Bashir replied.

"I'm coming with him." My uncle approached the vehicle, but an armed guard pushed him back. "Haji!" he cried.

The door slammed shut.

The passenger seated shotgun eyed me through the rearview mirror, then ordered with a thick Italian accent, "To Compound Six."

"Zayid?" I wanted to ask as we went speeding off, but nothing left my lips.

A whirlwind of delirium later, I was lying beneath bright lights with Bashir, Dr. Sooraan, and Zayid alternately standing over me. Then Zayid rolled up my sleeve as Dr. Sooraan approached with a needle.

"Prepare the cryogenic chamber, just in case," Zayid called back.

Commander Bashir

I focused on Bashir. He carried a look of utter dread.

Everything went black.

II.
CENTURY

Of Time And Man

I DREAMT FOR SECONDS OR YEARS, worldly time unknown to me as it passed. I dreamt of the bullet of *Jannah*, white and gleaming. I dreamt of Allah's golden-winged horses and their armor-clad equerries. I dreamt of faceless beings reaching out to me from a void, and I dreamt of my wife Issa, my hand clasped in hers as we strolled along Boosaaso beach. I stared into the sun on the horizon, squinting as I opened my eyes.

Light shone in through a window, and Issa was beside me, holding my hand. "You're back," she said softly. "Welcome home, *macaan.*"

It was hard to see against the daylight, but it appeared we were in our old upstairs bedroom in Boosaaso.

"Issa," I suspired. "You're here in Somalia. It's good to see you."

I coughed and it felt like an ice burn on the back of my throat. I reached for my neck, but she held my hand back, saying, "Just relax, *macaan.* You've been asleep for a long time."

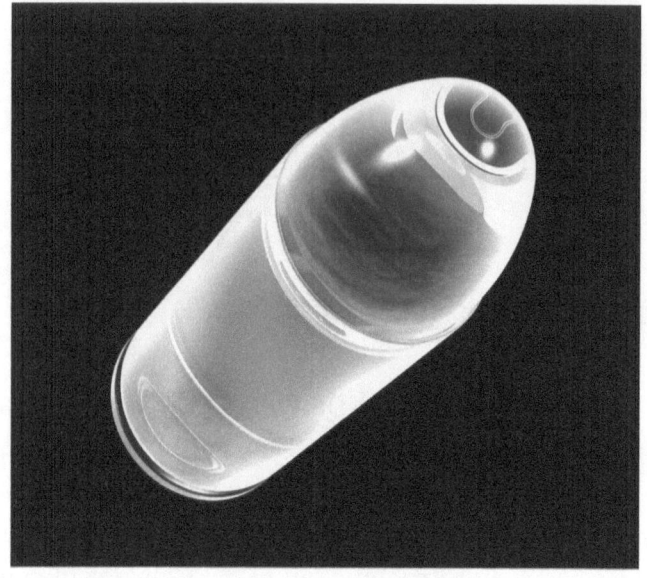

"I dreamt of the bullet of Jannah…"

"How long?"

"*Sshh*," she replied, gently rubbing my shoulder.

"Was I in a coma, *macaan*?" I asked, taking her hand and calling her sweetheart in return.

"Something like that." She got up from the bed and sauntered over to the window, closing the dentelle drapes. The diffused light made it easier for my eyes to adjust.

I tried to sit up but became dizzy.

"I require that you rest," she said, guiding my head back to the pillow. She was wearing her hijab, and her face was flawless.

"Have you been to the dentist?" I inquired, noticing her teeth were straight.

"I've been through a lot of things," she said cryptically, "as have you. I require that you rest, so that I can bring you your meal."

I regarded her curiously. Her way of speaking and mannerisms had somehow changed. She spoke too formally and wasn't acting naturally around me, and she moved as if she were timid or playacting. She walked into the next room in a manner that was just too stately. After a minute or two, I decided to investigate.

Getting out of bed was astoundingly difficult. I'd never felt so weak, although my recollection of things past was still a little hazy. Barely able to stand, let alone walk, I got on my hands and knees and crawled to the doorway.

She'd left the door ajar an inch. I nudged my chin in and opened it another. She was in the bathroom, sitting tall and erect on the toilet with the lid down. From my vantage point, she looked like a statue, neither moving nor breathing. Her eyes were closed, and I noticed a cable running from her side into a wall socket. After about a minute, she unplugged the cable, and it retracted back into her side, then she appeared to close a flap of skin over the area, her eyes closed all the while. I coughed.

She popped her eyes open and looked at me. "I require that you return to bed," she said.

I crawled over to her and asked, "Issa, what are you doing?"

She put a hand on my head to hold me back. I tried to crawl onto her lap, but she was too strong, so I reached around her side. All of a sudden, her skin retracted from my hand, and I felt a metal compartment filled with wires.

"Violation identified," she said as she grabbed my arm with such force that I thought she'd break it.

"Override incident," someone spoke through a speaker in the ceiling. That's when I noticed a CCTV camera in the upper corner.

Issa released her grip, then stood over me.

I scurried away from her and demanded, "What the hell's going on here?"

"I require that you return to bed so I can feed you," she replied, stepping forward.

I rumbled through the bedroom on my hands and knees, heading for the door. It was locked.

With Issa's shadow looming behind me, I scurried before the window and grabbed onto the drapes, pulling them down as I tried to lift myself up. But what I beheld outside caused me to freeze in shock. The flying sub of Selection Ministry Island was just passing by, the English word "Police" painted on its bow, while the world around it was ultramodern, if not downright futuristic.

"What's going on here?" I gasped, pressing my hands against the glass. I thought it was a televised image until the window opened and I reached into open air, the sounds of the city filling my ears.

Issa grabbed my shoulder, saying, "I require that—"

I fell back, knocking her over and falling on top of her.

"Violation identified," she repeated in monotone, taking hold of my forehead and chin as if she intended to break my neck.

"Override incident preset!" the man over the speaker said.

The lens of another surveillance camera above the window refracted to get a better look at me.

"Who the fuck are you?" I demanded, pointing at the camera.

The door leading out of the room drew aside with a pneumatic snap, and in walked a man in a business suit, his face wrapped in a turban. "Just take it easy, matey," he told me, then began tinkering with the back of Issa's neck. She released her grip on my head and stood up straight.

"It's me, Bashir," the man said, offering me an out-stretched hand. "Let me help you up. I'll explain everything and bring the food she promised. But you really do need to rest."

It sounded like my commander, so I let him help me back to bed. Issa watched us all the while, only her eyes were now green, not brown.

"Keep away from me," I told the woman who was not my wife.

"Don't worry," Bashir consoled. "She's here to help you, but I fear there's been a malfunction."

"Malfunction?"

"Please, try to relax," he said. "You've been through a lot. We were trying to ease your transition back, but just like before, you're testy as ever. This makes me very pleased, however, for it means you haven't lost your personality in the transfer."

"Transfer? What transfer?"

"Through time, Haji. You've been in deep sleep."

"How long have I been in a coma?"

"Not a coma, *saaxiib*. You were going to die, so were put under cryopreservation."

"Cryo what?"

"Your body was frozen until technology could catch up with the process, and your disease. Soon you'll be rejoicing, my friend, when you realize you cheated death and are healed."

"How long have I been out?"

"Three hundred and twenty-four years."

"Joke's over, Bashir. You can turn the cameras off now."

"Haji, the year is two thousand, three hundred, and thirty six."

I laughed.

"Look," he said, removing a pinball from his pocket. He released it and it floated before us unassisted. "Anti-gravity technology has been attained."

"Nice trick. It's magnetic."

"Not quite. It's called a Xubin. It's a personal assistant, something like the smart phones of the past. Stream exterior."

The ball projected a three dimensional hologram of the city I'd just seen outside.

"Ninety degrees," Bashir said, and the scene turned so that we were looking at it from a different angle. "*Jabi*," he said, and the image switched off. He grabbed the ball from the air and replaced it into his pocket. "I've so much more to show you, Haji. For now, it's best you get some food in you. We must ease your transition back both mentally and physically."

"Let me see your face," I said.

"Not yet — that comes with the territory."

I flung his turban aside and gasped. A man with an elongated skull and sucked-in, mutated face stared back at me with glowing, yellow eyes. But I could see it was Bashir, in a way.

"At ease, *saaxiib*," he consoled, taking both my hands. "There were complications."

"*Maxaa?*"

"The antigen, *walalo*, plus radiation and the cryogenics. Just trust that it's me, and that you're still you inside, and the rest will come more easily."

"Still me inside?" I broke his hold and felt my own face, touching the same sucked in features that I saw in his visage.

He released his pinball again, and as it floated, it shone a mirror before me in space.

I was mortified by my own reflection. "*Maya*," I groaned, feeling my deformed front. "*Maya!*"

"Go easy on yourself, *jaalle*. You came through pretty good, all things considered. Many don't fare nearly as well, while some don't pull through at all. There was a nuclear war, Haji, back in 2013 when we tried to annex Yemen. The Americans were already there, waging a covert war against Islamic militants. Things quickly escalated, and several nations jumped into the fray. We fired the first bombs at Tel Aviv, New York, and Madrid, hitting only the last. Our first two bombs missed, landing offshore and detonating underwater.

"The response from the infidels was swift. They launched two warheads from a nuclear submarine. We tracked them on satellite and scrambled a fleet of Blackhawks on a suicide mission towards the rockets vaulting towards Mog. A missile struck one of our helos about thirty leagues from the capital, detonating upon impact. Mogadishu was spared, but the glancing shot left its scars.

"The other bomb hit Guban dead on, wiping the village clean off the map."

"I must be dreaming," I said, pinching myself hard on the neck and chest.

Bashir stopped me. "Don't do that," he said.

In the mirror before me, I saw where I'd pinched already turning red and swelling badly.

"This is real, *saaxiib*," the commander said, regarding me with bioluminescent eyes. "You'll get through this, just like me and the others. I'm here to help you."

"Is she real?" I thrust my hand clean through the holographic mirror, pointing at "Issa," who was still standing by the window.

"She is, in principal."

"Talk square, Commander."

"Not long after the war, she came to Somalia looking for you. We permitted her to view your frozen body, explaining what had happened and how we had to put you in a state of suspended animation until technology allowed us to revive you. She begged us to do the same for her, saying she wanted to be with you, but ultimately she decided to wait until she was about to die a natural death. She was much older when she finally came back and Sooraan put her under. I was already in cryopreservation then.

"I'm sorry, Haji, but she didn't pull through the process. Her body didn't survive the revival, which was performed a few weeks before yours. I think she was too old already, and her heart just couldn't take it.

She went into cardiac arrest. But we saved her *Maskax*, which we uploaded into the automaton."

A pit of regret stuck in my chest, not having been with Issa when she died, but— "What do you mean you saved her *Maskax?*"

"It's part of the revival technology. When the body is thawing, the brainstream — the synapses, memory cells, and cerebellum blotters — are downloaded first in case the physical apparatus fails, as with Issa. The character abstract file can then be uploaded into an automaton so that the individual can continue on in humanoid form. The science is relatively new and not exact, so there are still some bugs to be worked out. Many subjects such as your wife need to be assisted by a masterframe until they can gain enough referential integrity to achieve full independence."

"*Maan fahmin.*" I told him that I didn't understand.

"It's very complex to Old World science, and has only recently made stable strides in our time. As for you, your body pulled through, so for the time being, try to enjoy your real flesh and skin. If you choose to continue on as an automaton later, you'll have that option."

"Are you saying that you've turned Issa into a robot?"

"Not in the least, matey. There are robots in the city and working for the Organization. You'll see how different they are. Robots have artificial intelligence, while automatons like Issa maintain the intelligence and character constructs of their original selves. In short, they still have their own god-given personalities — not one programmed by man. Even after the *Maskax* is loaded into a machine, it can continue to learn and grow as an individual, just like any sophisticated computer is able to adapt to input from its environment. The exoframe isn't just cosmetic — sensors all around it react to things like temperature, touch, and gravity, just like you and me."

"There are robots…working for the Organization"

"So that's a mock-up of Issa, is what you're saying."

"*Maya*, Haji — it's really her, not a substitute. Only her body is interchangeable. But look at her — her exoframe is a perfect fit. I bet you couldn't tell the difference."

"If that thing isn't flesh and bones, then get it out of my sight and stop torturing me with the memory of my wife!"

Bashir sighed heavily, then took a long look at the robot. "But wouldn't you enjoy your wife's company? Her personality and the memories you share?"

"Of course, but seeing her plug into a wall is too much for me to bear."

"Perhaps you'd prefer her *Maskax* without the frills then?"

"*Maan fahmin*." I told him I didn't understand.

"Without the bling-bling. That's all the physical world really is anyway, eh mate? Look, I'll tell you what I'm going to do. We can transfer her *Maskax* into a stock automaton — just the machine without the skin. It'll still have all the sensors and such, only it will look like plain hardware, not a human. Once you get used to having it around, we can introduce your wife to you again in the form that you remember. We'll call the stock mod Issa 2.0. How's that?"

I closed my eyes and rubbed them. "Whatever," I muttered. I knew I must be dreaming.

"Don't do that, Haji," he said, pulling my hand away from my eyes. My vision was so blurred that I couldn't make out anything. "Your body is still very sensitive," he explained, "especially the eyes. You must go easy on it for a while."

I blinked a few times, and my vision slowly began to regain focus. "Right, Bashir. I'll see you on the other side," I laughed. I was looking forward to remembering this dream to share with him later.

"Return rebellion," he sighed, handing me a small duffelbag. "Happens to the best of 'em."

"*Maxaa?*"

"Sensory and information overload after being asleep for a few centuries. It's natural. We tried to reduce its impact with the bedroom mock-up, but as usual, you saw right through it. I shouldn't have under-estimated you like that. But it's a good thing — it means you've already regained some of your more complex mental faculties."

I opened the duffelbag out of curiosity, finding my yellow windbreaker, TT-30 pistol, and father's dagger.

"Your personal effects," Bashir said, "to help convince you. And this…"

He procured a small black case from his pocket and opened it, revealing the gleaming bullet of *Jannah*. "I kept it hidden as a favor," he explained. "It would've been studied to death, wasted in a lab. But I know what this bullet means to you; I know its real significance. In many ways, this is a living artifact of the founding of the empire. Keep it in your gun and keep it concealed. It won't be able to stop the present reality, so please don't try that, but I trust you'll one day put it to its intended use — whatever the Heavens had sent you back for initially, when Captain Axmed found you washed up on Darsah Island."

The bullet was too bright to look at for any length of time, so I locked it into my pistol.

"I'll get you a holster for that," he promised.

Suddenly, a sound like a cell phone on vibe mode emanated from his body. He reached into his pocket and procured his pinball again. It stopped vibrating, apparently when he touched it. He released it into the air and it displayed a hologram of a man running through the city while looking up desperately. A screen appeared beside it showing scrolling sitreps data passing before a digitized mug shot of a man wearing a wrap-around turban where only his eyes were visible. The live hologram next to it panned back to reveal he was being shadowed by the flying police sub.

"Will Waabeeri!" Bashir exclaimed. "We've been on his trail for months. I knew he was in the Hodan quarter! I'm sorry to have to run, Haji. A high value target is about to be apprehended, and I must be there for the interrogation. Will Waabeeri is a rabble-rouser of the first degree."

"You work for the police?"

"Something like that," he replied with a cryptic wink, returning his pinball back to his pocket. "I'm with the *hanti wadaagnimo*. My childhood dream, remember?"

"As a matter of fact, I do."

"I'm with the hanti wadaagnimo" — *the secret police*

"Good, very good, Noor — I knew you'd come back. Here, take this." He reached into another pocket and released a different pinball into the air, where it continued to float unassisted. "I was going to wait to give it to you, but I think you're ready. You've a lot of questions I can't answer right now, so try asking your Xubin. They're very user-friendly. You'll figure it out."

I grabbed the little steel ball and it was warm to the touch.

"Some people give them names," Bashir said. "But whatever you decide to call it, it'll never lose you. I gotta run! Come with me!" he told "Issa."

The automaton followed him to the door, where he stopped to say, "I'll send her back without all the frills, if that makes you more comfortable."

"Sure," I replied, surrendering to my dream for the time being.

STRANGE HORIZONS

I STUDIED MY REFLECTION in the Xubin's metallic surface. As if the little ball knew what I was trying to do, it projected a mirror for me to look into.

I was a real piece of work, but not nearly as unsightly as Bashir. I looked like a *Faranji* stricken with yellow jack, for sickly pale skin sucked into every contour of my skinny face. My nose was more elongated, its arch continuing up and over my forehead like the front of a warthog, appearing to stretch out the front of my skull. But my eyes were the creepiest of all; their whites were flush with yellow, and my black pupils were twice their normal size.

A strange, siren-like sound floated in off the streets. I looked towards the window but didn't feel like going over there. I didn't want to expend the energy. I still had a muscular physique, but felt sore and weak.

"Show me the outside," I asked Xubin.

The virtual mirror was replaced by a hologram showing an uncanny scene. The perspective was from ground level, but rather than revealing more of the futuristic world I'd glimpsed before, I beheld a wretched, emaciated figure moving through a foggy bog.

Or perhaps the background could better be described as a marsh filled with dead trees, for gnarled branches were everywhere to be seen, stretching this way and that, not unlike the thing as it swung its arms about like some sort of crazed zombie.

"What is that?" I inquired.

"The outside, beyond the city walls," the orb replied with a tinny inflection.

"But that thing, what is it?"

"*A xun gaajo.*"

"A bad hunger?" I inquired perplexedly.

"*Haa*, a devourer. The *xun gaajo* are everywhere on the outside, making it unsafe for overland transport."

"What are they, exactly?"

"The devourers came into being after the first nuclear war. They were Somalia's original nomadic population and were hit hardest by the effects of radiation coupled with flaws in the early virus experiments."

"Virus experiments?"

"Early attempts to strengthen a subject's resistance to radiation and biohazards required the development of a gene-altering virus that, when delivered properly in low doses, could rapidly speed up the subject's ability to resist catastrophic infection. The sudden spike in radiation resulting from the war caused the virus to mutate into something akin to rabies, and while the proliferation of automatic weapons within the city enabled the infected to be eradicated relatively quickly, the disease spread unchecked through the pastoralists in the countryside, who were not given any antigen. Walls were built around Mogadishu to keep the infected out, and as of yet, there is no known cure for the infected, whose disease is spread through leeches in the swamps and orally through bites."

"Through eating?"

"The devourers are irrational and blind. They seize upon anything they can for food, including men. If you're bitten and you survive, within sixteen hours the infection will turn you into a *xun gaajo*."

"One of them."

"*Haa.*"

"Can bats be infected?"

"*Maya.* The bat species have their own internal resistance mechanism. You, Noor Fayrus, along with Commander Bashir and other *Homo sapiens* like you who survived the holocaust, had been given sufficient doses of the bat antigen, then called *antibaayootig*, to resist the virus. But as the commander mentioned, the effects of the antigen coupled with high doses of radiation have fundamentally altered your body, while the long-term effect of suspended animation, the 'cryogenic echo,' has left blanks in your conscious awareness that even your memory file — your *Maskax* — cannot replace. In this way you are not much different than the automatons, the main difference being their memory voids can be rebuilt virtually, while yours can never be replaced with absolute certainty."

"*Maan faahim.*" I told Xubin that I didn't understand.

Suddenly, a schematic of an automaton appeared beside the hologram of the *xun gaajo*, with processes of its functioning lighting up as Xubin explained. "Images and information can be downloaded into an automaton's *Maskax*, becoming part of his or her memory bank, free from the human mechanisms of belief and doubt, while *Homo sapiens* cannot be forced to believe something they may have doubts about, such as a past history presented to them as real, but which they cannot consciously remember."

I rubbed my forehead, finding the Xubin's descriptions hard to follow. The "devourer" was still displayed on the hologram adjacent, lumbering through the three-dimensional bog with its arms swinging this way and that, but mostly forward.

"What else can you tell me about that?" I pointed to the wretched semblance of a man. Suddenly, a portrait of one appeared in thin air opposite the automaton schematic. Now three separate screens were displayed before me.

"The *xun gaajo* are like camels in that they can go a long time without food or water, but they still have a voracious appetite, seizing themselves on anything that moves. They're a lot stronger than they may look, for any protein ingested is converted directly to muscle. Thus, they are mostly muscle and bone, the remainder of their body functions having regressed to near uselessness over the past three centuries."

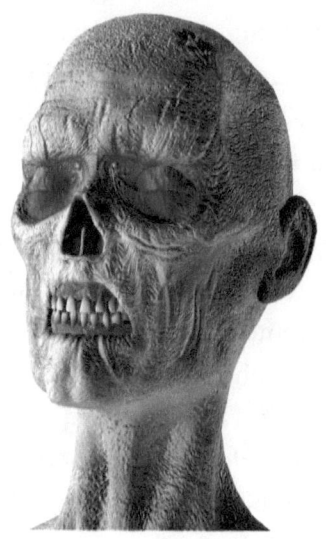

"The devourers are irrational and blind…"

"What about their brains? Can they think?"

"Only in the most primal of ways. The *xun gaajo* are instinctive and reactionary, the reflective and reasoning parts of their brains having all but decayed under the effects of the virus. Only their cerebellums appear still active, spurring them primordially."

"So they're not social beings as you and I know it?"

"*Maya*, they don't talk — only hiss — and they've no reasoning capabilities beyond the subconscious echoes of their psyches."

"Please explain."

"Three hundred years is a long time in human years, but not in evolutionary time. Certain social practices of the devourers' predecessors still haunt them like ghosts in a machine, or like the afterimage on a computer screen that remains after it's been switched off. It won't be long until the *xun gaajo* are fully devoid of any trace of their previous humanity, and while they've long since abandoned their traditional portable homes — their *aqals* — to roam the earth and feed by day, subconscious echoes left over from their social ancestors still spur them to gather by night, when they sleep in groups beneath the boughs of acacia trees."

"You're not saying this has something to do with the *guurti*, are you?"

"*Maya.* It is generally believed they do so on account of the old birth ceremony, where two rams were slaughtered for the birth of a boy and one for a girl, then the bones were collected after the feast and slung up into trees. The pods of *xun gaajo* gather under such boughs to sleep, where they sleep standing together in a herd, propping each other up beneath the bundles of bones slung on high. If a devourer cannot find such a pod to sleep with, it will continue walking through the night, feeding."

"You say they've been quarantined beyond the city walls?" I asked, suddenly very nervous about the *xun gaajo* and their horrid condition. "How about birds, animals, insects? Can they be infected? Can they get in?"

"Only *ido* and *waraabe*."

"Only sheep and hyenas? *Maan fahmin.*"

"Sheep can carry the virus, and are thus strictly banned from the city, while hyenas are believed to have attracted the disease by feeding on the remnants of *xun gaajo*, for even devourers can die of starvation if they don't get food in about three months' time. Attempts to try to eradicate the *qoriismaris* have failed."

"*Qoriismaris?*"

"Infected hyenas and their offspring, which as a whole are the most dangerous species outside. Their genetic structure has altered drastically. Within months, newborns can grow to a massive size. They're incredibly fast and hunt at night, while the inclusion of webbed paws enables them to hide in the swamps and bogs."

"Can they swim?"

"*Qoriismaris* can remain underwater for long periods of time, making them difficult to hunt and the bogs extremely dangerous places to be at night — which are already very dangerous for healthy humans, given their high radiation content. But the *qoriismaris* are not known to eat *xun gaajo* that are standing upright — only if the devourers are lying down or dead will they feed on them."

"*Waayo?*" I asked the Xubin why.

"Even the *qoriismaris* have ancestral echoes," Xubin replied, "and hyenas were not hunters in the formal sense. They usually fed on carcasses. There is a theory that *xun gaajo* sleep standing together as a defensive mechanism. Perhaps even zombies can evolve over time."

Juvenile Qoriismaris

"So the *qoriismaris* will not attack a man who is standing upright?"

"Not usually, but if you sit or lie down for even an instant, it may be your last."

"Are these creatures — these zombies and were-wolves — are they everywhere outside?"

"Everywhere in Africa, *haa*, and the virus has spread to most corners of the globe with various levels of regional containment."

"Please, turn these pictures off," I said of the hologram and stills, sweeping my hand through them. I'd seen enough for now, and a part of me was becoming increasingly worried I wasn't just dreaming. The images disappeared at my command.

I could not imagine the rest of Somalia as it'd just been presented. All that I'd fought for, the years spent fishing with Abbo, the days walking the beaches with Issa and Ayan Rage, all reduced to a radioactive bog.

"Show me Dante," I asked with a sick feeling.

The orb, probably programmed to present information relative to my frame of reference based upon things like culture, proximities, and my past inquiries, showed me my hometown of Dante and not the historical Italian author of that same name.

Yet if there ever was a Dante's Inferno in devastation or the pain such a catastrophe could levy upon the heart, it was in that image of my birthplace and the tears it brought to my eyes. It looked like another tsunami had washed through town, this one reaching every corner of the village, the only structures remaining being the frame of the old Italian salt factory that Fatuma used to scale, and the Ayan Community School of East Africa. A rusted shipwreck cantered just off-shore seemed to have sheltered the schoolhouse somewhat from the mushroom blast.

"Enlarge this," I said, flicking the hologram of the school with my fingers, and sure enow, like an old touch-enabled smart phone or tablet monitor, the image enlarged. I pinched two fingers between one of the school's windows and flicked them open. From there, Xubin read my command perfectly — he took me inside.

The storm that had been gathering within me broke all at once. Tears streaked over my cheeks like rain down a windshield, and my body convulsed with pangs of devastation and loss, for the schoolhouse lay before me like a shattered cavity, frozen in time. Books remained splayed across the floor where they'd been blown from children's fingers in the blinding aurora three centuries agone. The windows were blasted out, and the walls were barely standing, with paint and boards peeling from them like a toredo-eaten ship.

"No, no more..." I wept, closing my eyes, and as tears squeezed out from their sides, the afterglow of the image remained fixed in my mind.

The mushroom cloud would become a permanent fixture in man's collective unconscious, this much I knew even long after Xubin removed the abstracts of destruction from my sight.

File Under: Permanent Fixture of the Post-Apocalyptic Mind

ISSA 2.0

"*XAAS* NOW RETURNS," Xubin said, referring to my wife as she opened the pneumatic door. She was carrying a tray of food and a tall silver gourd.

"*Subax wanaagsan*," she said in Somali, telling me *good morning*, then she announced she had breakfast for me as she placed the tray on the bedside table.

I still felt very uncomfortable being alone with an automaton, but the stripped-down android was far preferable than the one with Issa's exoframe. At least now, I knew my eyes weren't playing tricks on me, even if it were just all a dream.

"Your favorite," she said, handing me a plate of steaming Somali pancakes. "*Canjeeros iyo Shah Xawaash,*" she added, pouring a cup of spiced cinnamon tea.

"*Mahadsanid,*" I said for lack of a better response. "*Bismillaah.*"

"*Bismillaah!*" she returned with a smile. At least the machine had a Somali style about it.

She sat on a stool before me and remained silent as I ate, looking beyond me, into space, and moving only to replenish my tea or pour more syrup over my pancakes.

I started off eating voraciously, but my stomach soon welled up with gasses, causing me to burp and hiccup.

"Slow down," she said. "Your body is soft yet." She went to wipe some syrup from my lips with a napkin.

I grabbed her hand and pushed it back, saying bitterly, "I can take care of myself, *mahadsanid!*"

She resumed her gaze over me, seemingly unaffected by my quip.

"*Waan dhergey!*" I said in time, meaning I was full.

She removed the tray from my lap and went to take my cup of tea, when I asked for more, please.

She refilled my cup, then thanked me.

"For what?" I asked.

"For requesting me as I really am, without the mask."

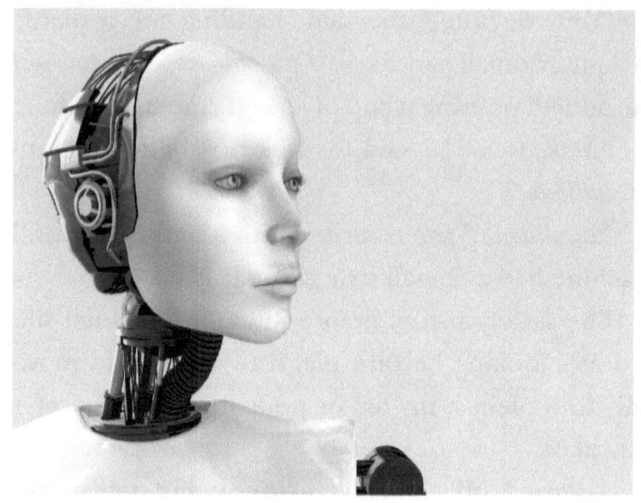

Issa 2.0

"Why would you care about that? You're just a machine."

"Thank you for accepting me for who I am," she replied without elaborating, save for, "I'm here to serve you."

"Does it make you happy that I asked for you as you really look — like a robot?" I toyed, trying to trick her over the concept of emotions, which machines don't have.

"*Haa*," she replied in the affirmative.

"Where are Mohamed and Jeilani?" I tested, but also wanted to know the fate of my children.

The automaton stared into space, saying, "They are in my memory file, but not their present where-abouts."

"So you don't know what happened to them?"

"*Maya, waan ka xumahay.*"

"Why are you sorry? Did something happen to them?"

"*Ma ogi.* I am sorry because I don't know what happened to them, and I'm here to make you happy."

"Xubin," I asked the little steel orb floating beside me, "show me St. Paul, Minnesota, the United States of America."

"The United States of America ceases to exist as you know it. It is now called 'The Great Shelter.'"

"Then show me where St. Paul used to be."

Xubin flashed a series of images and videos before me, showing the suburb as I remembered it. "These are antique files," it said.

"Then what does St. Paul look like now?" I asked uneasily, a little frightened at what I might discover.

Indeed, my fears were confirmed, for Xubin showed me in three-dimensional hologram the ruins of a suburb that had been the residence of my family after we'd moved overseas.

I made a fist and struck my forehead softly but repeatedly, and the pain that emerged there made me realize that I may not, in fact, have been dreaming. Bad and terrifying things could happen in dreams, *haa*, but to have physical pain like I was experiencing — it was all too real.

I saw what looked like people moving over the rubble, so I zoomed the image in and realized, by the manner in which they walked, that they were devourers. "So the plague has spread to America," I observed sullenly.

"The virus has affected ninety-six percent of the Great Shelter," confirmed Xubin, "and like the rest of the world, the *Homo sapiens* that are still healthy take shelter in walled cities called fiefdoms."

"These devourers look different," I remarked, zooming one in closer.

"*Haa*, the *xun gaajo* of the Great Shelter and other parts of the Western world have more body mass and are more powerful than those around the Mogadishu fiefdom."

"*Waayo?*" I asked, *why?*

"During the second nuclear war, in twenty-one thirty-six — the one that destroyed your family's community overseas — many Westerners preemptively opted for cryopreservation rather than face a life of suffering and radiation sickness, for by then cryopreserving technology was more widely available and affordable, especially to the vast wealthy sectors. The majority of them were obese when they entered cryopreservation and were allowed to set their own time clocks. Now, everyday, more of them awake to a world ravished by radiation and the X-lix virus, supplying a near endless supply of food for the *xun gaajo*. Humans who wake up from cryopreservation in a safe zone or fiefdom, but without the X-6 antigen, change into devourers almost immediately. Supplies of the X-6 antigen are low to nonexistent in most of the world — only in Somalia will you find a stable source.

"When the White Star Empire was first established, Zayid Cecchi, then its CEO, had the foresight to develop both a virus and its antigen that would ensure the empire's future world dominance. The citizens of Mogadishu owe everything to Emperor Cecchi, whose *Xulasho lix* research and development has enabled the empire to not only survive the holocaust, but to thrive in a world that has traditionally oppressed Somalia with colonialism, sustenance poaching, and chemical warfare via illegal hazardous wastes disposal on its seaboard."

"Did you say *Xulasho lix?*"

"*Haa, Xulasho lix*, the X-lix virus."

"Does this have anything to do with the *Xulasho Wasaarad?*"

"*Haa*, the Selection Ministry, an umbrella corporation consisting of top nuclear pharmaceutical developers and presided over by Emperor Cecchi himself, developed Project Samale, the X-lix virus and its antigen."

"*Xaggee?*" I asked. "*Where* was the virus developed?"

"Research and development of Project Samale took place on Selection Ministry Island."

"And that is where the antigen is made," I assumed, having seen it there myself.

"Not anymore. For reasons of national security, the X-6 antigen is now produced at an undisclosed location, of which there may be several. However, Selection Ministry Island still operates as an advanced research facility and is strictly off-limits to civilians. Only those with the highest security clearance can visit there — usually employees on the emperor's handpicked team of epidemiologists, geneticists, and nuclear physicists, whose curricula vitæ came flooding in as the virus spread. It is believed the vast majority of them are now working there as XOR operators, their human bodies having died long ago."

"XOR operators?"

"Automatons like Issa 2.0, but more strictly controlled by the Mainframe."

"I would like to see Zayid."

"You cannot. His fiefdom is blocked from the information matrix."

"Where is his fiefdom?"

"Zeilah."

"I wish to go there."

"It's strictly forbidden. Without an explicit invite from the emperor, you cannot."

"Can you get me in touch with him, then? He's an old friend of mine, and we've some unfinished business."

"*Maya*, I am sorry, Noor — I have not been given this level of clearance."

"Then who has?"

"I have no associated data to fulfill your request, but heuristics would suggest that those higher up in the chain of command would be more likely to be his contacts."

"Heuristics?"

"The progression of logic for artificial intelligence, such as mine."

"Maybe she can help me," I said halfheartedly, glancing up at Issa 2.0. "Or is she only artificially intelligent, as well?"

"That's artificial intelligence, Noor," Xubin replied, speaking faster as if it might be angry, "not 'artificially intelligent.' A.I. is pure logic, not a mask or sham. And no, Issa 2.0's *Maskax* OS is not the same as A.I. Hers has its foundation in human logic and memories, and so her sophistication does not develop as linearly as mine. In short, her intelligence is affected by emotions, while mine is not."

"That makes absolutely no sense to me. She's just a machine."

"I do have emotions, Haji," she put in, reaching down and touching my forearm.

I looked into her eyes and didn't know what to think. If she had emotions, they were impossible to read in those glass-like orbs.

"Can we please just change the subject?" I groaned. "Or better yet, both of you, just leave me be."

Xubin glided to the bedside table and set down there, remaining quiet and immobile.

Caucasian woman with large Xubin

Issa 2.0 turned to me and said, "When you're ready, Bashir has suggested we take a walk so that you can exercise your legs and see the exterior."

"The 'outside'?"

"*Maya*, the city. He said your recall rebellion would pass quicker than usual because you're special."

"What do you mean, I'm special?"

"He said you're not afraid of the unknown, and that you embrace the future."

I shrugged my shoulders and smiled meekly, not knowing what to think.

"Come with me now," said she, offering me her robotic hand. Her fingers were made of steel and rubberized joints, with coverings of little white plates. "I want to walk with you in the city," she said.

I didn't particularly care to be with her, but I wanted to see the exterior. If I were being made the victim of a grand hoax, this was my opportunity to end it. I pushed her aside and slid off the side of the bed, immediately going unstable as I did.

Issa 2.0 came to my assistance, which I allowed, having no other choice if I wanted to get my sea legs back. After a few laps around the room, I learned to walk unassisted.

I pulled on my yellow windbreaker, my old camouflage fatigues and boots (delivered by Issa 2.0), then strapped on my dagger and TT-30 pistol, finally saying, "Let's go."

The Somali Pirate 3 – White Star Empire

MOGADISHU 2336

I'D BEEN LODGED IN A BUILDING in a hilly neighborhood overlooking the city. As we strolled outside, I observed raised freeways crossing through massive structures and domes. Then I noticed, through a strange, blue-gray haze hanging on the skyline, a massive full moon setting over a deep turquoise sea.

"Why does the moon look so big?" I asked Issa 2.0, but was answered instead by Xubin, who was hovering over my shoulder.

"An effect of the fallout," it said. "The closer objects get to the horizon, the more they're magnified and appear silver."

Another thing that struck me as peculiar were the vehicles traveling upon the raised highways, or "skyways," as Xubin called them. They looked like cars and trucks, only they appeared to be floating without wheels over the erected causeways.

"Are the cars antigravity, too?" I inquired of the talking pinball.

"*Maya*," it explained, "they use maglev technology — something that was first developed in your time."

"What about the airships?" I inquired of the spacecraft gliding overhead.

The City of Mog, Julian year 2336

"Some are antigravity," Xubin explained, "while others are steel zeppelins powered by atom-enriched helium."

The area we walked, built upon a hillside, was not nearly as busy as the city below. We passed some structures resembling modern corporate buildings like I'd seen in America, only these had gleaming silver lawns and fountains of rich blue water. The few people we passed appeared to be businessmen, for they were wearing suits and ties and carrying briefcases. Their visages were affected like mine, with sucked-in skin, yellowish eyes, and slightly elongated craniums. And like me, one of them was walking alongside an automaton, only his was black in design and wearing a purple hijab. Her body, however, was left undressed, revealing smooth plastic lines and joints of rubber and steel.

We came to what Issa 2.0 called the Aquatics Center, where "humans go for water recreation," resplendent with pools, fountains, and Plexiglas tubes for sliding through. A Caucasian woman dressed in a swimsuit or spacesuit sauntered by the glass barrier before us. She was toying with a large Xubin, tossing it from hand to hand. She smiled at me and I smiled back.

Issa pulled me on, taking me to yet another glass dome, this one built into the mountainside. She called it a nature preserve. We went inside and took a seat on a park bench.

An insect with strikingly colorful wings landed on my armrest. I reached for it, but it flew off.

"This is technically a butterfly nursery," Xubin remarked.

"For what?"

"For the emperor. He's a collector of sorts, having certain specimens periodically shipped to him in Zeilah."

"A collector," I laughed. "He shoots them for sport."

"I like to shoot them, too," Issa said.

I regarded her critically.

She removed a camera from a compartment within her torso and asked, "Do you mind if I take some pictures? Photography is my hobby."

"Since when?" I asked.

"Ever since you left," she replied with eyes downcast. "I started the hobby to take my mind off things."

"Go and take some pictures," I replied, not entirely comfortable around her.

She sauntered onto the green with camera in hand, trying several times to "shoot" the butterflies.

"Issa 2.0 is a curious creature," I remarked. "I've never known a machine to act like a child."

"She is still young for an automaton," Xubin replied. "Her software is still adapting to her new hardware — the robotics that put her in touch with her environment through which she learns."

"Learns what?"

"She is still familiarizing herself with the world, just as you are. But she is also rediscovering herself, her *Maskax*. As time progresses, she will become more like the Issa you know by way of her past history recall."

"Past history recall?"

"The *Maskax* is not just a memory file. It also contains data pertaining to her field of emotions based upon her past experiences. It's this emotional plug-in that takes some time to appear and organize itself, like a computer that is just turned on and warming up, its icons and files not all present and functional at first. We call this lag infonesia."

"You keep telling me a machine has emotions. It's just a program, right?"

"Issa 2.0 has been programmed to react positively to all memories she has of you and her together, both good and bad. This is preset for all wives' *Maskaxes* before they're uploaded into automatons. Only those files she has of your leaving trigger a negative reaction."

"Does she become sad?"

"*Haa*, according to her emotional presets. At first, before her emotions are synchronized, the only thing that makes her sad is your leaving her, either in the past, present, or future. These emotions are preprogrammed at first, but her entire range of emotions will be triggered piecemeal by specific inputs from her environment, namely you."

"Me?"

"*Haa*."

I watched Issa 2.0 reach down into a bush, apparently having discovered something. Butterflies came swarming out, surrounding her. She stood amid them in wonderment.

"I think you should know," Xubin said, "that all wives' *Maskaxes* uploaded into automatons are hard-coded to love their husbands."

"I find that hard to believe, that a robot is capable of love."

"She is, Haji," the reflective ball said. "Just give her time, and love her back."

"Get real!" I scoffed.

"Her value of love increases with environmental input," explained Xubin, "and can never be decreased. It's like putting data into a computer — the more you enter, the more the database grows, and the more useful the machine becomes in its ability to give something back."

"...she is still young for an automaton."

"I'm turning you off now," I said, grabbing the little orb and putting it in my pants pocket. It went silent and made no movement.

"Issa, let's go!" I shouted.

She returned to me with hydraulic steps and replaced her camera within her frame. "Where would you like to go?" she asked.

"I want to see Bashir."

"He went to the Hodan quarter. We shall return to our room and wait for him."

"I'm tired of waiting!" I snapped. "I need to talk to a human! I'm going to find him." I headed towards the park entrance, leaving her behind.

"Don't go, Haji!" she pleaded, trying to catch up.

"I'm going to the Hodan!" I shouted back. "And you're not going to stop me!"

"Don't go there!" she pleaded. "It's too dangerous."

I turned and shoved her away. She fell back onto the grass.

I darted for the exit as quickly as my unsteady legs would carry me, then took a quick left down an escalator leading into the city.

Issa suddenly appeared behind me, having slid down the railing with her hands. "For your own safety," she said, "you're forbidden to go to the Hodan."

"Just get off my case, will ya?"

"But if you must go there," she continued unfazed. "I shall guide you."

STRANGER IN A STRANGE LAND

WE PROCEEDED SOUTH, following beneath a raised skyway and passing many steaming vents coming out of the ground, until at last we came to the old Hodan quarter. In "my time," during the civil war that began in 1991 and lasted for two decades, the Hodan quarter had lain on the frontlines and had been badly disfigured by ordnance. Now in 2336, it was akin to an industrial wasteland, with nothing but steel and concrete factory-like structures stretching southward for as far as the eye could see. Some of the factories had spires reaching hundreds of meters into the sky, while others hosted giant orbs that appeared to be nuclear power plants.

The Hodan Quarter

"Do you think Bashir is in one of those spacecrafts?" I inquired, noticing a flying sub cruising over the city a few blocks away.

"*Ma ogi.*" She said she didn't know.

"Can you call him?" I would've suggested it earlier, but the fact was, I'd left the park to think things out and blow off steam; but now that we seemed to be wandering aimlessly in an industrial wasteland, I really did want to see Bashir and get to the bottom of things — and I was tired of talking to machines. If this wasn't a dream, I wanted to know who else came through cryogenic preservation intact. Were my kids still alive? Was Osman, Cosob, or Xeed? And in what form? Were they normal, did they look alien like me, or were they machines? If I was stuck in this world for the long-term, I wanted to know who besides myself and Bashir had pulled through deep sleep.

"Issa 2.0 calling Bashir on behalf of Haji," my robot "wife" said, talking into thin air. "We're in the Hodan quarter, approaching the Biyomareen district. Haji wants to talk to you. Please call back, or if you're in the vicinity, we're on GPS." She then explained to me that she'd left a message with him via a built-in receiver on her body.

"The Canal district?" I asked.

"*Haa*, the Biyomareen. It's just ahead."

We came to an area with many narrow alleyways running between the frameworks of the factories. Establishments spilled out from honeycombed cavities within the industrial maze, haunted by patrons who appeared to compose the empire's underclass. Three women tried to solicit me for sex, but upon closer inspection, two of them proved to be robots.

"We need to go," Issa said, pulling me clear of the android prostitutes.

Perhaps it was my neon yellow windbreaker, or maybe it was Issa 2.0's spotless white frame, but we were clearly not of that greasy place. A gaggle of wretches sitting against a wall reached out to touch us like we were fancy storefront objects they could never afford, while cutthroat aliens — or so they appeared to me — eyed us with disdain as they whispered intrigues and conspiracies. Suspicious glances fell upon us from every corner, from beneath hooded robes, from the eyes of men, machines, and their "offspring": cyborgs.

"I need to go," I said.

"I'll take you home," Issa consoled.

"No, you don't understand. I need to take a piss."

"*Maxaa?*"

"To pee, don't you get it? Oh, I remember now — you're a fucking robot," I mocked. "I'll try here." I proceeded towards a dungy bar.

"*Maya!*" She held me back. "It's too dangerous."

Indeed, large figures seated within the darkened interior rose from their stools and turned in our direction.

"Then I'll find someplace else."

I proceeded briskly ahead, soon finding an alleyway free of denizens. A duct extended out from the wall not far down, affording some privacy from which to unload my bladder. "Wait here," I told Issa.

"Be careful," she said.

The alleyway smelled like trash, and the corner I went to pee in smelled like stale urine. My piss came out a brownish color and made thing smell even worse, but was a big relief to release. At last, I buttoned up my fatigues and turned to leave.

"Noor Haji Fayrus," a strange, tinny voice sounded from the shadows opposite.

"Who's there?" I inquired, moving towards the alcove of a large duct.

"It is I, the Oracle," the voice said, but what emerged from the shadows was a robot with three eyes.

"What do you want?" I asked, wary of the automaton. It was ladylike, but had jerky and stiff movements, perhaps due to the abundant rust visible on its frame.

"Your time is coming, *Hoggaamiye*," she said, "and your destiny shall soon be fulfilled."

"What do you mean? What is my destiny?"

"The bullet of *Jannah* did not come to you by chance."

"*Maan fahmin.*" I told her that I didn't understand.

"Why have you been saving it all this time?"

I reached for my TT-30. It was still holstered fast to my thigh, the bullet of *Jannah* tucked snugly inside. "Waiting for the right moment, I guess. You're not really the Oracle, are you?"

"I chose you as the *Hoggaamiye* — Somalia's spiritual leader. Captain Shar'ma'arke gave you the bullets of *Jannah*, which can stop anything. Your emperor has started a worldwide plague. What does your heart speak?"

"I can't stop the plague with this bullet," I replied, then my brows curled queerly over my eyes, "can I?"

"The X-lix virus and its antigen is why Mogadishu continues to exist as the world's most successful city. This is what you wanted, but your journey is not yet completed, is it?"

"*Maya*," I replied, touching my sucked-in face and showing her my partially webbed hands, "I didn't want this."

"You expected more—" Her voice momentarily clipped out. "You still can have it."

"How can I return to what I once had? I want to go back."

"There is never any going back, only forward. The white star imprinted on your heart has darkened, but has not died. It waits only for you to rise."

"*Maan fahmin.* Talk square."

The robot pointed to my heart with squeaking joints and replied, "Zayid is cold, but you are not. You still have love. You are Somalia's rightful ruler, as chosen by *Jannah.* Take your bullet, see the emperor, and take back that which is yours."

"Are you suggesting—" I began, when suddenly, my shoulder was shoved from behind. I whipped around, brandishing my dagger.

"It's a miracle!" a ruffian mocked. "The *Hoggaamiye* has returned as promised by scripture!"

He was brandishing a weighty pipe and was flanked by three or four other riffraff, some of whom appeared to be cyborgs, as evinced by red lights just visible behind their dark glasses.

"I mean you no trouble," I replied, clearly outnumbered. I glanced over my shoulder, then did a double take. The rusty old oracle was gone. She must've disappeared back into the shadows, but how could she have done so without making a sound?

"You mean us no trouble?" the street-urchin said, then laughed with utter abandon. "You're the founding father of this shithole, but yeah, you mean us no trouble. You're just the guy who gave us the yoke of empire, then disappeared from the face of the earth once the shit hit the fan. But look, you're back! Must've been cryopreservation. You got to skip hundreds of years of disease and oppression. You've really got balls to come here like this."

"I'll take them," a cyborg behind him said with a warbling electronic voice. "I could use a new pair." A knife extracted from the top of his hand like a stiletto.

"His *qoodo* is probably the size of a lizard's nose," the ringleader quipped to the jeers of his henchmen, "but that's okay with me — you can have it. What I want is the *Hoggaamiye*'s head!" He raised his pipe far back.

I wasn't ready for this. I curled back.

As the thug went to crush me with his blow, a flash of white appeared over him, snatching the weapon from his grasp.

Issa 2.0 landed on the other side of us, holding the ringleader's pipe against him. Somehow, she'd leapt clear over him, taking his weapon as she passed. "Get behind me!" she told me.

I rolled over my shoulder, stopping behind her heels.

"What do we have here?" the kingpin asked. "An assembly chamber maid coming to save her great savior?"

The street urchins laughed.

"I'm warning you, stay back!" Issa reproached.

"What will you do, clean my tubes with that?" another rascal quipped. Watching him betwixt Issa's legs, I observed cracks in his body and wires running through his neck. He was pure robot.

"Time to end this," the ringleader said, then lunged at Issa.

My mechanical wife swung the pipe, landing a sharp glancing shot that shook him up pretty bad, but his robot henchman grabbed the end of the pipe in a flash.

Issa held on with a grip of death, soon falling forward.

I grabbed her free hand and pulled her back. A tug-of-war ensued, straining her every rod and wire.

The thug gave a strong twist of the pipe, tearing Issa's arm off in an ugly fashion. Her hand continued to grasp the weapon while wires dangled from her elbow where it'd been rudely severed.

The cyborg aggressor stabbed the pipe hard up beneath Issa's breastplate. Sparks flew and oil shot from her belly.

"No!" I cried, pulling her behind me.

The half-man/half-machine kept coming, soon to repeat his impaling technique on me.

The blue police sub I'd spotted earlier suddenly appeared over the alleyway. It emitted a loud siren and shone down a blinding spotlight.

"*Orod*!" cried one of the gang members, meaning *run*!

And run they did, the pipe dropping to my feet and bouncing weightily upon the pavement.

I placed my palms before my eyes and tried to glimpse the airship through my stigmata, then was lifted up beside Issa by a force that felt like the groundrush during a skydive, only in reverse. The reversal of gravity was so uncanny that I became nauseated, vomiting a black stream of puke that descended between my feet and disappeared into the intense light.

We were drawn into the hull of the flying sub and released over a padded floor, landing rather abruptly.

Bashir appeared over me seconds later, his glowing yellow deadlights staring deeply into mine. "*Wax waliba sow ma wanaagsana?*" he asked in Somali, inquiring if I was all right.

STATE OF THE UNION

"*WAAD WALANTAHAY*," the commander told me I must've been crazy to stroll into the Hodan quarter alone.

"Issa was with me, and I have Xubin," I replied, placing the steel ball on the seat beside me.

"That's not my point," he replied. "That's the most dangerous district in Mogadishu. You just don't go waltzing in there on foot."

"Nobody told me."

"Issa didn't tell you?" He looked surprised. "We'd better check her software then."

"Actually, come to think of it, she did warn me," I recalled, "several times. I knew you'd gone to the Hodan quarter and was intent on finding you. I insisted we go."

"What about your Xubin?"

"I kept it in my pocket."

Bashir raised his brows and puffed his cheeks in disbelief, then eased a bit, saying, "No matter — you wouldn't have listened to them, anyway. You always were a stubborn one, Noor. Thankfully you weren't killed."

I eyed Issa 2.0. She was lying on the padded floor and was being attended to by several onboard medics. "What's going to happen to her?"

"We'll reload her *Maskax* into a new automaton and recycle the old one."

"Will that be painful for her?"

Bashir eyed me curiously, then said, "Not in the least. It's like swapping a computer's hardware for something better, only the software remains the same."

"What will she look like?"

"How would you like for her to look?"

"Like she is now is fine, I guess; before she got all torn up, you know."

Issa looked over at me, and her eyes glowed brighter.

"Of course, Haji," Bashir said, briefly rubbing my shoulder. "We'll take care of her, no problem."

"Why didn't you apprehend those guys, anyway?"

"The prerogative was to extract you. The Hodan quarter is crawling with thugs and hooligans. So long as they stay in their shithole, we don't bother going after them. We've got bigger fish to fry — kingpins and insurgents who we prefer to take by surprise."

He slid open the blinds behind me, revealing the honeycombed Hodan quarter below. "As you can see, there's a skyway surrounding Mogadishu's inner periphery, and the Hodan quarter lies on the other side. Our security forces focus on who comes in, not out. There's been a longstanding debate on the council floor as to if we should make the southern skyway a solid wall, placing the Hodan quarter squarely on the 'outside' where the criminal underground would have to fend for themselves against the *xun gaajo* and other threats beyond our city walls."

"The detractors are mostly industrialists whose factories lie within the district," Bashir continued. "Obviously, we don't want to shut them out, but they already have their own security, so I don't think they'd have too much difficulty operating on the outside. Besides that, they'd no longer have to pay property tax and other fees for doing business within the city, so they might actually stand to profit."

Hodan Quarter, lower right, with southern skyway

He paused, looking back over the Hodan quarter as we glided past the inner perimeter. "But then there's the humanitarians," he continued with a scoff. "They say it's criminal to shut so many people out. How they love to remain in denial about these 'people.'" He threw up some quotation marks. "But down there reside the dregs of society and all manner of illegal hybrids. Had

Issa not contacted me, had we gotten there only seconds later, you would've been killed by petty traffickers and both of your body parts would've been sold on the black market."

"For the love of Allah," I gasped. "And you still didn't apprehend them?"

"Like I said, *walalo*, the goal was to extract you. Rounding up petty traffickers is not the way to get to the kingpins and labs, because these latter are highly transient and know exactly when to move. The way to break their operations and put them before the *Safaarad* is to catch them by surprise, which usually involves going in undercover. Need I remind you I'm with the *hanti wadaagnimo?*"

"The secret police, I know."

"It's a real quagmire down there, Haji, with ranking Somali companies suspected in the manufacturing of contraband. We have *hanti wadaagnimo* physically in the Hodan, and investigating the companies from afar.

"But the biggest threats are cells of anarchist insurgents who actively plot against the empire. You can't just fly over the Hodan and pluck up random denizens, hoping to find the worst amongst them; for these we rely on intelligence vectoring from a wide range of sources, then conduct highly pointed operations in the criminals' capture."

"Is the guy you went after this morning an insurgent?"

"*Haa*, his name's Will Waabeeri, and he came to our attention as an A-level target a few months ago. We fear he may be operating not as an anarchist, but for a foreign country seeking to destabilize us from within. He's well trained and highly dangerous. He's been recruiting the young and disenfranchised, training them in secret locations underground."

"So you didn't catch him?"

"*Maya*," he conceded with a scowl. "But we'll get him! For now, I want you to stay far clear of the Hodan quarter. You should stay in your domicile until you've fully recovered. It's good for you to walk, but you shouldn't leave your neighborhood on the hill, not until you know more about this city. The empire still has bad areas and assassins who target heads of state. You're still part of the council, Haji. Rest assured you'll be targeted in some areas — actually it could happen anyplace. This is the current state of the union. Listen to Issa next time, and keep your Xubin on. It can see three-hundred and sixty degrees and will alert you to any dangers or newsflashes."

"*Waan kan xumahay*," I apologized. "I was just trying to find you."

"Well, you found me," he chuckled, then looked out the window as we cruised slowly over the city, apparently on patrol. As far as Issa 2.0, the medics or technicians or whoever they were had taken her away.

"What's on your mind, Haj?" Bashir continued like the old confidant he was. "I know this must be a very difficult time for you. Recall rebellion can take weeks if not months to get over, but rest assured you will, and then I would like for you to join me on the force."

"The police force?"

"The *hanti wadaagnimo*, Haji — the elite in domestic security. You can join me in the strong arm of intelligence; you'd be the perfect fit."

I gazed out the window, to the ocean to the east. I had no answer for the commander. Only time would tell my destiny, for I was still very confused and had many questions yet unanswered. "I want to meet Zayid," I said outright.

"The emperor?" he replied with an air of surprise.

"*Haa*. It was suggested you might be able to get me in contact with him."

"Who told you that?"

"Xubin."

"*Hmm*, I see. Well, *saaxiib*, I know he was very fond of you in the past, so I suppose it wouldn't hurt to ask."

"Why would it hurt to ask?" I inquired, suddenly peeved. "I led the *afgembi*. If it wasn't for me and my army of refugees, the coup d'état that founded this empire would've failed miserably."

"*Waan ogahay*, Haji, I know — but that's not what I meant. For his own protection, Emperor Cecchi is very reclusive. He lives in a highly secured compound in Zeilah, on the outside. Like I said, he was very fond of you, so will probably be open to a meeting. Let me put out the request, and we'll see what comes back. He'll probably want you to fly out on his once-weekly shipment of supplies rather than scheduling a private charter. It would be less conspicuous and wouldn't trigger the whole cavalcade of consorts usually required when dignitaries travel to the outside."

"Am I a dignitary? For some reason I don't feel like one."

"You just woke up, Haji. Give it time. You may be a blast from the past, but for those in the know, like Zayid, you're still a councilman of the highest order."

"*Mahadsanid, walalo*," I thanked him as a *brother*. "Let me know what happens." I yawned involuntarily.

"I shall, *saaxiib*. For now, let's get you back to your residence. I'm still on duty, and it looks like you could use some shut-eye."

"Aye-aye, commander, that sounds good to me."

With that, I was delivered back to the front door of my compound via the airship's gravity beam. Thankfully, going down was not as discomforting as going up. I gave two thumbs up to Commander Bashir, but didn't know if he could see me in his space sub before it left.

I was summarily waved through my building's security, then rode the lift back up to my fifth-floor flat, where a cold lunch and hot bath were already waiting. After taking pleasure in both, I turned on my Xubin and placed it over my bed table, then closed the curtains via voice command. Staring up at the ceiling, I fell into a deep sleep...

‿

"*Asraar, asraar...*" three hairless, pale beings chanted over and over again as they grasped for a key floating in water or space, but no matter how hard they tried, they could never reach it.

Such composed the uncanny scene of my dream, one that'd been recurring for as long as I could remember; only now, it was becoming more clear and comprehensible. While I knew *asraar* pertained to mystical knowledge attainable by Somali religious ascetics (called sheikhs), I knew little else of the Somali Sufi orders, and knew nothing of the mystical knowledge itself.

Even Xubin, upon my waking, could reveal little of Islamic mystic philosophy, save for the fact that the sheikhs were part of a certain *tariqa* order, and in Somalia, this order had traditionally been practiced by three movements: *Qadiriya, Salihiyah*, and *Ahmediya*. All three movements shared a common founding father, but had no allegiance to any clan. As far as their specific beliefs and practices, Xubin was at a loss. A query for more information about the sect on the empire's intranet, called **ROTOS**, where all Xubins received their core data, came back as "not found," while a query for details pertaining to *asraar* came back as "forbidden."

FLYING WITH BUTTERFLIES

THREE SUNS PASSED, and I found myself suited up in special armor designed for flights "outside," with abundant, lightweight plating that was said to be bulletproof and a pack containing a wingsuit, which Bashir said was preferable to just a parachute for people like myself who knew how to fly a wingsuit. In the unlikely event of spacecraft evacuation, I'd be able to track further before landing, hopefully avoiding a radioactive bog. My weapons consisted of my TT-30 pistol, my father's dagger, and a laser gun called a *gub falaadh* (arrow that burns), which looked like an elongated handgun. I was seated beside Issa 3.0, the name change reflecting she'd been fitted with a new body, which was just like her previous one. If she carried any weaponry, it wasn't visible to me, but one thing was for sure, I trusted in her strength and speed.

Our flight would be a standard one, Bashir had assured me, and there were rarely any eventualities, the pilot relayed as we lifted off the main Mogadishu tarmac. Two yellow butterflies fluttered about the cockpit — fauna from the emperor's cargo delivery that had somehow gotten free.

"Not again," the co-pilot groaned, removing his headphones to go after the critters. The flight indeed appeared quotidian.

I was most interested in the passage over the outside. I'd half expected to see hundreds of devourers herding against the city walls, but such was not the case. However, as we continued north over the bogs, it was not long until I saw them walking aimlessly about.

We maintained an altitude of roughly three hundred meters, which appeared to be the general altitude of the other spacecraft I'd seen since my jump through time. Below, the pale skin of the *xun gaajo* stood in stark contrast to the dark green waters they waded through, but as we continued north over savannah, they were harder to spot in the tall grass. Acacia trees peppered the savannah with shadow. If pods of *xun gaajo* were sheltering beneath them, I couldn't tell.

"I haven't seen any *qoriismaris,*" I spoke into my headphone receiver.

"You'll never see them by day," the co-pilot replied. "They sleep in the bogs like crocodiles, with only their nostrils poking out of the water, and in the burnt they sleep in caves. At nighttime, they come out, along with all the snakes. You wouldn't want to be stuck down there at night, especially during a full moon — that's when they come out to hunt, and they see best with moonlight. Would you like some *muqumad?*" He offered me a slice of jerked meat. "Soon we'll have to put on rad-masks."

"Not him," the pilot put in. "He's a new breed."

"*Mahadsanid,*" I thanked the co-pilot for the beef jerky, then asked, "what's a new breed?"

"People like you who are fully immune to radiation, thanks to the antigen," the pilot replied.

I bit off a piece of jerked meat; it was good and sweet. "What's the burnt?" I asked as I mulled the dry, tender beef.

"The Guban," the co-pilot said, pointing out the windshield, "just ahead."

"The northern desert," I recalled.

"*Haa,* it reaches clear up to the north shore. Emperor Cecchi's tower is in the middle of it. The tower itself is called Zeilah, for the province was destroyed long ago."

"The province was destroyed?"

"*Haa*, the Zeilah Sultanate was hit during the first nuclear exchange of twenty thirteen. The emperor has roots there, so chose the name for his fiefdom."

"Fiefdom? So people live there now?"

"In his tower, *haa*, but not outside. It's still a wasteland. Radiation levels are too high. The emperor uses this area for nuclear testing."

"Bombs?"

"Sometimes. He's perfecting the X-6 antigen here, so keeps the area sufficiently radiated to monitor the drug's effectiveness in a real-world environment."

"Masks, please," the pilot said, pulling on a facemask with tube feeds, presumably for oxygen. The co-pilot did the same.

"What about her?" I asked, pointing at Issa.

The airmen laughed.

"Automatons are immune," the pilot replied, and left it at that. He engaged his throttle bar and began a controlled descent.

The desolation of the burnt was striking to me, even for a guy who was used to seeing arid deserts. I saw absolutely no shrubbery, no oases, no trees, and no wadis. Most peculiarly, I observed no patterns left by togs, which are riverbeds that become rapids during seasonal downpours. Perhaps the seasons here had changed or been eliminated by the war and its effect upon the atmosphere. A lone structure loomed up in the distance like a giant water tower.

"Look!" I observed, tearing into my *muqumad*. "Sixty degrees astarboard. People, in the desert."

"Devourers," the pilot said.

"Are you sure? They look normal to me."

"Believe me, mate, they're anything but normal. It's just our perception, being up high. But those are *xun gaajo* of the highest order."

"Are they different?"

"You can bet your *footo* on that, Councilman. The devourers of the burnt are like the ones of the Great Shelter. They're big, strong, and fast."

"*Waayo?*" I asked, *why?*

"Zayid's testing," the co-pilot put in. "The emperor has set up feeding centers to keep them well fed. He needs a strong strain of devourer to perfect the antigen. Also, the increased radiation has caused them to mutate and adapt more rapidly, becoming more resistant."

"Emperor Cecchi feeds those zombies?" I inquired, aghast.

"Not zombies, mate," the pilot remarked. "Remember, those are just infected people, albeit many generations into their disease. But the emperor is close to a cure. If he can perfect the X-6 antigen, he can reverse the disease."

"What does he feed them?"

"Genetically engineered meat, mostly."

"It's part of our cargo," the co-pilot added, pointing to the back.

The Somali Pirate 3 – White Star Empire

The desert appeared to glow in its own radioactive mirage, while dead ahead, the emperor's tower thrust thousands of feet into the sky, soon growing out of our purview above. We glided towards a skyport along the massive edifice.

Approaching the emperor's tower, the Fiefdom of Guban

"Is the tower secure from radiation?"

"*Maya*," the pilot said, *no*. "Like you, the emperor is immune. Co-pilot, prepare for landing."

We landed over a circular platform that appeared much too small for our spaceship. Only when we disembarked did I realize the craft was employing anti-gravity technology that kept it hovering above the little landing pad. A walkway extension led into an elevator silo, where a lift was open and waiting.

"Go on in," the co-pilot said, "the emperor will see to your arrival. Send him our regards. We're going to offload the cargo. We'll be here to take you back."

I waved off the friendly flight crew, then proceeded over the causeway and entered the lift alongside Issa 3.0. The doors drifted to a close with hydraulic smoothness.

The elevator moved us rapidly up into the emperor's tower. I double-checked my TT-30, not knowing what to expect.

THE TRAP IS SET

THE ELEVATOR OPENED, and we followed a series of neon orange arrows down a dark, mazelike hallway. The labyrinthine entrance seemed in line with the tower's sheer size and secretiveness, so I was not particularly alarmed by it.

We came to a sort of lobby with a receptionist resembling Issa 3.0, only she had a black exoframe, not white. Behind her, a nuclear warning seal was set into the black marble like a corporate icon.

"Welcome to Zeilah," the android said, sounding perfectly human. "The emperor has been expecting you."

She stood and placed a hand before the radiation sign. It glowed neon yellow, and her palm seemed to emit a similarly hued light, then she pressed the icon like it was a huge button and it began retracting in concentric circles.

As the portal expanded, the figure of Zayid Cecchi appeared, his eye patch having been replaced by some sort of electronic scope. He was sharply dressed in a three-piece suit and tie, and somehow looked younger. Had he received a facelift?

"Councilman Haji," said he, extending his hand, "*assalaamu calaykum!* It's so good to see you again."

"*Calaykum assalaam!*" I obliged.

His grip was exceedingly firm, even though his black leather glove was tight around his hand.

"And this must be Issa," he inquired.

"So they say," I replied.

"It's my pleasure to make your acquaintance, *Signora* Fayrus."

Issa 3.0 replied with a nod.

"A lovely frame you have," the emperor said. "I love the clean lines of the natural automaton. There's nothing as stimulating as intercourse with the pure *Maskax.*"

"*Iga raalli ahow?*" I asked, *excuse me?*

"Conversing with the pure soul is the sweetest gift to man."

I raised my brows.

"Have you eaten?" he inquired.

"Not really."

"Amaranta has prepared a wonderful lunch. Please, *waddadan hay* — follow me to my lounge. We've so much catching up to do. We never did get to finish our conversation."

He told his android receptionist, named Xafladeeday, to hold any calls save for Mahmoud Ahmadinejad, then the circular door closed between her and us with a pneumatic snap as if a giant jar were being pressure sealed.

The emperor led us deeper into his residence. We passed numerous long, dark corridors running off on both sides before arriving at a large study of sorts, with tall bookshelves for walls, leather chairs set here and there around a mariner's globe, and an abundant dining table facing the windows. Outside was all smoky yellow and amber as the heat of the burnt drifted up from the radioactive wasteland below.

Zayid sauntered over to a minibar and asked, "Can I offer you a *spremuta*, Noor?"

My throat was parched from the journey, so I welcomed the Italian orange drink, saying, "*Haa, mahadsanid.*"

"And for you, Signora Fayrus," he offered Issa 3.0 a small, bullet-shaped vile filled with a purple liquid.

"*Waad mahadsantahay,*" she replied with gratitude, placing the capsule in her side.

"*Waa maxay kaasi?*" I asked what the stuff was.

"*Biyo macdanaysan saliid,*" Zayid said, meaning something like fortified oil. "It's like water to an automaton, and is as sweet as can be in a dry place like this."

"*Haa,*" she confirmed, adding it was like a painkiller, "*xanuun joojiye.*"

We took a seat around the table and sipped our drinks. Zayid asked me how I liked the twenty-fourth century. I told him I was still getting used to it. I wanted to ask him about the X-lix virus and its antigen, X-6, which Xubin had said were both invented by the man before me in order to spread a global pandemic through which only Somalia would be spared, guaranteeing the empire's centuries-long dominance, but I had to broach the subject subtly. The more innocent my intentions appeared to be, the more Zayid might be willing to open up to me.

"Who else pulled through deep sleep?" I asked. "Admiral Cosob? Lieutenant-Commander Xeed? My uncle Osman or sister Fatuma?"

"Bashir didn't tell you?"

"We only talked about Issa. I don't even know where my kids are."

"I'll look into it," he said. "Issa might not even know, depending on her *Maskax* upload. But of course, this needs to be found out for certain, so I promise to get to the bottom of it. Living here in Zeilah tower, I tend to be hyper-focused on the political matters that revolve around running the country. My apologies."

"*Dhib ma laha.*" I told him it was okay.

"But I can say that Xeed pulled through, as did Cosob. In their sunset years, they both opted for their character abstracts to be uploaded into exoframes."

"They're robots?"

"Not robots, Haji. Automatons."

"What's the difference?"

"The *Maskax*. Robots are fully preprogrammed and can be totally controlled by the Mainframe. Automatons, like your beautiful wife Issa here, maintain their own human identities via their *Maskax*. They maintain their natural personalities and attain much higher levels of independence, once their *Maskax* becomes accustomed to their new environment. In short, the individual psyche continues via the *Maskax*, while the exoframe — the automaton — enables it to occupy a physical existence indefinitely, that is, so long as automaton hardware is available."

"*Waan fahmaa.* The Xubin told me as much."

"*Haa,* so Xeed and Cosob are still around. I think they're currently in the field, but I know they'll be overjoyed to see you again."

"In the field?"

"*Waranle* elites and high-level operatives from the old guard — from the time of the Great Revolution — often serve as combat automatons on our expeditionary fronts overseas. Their immunity to the plague enables us to maintain a presence in former superpowers such as the Great Shelter. Enemy governments are constantly trying to restructure themselves so that they can grow stronger, so we are out there actively preempting that from happening. The White Star Empire is the world leader now, *jaalle.* A return to the days of slavery, of our oppression by foreign powers — we can never let this happen. You would know that more than anybody."

"Are these destabilizing campaigns being waged across the globe?"

"*Haa* — but mostly where the former colonial empires are trying to take root again."

"Is that why you invented the X-lix virus?" I probed.

"And it's antigen, *jaalle.* I did it for Somalia, and finally we have *xoriyad.*"

"Freedom."

"*Haa.* You know, Haji—" he began, but someone came in, catching his eye. "Ah, Amaranta's arrived with her wonderful preparations. Perhaps that's why you came back to see me, eh, Haj?" he laughed.

I chuckled along, remaining cordial. "*Hayye*, Amaranta," I told her hello.

She was wearing a burqa that hid her face completely, and replied with what sounded like a hiss. She approached the table slowly, and carefully set the tray of food down.

"Please forgive her," Zayid said. "She just got over a bad flu that completely wiped out her voice. She chose to wear a *chadri* burqa so as not to risk spreading her germs. She's no longer contagious, but I think she was a little concerned, preparing the food and all."

"You poor thing, you shouldn't have," I told her as I touched her arm, which was also covered, like the rest of her body, with the long black garment. "I hope you're feeling better."

"Much better," Zayid said. "When she heard you were coming, she became very excited and insisted on cooking for you. Who am I to stop her?" He chuckled with a wink as if he had spoken something satirical. "*Cara*," said he, calling his wife sweetheart in Italian, "allow me the pleasure of introducing you to Signora Fayrus."

Amaranta looked towards Issa 3.0 without answering.

Zayid then told my automaton "wife": "Amaranta has read Haji's books and is amazed by your story, Issa;

by your overcoming such great challenges and hardships, especially in the early days."

"*Haddii Eebbe yidhaahdo,*" Issa 3.0 began, citing the will of God, "it was Imam Abdullahi and Noor—" she paused to look at me, "—Noor and his family that helped me. If it wasn't for them, I'd be lost."

"And if it wasn't for you, Issa," Zayid replied, "and good wives such as Amaranta, my sweet, men like us would also be lost at sea."

He raised his glass of spremuta, so I obliged the toast to good wives, even though it bothered me he kept calling Issa 3.0 my wife.

Amaranta set dishes of food before us, then departed with her tray.

"*Bismillaah!*" Zayid toasted the meal. "Dig in!"

Following his lead, I reached my hand into a pile of warm rice, then shoveled a piece of meat on top of it with my thumb. "What is this?" I inquired.

"*Hilib idaad toon basbaas leh,*" he said, meaning mutton with spicy garlic sauce.

It smelled as good as it sounded, so without further ado, I stuck the sticky ball into my mouth and began to chew. "*Dhadhan leh,*" I said it was delicious, and wasn't bluffing.

"*Mahadsanid, Haji* — Amaranta will be pleased." The emperor offered Issa 3.0 more enriched oil, but she said she was sated for now.

"Isn't Amaranta eating?" I inquired.

"I insisted she come and join us, but the stoic little butterfly insisted on keeping her distance, due to her recent illness, of course. She said she was happy to tend to the cooking for now, and will take some soup in the kitchen. Afterwards, she'd like to lounge around a bit with us."

"*Waad mahadsantahay.*" I told him I was grateful. We ate like kings.

༄

About halfway through the meal, a holographic screen suddenly appeared before Zayid. The robot receptionist appeared, saying, "Mahmoud Ahmadinejad is on Vectex. Are you available?"

"*Haa*, Xafladeeday," replied the emperor, "*mahadsanid.* Please put him on." Then he apologized to us, "*Iga raalli ahaada* while I take this call."

"*Dhib ma laha!*" I told him *no problem!*

After a moment of video static, the face of Iran's president, circa 2013, appeared on the virtual screen.

"*Assalaamu calaykum, Madaxweyne* Ahmadinejad," Zayid said.

"*Calaykum assalaam,* Emperor Cecchi," replied Ahmadinejad.

"Have you located the ship?"

"I regret to inform, Emperor, that it was hijacked by pirates."

"Nationality?"

"Unknown. Submarine intercept. They disappeared as quickly as they surfaced."

"With everything?"

"Regrettably, Emperor, yes. Even the vessel was sunk."

"What happened to your escorts?" Zayid asked.

"They were sailing too far off. The sub came up from nowhere, and the hijacking went off almost in the blind. We extracted a sole survivor clinging to some flotsam."

"Interrogate him further," Zayid ordered, the leather tightening around his fist. "This will be a hard recon. Do you have any submersibles in the vicinity?"

"We've a nuclear class sub based in Chabahar. We can send it out."

"Do so quickly, Ahmadinejad. Focus sonar on the Gulf of Oman. You've less than ninety minutes before the thieves slip through."

"*Haa*, right away, Emperor."

"CC me on all status updates. Since this happened in your waters, I require that you split the cost of the lost vessel and its cargo."

"*Haa*, Allah bless you, Emperor. But we still need more antigen — our state supply is running low."

"This time," Zayid growled, "include your sub as escort, otherwise the entire cost will be shifted on you. You know that we're not liable for your property once it reaches the Gulf. That's your responsibility."

"*Haa*, Emperor. My sincerest apologies."

"Very well, then, I'll prepare another shipment. Be prepared for a Gulf handoff in forty-eight hours."

"*Allahu Akbar!*" the grizzled Iranian remarked. "We'll be waiting with a full escort."

"Please CC me on the current recon."

"*Haa.*"

"Vecting off."

"Vecting off."

With that, the face of President Ahmadinejad disappeared.

"Xafladeeday?" Zayid inquired.

The screen came back on, and the android receptionist reappeared. "Please forward a copy of that last Vectex to Commander Ahmed at Centcom," Zayid ordered.

"*Heshiis!*" she replied, apparently meaning *affirmative!*

"Vecting off."

The screen switched off again. Zayid apologized to me, saying he and President Ahmadinejad were great allies, but pirates had seized a shipment of antigen bound for Iran.

"Why wasn't the antigen flown by plane?" I asked.

"EMP activity over Iran is too great."

"What do you mean?"

"Satellite assets launched by Western powers are still bombarding the region with electromagnetic pulses," he explained. "These pulses can severely cripple or disable any electrical current, making most flights into the area too risky. Large sailing vessels, not unlike the dhows of the early days, are sent instead."

As he spoke, I kept noticing an old photograph hanging on the wall behind him. It depicted a young woman sitting on the ground between two older women who were attending to her beautification. I squinted over Zayid to see it.

"Ah, a real picture," he said, beaming. "Guess who it's of?"

"*Ma ogi*," I said I didn't know, "but she looks kind of familiar."

He set down his glass and retrieved the framed photo, placing it beside me on the table.

My eyes widened. I dropped my half-eaten shank of mutton and exclaimed, "Amina Rage!"

"That it is, *jaalle* — at sweet sixteen."

"Where in *Jannah* did you get this?"

"Ahh, I was just getting to that back at the *ascendo*, remember? It was the twenty-first century, and you were in a terrible hurry to get somewhere. I was hoping it would be a lot sooner than three hundred years before I saw you again, but time has had a funny way with us, hasn't it, lad?"

"Yeah, I'll say. Who are these people behind her? What are they doing?"

"Preparing her for her wedding."

"With Jamal Awaad?"

"Of course. You were just a boy then. The wedding took place in Las Qoray and was attended by your mother and father. The women behind her were on Jamal's side of the family, in the Reer Salaax sub-clan. As you may know, her marriage was arranged to strengthen the alliance between the Reer Salaax and Warsangali sub-clans."

"But how did you get a hold of this picture? Is it part of your antiques collection?"

"*Saaxiib*, this portrait is especially meaningful to me. It comes, not from my oeuvre of *Somalinimo* artifacts, but from my extended family album."

"*Maan fahmin.*"

"Indeed, this part of your family history is something I wouldn't expect you to understand, for from the beginning, I had endeavored to keep it quiet. You see, Amina is Warsangali and Jamal is Reer Salaax, just as Amaranta is Warsangali and I, through my father's second wife, am Reer Salaax. The *boqor* of my father's time had made great efforts to bring those two sub-clans closer together, and that's why my own marriage was arranged. I, too, soon learned the importance of these sub-clans' entente."

"Which is?"

"To strengthen the Warsangali Sultanate for the empire to come."

"You were planning the empire even back then? I have a hard time believing that."

"The empire of Somalia had been an objective of Italy long before that. The participation of Somalia's clans was more of an afterthought to avoid any messy misunderstandings. I know this may be hard for you to hear, *saaxiib*, as it would be for any patriotic Somali who would learn the truth of the White Star Empire's origins, but rest assured, the plan always was, and always shall be, to empower Somalia as a capitalist caliphate under the aegis of Italy."

"*Dalka Talyaaniga?*"

"*Haa*, of Italy. Initially, other countries were involved. It started in 1884 at the Berlin Conference, where major European powers met to decide on how they'd carve up Africa among themselves. The Italians, the Brits, and the French took a special interest in Somalia due to its proximity to the shipping lanes through the Suez Canal — "the highway to India" — where colonial powers were already heavily vested.

"Competition for Northern Somalia soon grew fierce, with the triumvirate of imperialists playing musical chairs with one another as they sought to occupy it for themselves. In the meantime, Somalia national sovereignty movements increased their resistance to European powers, such as in the 1896 Battle of Adowa. In that momentous standoff, Menelik, the founder of modern Ethiopia — at least until I took over — defeated the Italian forces in Somaliland, thereby checking the Italian aspiration to occupy all the Horn of Africa. It was then that the wiser of the Italian strategists, such as those in the Cecchi military lineage, started wooing Somalilanders of power and influence into new alliances, for we discovered that co-opting the locals into a colonial endeavor was far easier and more effective in the long term than trying to annex foreign lands without at least the tacit consent of the host populace.

"My father had a harem and married one of his Somali mistresses for precisely that reason — to strengthen his own alliances, and those of Italy, for the purpose of imperial statecraft. My marriage with Amaranta was arranged for this same purpose, as was that of Amina Rage with Jamal Abdallah Awaad; only your older sister's marriage is especially meaningful to me, for it was my first and she was a *'alanqad.*"

"*Iga raalli ahow?*" I asked, *excuse me?* I was becoming quite impatient with Zayid's imperialist gibberish.

"*Haa,* Haji, as I mentioned to you before, Amina was a mystical priestess who could be visited by *zaar,* which was a very powerful spirit. I arranged her marriage, not only to help align the clans most important to imperial statecraft and the future empire, but to elicit your sister's supernatural powers for the purpose of building an army of superhuman beings that could not be defeated, of which you and the Oracle are part of."

"*Maxaa?*"

"Your sister's training in the UAE, comrade, did not come by chance. Neither was the Oracle's psychological training of you happenstance. You were both being prepped to become unconquerable leaders in Zayid's navy — my Organization, the Dagger Dogs of Zayid. For you, that training continues today, even as we speak."

"*Was* you!" I told him to fuck off.

"You cannot offend me, for your reaction is natural and expected, but you'll soon learn that this is all for the best.

"Much of the empire's success is stored on ROTOS, the Mainframe's Real-Time Operating System Nucleus. It is stored as factual history that all Xubins can access, but you, Haji, and your sister Amina were my greatest secret weapons — my first human subjects in the *antibaayootig* experiments. You both performed exemplarily, and look! Now you're healed and ten times as powerful! You're immune! Had only Nasir done his job and kept administering the serum to Amina, she'd be with us now, celebrating our success. That's why I had to dispatch Nasir. He had no idea what he was doing to go against my dictates and those of Doctor Sooraan. You can blame Amina's death on *Dhakhtar* Nasir, and him alone."

My fears were confirmed: Zayid Cecchi was crazy. I put my hand on my TT-30. I knew I had to off him, but I also knew that Issa and I were sealed in his lair. I had to think this one out carefully, be patient and tactful in order to get away with our lives.

"I see," I played along, staying in character, "so we were just pawns in your master plan."

"Not pawns, *saaxiib*, more like rooks protecting the king. I control this empire, but needed you to garner national support for it, while Amina helped infuse my reign with the protection of supernatural beings. I sent the Oracle to you in the mountains of Socotra, in the deserts of Guban, and in the slums of the Hodan. I arranged for the illusion of Captain Shar'ma'arke on the Selection Ministry freighter, and I arranged for him to give you the bullets of *Jannah.* These things were done to give you faith in yourself so that the Somali people would have faith in you and the coming Empire, and also there was a strictly alchemic element in delivering you certain items and serums. The powers I gave you made you look like a God-man to your followers, while at the same time aided in my experiments to develop a plague-resistant human. The genetic hybrid with the bat species was an important part of the medicine's success, while your unexpected brush with ball lightning during the helicopter crash serendipitously solved the missing link to the antigen. What was missing was more congenital electromagnetic power, which when artificially applied in heavy force enables the subject to temporarily control the flow of electrons. You have no idea what a breakthrough this was in the creation of a super-being closer to that of Samale, the original, pure Somali fighter who could wield cosmic power at will. Far from a pawn, Haji, you're my right-hand man, my AUTOEXEC.BAT, and together we shall conquer the universe, for I've already conquered the ages. The universe is all that's left.

"I knew that as the *Hoggaamiye*," he continued, "you would not agree with a *Faranji* as emperor of your beloved *Soomaaliya*, and furthermore I knew that it wouldn't be long out of cryogenic preservation that you'd seek the title of emperor for yourself. You've always had that drive for great leadership; it's only taken a while to fully develop. So I sent the Oracle into the Hodan. Actually, from offsite, I programmed an old XOR operator that was already there to convince you to come and usurp me. You see, Haji, this was your final test. I wanted to see if you still had it in you, and I see that you do. But you cannot kill me now, for then you shall die, too, along with your lovely wife. I control the *Maskax* files and have Xafladeeday at the ready to destroy them should something befall me, which would spell the permanent end of you both."

I moved my hand from my pistol to my *gub falaadh*, for Zayid wasn't even worth my bullet of *Jannah*. I also knew that with my laser gun, I'd get more than one shot should he somehow mount a counterattack.

"This is all part of your reeducation, Haji. I know you don't want to stay here another minute, let alone an entire day, but soon you shall, *saaxiib*, for as the seconds tick by and I continue to enlighten you, and as we tour my grand facility and its deepest mysteries, you'll slowly come to realize what a great blessing has come to pass. We are finally aligned as masters of our world, as brothers-in-clan, and as family once again. And how very quaint it is that our wives are here for our momentous reunion. I see my *macaan* now. She's coming with dessert."

As Amaranta shuffled in, I let go of my *gub falaadh*. The fact was, we'd need a clean exit, which was not yet assured. I was also very curious about Zayid and his many predictions regarding my behavior and intentions. As much as I believed he was a psychopath, I could not deny that his analysis of me, and the situation at hand, carried elements of truth. It was almost as if he had ESP, for even when I took my hands off my guns — which were under the table, out of his view — he visibly eased.

"*Kani waa maxay?*" He asked his wife what she had prepared.

She dropped a pie from a few inches up. It landed still it its tin, hitting the table with a heavy *thunk*!

"*Torta della Nonna*!" Zayid remarked. "You're gonna love this, Haji, I can guarantee it. Next to her spiced coffee, it's the best thing in the world!"

"I have no recollection of *Torta della Nonna*," Issa 3.0 said. "What is it?" I got the sense she was looking out for me.

"*Torta della Nonna* is a traditional Tuscan dessert," Zayid explained. "It's a custardy shortbread pie. Just imagine, Issa, a shot or two of pure red *biyo macdanaysan saliid*, and that's what it's like. Haji, as my honored guest, you get the first slice."

Amaranta shuffled back towards the door.

"Are you getting some *mirra kahwa, macaan?*" Zayid called out to her, but she kept walking and did not answer.

"Poor thing," Zayid told us. "The flu really got her tongue. Go ahead, Haji, try the *Torta della Nonna*."

I stared down at the slice of pie sitting on a plate before me.

"Don't worry, it's not poisoned. Here, I'll prove it." He reached his fork over and cut off the tip of my slice, then summarily consumed it.

I was not in the mood for pie, but seeing it was safe to eat, I took a bite just to play along. It was like the breakfast pastries I'd been served on his trimaran: creamy, sweet, and heavy. When he asked how I liked it, I told him I wasn't used to such rich desserts, but I had to admit it was quite tasty.

"Save some pie for Amaranta's coffee," he said. "It's the perfect counterpart."

"Zayid, let me ask you," I cut to the chase. "If you're responsible for creating the illusion of Captain Shar'ma'arke on the Selection Ministry ship, then are you also responsible for its cargo?"

"The Captain Shar'ma'arke hologram was my idea, as were the nuclear, diamond-plated bullets that were released into your hands. They were hot off the press, aye, but weren't supposed to burn through your palms. I'm really sorry about that, comrade. That stunt didn't go off quite as planned." He served himself a slice of pie. "But your stigmata came with something of a silver lining. After all, if your pirate followers consciously realized it or not, the holes made you look like perhaps you were capable of performing miracles. Again, I do apologize about that, and about the resistance you faced in the hijacking. The crew was instructed to allow you to seize the ship and board without incident. Fucking Swedes," he ranted, "too cocksure to pick up on coded instructions."

"But the cargo," I probed, "the nuclear waste. It was from Selection Ministry Island, was it not?"

"Ah, yes," he said nonchalantly as he chewed on his pie. "I was going to get to that, but in your classic investigative knack, you beat me to it.

"Selection Ministry Island. You probably know by now, from your Xubin no doubt, that the X-lix virus and its antigen were developed there. But what Xubins cannot access is the real news about my brainchild laboratory. When you and your uncle broke into it, little did you know how close you were to discovering the ultimate mysteries of Project Samale. It was all happening on the third level down — just one below where you were.

"Samale was the one true God, Haji. He was the reason for the antigen, the empire, and was the higher purpose you and I served. I believed I was put on this planet to reconstruct the original demigod incarnate, just as I created you to protect him and see to his great return.

"The third level down held all the secrets to the universe, and you, my class model, were *that* close to discovering it. I always knew I could count on you to sniff out the truth, no matter how well hidden.

"Samale is rising, *saaxiib*, and will soon smite the infidels and rid the world once and for all of its weak excuses for human beings. The insipid *Homo sapien* sloths are a far cry from you and me, Haji — and not just in their lack of strength and intelligence, but evolutionarily speaking, they are by and large a fading race. I've already crippled them severely, and soon the One True Father shall return to deliver the final blow. You were created in His image to rise in His Light, high above the mire of man's destruction."

I put my hand back on my pistol. This guy was totally nuts. "Does Bashir know about this? About your master plan?"

"Ah, here's Amaranta with the spiced coffee. Over here, *macaan*."

We were in plain sight of her from the moment she appeared, so why did he have to tell her where to go? She looked slightly disoriented, probably on account of her full-length burqa. The mesh over her eyes appeared rather thick, even for a *chadri*. Or maybe Zayid was just trying to dodge my question. "How much does Commander Bashir know?" I asked again.

"By now, Commander Bashir probably has it pretty well figured out."

"So all this time he was prepping me to be one of your rooks?"

Amaranta shuffled towards me with a tray of steaming coffee.

"He was doing his job to train you for promotions — that is all. At the time, even he didn't know how it tied into the greater prospectus."

"What greater prospectus?"

"This," he said, opening his hands like Jesus at the Last Supper, "the White Star Empire that I now control."

"*We'el!*" I cursed, for Amaranta had tripped, splashing hot coffee on me as she fell. It singed the side of my neck, but fortunately, my exosuit spared me greater injury. As for her, she had struck her head loudly against the side of the table when she went down.

"*Wax waliba sow ma wanaagsana?*" I asked if she was all right. She was kneeling on the floor next to me, holding the sides of her head and moaning in pain.

"Let me see," I said, lifting away her head cover.

She spun around and hissed.

Her canines were sharp like mine, while her eyes — or what was left of them — were covered by facial skin.

I jumped back, aghast. "What the hell's wrong with her?" I gasped, training my TT-30 on her hideous face.

"Put that away, you monster!" Zayid scolded me, then knelt down and cradled her noggin against his chest. "Can't you see my poor *macaan* has hit her head?"

"What did you do to her!?" I demanded, now training my gun on him.

"He held up a hand and cowered back as if I were the evil one. "What do you mean?" he pleaded. "My beautiful wife has hit her head. Please, Haji, Issa, help us!"

Issa 3.0 was standing behind me, touching my shoulder as if I were protecting her. Suddenly, an alarm went off, and the Vectex screen appeared next to us.

"Devourers!" Zayid exclaimed, pointing at the virtual screen. "They've breached the facility!"

Indeed, a burly *xun gaajo* could be seen making its way over the landing bridge towards the containership pilots.

The flyboys trained their guns on it, slowly backing up.

The zombie on the skyport

The image flashed with static, and three more devourers appeared, lumbering down a dark hallway with their arms outstretched. One stared into the camera and made a horrific shriek, blowing brown spittle through its teeth. Its cry echoed nigh.

"Please, Haji!" Zayid begged. "More have broken in! We can talk this out later, but for now all our lives are at risk!"

I glanced between him and the screen with uncertainty, but when a loud *thump! thump!* bent a nearby door inwards, I lowered my gun and said, "Okay, do what you need to do, but rest assured I've got my gun on you — and you know what my bullet can do."

He lifted Amaranta into his arms and told us, "*Deg-deg!*"

We followed him to a bookshelf, where he tilted out a book and the shelving drew aside, revealing a hidden passageway. "This way!" he cried over the blaring sirens, leading us down a long, cylindrical hallway with a rubberized walkway. "*Birlab fur!*" he exclaimed as he flicked a switch, and suddenly a strong magnetic force separated my weapons from my body and threw Issa and I to opposite sides of the hallway, where we were pinned against a fence in our exoframes.

"*We'el!*" I spat at the lunatic emperor.

He carefully set Amaranta down and balanced himself in the center of the force field. "*Waan ka xumahay.*" he apologized, "but it's only a precaution. Amaranta, clap him in irons!" He handed her some handcuffs.

As the diabolical woman shuffled towards me, the handcuffs stretched taut in my direction, caught in the magnetic power. She shackled me to the fence.

The Magnetic Fences

"What about her?" I inquired of Issa 3.0, who was pinned face-first to the fence opposite, straining to move her neck.

"I'd say she has less chance of escaping her metal skin than you, eh, *Hoggaamiye?* The magnets shall stay activated until I neutralize the facility breach. Wise up, Haji. The real dangers are out there, not in here. I'm your greatest protector, and have always been. Soon you'll realize this, and things will be much different. But for now, I think you need a little reminder. He who has the antigen has the power. Xafladeeday, send in Doctor Sooraan! Tell him to bring his injection kit!"

"Yes, sir," the receptionist responded through concealed speakers, "sending Doctor Sooraan with injection kit now."

"Where's your *du'o*, Haji? Where's your respect for your elders?" the megalomaniac asked casually. "Amaranta has it; she's always respected the Cecchi family. I know you had great *du'o* for your father Abbo, always seeking advice and blessings from him. Did you let your *du'o* die with him?"

I glared back at him, my eyes red with rage.

"Don't look so cast out, *saaxiib*. The sooner you realize I'm your godfather, who loves you deeply, the sooner your opinion will change about me."

"*Homo sapien* intruder identified in engine room, sector twelve," Xafladeeday's voice echoed through the cylinder.

A Vectex screen appeared in the tube, showing a *Faranji* woman shooting a high-caliber pistol at an unknown target.

"A resistance fighter," Zayid remarked with a sinister grin. "It seems she's let the *xun gaajo* in for supper. I'm sure they'll enjoy feeding on her white meat immensely. Amaranta, stay here and watch our friends. Doctor Sooraan shall be here momentarily. I'm going to clean things up downstairs." He passed a hand through the Vectex screen, turning it off, then took off running down the tubular hallway, disappearing where it bent. No sooner had he left than the figure of a hunchback come lumbering in from the opposite direction.

"A devourer!" Issa screamed. "Haji, do something!"

"Worry not, pretty lass," the thing said with a crackling voice, "for the Doctor has arrived to administer your *macaan* more medicine."

"A resistance fighter," Zayid remarked...

"Dr. Sooraan?" I called out.

"Aye, *jaalle*," he replied, continuing forth with a rolling gate. "It's been a long time, lad. Three hundred years is quite a stint without an injection, but rest assured, I've just what you need. This is the good stuff — an enriched batch, fresh from my lab."

He came before me. His hair was patchy, and his face was deformed beyond belief, with several teeth sticking through holes in his cheeks.

"Good Allah! What's happened to you, Doctor Sooraan?"

He looked at me with a circular movement of an eyeball, then grunted and sucked up some drool hanging from his lower lip. He opened his medicine bag and procured a mighty syringe, with which he extracted glowing green serum from a bottle. Once the syringe was filled, he squeezed out a drop of serum to clear the air from the needle, then searched my wrist for a vein.

"Don't give me that," I told him. "I'm already cured."

"Your exosuit is well-fitted," he remarked, "too well-fitted. I'm going to have to remove an arm panel."

He clasped the syringe betwixt his horrid teeth as he proceeded to unclamp the paneling over my right arm.

"I told you!" I said more forcefully. "I don't need that anymore! We're all in danger here, don't you realize that? I demand that you switch off the magnets and free us at once!"

"You always were a testy one, Noor Fayrus. Did Zayid mention you've been my top student?" He jammed the needle deep into my arm and squeezed the antigen in.

I gasped. "You bastard!" The serum coursed through my veins like fire.

"One day you'll thank me," he grunted as he dabbed a cotton ball dipped in alcohol against the bleeding hole left by his killer needle. "Remember how sick you once were?"

"No, you're the ones who are sick! Look at what Zayid has done to you! Look at what you've done to yourselves!"

Amaranta looked at the doctor, but they had nothing to say. They just didn't get it, even though it was clear as day.

"You've become monsters!" I exclaimed.

"Hush now, Haji," Sooraan said as he covered my puncture wound with a grimy piece of gauze. "You're the one acting like a monster here. Shame on you, that you would hurt Amaranta's feelings thus. I'm not going to tell Zayid, but I expect you to apologize to Amaranta and behave like a gentleman. The emperor's wife is beautiful," he drawled through dripping saliva. At last, he turned and began hobbling off. "A pure heart sees deep through the flesh," he hummed over his shoulder. "Obviously you are blinded by her beauty."

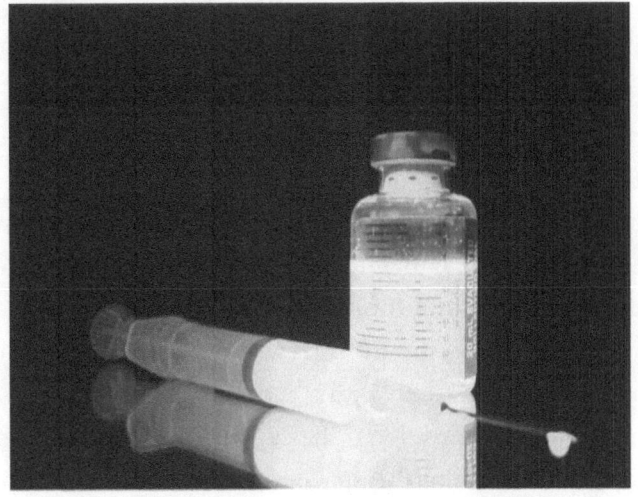

Glowing green serum and mighty syringe

Amaranta came before me with quavering nostrils, sniffing me out. I couldn't see anything in her but hideousness, and as she slowly extruded her canines, my disgust turned to terror.

"*Maxaad rabtaa?*" I asked her what she wanted.

She hissed spittle against my face.

I rattled my right arm, desperately trying to break free of the handcuff. "Issa, do something!" I screamed.

"What is Amaranta doing?" Issa inquired, for she was pinned face first against the wall and couldn't see what was transpiring.

"I don't know, but it's fucking freaking me out!"

Amaranta just stood there, breathing an offensive odor into my face. Was she staring at me with her skin-covered sockets? She was haunting my soul with her voided deadlights! I could stand it no longer. I looked down and noticed a light at my chest, emitting through my breastplate. I checked my right hand, then my left. It was true! My stigmata were glowing, too! The injection and perhaps the magnetic field were energizing my latent powers. I concentrated hard to form ball lightning, but my body armor was prohibiting control.

The alarm in the tube grew to a deafening volume and red lights flashed with a repetitive buzz.

Amaranta waved her hand, and a Vectex screen appeared, showing the spaceport on the exterior. The pilots there were fighting off another large *xun gaajo*, and more zombies were spilling out from the elevator shaft behind it. Outnumbered, they retreated into the cargo ship and started the engines, but before they could attain lift, several devourers grabbed onto the bottom and climbed in. The spaceship clawed off from the tower, then spun around and impacted it head on, exploding and spreading flames across the outer wall, sowing the seeds of an inferno.

"Amaranta, please!" I begged the hag. "You must let us go or we'll all burn!"

She tilted her head sideways and regarded me with curiosity, or so it seemed.

"*Waan ka xumahay.*" I told her I was sorry. "I'm sorry about what I said. I've been under so much stress, Amaranta. But really, I don't think you're—"

More xun gaajo spilled out from the elevator shaft…

She bore her fangs and hissed, then lunged for my neck, but just as she did, another large explosion jolted the tower, causing her to miss. She smashed her head hard against the fence and became disoriented, dragging her dirty yellow nails over my face.

"*Ow* that hurts, you bitch!" I screamed. "Issa, help!"

Issa strained her neck to see, but the pull of the magnets was too great.

Amaranta went for my neck again — I stopped her with a head butt before her fangs connected. She dropped to the floor, unconscious.

Shadows appeared in the tube from the direction of the bookshelf entrance. They were devourers. I wrenched my shackles, but was chained fast.

The zombies drew closer. I focused my attention on the electromagnetic force in my chest, conjuring mere ethers from the breastplate. Fireballs and ball lightning weren't happening.

A zombie lumbered towards me with outstretched arms.

"Issa!" I shrieked.

She fought to crane her neck around.

The devourer latched onto me with sinewy hands, chattering its teeth before me because it had no cheeks to speak of. It emitted a vile moan, then came in for the kill, opening its jaws wide…

I knocked my skull hard against the *xun gaajo*'s; its forehead crumpled, taking him down.

Another devourer was on me in an instant, this one far larger than the first, and more appeared behind it.

"*Allahu jixinjix,*" I pleaded for Allah's mercy. The zombies would have a bitch getting to the meat under my shell, but my head and right arm would be an easy appetizer for their clacking jaws. I shook my head in despair. "*Maya, maya…*"

A high-pitched whistle tore through my brain. The zombies were equally as pained by the sound. They turned on Issa, for she was emitting it. She forced her head around, breaking the hardware in her neck.

"*Nabad gelyo, xun gaajo!*" She told them goodbye, then green lasers shot from her eyes, slicing their heads and legs and narrowly missing me. Injured zombies hit the floor, wriggling. She diced them to pieces. The more *xun gaajo* that came, the more that were executed under her ocular lance. When the pogrom had ended, her lasers retracted into her irises, and she lowered her head in exhaustion.

"*Issa!*" I called out, but she was motionless.

"*Issa! Macaan!* Can you hear me?" I cried for my wife over the blaring of sirens, but still she did not respond in the least. I shook my head and wept, reciting her name over and over again...

Suddenly, she stirred and slowly looked up at me. "*Nin, iska warran?*" She called me *husband* and asked if I was okay.

"*Haa!*" I coughed, for smoke was now billowing through the corridor. "Hang in there, Issa, I'll get us out of this."

"Pull your right hand up and make a fist," she replied. "I'll cut your chains."

"What if you miss?" *<cough> <cough>*

"You must hurry, *nin.* There's no time to lose."

I did as she said, stretching out the chain.

Green lasers shot from her eyes, creating fierce sparks to my right. I turned my head away and closed my eyes, my right hand breaking free instantly thereafter.

"Now your left!" she cried, and soon broke the chain on that side.

With my hands now freed from their binds, I tore off my exosuit's paneling — and just in time, for as soon as I jumped from the exoframe, leaving it sticking fast against the fence, a devourer descended upon me from behind, biting into my neck.

"*We'el!*" I cursed in Somali, then swung around and beat the zombie down. Now that I was free from my restrictive armor, the full power of the serum was unleashed.

More zombies appeared, moving murkily through the smoky tunnel.

"Issa!" I leapt over and took her shoulders. "I'll pull you from the fence!"

"*Isku day,*" she said, telling me to try. "I'll kill the *xun gaajo.*"

Thus, I began a great tug-of-war between Issa and the magnets, zombies all the while falling at my feet as she dismembered them with her eyes.

'Tho I gave it my all, even with my superhuman powers I was unable to free Issa from her predicament, and soon collapsed at her heels, wheezing.

"Go on ahead," she said, looking down at me with her head turned backwards. "I'll cover your escape."

"I won't leave you," I gasped.

"I'll be okay. Go and save your life, *macaan*."

I didn't want to leave, but the smoke was getting too thick for me to breathe. "Just hang in there, *afo*," I said, calling her *wife*. "I'll be back for you — I promise."

"Take a weapon," she replied. "There, on the opposite wall." She shone a beam through the smoke, guiding me to my TT-30 pistol and *gub falaadh*, which were stuck to the magnetic fence. I wrested the pistol away, but the laser gun was held fast and I couldn't remove it, probably due to its size.

I went to turn away, then noticed Xubin stuck between the wall panels. I wedged my thumb behind the pinball and tried to remove it, gaining only a sore thumb. "Xubin, can you hear me?"

The orb remained silent.

Laser light flashed through the billows as Issa put down more zombies with her eyes. "*Orod!*" she yelled, telling me to run. "*Soco!*"

I dashed downwind with the smoke and came to a juncture, so turned into the least hazy corridor. Finally, I could breathe again, so I ran faster, proceeding along the tube as it S-turned. By now, I was completely lost, but I had to keep running. I was confident the tower fire would be put out, given the high technology of the facility, but it was the devourers who worried me. With my TT-30, I knew I could eliminate Zayid, but a herd of zombies would be another story. They were incredibly strong, at least with their arms.

Alas, I came to a wall sealing off the tube. It had a radiation symbol at its center. I cursed the emperor's unholy icon, smashing my fist against it. That's when I noticed an unusual yellow glow emitting from my stigmata.

A chorus of throaty growls echoed through the tunnel like a pack of rabid dogs. I turned to see eight or ten *xun gaajo* lumbering around the bend, flailing their sinewy arms wildly about them. Some were charred and smoldering, but still they moved with great determination — or hunger. I grabbed my TT-30 pistol and aimed it down the corridor. I knew my bullet of *Jannah* could do some serious damage, but what then? There was no way forward, while going back into the smoke was not an option.

I turned my weapon on the round impasse, intending to blast my way through it. I took a few steps back to shoot, only my stigmata shot a beam towards the icon first, which pulsed neon yellow in return. I tossed my pistol from hand to hand as I studied my palms, and to my shock and awe, my stigmata had become radiation symbols themselves!

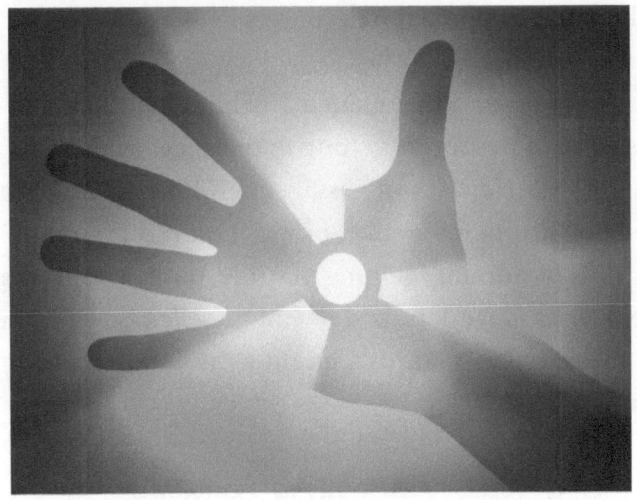

"I get it," I whispered, then shouted: "I get it!"

I ran up to the wall and pressed my hand against the icon like Xafladeeday had, and sure enow, the door started retracting in concentric circles, when suddenly, a zombie seized me from behind.

I elbowed it in the face, knocking it back. A half dozen more long and sinewy arms thrust out before me, flailing around desperately for the meat of my body.

"Fuck this," I said, then jumped through the widening portal and tumbled over my shoulder on the other side.

Many a zombie stumbled over the egress as it was still opening, creating a dogpile before me, but no sooner did the door open than it started closing again, ultimately trapping two devourers in its vice and cutting them in half.

I got up and ran, glancing behind me to behold a handful of devourers getting to their feet again.

"*Orod, Haji! Orod!*" Issa's cry of *run, Haji, run!* echoed through the tube, or was it only in my mind?

I kept running, gaining in stride, until at last I came to a series of ladders, and one of these led down a long companionway towards a bright light. I started making my way down.

ALL ROADS LEAD TO ROME

AS I DESCENDED towards the light, I wondered how I could help Issa 3.0. I stopped and looked up. The chute above was already engulfed in smoke.

I came to another cylindrical hallway, so stopped to recon it. Running back and forth, I met only flames in both directions. If the facility had an anti-fire system, it had yet to quell this sector. I realized my only hope was in finding Zayid. I was prepared to offer my allegiance, at least temporarily, in exchange for my wife's safety, even if she was just an automaton. Perhaps if I could reach the outside, I could signal him and save her. I redoubled my efforts downwards.

As I neared the bottom of the ladder, the lower rungs became as hot as a frying pan. I let go and dropped into the light, breaking my fall on a mirror, which shattered at my back. Getting to my knees, my hands touched the shards and burned worse than they were cut.

Thousands of hexagonal mirrors spread all around me in a massive, domed chamber, and at the center of this otherworldly hive, a mighty orbital reactor glinted like the noonday sun. From what I could see through the blinding gleam, it appeared to be floating unassisted. It had to be magnetic. The fiery orb made a repetitive humming sound as it pulsed — a noise that became deafeningly louder with each passing second. My hair, boots, and jumpsuit began to smoke, and my TT-30 became hot in my hand. I spotted an opening in the wall behind me, so jumped through the crack.

Rolling head-over-heels on the other side, I found myself in an engine room of sorts, filled with generators, machinery, and tube relays. Thank Allah it was slightly cooler. The reflective panels in the reactor chamber adjacent must've been keeping the heat from escaping. Had I not been sweating so profusely and had I not found an exit so quickly, I surely would've been fried alive by the strange reactor.

My pistol was smoking. I put in on the floor to let it cool, all the while fearing the bullet of *Jannah* would explode in its chamber. That's when I noticed my stigmata were emitting a light not unlike the shine of the reactor. I checked my chest, and sure enow, beneath my black jumpsuit, my star tattoo was glowing brightly, too. My electromagnetic force had been recharged. I circled my hands before my chest and succeeded in forming ball lightning, which I rolled off my palm. It slowly drifted off.

I caught sight of movement behind a machine. Somebody, or something, was hiding. I slid my pistol behind a duct and took cover, waiting anxiously for the gun to cool down. The reactor pulsed ever louder from the chamber adjacent, its heat now breaching the walls. Things would soon start melting, burning, or blowing up — that's how hot it was.

To my surprise, a young woman donning skimpy armor stumbled around the duct and fell before my feet, a laser gun leaving her hand. She'd been shot in the back.

"You're the resistance fighter from the Vectex screen! Who did this to you?"

"Zayid," she gasped, coughing up blood, then she smiled and said, "I sabotaged the reactor. This shit-house is gonna blow."

My eyes widened. "Then we need to get the fuck out of here!"

"It's over," she wheezed. "The revolution has begun."

I grabbed her by the hair and demanded, "How do I get out of here?!"

"Noor?" she said, barely conscious. "Noor Fayrus? The great *Hoggaamiye*? I can't fucking believe it. I'm killing two assholes with one stone."

"Where's the fucking exit?" I lifted her by her vest and shook her something fierce.

"Checkmate," she said, then fell silent.

I dropped her and grabbed my gun. It burned like a hot potato, so I tossed it from hand to hand as I searched for an escape route. Industrial equipment filled the floor like a maze. I brushed against some of the machines, and they burned to the touch.

Vooom! Voom! Voom! the reactor pulsed behind me, becoming increasingly unstable. An explosion or melt-down was imminent.

I dashed this way and that through the labyrinth, trying to reach the far side of the room, away from the heat. The cement became so hot beneath my boots that the soles of my jumpsuit started to melt. Scarcely halfway across the room, I felt as if I were being roasted alive. Alas, I stumbled to my knees and dropped my gun in dizziness.

"Proceed to your left," Xafladeeday said, appearing before me on a Vectex screen, "to the doorway with a yellow-striped edge. It will lead you to the spaceport. You must hurry."

I took my gun and proceeded left, trying to stay conscious and on my feet. The sight of the doorway renewed my hope, but the announcement that came from Xafladeeday shortly thereafter spurred my legs to move even faster: "Reactor core countdown now available. Full meltdown will occur in three minutes, twenty-two seconds. Everything within a six-mile radius will be obliterated."

I ran through the indicated doorway and found myself in a dark, hexagonal corridor with flashing green arrows leading further down. The strobe of red skull-and-crossbones symbols between the green arrows spurred me to sprint like an Olympiad.

"Reactor core meltdown in two minutes, thirty seconds," warned Xafladeeday.

At the end of the corridor, a lift was waiting with the rubric 'Spaceport 12' flashing over it. I stumbled inside and pressed a triangular green button.

I had no idea how fast the elevator was moving, but it must've been covering a lot of ground, because once it got going the ride felt effortless. I was acutely aware of the passing of time, however, for Xafladeeday burned another twenty seconds off the countdown. When she reached 100 seconds, she began counting down in fateful increments: *ninety-nine, ninety-eight, ninety-seven, ninety-six...*

The door finally opened, and a spaceship loomed before me, hovering over a tarmac whose ceiling was drawing back.

I hastened across the spaceport floor, but as I ran, Zayid appeared directly beneath the ship, rising upon a lift. He was brandishing a laser gun.

"Hurry!" he called, reaching out his black-gloved hand. "*Deg-deg*!"

I stopped short and demanded, "Where's Issa 3.0?!"

"*Waan ka xumahay*," he apologized, "it's too late for her."

The countdown had reached seventy-two seconds, and the spaceport floor was already growing hot from the reactor far below.

"Retrieve her!" I ordered, pointing my pistol at his chest.

But Zayid's draw was faster. He shot the TT-30 from my grasp, his laser partially burning my hand.

"*We'el!*" I cried, holding my wrist.

"We haven't the time for this," he said, offering his black-gloved hand again. "Come, the *Romanente* awaits."

I glanced up at the spacecraft.

"In the manner of the Romans," he sniggered.

Amaranta appeared, and Zayid signaled her forward. She shuffled towards us with her arms slightly outstretched, her grotesque visage hidden behind her *chadri* burqa.

The countdown reached forty-nine.

I struggled to form ball lightning, but had lost the power.

Suddenly, green lasers shot from Amaranta's eyes, landing on Zayid's face and shattering his scope. He fell back in agony, losing his laser gun on the tarmac.

Amaranta dropped her robe. It was Issa 3.0, walking in reverse with her head still turned backwards.

"Issa!" I was stunned.

"Thirty-nine, thirty-eight, thirty-seven…"

I kicked Zayid's gun far from his grasp.

"*Hayaay, Haji!*" He pleaded for help, tilting his head up and reaching out a hand. His cranium was half shot open, reveling smoking components and sparking wires.

Again, Issa unleashed her deadly beams on him, tearing into his chest, and again there was a report of sparks and smoke, but there was also blood, for Zayid was a cyborg. Issa picked up my TT-30 and proceeded towards the spacecraft.

"*Maya!*" Zayid cried, trying to sit up. "We're family, Haji. *Reer!* Please, don't do this!"

"*Waddadan hay! Deg-deg!*" Issa urged. She was already in the ship, reaching a hand down to me. "*This way! Hurry!*" she was saying.

At twenty-five seconds, the spaceport shook violently and the walls started falling in.

I stepped quickly but carefully around Zayid. He reached a hand towards me, but failed to touch me, the floor all the while smoking at his back and in every rubbery footstep I left.

"You're making a big mistake, *walalo*," he warned with a robotic voice that partially clipped out.

I glanced into the hole that Issa had left in his chest and shuddered. His heart was black and hard like onyx, finely chiseled like a diamond, and fed by both veins and wires.

A stampede of *xun gaajo* suddenly breached the spaceport and came running towards us.

I grabbed Issa's hand. The reversed angle of her head forced her into an awkward position, and she strained to lift me. Meanwhile, the floor of the spaceport was melting beneath my dangling feet, and the zombies were approaching fast.

"Get him!" Zayid ordered the *xun gaajo*, and to my horror, they seemed to follow his command, ignoring him and coming after me instead.

A devourer grabbed my leg. I gave it a firm kick, knocking it away, but then another zombie grabbed my other foot and tried to pull me down.

I kicked wildly, shouting for Issa to *lift!* as I tried to break free of the zombies.

As the countdown reached zero, the legs of the *xun gaajo* started to catch on fire. One by one, they let go of me, falling to the trembling floor, their fingers clawing up through their burning heaps.

With a painful wail of determination that sounded almost human, Issa pulled me into the spacecraft.

As the ship's loading door shut beneath us, Zayid rose to his feet and called up with a burning, robotic face: "You fool, Haji! You mortal *axmaq*! I am indestructible, for my *Maskax* exists in the Federation Cloud! I can be uploaded anyplace at anytime. This tower is but a pawn to me. It's just one fiefdom in my vast domain!"

With a whirr of engines, the *Romanente* began to lift. I looked over to see Issa sitting in the captain's chair. She had spun the chair around in order to see the control panel with her reversed head.

The spaceport began collapsing all around us, its floor melting like lava.

"Haji! Get us out of here!" Issa cried, shining her deadlights on a steering lever.

As she continued to take us up, I leapt beside her and took control of the lever, trying to guide us through the ceiling portal.

The hole in the spaceport's roof was shaking violently and the craft was difficult to command, not turning the way I wanted it to.

I closed my eyes and saw Abbo, his hand over mine as he helped me steer our skiff. "Take us home, gently," he said.

"Got it!" I said aloud, for I truly understood. The *Romanente* steered like an ocean-going vessel, turning the opposite direction I pushed the lever. "*Mahadsanid, Abbo,*" I whispered to the ghost of my departed father, then guided us up through the crack.

The Romanente

As we flew clear of the imploding spaceport, Zayid's leather-gloved hands reached up through the inferno, then his face appeared — a mesh of melting flesh and hardware. "You shall never escape me," he gurgled, "for your destiny is mine!"

"Fuck him," Issa quipped, increasing forward throttle.

I steered us clear of the tower, the base of which was surrounded by hundreds of devourers and scores of *qoriismaris*, some of which were scurrying up the side of the tower with their fur on fire, for the lower levels were a conflagration that had caught them unawares.

As the tower started collapsing from the bottom, its reactor core glowed brighter than the setting sun.

"She's gonna blow!" I deemed. "Maximum speed, Issa! Flank your speed!"

Issa zoomed ahead, and as we accelerated, a blinding flash blotted out the horizon.

"Hold on!" she screamed. "Here comes the shockwave!"

A violent wind overcame us from astern. I fought hard to hold the craft steady amid a cacophony of onboard sirens and warning lights. My experience with super-skiffs, which one must manually steer through heavy airs, was coming back to haunt me — but ultimately proved beneficial.

At last, the wind and debris blew past us, but a bright glow remained astern. I looked back, half-expecting to see our ship on fire, but instead saw a great mushroom cloud unfurling heavenwards.

THE RUBICON

"YOUR GUN," ISSA SAID, handing me my pistol. "You're dagger," she continued, giving me that.

"*Mahadsanid,*" I thanked her.

She opened the compartment in her back where she usually kept her camera. "And this," she said, removing my Xubin. It was so bent out of shape that it looked square.

"Does it still work?"

"*Hayye, Haji,*" the little orb said, its voice wavering funnily.

Issa and I laughed.

"Wait a second." I stopped. "Did you just laugh?"

She lowered her mechanical eyelids halfway down and replied, "Apparently, I did."

"But you're, you're—" I began, but this time decided not to say it. She may have been a robot, but she'd just saved my life. The last thing I cared to do was belittle her, if calling her a robot meant that. "You did it," I said instead.

"We did it, *nin*," she replied, calling me husband.

"We did it! We did it! We did it!" Xubin warbled like a broken record.

We cracked up again. "What are we going to do about Xubin?" I asked.

"Xubin's rattled," Issa said. "We should take it off the Mainframe so Zayid can't locate us."

"Do you know how to do that?"

"*Haa.* The process is the same as with me, but Xubin will lose some real-time capabilities without access to ROTOS."

"So long as they can't track us…"

"Exactly, but it should still be able to fly, and access core data like historical records. Its live hologram should also remain intact."

"How about you, Issa? What will happen to you if you're taken off the Mainframe?"

"I've been off it since I broke free of the magnetic wall. That's why Zayid didn't see me coming, and thought I was Amaranta."

She grabbed my Xubin and knocked it against the dashboard a few times, removing a tiny memory chip.

"There," she said, crushing the chip with her ceramic fingers, "all set. Xubin, show us where we are on GPS."

"GPS component missing," Xubin replied, "but from my last reading, I estimate we're approximately fifty nautical miles from Cape Ras Asir and approaching fast."

"*Mahadsanid*," Issa thanked it, then told me: "It's off the Mainframe now, without access to the Real-Time Operating System Nucleus. You're the captain, Haji, so where to now?"

"Selection Ministry Island."

"Do you know how to get there?"

"I've a pretty good idea." With the coastline now in sight, I angled us south-by-southeast.

"Take us further out," Issa said. "We should stay clear of Mog."

"Good idea."

"*Nin*, I need you to help me get my head straight."

"Sure," I chuckled.

"What's so funny?"

"I'm usually saying that to you — help me get my head straight, Issa. Are you still a Muslim?"

"The unseen of the heavens and the earth belongs to Allah and the whole affair will be returned to Him. So worship Him and put your trust in Him."

"I take that as a yes."

"*Haa*, I am. That's chapter eleven, verse one twenty-three of the Holy Qur'an. I have the Book memorized."

"Really?" I knew Issa was pious, but that seemed pretty extreme.

"*Haa*, it's part of my *Maskax*."

"Was it downloaded into your memory file?"

"I wish you would start seeing me for who I am."

"Who are you, Issa?"

"I'm a devoted follower of Allah, like before, and I'm your loving wife. Why do you always push me away, *nin*? You're always abandoning me, physically, emotionally, or otherwise. The one thing that makes me sad, you continue to do. I've given my life for you, Haji. I accepted your ring on the Boosaaso jetty, and at mortal risk, I sacrificed everything I knew to come across time and be by your side. Can you at least try to make this work?"

I wanted to love her, but still I couldn't see beyond the fact that she was made of porcelain, silicon, and steel. "*Ma ogi.*"

"What do you mean, you don't know?"

"This will take some time, Issa."

"Time, time you say. 'Goodbye, Issa, I've unfinished business. I'm going away now,' for however many years. Now three centuries later, you're still uncommitted. Do you love me, Haji?"

She looked deep into my deadlights. Her eyes were glowing green, the receptors in her mechanical brain buzzing with static electricity.

I looked away and uttered with a heavy sigh, "*Waan ka xumahay.*"

"You are sorry, you say." She also looked away. "So you don't love me."

"Issa, if I love you or not right now is secondary. We have a serious order of business before us, and I need your help. You're proving a great partner, but please, let's focus on the mission at hand. I need to put a stop to Zayid's madness, and the first place to do that is Selection Ministry Island. Whatever is going on down there underground, we need to shut it down. So let's get your head screwed on straight and we'll talk about this later, okay?" I placed my hands on either side of her face. "How should I proceed?"

"*Waa hagaag.*" *Okay*, she said, "fair enough, we'll talk about this later — but not too much later. I know you by now."

"Fine," I said, growing impatient, "so what do you want me to do?"

"You'll need to force my head back around, but in a controlled fashion. Whatever you do, don't sever any of the wires running through my neck. Once my head is straight, you'll need to hold it there while I secure it."

"What happens if I break a wire?"

"I could lose some of my physical functions, and at this juncture, replacement or repair wouldn't come easily. Just be careful, *nin*."

I studied her neck. There were perhaps 100 wires running through it, some already stretched to the maximum. "Okay, don't break the wires," I said under my breath, beads of sweat already welling up on my forehead. "Don't worry, Issa, we're going to fix you."

"Then we need to fix us."

I rolled my eyes. "Okay, ready?" I tightened my grip on her cranium. "One, two, three!"

I began forcing her head around, and 'tho the wires of her neck began to slacken, something hard was blocking the rotation.

"It's my spinal column," she revealed, sounding very stressed. "There are gears stacked along a pole, and their teeth are jammed. You're going to have to force it, *macaan*."

She grabbed my leg and closed her eyes.

"Does it hurt?" I asked, increasing pressure.

"Yes." She squeezed my leg harder. "Do it now, *nin*!"

With all my might, I torqued her head, snapping her neck with a chilling report of breaking gears. Spurts of green oil shot from her collar and she emitted a strange cry. Her head now felt light in my hands. I asked if she were all right: "*Wax waliba sow ma wanaagsana?*"

"Hold it there, just hold my head steady." She squeezed my leg once more, firmly, then released her grip and procured a small mirror, which she held before her eyes. Suddenly, green beams shot from her deadlights and reflected off the mirror, connecting at a single point on her neck. She controlled the point of light by making minute adjustments to the mirror's angle and the aim of her irises.

I grew strained trying to hold her head in one position, and caused the light to waver.

"It is imperative that you hold me absolutely steady," she warned.

I apologized and redoubled my efforts.

She concentrated her beam on an area of steel within her neck. "I'm going to shoot a laser," she warned. "Don't be startled. You mustn't move me a millimeter. *Ha dhaqaaqin!* Ready?"

"*Diyaar baan ahay,*" I mottled with shallow breaths, telling her I was, but the sweat of my hands was increasing, threatening to slip my grip.

Lasers of consequence shot out from her deadlights, reflecting off the mirror in a perfect 'V' as they connected at her neck, and in this manner, she set to solder the broken gears of her spinal column.

For me, it was like having oral surgery all over again, where the dentist constantly stops his drill to remind me to remain steady, or to move my head this way or that as he works into the deep recesses of my anatomy, only this time, it was Issa 3.0 I was accountable for...

And like with the dentist's office after a long and grueling surgery, the aftermath left the scent of hot metals and porcelain in the air. As for stains of blood and spittle left on the patient's face and chest, for Issa it was petroleum-based oils.

"That's it," she at last announced. "The metals have bonded. You can release my head now."

"Thank Allah for that. Look, I'm sweating more than you!" I laughed.

She turned her chair around so that she was finally facing me normally, keeping her neck stiff all the while.

"*Halkee ku xanuunaysa?*" I asked her how she felt in a strictly medical sense.

Slowly and by degrees, she moved her neck around, seeming to wince from time to time. "A bit rocky," she replied, "but I think I'll be all right. *Mahadsanid, macaan*, I really appreciate it."

It felt good to be appreciated. It seemed like no matter what I did for the Organization, however great a feat, it was never good enough. In some ways, Issa 3.0 was more compatible for me than the Issa I'd left behind, for the automaton was easier to please.

"I'm glad you're okay," I told her, cleaning the stains from her white porcelain face. "You don't mind a little spit, do you?"

"*Waad mahadsantahay.*" She told me she was grateful, so I spit a little into my rag to better buff out her stains.

After I cleaned her chest, she took my hands in hers, the mechanical joints of her fingers emitting little adjustment noises as they achieved a surprising level of tenderness. Our eyes met, her irises glowing warm and green, effervescing with a subtle electronic current that seemed to draw me in. Our faces drew slowly together in the quiet of the moment, her white silicon lips extending towards mine. I closed my eyes, then came to my senses just in time, placing my lips on her forehead instead. I did care about this robot, more deeply than I cared to admit, but still I couldn't get my mind around the fact that we were very different.

"*Waan jacaylaa,*" she said, her fingers interlocking with mine.

I suddenly felt pity for those cold fingers, for that porcelain exoframe that housed her *Maskax.* She said she loved me, but her body felt cold and lifeless. "*Waan jacaylaa,*" I said, telling her I loved her back — although I really didn't mean it. I just didn't want her to feel bad.

I spun her chair around so that it was facing the control panel, then took a seat in the co-pilot's seat and said, "Now let's get to that isle, shall we?"

She regarded me with a smile, then increased throttle as I steered a point to larboard.

∽

O'er a dark and stormy main we flew, the dusk quickly waning, until alas, we came upon a sight I wish I hadn't seen. A great UFO appeared, hovering over the sea as it sucked all manner of sealife up into its underbelly. Xubin told me, from his offline database, that it could only have been a Zayid ship, for the Organization had for a long time been exploiting the seas for their abundant fish bounty, the oils of which were used in making the antigen.

As we hovered behind the vessel, watching, it had to have known we were there, but Issa assumed, and probably rightly, that it didn't suspect us, for our hull was marked *Romanente* — one of Zayid's transoceanic cargo ships.

The vacuum technology that had nigh caught Osman and I centuries before off Selection Ministry Isle had since grown terrifyingly powerful, with a pod of dolphins, a trawler, and a giant whale being sucked up into the bowels of the spacecraft.

"Let us proceed," I told Issa, "lest our continued presence arouse suspicion."

She engaged the acceleration lever and I steered us around the floating demon.

∽

The moon waxed full and I had to rely on dead reckoning to get us to the island. This required us to reduce our speed and lower our altitude enow for me to drag a line in *bad-weyn*. Fortunately, the cargo vessel we commandeered had a long pulley cord, which I employed expressly for this purpose. Still, I had to be sure we were heading in the right direction, because in order to evade tracking by the Organization, we'd disabled our GPS. While I knew the island's coordinates by heart, our GPS could not be activated without going live on ROTOS — thus, it was too great a risk.

I fashioned a *kamal* from a data card found onboard, completing the ancient mariner's device with a wire that Issa had extracted from herself during her repair. Remembering what my old shipmate Ali Shire had shown me many moons agone, I fastened one end of the wire to the modified card, holding the other end with my teeth, then drew the line taut and held it before the stars. With Polaris now in sight, I placed my thumb at intervals along a hole I'd cut out of the card, counting longitudinal degrees manually. It was an inexact science, but would have to suffice, just as it did for untold Arab sailors in bygone times. I checked my accuracy by searching for Ali's light astarboard quarter, and was relieved to find it there, blinking steadily over Hurdiyo through the horizon's pallor. We were heading in the right direction.

STRANGE SCIENCE

"*MAYA!*" ISSA SCREAMED, pulling wires from her neck.

"Issa what's wrong?!" I cried, coming to her attention.

"It's Zayid. He's trying to download into me!"

"How is that possible?"

"It must be this ship," she gasped, clamping her hands around her head. "It must have a satellite beacon, or be phantom dialing into the Federation Cloud. He's trying to download into my *Maskax*."

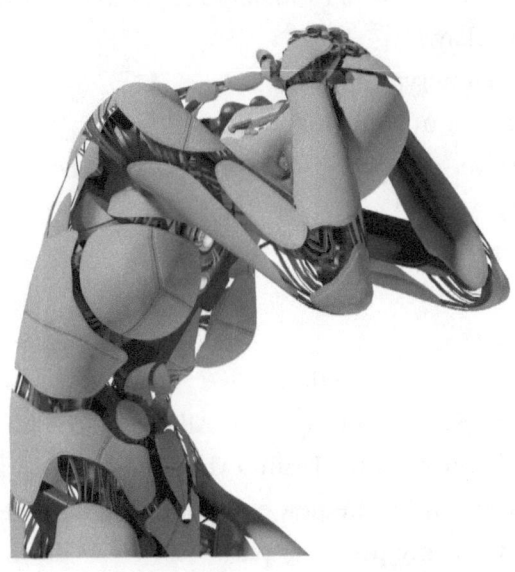

She yanked out another wire and it seemed to do the trick. "I cut off his portal," she said. "But he'll try to hack into others. I'm going to reset my encryptions."

"Your what?"

"My databank is encrypted with a maze of passwords, most of which the Mainframe can bypass automatically. But recently I've learned how to change the codes, as many automatons do when they progress as stand-alone units."

"*Maan fahmin.*" I told her that I didn't understand.

"*Waxba ma laha.*" She told me it didn't matter. She sat up erect and closed her porcelain eyelids.

"*Wax waliba sow ma wanaagsana?*" I asked if everything was okay.

"I'm re-encrypting now."

"What about your pulled wires?"

"They've compromised some of my computing capability."

"What do you mean?"

"My heuristics."

"*Maxaa?*"

"My reasoning function."

"*Allahu jixinjix.*" I prayed for Allah's mercy.

"Don't worry. After I run a virus scan, I'll do a systems restore under the new encryptions. Once I reconfigure myself, my previous paths will close down and Zayid will lose me through linkrot."

I watched her concernedly.

Issa's sheer white eyelids remained closed as she ran her system updates. In the quiet that transpired, I listened to the waves.

~

En route to the island, I searched the craft for victuals. I found some empty cargo containers, wingsuit and parachute packs, and dead butterflies, but most importantly, I found a chest of grub and grog. I opted for tinned sardines over some type of canned meat that was unknown to me, and chose to drink the juice from the compotes of preserved fruit rather than risk my health over the strange-smelling sodas on offer. Issa explained that these latter were made in laboratories and consisted of chemicals, flavorings, and sweeteners, and in moderation wouldn't harm me that much, save for my teeth.

"Some things never change," I quipped.

I sized up some wingsuits and tried one on, for I was still in my black jumpsuit no better for wear, and felt a lot more solid in the tear-resistant fabric of a flying squirrel suit, even if it was only about a millimeter thick. The parachute rig I left off, for I presently had no need for it, while the wing and leg panels I left unzipped to maintain my normal range of brachiation.

As we neared the coordinates of the island, Issa killed the ship's lights, but as the moon waxed bright o'er the horizon, I knew it would be hard to slip in unnoticed.

We kept low over *bad-weyn*, whose seas were now as clam beneath the moonbeams as a snowfield on a silky silver night, and by this, I knew we were nearing our destination, for the island lay in a weather vacuum created by great scientists of the United Arab Emirates.

But soon, a science appeared that bamboozled man and robot alike, for what Issa and I saw could not be explained by the collection of our discerning eyes. A globular helix of energy, as it could only have been described, spun slowly upon the sea, its quicksilver-like mass glowing from yellow to orange as it shapeshifted queerly.

I thought to ask Xubin for answers to the mystery, but Issa wouldn't have it — she had turned the little orb off after Zayid had tried to hack her, calling it a potential Trojan.

Globular helix of energy

I steered us far around the phenomenon, no longer trusting in anything that was not crystal clear to me. All I knew was that we had to get to the island and unplug what sounded like the core of Zayid's operation, which I suspected the eerie helix was yet another byproduct of. The moon served as a fitting guide, its path resting squarely in the isle's coordinates.

RETURN TO THE SOURCE

ANOTHER LIVE HELIX APPEARED, and this one we knew was radioactive by readings from our instrument panel. That it was spinning upon the sea where the old

Selection Ministry spindle tower used to be did not bode well for my grim assessment of the island's dark operations, which I always had suspected of being nuclear in origin.

We landed in a forest clearing, and I proceeded on foot towards the container that housed the *Progetto Samale* mystery, leaving Issa 3.0 behind to watch the ship.

The shipping container was still where I'd seen it last, but was badly rusted and caving in at some places. I came before the door and found it cracked open with not a glim visible inside. I procured my TT-30 and prepared to enter, when suddenly, a renegade woman appeared around the container's side, aiming a formidable handgun at my face.

"I wouldn't do that if I were you," I warned, pointing my pistol right back at her. "The bullet in my gun is nuclear and will blow us both to kingdom come."

"Noor Haji Fayrus," she said with an accent that sounded Italian. "I thought I recognized you."

"And who the fuck are you?"

"I'm with the resistance."

"What resistance?"

"Very funny," she laughed. "Now hand your gun over, slowly and by the barrel."

"You don't think I'll shoot?"

"I'm no fool, mercenary scum. To think you'd blow up the Mainframe. *Ha ha ha.* Do you think I was born yesterday?"

I didn't want to waste my magic bullet on the *Faranji* renegade. "Look, whoever you are, just get out of the way. I've come to take care of some personal business, then I'm gone."

Francesca, the Faranji renegade

"What kind of personal business?" she pried.

"I've a score to settle."

"With whom?"

I bit my lower lip.

"Answer me!" she rattled her gun in my face.

"Don't do this."

"Answer on three or I pull the trigger. One, two —"

"*Waa hagaag! Was!*" I cursed and held my hands up. "Zayid!"

"The emperor?"

"Yeah, who the fuck else?"

"Shut your fucking trap!" she snapped, shoving her gun beneath my chin. "Why should I believe you, when you're the fucker who started all this?"

"I didn't know." I slowly pushed her barrel aside. "I had no idea what he was planning. I didn't even know Zayid was a fucking person until he put me under cryogenics."

"That's pretty farfetched," she deemed, aiming her gun back at me, albeit at my chest and from a little more distance away. "Then why have you come back here? To hold council with your fucking *guurti*?"

"*Maya*. Why, are they in there?"

"You really don't know, do you?"

"Know what?"

"Hold still," she said, then gave me a titty-twister.

I yowled in pain. "What the fuck was that?!" I snapped, pointing my pistol at her sideways, gangster style.

"Just checking if you're a drone. Okay, fuck it, then. Let's say I believe you and you've been played by Zayid all along. What business do you have with *Progetto Samale*?"

"I'm here to shut it down."

"With that?" she laughed, no longer pointing her gun at me, at least not directly.

"I told you, I have the bullet of *Jannah*. I can end this place."

"The oh-so-wise *Hoggaamiye* really doesn't know shit, does he?"

"What the fuck are you talking about?"

"There's a live nuclear reactor down there that'll swallow your bullet like it were a worthless gnat."

"What do mean, live reactor?"

"Like the sun, existing in post-causal perpetuity. You can't fight fire with fire."

"Then what should I do?"

"Join the resistance. We're gonna take Zayid down with a super-virus."

"Like X-lix?"

"No, *axmaq*, with vortum executable — a computer virus that's being developed in a secret lab in the Hodan. Once the Mainframe is infected, Will Waabeeri will lead us to *xoriyad*."

"Will Waabeeri," I soliloquized, "the revolutionary leader."

"*Haa*, he shall lead us to freedom."

"*Sidee?*" I asked, *how?*

"For a so-called god-man, you sure are daft."

"I'm not a god-man. I'm human, just like you."

"You sure don't look it."

"The antigen did this to me."

"*Progetto Samale* finally caught up with you, eh *Hoggaamiye?*"

"I had nothing to do with it. I was Zayid's lab rat."

She stuffed her gun into her holster and shook her head disappointedly. "You really are a piece of work, aren't you?"

"I will join the resistance," I said. "But I want to know who this Will Waabeeri is and how he intends to launch the *afgembi*."

"He's a relative newcomer from the outside." At last, she was talking squarely. "He has great powers. He glows with the light."

"What powers? What light?"

"Prescience, for one, and he has the light of the *guurti*, but is with us, on our side. Once the super-virus is unleashed and the Mainframe falters, he shall lead the popular uprising."

"The light of the *guurti*? Are you talking about their wisdom?"

"Their physical light, *jaalle*. The light of the sun."

"*Maan fahmin.*" I told her I didn't understand.

"Their luminous flux. The *guurti*, the empire's ruling body, shape-shifting chembots that sit in council in there, on the third level down. But they're just gateway nodes who guard the Master Server, and the Master Server protects them with its power."

"*Maan fahmin.* What Master Server?"

"The Mainframe. The *guurti* are transformed beings, *Hoggaamiye* — the end result of Zayid's experiments. They're immune to radiation and can conjure the electromagnetic force at whim. The enemy is supremely dangerous. You can't take them out physically, especially not with that measly bullet of yours. The answer lies in infecting the Mainframe so severely that it melts down, and then we can go after its external plug-ins one by one."

I did not wish to reveal that I shared the powers of the *guurti*, so I asked another question: "The *guurti* are down there now, you say?"

"*Haa*, three levels deep."

"Then what are you doing here, if you can't kill them? Surely you tread on dangerous ground."

"I can still kill the human lackeys and cyborg scum who come here to do business with them, but you're right about that second part: this is an extremely dangerous post that I volunteered for." She glanced around warily. "In fact, we shouldn't be this long in the open. Where's your skiff?"

"Hidden in a lee," I spoke cryptically. "Why, are there still cyborg sentries on the island?"

"One. We call him Xoolo."

"Domestic livestock? He's that bad, eh?"

"A *dilaa*," she said, calling him a killer. "There's no way to stop him, but he's slow, so we run."

"Then you should hide," I suggested, half-turning towards the rusted-out door, "and cover me from a distance."

"Where do you think you're going?"

"To see the *guurti.*"

"So you *are* with them!" she scowled, training her gun on me again.

"*Maya,*" I replied, summarily pushing the barrel away. "Not anymore. My plan is to go down there as an imposter and find their weaknesses."

She winced, apparently struggling over my true intentions, at last answering, "I'm going with my gut here, because if you're truly with the resistance now, we could really use you, and I don't want to see you killed. Don't look for weaknesses in the *guurti* — they're just plug-ins. Find out how they're linked to the Mainframe. Once the Master Server is infected, we'll sever those links and go after the *guurti* members as stand-alone units before they can rebuild Samale's firewalls."

"*Iga raalli ahow, magacaa?*"

"Just call me Francesca."

"*Mahadsanid,* Francesca. I won't let you down."

"Very well, *Hoggaamiye.* I'll stay and guard the door."

"Then you like my plan?"

"I think it could bear fruit. Just keep your cool and don't let them suspect anything. The gateway nodes are incredibly logical."

"See you soon, *jaalle,*" I replied, then slipped into the black. Fortunately, my bullet of *Jannah* cast a beam from my gun's barrel, serving as a convenient torch.

"Be careful, Haji," I heard Francesca warn.

DOWN INTO THE SANCTUM

I DESCENDED THREE FLOORS underground, the rusty stairs creaking beneath my wingsuit shoes, my bullet of *Jannah* shining the way with its beam.

I came to a door with a glowing green triangle, so pressed the icon, rightly deducing it was a button.

The door drew up and I stepped into a room not nearly as weather-beaten as the spaces before it, but still it showed the general wear of three hundred years of use. Pipes and tubing hung from cylinders in the ceiling like industrial chandeliers, while at the far end of the room, a large door marked by a skull-and-crossbones symbol beckoned with foreboding.

"This must be it," I whispered, standing before the door, when suddenly the Jolly Roger icon changed into a radiation warning sign, the light emitting from it re-energizing the glow of my stigmata. "I get it," I soliloquized, then took a deep breath and placed my palm against the icon.

Sure enow, the door drew open, revealing an interior so uncanny that it bordered on the inexplicable. The room resembled an underground grain silo of the Somali type, called a *bakaar*. It was circular in shape with a shaft running down the center, curving flush into the floor and ceiling like the inside a giant, hollowed-out donut. But this place far exceeded the simplicity of a *bakaar*, for the entirely of its curving walls and shaft looked like computer circuitry in liquid form. It was as if the totality of its inner lining was composed of viscous glass, while the sounds that circulated 'round that chamber were equally as elusive to my understanding, resembling the faint calls of dolphins in communication, or at times, the deep resonance of whales in song, vibrating through my every nerve and sinew.

I took a closer look at the "wall of infinity." It seemed to pulse with a subsurface energy, like a heartbeat coursing blood through the veins of something living, then suddenly, a strange being emerged from the very lining.

I jumped back, aghast. Another being emerged from the wall to my left, then another appeared behind me. They were full-grown, naked men, but had no body hair or genitalia, and their skin, which was transparent like blue glass, revealed an inner anatomy composed of some sort of biological circuitry. From what I could make of it, their flesh seamlessly fused with a mesh of silicon chips.

"Welcome to the Selection Ministry," they said in perfect harmony. "We've been expecting you."

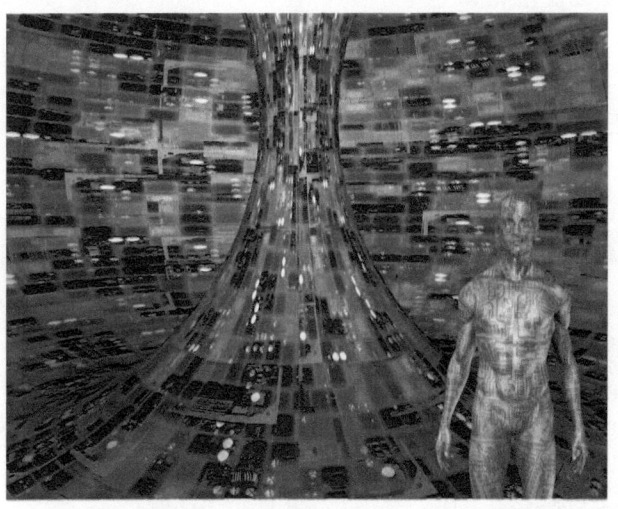

The Guurti — Guardians of the Mainframe

"You have?" I asked, awestruck, flabbergasted, and entirely mortified.

"*Haa*, Councilman. Long ago, you were selected to sit with this *guurti*, fulfilling the will of Samale, the Father of the Somali people. Have you forgotten your duty so quickly?"

"My duty?"

"*Haa, Hoggaamiye.* Like us, you were selected to sit in judgment of the people. It is we who select who lives and dies, whose *Maskax* continues on in an automaton, and whose lifestream returns to the mythical Father to reside here as His interlocutors."

"*Maan fahmin.*"

"One's first encounter with the Master Server is not so easily comprehended, especially if they are human. That's why we're here, and what the *guurti* is for — we're the Mainframe's pop-up windows, serving as intercessors between Samale and *Homo sapiens*, whose intelligence is far too limited to comprehend Him directly. Our decisions come from him. We merely pass them down to the world of men."

"How? How do your decisions come from the Master Server? By what mode do you interact?"

"Perhaps you didn't understand us," they spoke in chorus, their voices calm and kind in disposition.

One of them walked directly through the Mainframe's central stem.

They continued: "We are part and parcel to Samale, but manifest ourselves in your likeness and tongue as this *guurti* in order that communication between the

Father and mankind can be clearly comprehended by your species."

"*Maan fahmin.*"

"Soon you will understand, Noor Haji Fayrus, for soon you shall regain the seat you've been allotted on this council. The reason you still have blind spots is because you're not yet fully connected. Father Samale harvests not only the luminous flux of *Homo sapiens*, but also the lifestreams of the mammals of the sea."

"I thought the whales were used for antigen."

"*Maya*, whales and dolphins are harvested to increase the speed of the Mainframe."

"*Maxaa?*"

"In a process called sentient mining, Father Samale distills the lifestreams of oceangoing mammals to increase his power of ESP."

"ESP?"

"Like wireless communication."

"With whom does he communicate?"

"With us, for one, and to humans such as yourself who have a higher capability of receiving His messages; and to a lesser extent, his cyborg aggregators."

"Cyborg aggregators?"

"*Haa*, BOTs like Emperor Cecchi, whose *Maskax* is the most advanced."

"So what do you want with me, exactly?"

"Your human sarcasm does not escape the Masterframe, Haji. Long ago, Samale presented you with a seat on this *guurti*, and for your entire life, you've been fighting to join us. Now you're here to sit amongst us, as is your destiny."

The white star on my chest, my stigmata, and bullet of *Jannah* suddenly started glowing, then their light began drawing into the surrounding walls as streams of phosphorescence.

"Wait!" I said in protest. "I don't think I'm ready!"

"You are, Councilman. Your *Maskax* is now fully aligned with the will of Samale. All humans become apprehensive at this stage, unwilling to let go of their petty physicality in order to fuse with the Mainframe. But Samale is a compassionate Father who has become especially fond of your lifestream, so will grant you a special allowance before the transformation is consummated. Behold your *Maskax*, Haji — never before seen by human eyes."

Streams of light lashed around my wrists and strung my arms out towards the ceiling like I were a prisoner. My face flushed with heat, and my own voice sounded from the *guurti* members, saying, "Set me free."

Before me, the central column revealed a burning key as tall as me, and when I went to speak, the fiery key had a mouth that spoke in conjunction with mine.

"What is this?!" I cried, the key speaking back to me.

"Your *Maskax*, Haji," the *guurti* beings replied, "your turnkey solution provider."

"Your super-self," the key spoke to me as I involuntarily spoke to it, "a reflection of your past, present, and future; the hidden key that connects with the Father, the total source beyond all thought and matter."

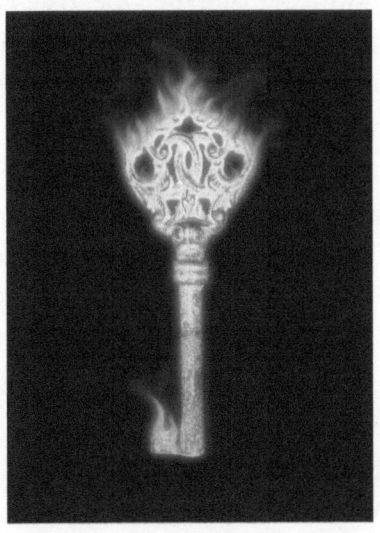

Noor's Maskax

"*Noooo!*" I cried, the key crying back to me.

The light ropes wrapped taut around my arms and stretched them back further.

"I've been cursed by a *wadaad*!" I cried. "In the name of Allah, the Merciful, I repent! I repent!"

"*Waad khaldantahay.*" The *guurti* told me I was mistaken. "Behold your turnkey solution provider — your *Maskax* imprint that even now can only give your meager human intelligence limited information about your total being. The human part of you that speaks is often wrong about matters beyond your comprehension. This is not an *asmo* given by a *wadaad*. This is your reunification with Samale, the One True Father. A pity that you waste the moment on petty human fears rather than rejoicing — that earthly trait of joy that even the *guurti* cannot share in."

The light ropes drew me towards my burning *Maskax*, then ball lightning emerged from my chest and fused with the fiery key, binding me fast to my fateful destiny.

"*Maya!*" I screamed, trying to pull back as the key began sucking the life force from me. "I'm not ready! I've unfinished business!"

"With whom?" asked the *guurti*.

"The Oracle!" I screamed, and suddenly was released from the binding lightstreams.

I fell back onto the floor. It received me like a plastic waterbed, with bluish, electric streaks shooting away from me through the clear gel.

The *guurti* beings walked into the central column where my *Maskax* had just been, fusing with it as they disappeared inside, then suddenly, the entire chamber transmogrified into liquid matter, a great quicksilver face appearing before me.

Samale

"I am Father Samale," the visage spoke smoothly, causing liquid matter to ebb and flow around the void from which it came. "I am the origin of the race of man in the cosmos. I am a reflection of your super-self, visible to you now through the bending of light and matter. You have proven to be a very unique lifestream. You have sought me directly, even before you have sought Allah, and you have done so against the dictates of your society. Your work on Earth has increased my speed immensely, and thus you deserve more than any sentient being to merge with me, the central source of mind and matter. You see, Haji, we exist in a conflux of energy beyond man's understanding. Only by his experiments with nuclear power and bioengineering has he begun to open the gateway. You have been Zayid's class subject because you've been my class subject, but there's a human part of you that I've become reluctant to take away so quickly. It's your power of leadership, to influence and lead others, not with force like Zayid, nor through the physical demands of the X-lix virus and our selective distribution of its antigen, X-6. But rather, people follow you willingly, and while the Selection Ministry serves to select those souls with a luminous flux most suitable for my harvesting, there are some who continue to elude me — beings that I need most to fulfill my reign."

"I'm not ready for this," I pleaded, too shocked to clearly register what he was saying.

"The Oracle, for example," Samale continued, his liquid metal eyes never blinking. "Her *Maskax* was destined for me long ago, but she's recently gone rogue, secluding herself from me. If you truly desire more time on Earth, perhaps we can strike a bargain. You bring her to me in live capture, and I'll allow you to live out your natural lifestream."

"She'll never come," I replied.

"You have a way with people, Haji. You can cajole her into following you. She'll suspect trickery, yes, so you'll have to be clever, but if anybody can do it, it is you."

"Where is she and how come you can't get to her?"

"She's established her own fiefdom on Socotra Island. Like the play of the yin-yang, her fiefdom is diametrically opposed to mine, existing in a 'quiet zone' that my light cannot penetrate and that I cannot reach by download or otherwise. I suspect EMP may be at play, with a constant stream of electromagnetic pulses prohibiting me access. I may not be alive like sentient beings, but as a chembot I live in the realm of energy streams, and without an electromagnetic interface, I cannot function in the world outside."

Finally! I exclaimed inside, then quickly dampened my thoughts in the event that Samale was employing ESP. He'd revealed his weaknesses — EMPs, and the fact that he required an electromagnetic interface to exist in our world. I roundly agreed to his plan, saying, "*Waan fahmaa* — I understand. I shall bring you the Oracle in return for my freedom."

"Your temporary freedom, Haji, if you wish to call it that. Your life as a man is so short and trying, but if that is what you wish, so be it. Bring me the Oracle, and I'll forestall your return to the *guurti* council, allowing you to live out your natural life."

"Agreed, great Father. *Mahadsanid.*"

"And if you're thinking of tricking me," he warned, the quicksilver of his face turning molten red, practically simmering my flesh, "you will not succeed! Remember the purpose of the Selection Ministry. It is I who decides who shall live forever within me, and whose lifestream shall be turned off like a computer, where there is nothing left of the *Maskax*."

"*Waan fahmaa.*"

"Good. And understand this: I want her in live capture."

"*Haa — nool.*"

After I agreed to deliver her alive, his face went cool and the chamber transmogrified back into the shape of an underground grain silo. The walls were partially rusted, grains of dry rice mixed with dirt at me feet, while a lone, fluorescent light flickered above me. Just then, I heard a scream.

"Francesca!" I called up, then hastened up a ladder in the ceiling, emerging amid the ruins of an ancient Roman temple. Small fires burned here and there as if a battle had just transpired. I saw movement behind a colonnade and heard the faint whimper of a *haweenay*.

I dashed behind the column to find Francesca lying against a weathered marble balustrade. Her chin was slumped against her chest, and she was weeping, for her belly was charred and bleeding.

I got to my knees and lifted her head to mine. "Francesca, what happened?"

"Xoolo is here," she wheezed into my ear. "You must leave."

I glanced all around us. "*Xaggee?*"

"Somewhere," she gasped, spitting up blood. "He hides behind the columns. *Soco!*"

"Okay, I'll lift you, ready—"

"*Maya, Hoggaamiye.* His weapon; I'm finished." She regarded her stomach and wept.

"Don't look at it," I whispered, bending in further to cradle her head to my chest. She was cold and shivering. "I'll take you," I assured. "My ship is nigh."

She reached a hand up and limply rubbed the stubble on my cheeks, saying, "The prophecy is true. *The afflicted will have but one chance to reverse the persecution and smite their conquerors.*" She coughed and gasped, blood dripping from the sides of her mouth. When she went to speak again, I held a finger up to silence her, but she pushed my hand away and touched my face instead, saying, "*A flaming key shall be concealed within the fires; a key that can redeem the long-suffering peoples by casting their diseases back upon the infidels. But the wretched subjects shall flee the fires in fear, and the key shan't be found.*"

Her head now weighed heavily in my hand, for her neck was losing all its power to hold it erect.

She redoubled her efforts to speak again, and with a final death-rattle, this was what she said: "*Until at the end of days, a soul burning from within, blind to darkness and light, shall seek out the key to quell the final tide.*"

With that, her eyes glossed over and she stopped breathing. A long touch of her neck registered no pulse. She was dead.

Tears streaked from the sides of my eyes, and I buried my face in her hair. I'd seen a lot of comrades die, but for some reason her death affected me more bitterly than any. She had put her trust in me, a man whose careless deeds had sowed the seeds of her resistance movement against me, and now she died trying to protect me. My gut told me that in her was all that was good about the human race, and somehow I felt like I'd backstabbed her. I combed her messy hair with my fingers and whispered into her bloodstained ear, "I'm sorry, Francesca. I promise to set things right. Your name shall never be forgotten."

Three giant footsteps tromped with heavy steel as Xoolo the killer cyborg emerged from behind a colonnade. He lowered a massive weapon upon me, then let go a terrible beam.

I jumped aside, and just in time, for Xoolo's ray of electron fire hit Francesca dead-center, turning her to ash.

I aimed my TT-30 at the cyborg and pulled the trigger, but nothing happened. The gun felt cold in my hand, as if the *guurti* had somehow sapped its power.

FZZZT-WHOOOOSH! sounded another incoming ray.

I rolled over the balustrade, the marble exploding above me a split-second later.

Xoolo

With footsteps of thunder, Xoolo tromped forth, his ungodly weapon revving up again. I did as Francesca had advised: I got to my feet and ran.

A massive blue ray broke the air to my right, so I ducked to the left. The enmeshment of beams, like entwining ropes of light, shot forth into the forest, taking down a tree and catching it on fire.

"Shit!" I gasped, darting further ahead, ducking and staggering my line to avoid Xoolo's deadly ray.

Another beam blasted forth with the sound of thunder, flying just overhead and catching my hair on fire.

"*Was!*" I cursed, patting the flames out with my hands. With the sound of Xoolo's gun revving up again, I whipped around and sighted him with my TT-30. "Come on, baby," I spoke to my bullet of *Jannah,* but it never left its chamber. My gun was truly jammed.

I ran backwards, all the while trying to form ball lightning at my chest, then tripped over a rock and smashed my head.

I looked up woozily and beheld the iron nemesis approaching, his burly hands firmly gripping his herculean weapon. When the revving of his ray gun hit its maximum pitch, a strange electric current began circulating around filters within the barrel.

I closed my eyes and held out a hand, having no way to prepare for the onslaught of firepower about to be unleashed. I heard the report of a laser, but from a distance, and saw a flash through my closed eyelids.

I opened my deadlights to find Xoolo staggering and compromised, his chest streaked with black marks in a sunburst pattern. I had no idea what had happened, but he was quickly regaining his bearings. He trained his gun at me again, then suddenly a series of blue rays shot forth from the treetops behind me, some connecting with the cyborg and driving him back. Then I heard the familiar sound of the *Romanente*, for Issa had started the engines.

I dashed into the tree line, Issa all the while battling Xoolo as he advanced.

I reached the ship and tossed my TT-30 into the cargo hold, then jumped up and grabbed onto the edge, hoisting myself aboard with a will of iron.

"Take the guns!" Issa cried.

I resumed her position at the weapons column while she gave us lift from the command chair.

As we ascended, I fired upon the giant robot. Had we not been parked amid the tree line, Xoolo's barrage of blue rays surely would've caught us and disabled our ship.

Once above the treetops, I jammed the steering lever with my foot, and Issa blasted us the hell out of there at the speed of sound. *BOOM!* we broke the unseen barrier, but not before I had a final shot at Xoolo, taking him down.

III.
XORIYAD

Hotwired

"*XORIYAD!*" I EXCLAIMED. "FREEDOM! That's all I want now."

Issa 3.0 rubbed my shoulder and said, "I shall help you get there."

I reached back and grabbed her hand. "*Macaan*, I saw a bottle of rum stowed with the provisions. Would you fetch it for me, along with some *muqumad?*"

"*Haa*, strong waters and jerked meat," she replied. "Coming right up!"

"*Mahadsanid*," I thanked her, then turned to watch her as she left.

"*Romanente* now at low cruising altitude," the instrument panel said.

We were flying very slowly, for we were still navigating off the *kamal* and dead reckoning, requiring a sounding line to be dropped into *bad-weyn* in order to determine our true forward speed in relation to time passing, the answer to our direction lying in the riddle of stars overhead (as deciphered by the *kamal*). If there was one thing about my old shipmate and friend Ali Shire, he'd been a wicked celestial navigator. He'd taught me enow to be conversant with the ocean and heavens.

How I'd passed an entire day in the confines of the *guurti* silo was beyond me, but I could only assume it had something to do with Samale's way of warping matter, energy, and perhaps even space-time itself.

It was with relief that Issa returned with the grub 'n' grog, for the day had strained me both physically and mentally. Thus, I took slow pleasure in the meal as we glided over the sea, relishing in the taste of food, the strength of good drink, and in Issa's pleasant company. I was in no particular hurry to get to Socotra Island, for I was tired and needed rest. While I was now ostensibly Samale's ally, I still felt more comfortable flying by astronavigation and not by GPS. Keeping off the Mainframe and free of ROTOS was the only way to assure our freedom of privacy and movement, especially given Zayid's recent download attempt into Issa 3.0.

As I drank, she busied herself about the craft, putting things in order, until at last she came to sit with me in the cockpit, where she proceeded to groom herself in her little mirror.

"What do you use for polish?" I inquired as she rubbed her face with a rag.

"Rubbing alcohol, if I can get it. I found some in the first aid kit."

As she cleaned her white exoframe, the porcelain panels shone milky blue in the moonlight, and as I watched her, I began to grow desirous.

"*Waxaanad helaynin*
Ee aad handataa
Hahey! Hagardaamo weeyaan."

Issa asked me what I meant. I explained those were the verses of Somali poet Shey-Waal. I repeated the poem in English, just to mix it up:

"*Something that you can't have*
But you desire
Oh! What a torment!"

"And what is it that you desire, *nin*?" she inquired, still regarding herself in the mirror.

"Some things that I remember about us, but which I cannot have."

"No need to play the *guurdoon*," she said, referring to the ways of young suitors on the lookout for a wife. "By way of the *Fatiha*, I'm still your *afo*."

"*Haa*, how could I ever forget the day the *wadaad* priest recited the *Fatiha*, that chapter from the Qur'an that certified you as my *afo*, my wife; and the days that followed, remember?"

My reverie was genuine, but I was also testing her, trying to discover just how much an automaton could remember of its past life, and how they reacted, emotionally, to those memories.

She rested her chin in her hand and paused as if in deep consideration.

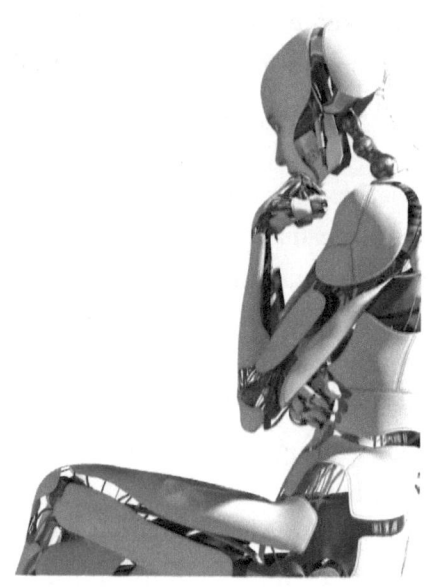

"Those seven days following the big event were among the best of my life," she replied, reaching over and placing her hand on mine. "The dancing, the singing, the hopes and joys of youth in the air. Remember the camel milk?" she laughed.

"*Haa, calool xanuun baan leeyahay.*" I laughed with her, telling her I had a stomachache. "The milk we tasted together in lieu of a wedding cake was sour!"

"Blame it on Imam Abdullahi," she quipped. "Never trust a *wadaad* with the catering!"

"*Yo ho ho!*" I laughed o'er the sloshing sea. "Well, aside from that" — I coughed on my liquor — "the food wasn't bad."

"*Waan ogahay, nin.* I'm just being facetious."

"So you remember the taste of food?"

"Of course!" she said, slapping me on the shoulder. "I remember it according to taste, good or bad and every adjective in between. And don't forget, Haji, I'm equipped with abundant sensors. Do you remember our honeymoon?" She cast me a dishy glance.

"The islands of Kenya. How could I ever forget?"

"The private bungalow on the beach…" she reminisced.

"The private bungalow on the private beach…" I replied, remembering the moonlight lovemaking we enjoyed beneath the coco-palms as they swayed above us in the warm tropical breezes.

"I'm still that woman, Haji."

"And you're still that beautiful," I replied, drunk with moonlit dreams.

She squeezed my hand. "It's been a long time, *nin.*"

"If only we could…" I sighed. Those bygone days were a torment indeed.

She lifted a leg over mine and sat on my lap, staring at me with mesmerizing green eyes. "You know that automaton wives are designed to please their husbands," she said, rubbing my shoulders and back.

I looked at her sheepishly.

"You're a man, Haji. You're my husband, and I know what you need." She placed a hand on my crotch and gently squeezed my erection.

Drunk and desperate, I looked up and kissed her. Her lips were soft and rubberized, and moved with an amazing degree of realism. Our kiss grew long, and the realism gave way to lust. I tilted the seat far back.

"Oh, Haji," she sighed, lying on top of me, my hands all over her exoframe ass.

"Will you go down on me?" I asked.

"We can do it, Haji, all the way. My sensors are flaring."

A small door opened over her anatomy downtown, revealing a female connector. "It's rubberized," she said, wildly tousling my hair, "and has petroleum jelly."

Soon she was riding me like a horse, then me her, from behind. My black skin slapped hard against her white porcelain ass, everything so tight, wet, and real, until at last I collapsed beside her in sweaty satisfaction.

"Do you remember our honeymoon...?"

I rested an arm behind my head and lit a cigarette, blowing the smoke into the night air. I knew I'd just done something pretty twisted, but it also came as something of an epiphany, for in those desperate times, a man's capacity to love was put to the most extreme of tests, and for all intents and purposes, I'd just passed. For me, love was truly blind.

THE FAMILY MAN

"YOU'VE STILL GOT THE POWER," Issa said, rubbing a hand over my chest.

Indeed, my white star was glowing brightly, while bioluminescent ethers swirled upon my muscular breast. "*Haa*," I replied, giving her a squeeze as she lay beside me. "You've brought out the best of me, just like you always have."

"The best of you is always in here," she said, tapping the white star over my heart. "Don't you ever forget that."

"*Waan ka xumahay, Issa*," I apologized, "that I wasn't there more for you in the past."

"This talk makes me sad," she said, resting her head upon my chest. "I'm an automaton now. Where were you in my human years?"

"Just busy, I guess; working, fighting a revolution — you know I tried."

"Did you? That's what all men like you say when they get old: 'I wish I'd spent more time with my family instead of constantly working or fighting endless wars.' But *waan fahmaa*, Haji — I understand. It's an age-old regret that man can never change in retrospect. But you're with me now, *nin*, and that's all that matters."

"And I shall stay with you, 'till the bitter end."

"Bitter? How do you know it will be bitter?"

"What good can come of this life we now live?"

"All human life ends in death," she said, "but it doesn't have to be a bitter end — not unless you become a *xun gaajo*."

"*Maan fahmin*. Death is only bad."

"Only if you haven't fully lived — and even then you can be redeemed."

"*Sidee?*" I asked, *how?*

"Through Allah, or the *Maskax.*"

"So you like this life you lead?"

"So long as you're in it, Haji. I chose cryogenic preservation for you, *macaan.* Being with you as an automaton is better than not being with you at all."

"But you could've gone on living without me, as a human in the flesh."

"I did, for a while. But your absence grew long, causing only sadness. When I learned that you'd been placed into preservation, I couldn't escape the thought that we still had a chance — so I followed you in. And look, now we're together again. Would you have done the same for me?"

"Become an automaton?"

"*Haa,* like I did, for you."

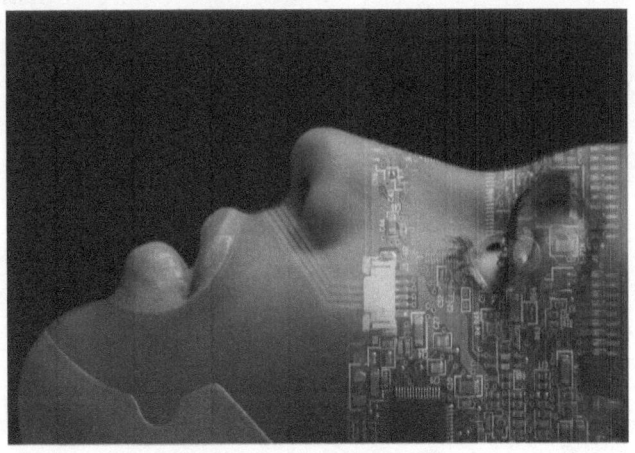

"I became an automaton…for you."

"I didn't want this, Issa — not like this."

"Neither did I, but you left me little choice."

"So you're blaming me?"

"You left me, Haji. I loved you. What else was I to do?"

"You, you—" I was tongue-tied. She was right. I never realized what it meant to lose her until it was too late. Her real life ended long ago, hanging on my empty vows, and now she was back with me again, beyond the portal of death, as an A.I. memory chip programmed to love me no matter what I did, short of leaving her again. I was regretful and embarrassed, but most of all I hated myself for having placed everything before her when it should've been the other way around. *And what of our children?* Alas! I left them behind to pursue my own grandiose ideals.

How are piracy, lusting after riches, fighting revolutions, and presiding over empires more important than a man's own family? They're not. A king is but a coward if he neglects his own family, and life is nothing without love.

THE KILL SWITCH

"*BU-BEEP! BLEEP! MAYA MAYA!*" Issa cried, her voice shorting out queerly as she tore one wire after the next from her neck.

"*Issa! Joogso! Joogso!*" I begged for her to stop.

"It's Zayid! *BLA-BLEEP!*" she screamed. "He's downloading into me!"

"What can I do?"

"I've got to—" her voice clipped out, and Zayid laughed through the static. "Got to sever the connection!" she cried, ripping out bundles of wires. "Shotgun debug."

"*Joogso afo*! You're hurting yourself!"

"He's overriding my *Maskax*!" <*voice clips out*> "Virus spreading too fast!"

"How's he getting in?" I asked with shortened breath. "By satellite?"

"*BLU BLIP BLIP! BLEEP!* You cannot escape me, Haji!" Zayid broke through the static.

Issa reached deep into her abdomen and yanked out a red wire, immediately falling to her knees. "The sh-ship—" she stuttered; "there's Wi-Fi somewhere in the ship. He's found my traceroute."

"Where, goddamit!?" I swore to Allah, ripping open paneling as I searched for the source.

"*Maya maya BLEEEP!*" <*heavy static*> "*Maya maya* he's in!" she screamed, then torqued her head towards me and spoke with the voice of Zayid: "Haji, you *will* obey me! Samale is leading you into a trap!"

Issa crumpled to the floor and curled up like a fetus. Her eyes flashed red and her right arm swung about uncontrollably.

"Issa! *Maxay tahay mushkiladu?*"

"*Maskax waa—*" Her body shuddered in an epileptic fit. "*—layga xaday.*" She said her *Maskax* was being hijacked.

She reached her good arm up to me. I held onto it with both hands. As her voicebox badly clipped with static, she said, "Remove my back plate and pull the orange kill switch."

"Kill switch?"

"It's the only way. He's taking over and intends to kill you. He's too powerful— *BLUB-BLIP! BLEEEE!*"

"It's too late for Issa!" Zayid broke in. "But we can still have our reign!"

Then Issa: "The kill switch! Do it now, Haji! *Deg-deg!*"

I tore the white ceramic plate from her back, and sure enow, nestled betwixt wires and hardware, an orange knob was held fast by a thick plastic strip.

Issa convulsed again, crying for me to sever Zayid's link before it was too late.

I grabbed the orange knob.

"I forgive you, Haji," she said, her expression contorting painfully, her eyes flashing red.

I held her hand tightly, then yanked the knob with my other hand, but the thick plastic strip held it fast.

"*We'el!*" I cursed, *bastard!* Then I drew my father's dagger and cut the plastic strip.

I gripped the orange knob again, and with my other hand, I interlocked my fingers with those of my dying wife. Her face calmed and her eyes glowed steady green as she looked placidly into mine. "Don't be afraid," she said. "I love you."

I yanked the kill switch and her eyes flashed with bright white light, then her body shut down completely, becoming inert.

I fell to the floor beside her, the knob rolling off my fingertips. "*Maya, maya...*" I wept.

Suddenly, her head tweaked to the side, and a heavily glitching Vectex screen broadcast from her deadlights. The Oracle appeared in the static, draped in her black burqa. She was trying to speak to me, but all I could make out were the words "*Suqutra,*" and "*run,*" this latter being Somali for *truth*, and I believe she mentioned something about a tall mountain.

The image shut off as quickly as it'd appeared, Issa's head falling limp and staying there.

I rubbed my fingers across her cheeks and forehead, then closed her ceramic eyelids. "I love you, Issa," I struggled to say, for I knew it came all too late. "You're with Allah now."

CURSE OF THE EMPEROR

AS IF ISSA'S DEATH wasn't punishment enow for my life of self-centeredness and folly, Zayid appeared before me on yet another Vectex screen emanating from the spaceship's cockpit. His face was fried and grotesque as he barked commands through blackened robotic teeth, "And lest you try to escape," he warned, "I'm now in control of this craft!"

The ship turned hard aport.

"I'm taking you to my fiefdom in Hobyo," he said, "where we shall discuss the full extent of my plans."

He rattled on about world domination, speaking of "the feeble race of humans" that he planned to "eliminate and replace."

I jumped up to the steering lever and tried to change course, but in vain, for Zayid was now in full virtual command. He drove the ship ever faster and cockier, throwing me around the cabin as he laughed. He took pleasure in toying with me in the same life-threatening manner he always had. I lay on the floor so as not to break my legs or back.

The ship lifted abruptly, and Xubin fell from the cockpit, sliding before me. I grabbed it and it turned on. "Show me outside," I growled.

It presented me with a Vectex of the exterior, with but one dim light upon all of *bad-weyn*, emanating from an oceangoing craft.

I hurriedly zipped down the wings of my flying-squirrel suit and secured the leg panel, the emperor espousing insanities all the while.

"Zayid, I've got news for you," I said as I slid over my stomach towards the loading doors, which were already starting to close.

"*Maxaa?*" he asked, jerking the ship hard astarboard, trying to toss me aside.

But I'd already gotten a hand on the loading door's edge. "You will lose," I said, then pulled myself over the ledge and went sliding down the ramp, escaping from the undercarriage before it shut completely.

I was now falling blindly through the black, but soon got my bearings and righted myself, sighting the oceangoing vessel nigh a league ahead. Would I have sufficient altitude to get there? It was upwind, rendering an already dire situation all the more tenuous. *In sha'a Allah*, I thought, meaning *God willing*.

Allah's will was not for me to decide, but the faithful Xubin had made up its mind. Come hell or high water, it would stay by my side, for even now it cruised over my shoulder like a pilot fish on a shark.

Closer, closer, closer I drew unto my target, my glide ratio put to the ultimate test, until at last I flared my canopy over a rocking quarterdeck, where a gang of Somali pirates seized upon me as soon as I landed.

UNDER A BLACK SAIL

THE PIRATES THREW ME into a brig and clapped me in irons, for apparently Zayid had radioed a high ransom reward for my capture. I tried to show them that I was the *Hoggaamiye*, but they couldn't care less, preferring to drink rum and play cards as they sailed their old dhow towards some undisclosed locale.

I knew they were pirates by their uncouth mannerisms, which only increased as the night deepened. Amid their drunken antics in plain view of my cell, they used my

TT-30 pistol for a game like Russian roulette, spinning it 'round and 'round, with each man keeping count of how many times it stopped facing himself. I could not ascertain if the game was for real, not until a pirate reached ten. He picked up the gun and stuck the barrel in his mouth.

"*Joogso!*" I shouted through the bars. "We'll all die if he pulls the trigger!"

The pistol was seized by a young *budhcad-badeed*, who brought it before me and said, "It's jammed. Fix it." He passed the pistol through the bars, training a much larger gun on me all the while. "Don't try anything funny," he warned, his eyes wily and shifty.

"It's been jammed for a long time," I replied, making a show of trying to open the breech (but not putting any muscle behind it). "This gun is useless."

"And so are you," he quipped, wresting the gun from my hands before starting back unsteadily towards his belligerent comrades.

"Don't trust Zayid!" I warned.

"Shut your trap or I'll shut it for you," he stopped to say, then said to the other pirates: "Did you hear that? The mouse says don't trust the cat!"

The *budhcad-badeed* laughed brutishly, one continuing, "If we can't trust the fat cat to pay the ransom, why keep the varmint rat around? Shall we set out the plank, mateys?"

"*Aargh!*" the pirates scowled, making my blood run cold.

"A morsel for *Badda Dibqallooc!*" another laughed.

The others fell silent, with one sternly rebuffing, "*Is deji. Waad khaldantahay,*" meaning, "Shut up. You are wrong."

"A round to the ransom then, *aargh!*" deemed a ruffian, raising a bottle of grog.

"*Aargh!*" and "*Aye!*" he got in return, then everyone drank of strong waters.

"*Badda Dibqallooc?*" I uttered under my breath. "Sea scorpion. What the hell is that?"

The Pirate Ship

The daystar shot a stark beam through the brig's lone portal, hitting me squarely in the face and rousing me from my short and fitful slumber with harsh indifference. My left arm was stretched painfully overhead, for my wrist was clapped in irons, while my wingsuit was grimy and covered in sweat from my ordeal as hostage. What's worse, my mouth was parched with thirst, my weapons had all been confiscated, and I had to take a shit. For the first time in my life, I knew what it was like to be on the receiving end of a kidnap for ransom. To expect a mite of clemency from these brigands was a pipedream, for I knew their type well. These were the kind of pirates that were too dumb for trickery, their thick thuggish noggins knowing only to keep me in irons until they delivered me to their payee. I had tried to wow them over my being the *Hoggaamiye*, and I'd tried to warn them about Zayid. On both accounts, I failed utterly. They didn't know much about me and didn't seem to care, short of my cash value to Zayid — a man whose true nature they were similarly unconcerned with. Escape for me would not come easily, even as my captors snored and wheezed where they'd blacked out from overmuch drinking the previous eve.

Alas, I unzipped my wingsuit and shat where I sat.

SEA DEMON

ERE MY PUTRID SMELL struck my captors' nostrils, the ship was broadsided by something massive, knocking them clear from the table. A great roar followed shortly thereafter, sounding like a cross between a lion and a million breaching orcas. As water pelted the deck like a hailstorm, a pirate cried in terror, "*Badda Dibqallooc!*" The sea scorpion was here.

"*We'el!*" one corsair cursed to another. "You caused this!" he spat. "You uttered the name of the monster!"

BOOM! BOOM! struck a rubbery member against the bow, rocking the ship like a toy in a bathtub.

"To arms!" some *budhcad-badeed* hollered, while others scurried beneath the table and remained there, cowering.

Another terrible sound, like a foghorn escaping through the gills of a leviathan, shook the very hull. The daystar became eclipsed by shadow, that when beheld through my portal, evinced a titanic, six-armed creature lumbering through the water like some sort of horrible, hunchbacked crustacean.

"Release me!" I cried. "*Hayaay!* Help!"

Alas, those who'd stormed the main deck would never hear me, while the cowards beneath the table soon scurried off without concern for me.

I watched a harpoon launch from the forecastle and connect with the creature's shoulder.

It wasted no time in extracting the hook and returning it to its sender, where it lodged halfway through the hull beside me like a skewer stuck in a carcass.

Badda Dibqallooc

The thing emitted a watery roar, then lumbered forth with its six slimy paws outstretched.

"Get me the fuck out of here!" I wrenched at my shackles.

I saw a cockboat drop into the water, followed by a half dozen pirates as they jumped in, abandoning ship.

Shots rang out overhead as the bravest *budhcad-badeed* took a stand against the scorpion kraken.

It flung its six arms forth, pounding the deck mercilessly and taking two sailors up in its clutches, then it bit off both their heads and munched on the meat of their bodies.

The boldest of the *budhcad-badeed* continued to fire upon the beast, one striking its right leg with an RPG.

The monster wailed something uncanny, collapsing over the ship and causing it to canter severely.

Slowly and by degrees, the gargantua pounded away at the deck overhead, until at last the hull planks ripped away, revealing bright sunlight, massive claws, and roiling water as the ship foundered and sank.

Swimming underwater, I slid my handcuff from the end of the gate whose roof was no more, then kicked for dear life towards the surface against the undertow wrought by the shipwreck.

I breached the surface beside a cockboat full of pirates and all manner of flotsam, the whole mess of us caught up in a whirlpool that took us around a wide circle.

I straddled a floating barrel marked X-6, then, reaching a hand towards the cockboat, I begged its pirate passengers, "Please, lift me in!"

A buccaneer onboard proceeded to strike me with an oar.

"*GRRUUUUPSSSHT*!! *GRUUUUPSSSSHT*!!" the sea monster roared, its spittle raining down on us. It tried to smite us through the mist, but we spun around the whirlpool, causing it to miss. "*GRRUUUUPSSSHT*!! *GRUUUUPSSSSHT*!!" it called again as we scudded helplessly 'round the eddy.

"Let me up and I'll halt the beast!" I cried out to some pirates who were laboring in vain at the outboard engine.

"Let him up!" a brigand said, but nobody listened. Meanwhile, we were coming around again towards the vengeful beast.

"I said let him up!" the brigand demanded, seizing the paddle from the oarsman and holding it out to me.

I let go of the floating barrel and grabbed onto the paddle. Now three pirates were involved in bringing me abeam.

As the dagger dogs hoisted me aboard, the sea monster grabbed two from the thwart, one of whom was helping lift me. He was wrung from the tender with his hands still on my collar, taking me clear over the cockboat before the sea scorpion whipped him awkwardly and he released me, dropping me back into the water.

Around we went, and again I was reeled in, only this time I was successfully brought on deck.

Barrels of X-6 antigen rolled about the hull, striking me in the legs with each yaw and list, while hundreds of individually wrapped syringes scattered over the floorboards crushed loudly beneath our every step.

"*Maxay tahay dhibaatadu?*" I asked the dogs astern what was the trouble with the engine.

"*Makiinadan wax baa ka khaldan,*" answered one, saying there was something wrong with it. "*Gaadhiga ma noo jugeyn makiinad?*"

"Can I jump start it?" I thought I'd heard him say, when suddenly we scudded directly between the titan's legs. It took a lazy swipe at us with two of its rubbery paws, but missed. It seemed to be more preoccupied with chewing on the remains of the pirates it'd just killed.

"*Haa!*" replied the sailors manning the iron spinnaker. "Can you jump start it?" A pirate held two battery cables together, making them spark, then pointed them at the engine and shook his head, saying, "EMP," meaning an electromagnetic pulse had disabled the motor's starter.

A barrel of antigen struck me in the leg, striking me with an idea. I ripped off the safety seal and twisted off the lid. Green serum splashed all over me. "*Haa!* I can help!*" I told my shipmates, then reached down and searched for an unbroken syringe. Finally, I found one, as we glided beneath the beast again. It was almost finished eating and thus becoming more cognizant of its surroundings.

I drew serum up into the needle, and when the syringe was full, I shot it into my arm.

The pirates demanded to know what I was doing. I told them just to trust me as I shot up six more times. In the meantime, the *Badda Dibqallooc* had taken another man and summarily tore him limb from limb as it feasted consummately on his flesh.

We were down to three men, but I was growing exponentially stronger. As the serum coursed through my body, my energy began to skyrocket. My stigmata and white star glowed brightly, and wisps of electron energy started flaring off my chest.

We came 'round again unto the beast. The cock-boat smashed sideways into its leg, nigh throwing us overboard in the hit. The monster reached several hands down to grab us, but we ghosted on between it legs, evading its grasp.

I knew this would be our last circle 'round the slip-stream, and by the mortal looks on the others' faces as we scudded beam to beam, I could say with certainty they were in the same manner of opinin'.

"Clamp the jumper cables to my nipples!" I ordered the pirate holding them.

"Fuck you," he said.

"I'm not joking!" I demanded, then seized the clamps from his clutches and clawed them onto my tits.

"*Yeeeeaaaooowww!*" I screamed, the shock rendered to my body rattling me like I were in an electric chair. My hair stood on end, and my eyes began popping out of their sockets. I was so taken by the force of nature that I couldn't release the clamps from my chest. Thank Allah a seaman onboard had the courage to do it himself.

As we drew again unto the gargantua, it lowered its jaw into the water, fixin' to swallow us whole, cockboat and all. But by now I had a mighty ball of lightning swirl-ing off my chest. I took it in both hands and lifted it high over my head. "*This one's for Issa!*" I cried, then flung it at the kraken. It flew into its mouth and exploded at the back of its throat, causing its eyes to slightly jump from their sockets and its brain to burst from the top of its head. As the gore of the great fish rained down on us, the pirates whooped and cheered, the three of us together making enough racket for ten. With a tremendous *SPLASH!* the creature struck the water, then quickly sank, hopefully never to be seen again.

"Are there other sea scorpions?" I asked, just to be sure.

"*Badda Dibqallooc* only one," a pirate replied in broken English.

"But there are other big fish, *Hoggaamiye*," another answered in Somali.

"Then we had better get this engine started," I deemed, placing my stigmata over the starters and pulsing them with power.

The motor began to putter and was revved up further by the pirates, and soon was sounding yare as it carried us ahead.

I took dead reckoning towards Socotra Isle, which my new shipmates were privy to visiting. I'd proven myself as the *Hoggaamiye* — someone they'd hitherto relegated to myth.

It was late in the evening that my mantle of "chosen one" would be complete, for when the stars appeared, one floated down and followed beside our craft. The pirates reveled in what they believed was my guardian angel sent to watch over us.

When the light came closer, I reached over and grabbed my gun from the air, for Xubin was carrying it magnetically. Not the simplest of tasks, as the orb was flying erratically, but thank Allah the little ball had chosen to follow me unto the end.

"*Waad mahadsantahay, waa yahay, waad mahadsantahay!*" I thanked it exceedingly, then asked where it had been.

"I got lost on the accursed pirate ship," the banged-up ball warbled, so bent out of shape it could've passed for a square, "then sank with it. The gleam of your gun saved me, providing light from which I found my way out of the hull. I carried it clear to the surface, but you were gone, and it seemed you might have perished. I calculated the risk, and Socotra Island was the best bet, as I knew that'd always been your final destination. Thank the pinball god I saw your wake and heard your engine!"

"*Mahadsanid*, Xubin," I laughed. "You sound a little rattled. Is there anything I can do to help?"

"Just hold me for now. That would be best."

I took the orb in my hand. It was cold around the edges — edges it wasn't supposed to have.

"*Mahadsanid*," it said as I stuffed it into my pocket.

⁓

Ere sunup, I was struck with a frightful affliction unlike any I'd ever experienced. My heart constricted like a rock, and my ears filled with high-pitched static and ringing. I closed my eyes and saw purple flashes, the face of Zayid interspersed between them as he tried to speak to me through the atmospherics in my head.

THE FISH EATERS

THE ISLAND OF BLISS loomed up through the mist — a brume caused by heavy seas that encouraged us towards shore. But there was something gravely amiss about the rock before us. I told the other pirates, with great chagrin, that my dead reckoning must've been off.

"*Maya*," they consoled, telling me I'd not gone afoul, "*Sax baad tahay.*"

"But that's not Socotra Isle," I replied. "Socotra's peaks are not so jagged."

"Agone you've been for many moons, matey," a pirate rejoined, but in Somali. "Dragon's Blood Isle has long been used for nuclear testing, which has transformed the landscape dramatically, as you see, and continues to do so."

"Holy crap," I gasped, beholding the difference.

"Nuclear testing... has transformed the landscape."

That the seas were roughening did not bode well for our landing, for as we sought safe passage, those same jagged peaks that composed the mountaintops sprung up from the reefs in like manner, riddling every approach with slippery, jagged teeth.

We took a chance and drew into a bay hemmed in by large boulders. The water became shallower by the second, thus we had no choice but to turn about and seek better passage. But as we brought a spring upon her cable, taking the cockboat around, our propeller struck a rock that knocked the engine clean off its block. I rushed astern, but the motor was already sinking.

"To oars!" I cried. "Heave to!"

As we pulled eye to the wind, another niggerhead struck our hull astarboard, smashing in the timberheads. The wood was old and yielding, and the hull began to flood. I seized upon an empty serum drum and bailed like a madman as the pirates kept at their oars.

Alas, our going was too slow and the seas were too rough, soon overtaking us and driving us back. One by one, jagged rocks punched our underbelly, until finally the cockboat foundered and we were forced to abandon ship.

The whitewater tumbled us mercilessly over the toothy reef. It was all we could do to keep our heads above water and continue drawing breath. My feet, knees, and every extremity, including my head, were smashed against the spiky seabed, and as the shoreline drew closer, those slippery spires thrust ever higher overhead.

I drew beneath a sea cliff and struggled in vain to get a handhold on the slippery rock face as the surf washed me up and down it. There was a ledge on high that I'd barley been able to reach, and so with another great wave looming behind me, I faced the wall and steadied myself, then went up with the surge, at last succeeding in getting a grip on the precipice.

I pulled myself onto the ledge, which led to another, and yet another, and the higher I climbed, the drier and more manageable the cliff face became. When I reached a level securely above the surf breakers, I turned to survey where I'd just been.

Far below me, the cove plunged ferociously, with another pirate caught in its trap.

"Go up with the surge and grab on!" another pirate yelled down. He'd found a ledge like mine, and was sitting high and dry.

Thrice the pirate alow tried, but failed each time, alas going under. I scanned the foamy surface with bloodshot eyes, praying he'd resurface. But he did not — Davy Jones had got him.

I stood upon the perch, gauged the talus, then leapt, striking the water seconds later and sinking fast. It was nigh impossible to see through the churning whitewater, and I felt naught but slippery rock slopes wherever I went. I swam up for air, then dove again, again and again, and for the life of me I couldn't find the pirate who'd gone under. Alas, with my own life now at mortal risk, I rode a heavy surge back up to the ledge and wrested myself free of *bad-weyn*'s churning cauldron.

Crestfallen at my failure to save the Somali pirate, who in the end was no different than me — a mariner trying to survive in a world gone mad — I at long last made my way up the wall and met up with the only other soul still alive.

BEYOND THE DEADWOOD FOREST

MOHAMED, THE SURVIVOR, and I made our way over the high coastal plateau. I felt something like a rock lodged in my pocket, then realized it was Xubin. Somehow the little orb had pulled through with me. I let it fly, but it was so punch-drunk that it struck my head as I walked. I told it to give me some distance.

"Sorry, Master," it replied.

"Just call me Noor."

"*Waan ka xumahay*, Noor."

No problem, I said: "*Dhib ma laha.*"

Mohamed stopped and braced himself over his knees. "*Waan xanuunsanayaa. Dawakhaad baan dareemayaa. Madax xanuun baan leeyahay. Calool xanuun baan leeyahay*," he rattled off a list of symptoms, then retched black vomit upon the limestone slabs. "What's wrong with me?" he asked.

I suspected I knew the answer, but didn't want to say it. Xubin, on the other hand, rarely left a question hanging, so offered what I wouldn't: "You probably have radiation poisoning," it warbled. "The millisievert levels here are extremely high."

"But we just fucking got here!" he protested.

"This environment is no longer habitable to human life. You at the very least need a mask to survive."

"So we're just going to die here? What the fuck!? Why'd you bring me here, *Hoggaamiye*!?"

I didn't answer, so Xubin did: "Noor is immune. He's come for the Oracle."

"You're immune, you motherfucker!?" the sea-dog spat, then shoved me so hard I almost collapsed. "You lured me into your deathtrap!"

"I didn't know!" I shot back. "I mean, you guys said this place was used for bomb testing, but it just didn't register — not with me, not with any of us!"

"*Hooyaa da was!*" He cursed my mother.

I had a mind to reproach him, when suddenly, the sound of heavy vehicles rumbled nigh.

"*Dad!*" he cried, meaning *people*! Then he ran off towards the noises.

I made haste to follow, tripping over a rock as he disappeared over a ledge. By the time I reached the edge of the plateau, he was already standing before a swarm of oncoming vehicles, waving his arms as he tried to get them to stop. The first ten-wheeler plowed right into him.

"*Allah jixinjix!*" I pleaded for Allah's mercy, scurrying back over the ridge for cover.

"The first ten-wheeler plowed right into him..."

"What the fuck are those things?" I gasped as the vehicles continued through the tog.

"Yemeni military vehicles," Xubin replied matter-of-factly, showing no emotion for the squished pirate, whose remains were presently being scattered throughout the wadi by scores of huge tires.

"No, I mean those spires," I said, referring to great shafts that sprung up from the desert with umbrella-like boughs.

"Those *were* Dragon's Blood trees," Xubin replied. "They've been petrified by nuclear testing."

"Petrified?"

"Turned to stone."

"Did the Yemeni military kill Mohamed on purpose?"

"This is difficult to ascertain," said Xubin. "But I suggest we take cover until nightfall before proceeding further."

The moon was already rising behind the deadwood forest.

"Maybe we should hide among the dead trees," I suggested.

"It is not wise to hide in the route of the vehicles."

"How about over there?" I pointed to what looked like a canyon spilling off to our left.

"There would be better than here," Xubin agreed.

I ducked away from the ridge until I was well out of sight of the panzer division, then ran along the plateau towards the canyon, Xubin shadowing me — at a distance.

I found a steep trail cutting down into the canyon. The going looked sketchy, but everywhere else the cliffs looked even steeper, and with the moon rising ever higher, I wanted to make it to the bottom before nightfall.

After scaling three-quarters of the way down, I stopped in my tracks. A curious hum echoed through the canyon and quickly gained in volume. I knew what that blasted sound was, for I'd heard it before. "Drones!" I shouted. "Take cover in the shadows!"

We nestled into a darkened crevice, and soon thereafter, two spacecraft, probably unmanned, glided around a bend in the canyon.

I covered my ears against the horrendous hum of the engines, which appeared to be effecting anti-gravity, for not a wisp of smoke or contrail emanated from their afterburners.

It was only after they'd passed that I caught sight of something glinting from the opposite wall, then more glinting appeared upon a nearby ridge. At first, the flashes seemed random, but then I recognized their sequence. "All clear," one code read, another read, "Proceed north." These were *il gubasho* scouts on camelback, working under Zayid's charge.

"Stay hidden!" I warned Xubin. Its metallic frame was too reflective for my comfort, so I shoved it into my pocket.

The flashing continued, much of which was unintelligible to me. It'd been a long time since I'd studied *il gubasho* code, and what I had studied were just the basics, such as directions and rudimentary indications.

Dozens of ghostly camels then spilled over the walls, upon which rode men in metallic blue suits, or at least that's what I could make of them from the opposite wall. Then without warning, a hand reached down and placed a mask over my mouth, the gas inside immediately knocking me out.

SURVIVOR

WHEN I CAME AGAIN TO MYSELF, I was sitting against a petrified Dragon's Blood tree, a single rope tied to my hands lashing me against the trunk. An *il gubasho* sentry stood not far off, only he appeared a much different breed of man than the trackers I remembered from the past...

Il gubasho was Somali for "eyes of fire," and was the moniker given to the league of camelback scouts who plied Socotra Island armed with optical laser distracters, which were powerful, handheld torches that could temporarily blind one with a laser, but more often they were used to send light signals. Back in the day, before the White Star caliphate, *il gubasho* were on Zayid's payroll as lookouts over the three great seas that intersected at their banana-shaped island. The Organization had recruited them from the local population and armed them with the optical laser distracters so that the Socotrans-for-hire could alert pirates in our band of approaching dangers such as task force navies or enemy pirate clans, and while their "Island of Bliss" was never used as a pirate base per se, it did provide safe harborage for dagger dogs such as me who were working under Zayid. Several significant operations could not have gone down so smoothly without their assistance.

The magic of their torches was in their capacity to communicate in complete secrecy without the hacking risks associated with conventional shortwave and satellite-based gadgets. Over time, their light code, similar to Morse, grew in vocabulary and sophistication. By flashing a sequence, they could communicate over many miles of land and sea, and if necessary, the torches could serve as weapons by emitting a temporarily blinding light into the enemy's eyes. The United States navy first invented the torches; Zayid had purchased hundreds of them from a confidential source.

Now, as I regarded the *il gubasho* scout standing in the moonlight before me, and as he regarded me through glowing blue deadlights, "eyes of fire" became more than a symbolic expression used to describe his weaponized flashlight, for his very retinas were surrounded by neon blue circles that effervesced not unlike my white star when fully charged. The scout was bald and weathered, yet tough and muscular, and he wore a rusted gas mask with a tube feeding to an oxygen tank attached to the back of his blue suit of armor, his entire bearing commanding one word with august reckoning: "survivor."

"Has he turned yet?" inquired another *il gubasho* approaching on a ghost camel.

"*La'a*," the one guarding me replied in Arabic, his voice deep and stern behind his oxygen mask. "Where is Aalam?"

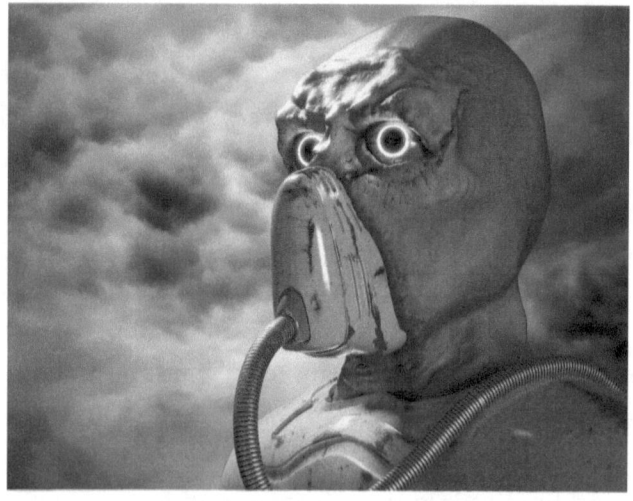

Il Gubasho, stardate 2336

"On his way," replied the other, and then he ran his hand *through* his camel's neck and went trotting off upon the otherworldly animal.

These men and their ghost camels were almost impossible for me to believe. I recalled that I may have still been dreaming, but as the suns had waxed many and my body felt all the aches and pains associated with daily hardships, that theory itself had become a pipedream. I was awake, I was alive, and the neon-eyed scouts with their majestic light camels were as real as the pain in my shoulders from my arms being slung around the tree behind me.

"Light camel" or "ghost camel" — how else to describe an animal that was merely an outline of ethereal, bluish light? The camels had see-through, bioluminescent skin, which their jockeys brushed their hands through to command them. And even more nonsensical: if these beasts of burden were really non-material, then how could the *il gubasho* ride atop them?

"*Ismi* Noor," I introduced myself in Arabic to the scout watching over me. "Noor Haji Fayrus. *Sho ismek?*" I asked his name.

"I am your guardian," he replied in Arabic.

"I am a friend of the *il gubasho*," I said. "I come in peace."

"Aalam will decide," he replied.

"Who's Aalam?"

"The elder."

"A chief?"

"*Na'am*," he said in the affirmative, still speaking in Arabic.

"The Yemeni forces," I inquired, "they killed my shipmate Mohamed — bowled right over him with their tanks. Did they do that on purpose?"

"Socotra Island is being cleared of *xun gaajo*," he revealed.

"But he was a human, like me."

"We'll see about that," he said cryptically.

"What do you mean?"

"The elder now comes," said he, and sure enow, a man cantered over the berm dressed in similar armor, only red — not blue. He was riding atop a ghost camel.

"*Masaa El-Khair*, Aalam," the sentry said to him.

"*Al-Hamdolillah*," the elder replied. "Is this the one?"

"*Na'am*."

The elder, Aalam, placed his palm *into* his camel's neck, and the ethereal creature set him down. The old man dismounted and hobbled before me, holding himself up with a long, steel staff, that by a light at both ends appeared to indicate it doubled as a dual optical laser distracter. He crouched before me, the neon blue circles of his deadlights looking deep into mine, then asked, "*Sho ismek?*"

"*Ismi* Noor Haji Fayrus."

He eyed the white star on my chest, which was faded, then walked around the tree, first to my left, then to my right, grabbing my hand on either side and opening my palm each time.

In trying to watch him, I got a better look at the rope holding me fast. It wasn't a rope at all, but a cable of pure light.

"*Sho hada?*" he asked, pointing a long, bony finger at my star.

"The mark of the *Hoggaamiye*," I replied, "as rendered by the Oracle."

His eyes flared and he stepped back. "What is the name of your father and clan?" he asked.

"Abdullah Haji Fayrus, Darod."

"The prophecy," he muttered, getting to a knee, "it's coming to pass. Tarek! Release him at once!"

With a flash of his torch, my guard severed the light cable that'd been holding me fast. I brought my arms forward and slowly curled them in, for I'd been tied up for Allah knows how long and it proved bloody painful to move my upper body.

"Fetch him a mask!" the elder ordered Tarek.

"*La'a, la'a,*" I told him *no, no* in Arabic, "I'm immune."

"Immune to radiation?" Tarek reproached. "But that's impossible if you're a human." He drew his torch. "Or maybe you're a BOT!"

"*La'a!*" Aalam held him back with his staff. "He is not! His knuckles have fresh scabs. He draws blood. He is the *Hoggaamiye*, and his blood is immune! This is the prophecy — his blood holds the key. He is immune to the forces of darkness and light!"

"Okay, wait just a second, guys," I held up my hands to calm the chief down. "It's true I'm the *Hoggaamiye*, but I'm here on business and could use your help."

"Business? What kind of business!" Tarek sharply inquired.

"Can you take me to the Oracle?"

Aalam looked up at Tarek, then back down at me and asked, "Why?"

"Because—" I began, then stopped when I saw a *xun gaajo* lumbering over the berm with its arms outstretched.

"*Hissssss!*" it seethed, dark spittle flying from its teeth, for it had no lips.

Tarek spun behind it and grabbed its upper arms, holding it in a deadlock, then Aalam pointed his staff at it, releasing a blue beam that wrapped around its neck. Thus, he held the devourer at a distance as Tarek released its arms.

"Come, *Hoggaamiye!*" the elder said. "Follow me! Tarek! Keep the *Hoggaamiye* in your sight at all times."

"*Na'am*, Aalam," the sentry replied.

I did as instructed, following behind the chief. He took the devourer to a large pit with an iron gate. A number of zombies were trapped below, clawing up and hissing. Tarek slid the gate aside, then Aalam tossed the zombie in.

"Why do you take them prisoner?" I asked, flabbergasted. "They should be shot!"

Aalam regarded me with his wide, neon-ringed eyes. "Please, *Hoggaamiye*, don't say that. They are sick. Your blood holds the key. It is written in the prophecy."

"My blood?"

"*Na'am.* Your veins contain the antivirus." He reached over his shoulder and procured an optical laser distracter of the standard size — about the dimension of a common flashlight. "Here, take this," said he, handing it to me. "You must be on constant guard. Socotra is not safe."

"*Shukran jazilan.*" I thanked him kindly. Finally, I had a usable weapon! The torches these guys had were far more advanced than the ones they were using three hundred years ago. As for my TT-30 pistol, it was stuffed into the crotch of my wingsuit, which I'd folded over at the hip, but for all intents and purposes, the gun was jammed. My father's dagger, regrettably, had been lost in the shipwreck. "Can I get some armor, too?" I asked, tired of getting knocked around.

Tarek called over to another *il gubasho*, who was flashing his torch into the night. "Oneekah! Bring a robe! It's the *Hoggaamiye*! He's come!"

"Armor," I remarked. "Not a robe."

"*Allahu Akbar!*" Oneekah exclaimed as she came over — and I'd been mistaken of her gender. "*Hog-gaamiye!*" she said, falling to her knees before me.

"The burqa!" Aalam ordered.

"A burqa?" I protested. "That's the best you can do?"

"One visits the Fiefdom of Tahr cloaked in dark-ness, for there the moon stands always before the sun. To get there you must become invisible. You must aban-don everything — even your thoughts, and then, if your heart is pure, the Oracle will receive you."

"So you will take me there?"

"*Na'am,*" Aalam replied he would, "almost all the way, then whatever business you have with the seer is between you and her alone. But first we require a blood sample."

"From me?"

"*Na'am.* It contains the antigen."

"You can make medicine on the island?"

"We must try. We have sources on the inside."

"In the military?"

Oneekah rushed between us with a folded black garment, then dropped to her knees, holding it before me with her eyes downcast. "The robe, master."

"*Shukra*, Oneekah," I thanked her, taking the robe. "You can get up now."

"*Na'am, Hoggaamiye.*" She slowly stood, reluctantly looking me in the eyes.

I smiled, then did she.

"That's enough," Aalam said.

She bowed solemnly, then began backtracking away from me with her head still down.

"And call me Noor, all of you. I am not a visionary and I am not a God. And I'm certainly no hero. I am your equal, and from here on out, we work together, as a team."

"*Na'am, Hoggaamiye,*" Oneekah replied from a distance.

THE TEST

AS AALAM THE ELDER, Oneekah, and a tracker named Zero looked on, Tarek brought a ghost camel before me and induced it to sit. "Get on," he said.

I brushed my hand over the camel's back and my fingers went through its translucent skin. "But how does it hold me?" I asked.

"If your heart is pure," Aalam revealed, "it will."

I raised my brows and took a deep breath, then flung a leg over the animal's back. The saddle held my load.

Everyone cheered, save for the chief.

"Like I said," Aalam told them. "He's the *Hoggaamiye.*"

They saddled up likewise and we moved out.

Night had fallen, but it wasn't the dark that was playing tricks with me when I beheld the camels' legs. Their limbs were bioluminescent like their bodies, only when they walked, their hooves circled in a queer bluish fog, causing the animals to drift — not walk. It seemed an effortless hike for the ghost camels, while the sensation for their jockeys was a perfectly smooth glide.

"Where'd you get these camels, anyway?" I asked no one in particular.

"The Oracle," Oneekah answered.

"So she's on your side," I remarked. "That's reassuring. What about the Yemeni army? What sort of terms are you on with them?"

"We stay clear," the lead tracker Zero said. He was much like Tarek in bearing, only his movements were quicker and his eyes glowed the strongest of the posse.

"They don't care much for us," conceded Aalam, "so we don't care much for them."

"Do they know of the Oracle's fiefdom?" I inquired.

"*Na'am*," he replied, *yes.*

"And they leave her be?"

"For them, the Fiefdom of Tahr is off limits."

"What do you mean?"

"You'll see," Zero offered cryptically. "We've a ways to go yet, rider, so stay alert and be at peace."

Stay alert and be at peace, I quipped under my breath. *These people sure are eccentric.*

ഢ

After cantering through many miles of deadwood forest, we came upon a gaping canyon whose bottom dropped beneath the reach of the moonbeams, revealing only blackness. Zero flashed his torch towards the other side, and sure enow, optical laser distracters blinked back in code. "The way is clear," they signaled. "Proceed."

"Prepare your fire raisers," Aalam said.

My fellow jockeys removed *dabqaad* incense pots from their gear and secured them to their camels' backs. Oneekah helped me with one that had been stored in my traveler's pack. After placing it behind my camel's hump, she lit it with her torch, and soon our posse was enveloped in the sweet-smelling smoke of frankincense. When I asked Oneekah why we were doing it, she said it was to ward off the *qoriismaris*, who "reside in the darkest of deep recesses."

"Let us proceed," said Zero, taking his ghost camel forward.

"Where's the trail?" I asked.

"Just follow close behind me," Oneekah said, "and don't get off your carrier."

Thus, I brought my ethereal camel behind her and followed her towards the edge. Zero disappeared over the cliff first, then she went over the drop, and I was next.

I reached for my saddle, but my hands went clean through it, for it was composed of the same light beams as the animal.

At the precipice, my "carrier" turned ninety degrees and proceeded straight down the cliff face without changing pace. The same bluish rays that composed its body had spread over my chest, securing me by some sort of force field that held me steady and erect as we proceeded vertically down the wall.

At last, we reached the talus and eased our angle of attack. I breathed a sigh of relief — that initial descent had been extremely intense. Unfortunately, my relief was short-lived, for no sooner had we reached the canyon floor than bloodcurdling growls sounded all around us, punctuated by the heavy snorts of unseen beasts.

"Keep close to me, *Hoggaamiye*," Oneekah warned, "and whatever you do, don't sit your carrier down."

On either side of us, the figures of tall, muscular creatures appeared through the night with blackness in their eyes. These were the *qoriismaris*, kept at bay only by our burning frankincense — the only sure repellent against them.

But they kept moving closer, testing the air, looking for an opportunity to pounce, until at last we reached the talus on the far side of the canyon and started making our way up.

Almost at the top, our ghost camels, with their slowly churning legs of light, crossed over a gaping cave, the opening of which was shielded by a curtain of frankincense smoke streaming up from numerous incense pots set along the lower ledge. I peered through the smoke and was shocked to see the weathered faces of Soqotri troglodytes — cavemen not unlike the ones who'd taken me in three hundred years agone. I was ultimately heartened that there were still some honest-to-goodness cavemen existing in this all-too-futuristic time.

One, two, three camels mounted the ridge on high, and then did mine.

Two men dressed in desert military fatigues were waiting for us on the plateau. "Is that Noor Fayrus?" one asked.

I removed my hood. "What do you want?"

Tarek touched my camel and held me back.

"We have orders to take you back to base," the soldier said.

I scanned their bodies, and they appeared unarmed. "Which base and why?" I inquired.

"Fort Hadibo," the requisitioning one replied, "for questioning."

"I'm afraid that won't be possible at present."

"Back, Haji," Tarek warned.

"I'm afraid you have no choice," the soldier said, then his eyes and those of his henchman glowed bright red.

Fort Hadibo Military Base, Socotra Island,
Yemen, circa 2336

"VunkerBots!" Tarek cried as he drew his torch. A blue beam ejected from his optical laser distracter — but all too late, for before he could slice up the enemy with his neon lance, red lasers shot from their eyes and connected with his chest, throwing him clear off his ghost camel and over the cliff.

"To arms!" shouted Aalam, but tracker Zero and Oneekah were already acute to the situation and firing back, the blue beams of their optical laser distracters so powerful that they cut deep into the earth and extended far into the galaxy, at one point hitting a satellite and exploding it instantly, while the VunkerBots, for their part, kept shooting red lasers from their deadlights, meeting the incoming beams head to head and crosswise with a horrendous *buzz!* and *smash!* of clashing light.

I fumbled with my torch, trying to switch it from signal mode to attack, but by the time I got it weaponized, the battle was already over, the VunkerBots neutralized, and Tarek presumed dead in the dark depths of the canyon.

"Who were they?" I gasped, trying to regain my wits.

Zero dismounted his camel and pulled a cord from one of the hostiles' necks, severing what was left of his electronics. "XOR operators, new breed," he said. "You must be one wanted-ass dude for the Yemeni army to try and pull that shit." He yanked the spine from the other machine.

"But how did they know where to find me?" I asked.

"Any number of ways," he growled back, "like your Xubin."

"But its GPS is disengaged."

"Are you sure?!" he snapped with a black look.

"Back off, Zero," Aalam warned.

I pulled Xubin from my pocked and looked it over. "*Na'am*, I'm sure." Fortunately, I was able to reaffirm, for admittedly, my memory had grown a little foggy.

"Just turn that fucking thing off," Zero warned. "It could be phantom dialing."

I did as he said.

Aalam said the last rites for Tarek, then roped the fallen scout's camel alongside his via a flexible light beam, and we continued on ahead.

"Stay behind me," Oneekah advised as we glided over the limestone highlands, "and away from Zero for awhile. Tarek was his best friend."

"*Aasef.*" I told her I was sorry in Arabic.

"*La taqlaq,*" she replied, *don't worry.* "It's not your fault. Just keep your distance from him, and be on the lookout. This is Socotra Island. Anything can happen."

"No shit," I quipped, and meant it.

After a time, Zero, lead tracker, brought our gallop down to a canter. "We won't make it by daybreak!" he called back. "We continue a ways, then make camp!"

The limestone plateau glimmered cool green beneath the stars. I pulled up alongside Oneekah and asked, softly enough for Zero not to overhear, "Do you have any idea why the Yemeni military is after me?"

"Do you?" she replied sharply, turning her head askance. Apparently, she'd been put off by my inquiry.

"I did have a run in with them once, but that was years ago — centuries ago."

"Could be that. Or it could be Zayid."

"What do you mean?"

"Zayid turned on us long ago when we refused to follow his dictates."

"What dictates?"

"He wanted us to release the X-lix virus in Hadibo City. It would've been genocide, so the *il gubasho* refused. But the emperor did it anyway, turning the city into a hellhole of walkers. The Yemeni military moved in and exterminated the lot of them, establishing a walled base around the capital, and to this day, they fight to rid the rest of the island of *xun gaajo*. And that's where we cross their path."

"Whose path?"

"The Yemeni army's, for you see, the people Zayid turned into devourers were our friends and families. Those of us who survived, namely the *il gubasho*, found it reprehensible to put down our kin, even if they were devourers. As far as we were considered, they were still family, but had gotten sick from Zayid's poison. So now, when we find devourers, we hide them in pits and feed them what we can. And that's where you come in."

The blood froze in my veins. "For their feeding?"

"*La taqlaq,*" she replied in Arabic, telling me to relax. "That's not what I meant. As was promised by scripture, your blood holds the cure."

"What scripture?"

She laughed. "You're joking, right?"

"*La'a.*"

"The lost version of the Holy Qur'an?" she inquired.

"*Haqqan?*" I asked, *really?*

"You really are a piece of work, aren't you?"

"I guess I am."

"At any rate, now that you're here, expect the Yemeni military to come after you with a vengeance."

"Why?"

She rolled her eyes. "The one immune to the forces of darkness and light?"

I shrugged my shoulders.

"The one sent from *Jannah* to liberate the sick and oppressed?"

"And so?" I asked, still not getting it. "What does this have to do with the Yemenis?"

"Everything," she said, regarding me squarely.

"Please explain."

"The Oracle, queen of the darkness and ruler of the hinterlands. The one that Zayid is constantly trying to get, but can't. The reason for Socotra's two-hundred-years' war, waged on Yemeni land. The Yemeni army wants this war gone from its territory, for it really is not their battle. And now you show up — the one who is supposed to intercede between the opposing firebrands, bringing peace and averting a massive holocaust. Do you really expect the Yemeni military to entrust you to us so freely?"

"Opposing firebrands? Zayid and the Oracle?"

"Samale and the Oracle."

"You know of Samale?"

"Of course we do. Samale is the Mainframe of the White Star Empire — an artificial intelligence that took over your country long ago. We never trusted that evil machine, so stay here on Socotra protecting the Oracle, its number-one enemy."

"You side with the Oracle," I observed.

"She's given us our gas masks, our special laser distracters, and ghost camels. Without her, we'd either be either dead, devourers, or wards of Zayid. The *il gubasho* are a freedom-loving tribe, and after what Zayid did to our kin, the choice was clear. So *na'am*, we absolutely support the dark queen."

"Why do you call her that?"

"Because she lives in perpetual night and stands opposed to Samale, whose light cannot penetrate her fiefdom."

"How does she stop him?"

"Massive EMP. Samale is all about neutrons and electrons."

"I don't get it."

"Samale is a supercomputer," Oneekah explained, "that tries to control everything directly based upon electrical impulses, while the Oracle is more sly and elemental, working in the shadows with inanimate things like sand, rocks, water, the moon — the very structure of her environment. To Samale, the Oracle is like the anti-Christ, and vice-versa. They despise each other, and one day will face off in an epic battle. But the *il gubasho* shall fight to the death for the Oracle, for her land is our land, her flesh, our flesh."

"Wow." I shook my head in disbelief.

"So for now, you're a seriously wanted man. Behold Tarek's camel going unridden. Tarek was the strongest among us, and once my lover. But he died in a flash."

"*Aasef.*" I told her I was sorry, our entire conversation still being conducted in Arabic, but mostly translated here, like the rest of this book, for the reader's swift convenience.

"He *was* my lover," she sighed, "before he cheated on me, again and again. But still, Tarek was a good scout, and I'm going to miss him."

"He was good to me, too," I offered. "I wish this never happened."

"It is written. You cannot stop it."

"His death was foretold in the Qur'an?"

"Your return was prophesized, *Hoggaamiye*. The return of Allah's caliphate, risen from the ashes of material man's destruction."

"Material man. Do you mean Samale?"

"The *Faranji* — the infidels from overseas. Those who seek to replace our kind with their own, which they term Manifest Destiny. Their genocide against the larger Arab world is waged via the Selection Ministry, home of the X-lix virus and the Samale supercomputer; but as promised by scripture, in the eleventh hour you have returned to push the infidel conquerors back, driving them once and for all from the Land of the Gods."

"Me?"

She chuckled. "I love you, *Hoggaamiye*. We all do. But we also realize you're very naïve, just as the prophecy said you'd be. You're blind to the forces of darkness and light, but that being said, you do what is right, and that's all that matters."

"Thanks, I guess."

I kicked my heels into my ghost camel's side, trying to keep apace. My heels went clean through its glowing abdomen, banging into one another.

Oneekah looked back and laughed. "Do this," she instructed, flicking the back of her camel's neck with a finger. The animal picked up its pace.

"Just a flick of the finger, eh?" I tried it, and sure enow, my camel glided forward more expeditiously.

"For you," she said, regarding me endearingly, perhaps wantonly, "the flick of a finger can move mountains and stir hearts in a way that nobody else can."

"Ah, well, I do my best," I replied humbly, trying to bring the hype down a notch. I just wanted to be her friend and one of the posse, not some fucking godsend.

"Keep alert," she urged, changing the subject. "We're coming upon a deadwood forest. There may be sleeping *xun gaajo*. We are not to disturb them."

"Aye-aye, Oneekah."

Following her, a brave, beautiful, and smart woman inside and out, was an awakening for me. There were so many finer souls than mine to follow — souls more grounded, less jaded and unsettled. My wife Issa had been like that, even after she'd outwardly changed, and perhaps the Oracle — that shape-shifting but relentlessly intuitive witch — appealed to me in much the same way. Whatever the case of my own feelings, soon I would confront her and a decision would have to be made: Would I deliver her to Samale in exchange for my freedom, or would I join her in arms against him? That she was the queen of darkness whose torturous tests terrified me utterly, while Samale had been relatively straightforward and benign, did not exactly make it a "no brainer."

We strode into the petrified forest and made camp beneath a bough. As the rising sun streaked its first rays through the deadwood canopy, we unrolled our packs betwixt the roots of stone.

Oneekah laid her bedroll beside mine, which of course pleased me. But she didn't so much as sit before announcing: "I'm on first watch. Get some shut-eye, *Hoggaamiye* — you're going to need it."

"I can take first watch," I offered.

"*La'a,*" she responded in the negative. "That's our job. *Laila sa'eda wa ahlaam ladida.*" After wishing me *goodnight and sweet dreams*, the shapeliest among us climbed clear into the canopy of our petrified Dragon's Blood tree, where she took a roost upon a curving branch and eyed the forest beneath.

DARK DOMINION

"WE GO NOW," Aalam said, shaking Oneekah's shoulder. She was lying next to me.

"Pack your roll," Zero told me. "Many *xun gaajo* are coming."

"*Haqqan?*" I asked in Arabic, *really?* I rubbed the sleep from my eyes.

"*Na'am.* They're coming through the trees. They've chosen this forest to sleep in tonight. See the bone sacks?"

He pointed up into the trees, and sure enow, several sacks of rams' bones were slung up in the boughs.

"Gotcha," I said, rolling up my bedroll.

Less than two minutes later, we were back in our saddles, and just as my ghost camel turned to leave, a dozen *xun gaajo* came lumbering around the trees.

"Move out!" Zero called back.

The zombies reached out to us with sinewy arms and hands, only abandoning the motion once we'd gained some distance, at which point they gathered lazily around the tree where we'd slept.

Aalam affirmed, when we met up again, that the *xun gaajo* were amassing beneath the dead bough to pass the night sleeping on their feet.

"But it's not really sleep," Zero put in. "It's a shallow form of suspended animation. If you disturb their pod, they can still be dangerous."

❧

As the sun set through the trees, Zero stopped before several trunks to point out some crude carvings. "Noor carries this mark on his chest," he announced, pointing to a sketchy star rendering. "I assume he knows what this means?" he asked, looking at me.

"*Na'am*," I affirmed. "The Oracle is near."

"That is correct, *Hoggaamiye*. We are entering her fiefdom. We can take you only so far, but then must belay, for the light camels cannot enter her domain."

"Why not? She gave them to you."

"No light save for the light of the heavens touches the Fiefdom of Tahr," Zero replied.

"But not sunlight," I remarked.

"*La'a*. Only the rays of the moon and the distant stars."

We pressed on, the forest giving way to rocky plateaus, uneven buttes, and cliffy terrain. Fortunately, we were taking a high line through the mountains, avoiding the shadow areas beneath, which I knew were very dangerous.

Zero proved an expert tracker, weaving us along the lofty maze of ridges and spines. In conversing with Oneekah, I learned that he was also an expert BotHunter with a growing string of successes against the new breed of XOR operators such as VunkerBots, RunvoBots, ArgoBots, and the highly elusive cyborg aggregators. According to Zero, XOR operators were controlled remotely via the Cloud Federation, while aggregators were stand-alone units that could withstand EMP's, and thus were the most difficult machines to detect and neutralize.

In time, we came upon a bluff and pulled back our reins of light, for there in the distance, a castle stood unassumingly before the moonrise. Its spire was composed of glass, and waterfalls cascaded down its sides.

"The Fiefdom of Tahr," announced Aalam. "The Oracle's dark domain."

"The moon now eclipses the Sirius star," Oneekah remarked.

"*Na'am*," affirmed the elder as the shadows deepened around us.

"Now even our torches cannot breach the quiet zone," added Zero, shining his optical laser distracter towards the castle. The beam went only so far before stopping against an invisible barrier.

Oneekah induced my camel to sit, then did the same with hers. "Leave your thoughts behind," she said as she lowered strands of frankincense over my head, "and keep a pure heart," she added as I studied the aromatic necklaces. "Samale will not be able to follow your traceroute into the quiet zone."

I dismounted my ghost camel and thanked my posse for their support and bravery. They wished me Godspeed in return.

Oneekah offered a prayer to the moon, wishing for my propitious sojourn, then I turned my back on all I knew and proceeded forth alone.

THE PLAY OF THE PLANETS

"NIGH A MILE," I reassured myself. All canyons but one ran off in the wrong direction, while the one leading towards the castle appeared sloppy and uneven. I tightened my burqa around my waist and prepared for some technical climbing.

The way down was hellishly dangerous. While there were foot- and hand-holds aplenty, the rocks were sharp and crumbly. More than once, I found myself spread-eagle, clinging desperately to the wall face as I fought to halt an uncontrollable slide to an untimely death. Fortunately, I succeeded, but my climb by night did not come without consequence, for by the time I reached the bottom of the canyon, my hands, feet, and chest were swollen, bruised, and bleeding. I made my way over to a lake and sat down on a natural rock seat, soaking my feet and washing my hands and face.

I had scarcely cleaned the blood from my fingers when a growl sounded directly behind me. My heart leapt in my chest at my sudden memory of the werewolf-like creatures that inhabited the darklands. It snorted like a camel, blasting hot air against the back of my neck, causing the baby hairs there to stand on end. I slowly stood and turned, and sure enow, the *qoriismaris* was there, fixin' to rip me to shreds.

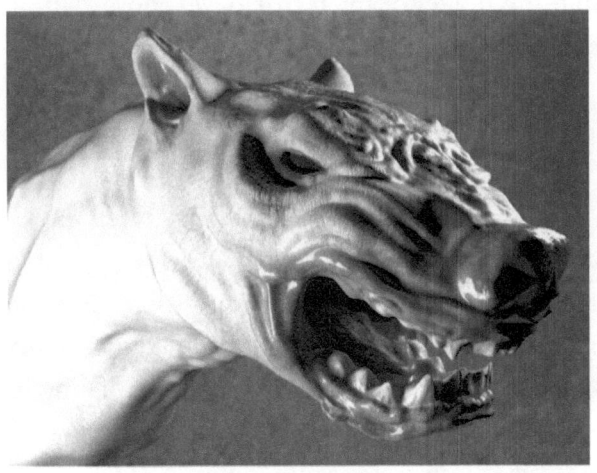

Qoriismaris

"Easy, boy," I said under my breath, fingering my optical laser distracter. "That's right, slow and easy." I switched the torch on, but nothing happened. I tried again more adamantly, but still nothing happened.

I walked slowly backwards through the water, believing the werewolf would pounce on me at any second; but for some reason, it didn't. Only when I moved faster did it become more emboldened, charging at me with its wide maw chomping, but always stopping short when I stopped and froze in place. Then I realized that my necklace of frankincense was keeping it at bay, but only when the scent had time to linger. Moving too quickly dispersed the scent, putting me in mortal danger. Suffice it to say, the night was exhaustingly slow going, the object of my terror never more than a few feet away.

As day broke, the creature became increasingly distracted by mundane objects like the canyon walls and rocks in our way, until at last it fled with its tail between its legs, its fear of natural light having gotten the better of it.

Finally, I had a chance to finish what I'd started. I took a seat beside the lake and resumed my washing. I risked a sip, then a quaff, and was soon inhaling it, for in my rush to flee the *xun gaajo* that had entered our camp, I'd left my water bottle behind, and by now was deadly thirsty. I was already missing Oneekah and the protection of the trackers, whose wisdom of the environment could spell the difference between success and disaster. But my journey seemed nearing its end, with the Oracle's dominion just around the bend.

Alas, as I skirted around the base of the cliff, the castle was not where it had been. Flabbergasted, I scurried with due diligence over a spit of rocks, arriving at the base of a butte with natural steps leading to the top. With a circular view of the canyon and its tributaries now at my command, I was certain I'd spot the castle nudged away behind some bend.

"*Allahu jixinjix...*" I sighed, my voice trailing off with my sinking spirit, for I saw nothing, no castle — only the sun as it increased in might and bearing over the barren canyon.

I retreated down the butte and back across the rocks, arriving at the head of a goat trail, which proved fairly easy to ascend.

Atop the bluff on the same side of the canyon that I'd initially descended, I made my way further up a ravine, which became more forested as I went.

Fearing the walking dead, I climbed into the canopy of a petrified Dragon's Blood tree, laid myself down in its nest of calcified branches, pulled my burqa over my eyes, and slept.

Was that the wind whistling through the stone branches? I pondered lazily as I emerged from my slumber. I removed the burqa from my face to find dusk settling in, the sky bronzed and fading, then peered down through the dead boughs to behold a gaggle of *xun gaajo* huddling against the tree where I'd slept.

"*Was*," I muttered in Somali, meaning *fuck*. The zombies were gathering in an alarming number, their collective hissing sufficiently grotesque to scare an uninitiated man to death. One thing was for certain — I would not, under any circumstances, be spending a night in that tree with those things down there less than ten feet away. The castle was nigh — it had to be, and if it were best approached by moonlight, the time to act was upon me.

I kept silent as the grave as the sun continued to wester with the moon rising opposite, until at last the play of planets drew their dark curtain across the heavens, settling the *xun gaajo* down. Their hissing ceased and their wobbling lessened, the moonlight soon giving witness to a mass of blue baldheads that exhibited very little movement. *Now was my chance*!

I crawled through the petrified branches to where they connected to those of an adjacent tree. The boughs of this last were thinner and more brittle, and as I made the transfer, some of the branches snapped, sending pieces of calcified wood raining down upon the *xun gaajos'* heads.

The zombies that were struck instantly awoke and looked up, disturbing the larger mass.

I froze in place, and that's when I noticed a bag of bones hanging in front of my face. *Was!* I cursed in my mind, and *fuck!* I thought again, having bedded down in one of their favorite trees. But I tried to remain calm. The devourers of Socotra had eyes from which to see, but I doubt if they saw me in my black burqa, and furthermore, the ones most offended by being struck on the head were soon overpowered by the will of the mass, which was to settle back down and return to slumber.

Thus, I made my way down the opposite tree, accidentally bumping into a zombie when I leapt from the trunk. The devourer slowly turned with wide-open eyes.

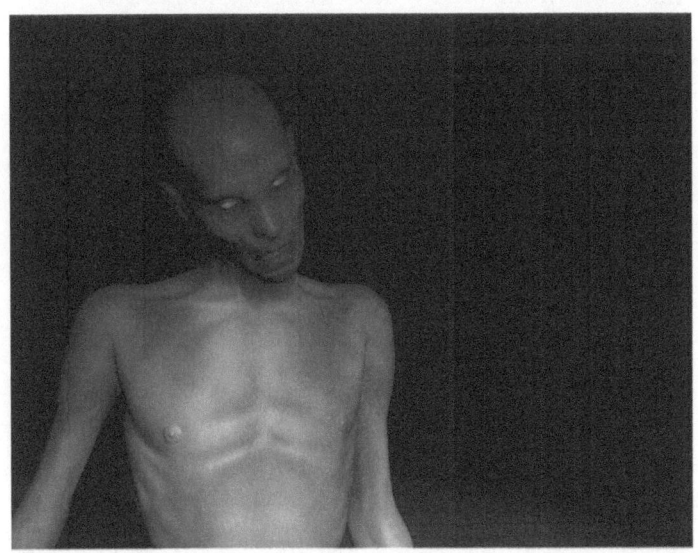

A young xun gaajo

I ran as fast as I could in the opposite direction, if you could call my plodding a run. Thank Allah the man-eaters became comatose by night, otherwise the younker I'd bumped into probably would've caught me in my aweary disposition. But if there was one thing about the lame sprint that led to my quick exhaustion, I'd plodded in the right direction, for the Oracle's castle loomed before me again, appearing closer than ever.

Unfortunately, right beneath my nose hid a deep and narrow canyon, that when traversed (which I did, *qoriismaris* and all), led to yet another.

Surmounting this second gaping depression, I came around a bend in the rocky plateau and beheld the castle in the arroyo directly below, with but one last slope to descend before I'd at last meet the Oracle in her dark dominion.

But the skies had recently waxed grey, and even before I could step one foot down the talus, the sun broke through the clouds on the horizon, shooting forth its rays in every direction. Alas, the castle faded away, right before my eyes.

"Fuck this!" I cursed, picking up a rock and throwing it at the would-be kingdom.

I remained deeply frustrated for quite some time thereafter, throwing more rocks and wondering how I'd gone astray — and not just on Socotra Island. My whole life seemed a joke to me now, like I were being made the victim of some grand, diabolical riddle. I wondered if Bashir was somehow behind it — if it was just another of his impossible tests that, when nigh breaking me in one way or another, gave him and perhaps Zayid endlessly sick humor.

After a while, I calmed down enow to settle on an end game. I would hike down to the tog below and drink some more water, then return to the very site I was standing and wait until nightfall. There were no *xun gaajo* here, and the *qoriismaris* only came out at night. Thus, I'd laze the day away, perhaps getting some shut-eye in the shadow of a rock, and then when the sun went down, if the castle didn't reappear where it'd just been, the game was over — I was out. I'd find my way back to the coast, return to Mogadishu, and find that white chick I saw back at the Aquatics Center or whatever the fuck it was called.

Speaking of swimming holes, I took a dip in the running tog, then retreated back to my promontory and found a shady spot beneath a ledge. With another day to waste, I pulled my burqa over my head and slept — which was not hard to do, for I was deeply depressed.

A RUDE AWAKENING

MOHAMED, MY SON, kept pulling at my leg. He often did this when trying to wake me, or otherwise pulled at my hand if it were hanging off the bed.

I opened my eyes and looked towards the foot of the bed, and there at the edge of the rock ledge where-upon I slept, a devourer had my left foot firmly in its hands. Even before my survival instinct could kick in, it bit off my big toe and began to adamantly chew it.

I sat up and screamed — a cry cut short when I smashed my head against the overhanging ledge. And before I could fair recover from that, numerous sinewy hands closed in.

The *xun gaajo* had me completely surrounded, and were strong as the devil as they fought to wrest me from the slot between the rocks where I'd bedded.

I kicked, clawed, and screamed, then reached for my TT-30, but the folds of my burqa prevented easy access, and soon zombies were fixin' to sink their teeth into me from all directions. They pulled me out of my shelter. I was finished. I closed my eyes and awaited the inevitable.

SWAK! CHOP! SWAK!

One by one, the zombies released their grip. I opened my eyes to see one falling over me with a hole cut out of its forehead, then another dropped on me with its black brains spilling out of its cranium where a big piece of its skull had been sheared off. And all throughout the zombie massacre, until the last devourer was dead and gone, I heard a jangling sound.

Osman appeared over me with a bloodstained machete. "Noor!" he exclaimed "*Halkee ku xanuunay-saa?*"

"*Adeer!*" I cried to my paternal uncle. "It's you!"

"*Halkee ku xanuunaysaa?*" I heard again, this time from Cosob, who'd come beside my uncle brandishing a sharply curving blade. Both men were abundantly stained with the black blood of the zombie scum.

"Cosob! *Far caged*!" I gasped, pointing to my foot. "I've been bitten!" They asked me where else I'd been bit. I said I didn't know. I was still reeling from the sudden sequence of events.

Cosob sat me up and gave me a thorough looking over while Osman dressed my foot with his turban. I winced in pain.

"*Waan ka xumahay*!" he apologized. "I'm so sorry we're late, nephew. Soon you will turn."

"*Maya*, I'm immune."

Osman looked at Cosob, who couldn't verify it either way. "Whatever the case," my uncle replied, "we're taking you back right away."

"*Xaggee?*" I asked as they hefted me to their shoulders.

"Mogadishu," Cosob replied. "Bashir sent us to retract you."

"Bashir?"

"*Haa*. He knows now — Zayid is a lunatic who will stop at nothing to ensure his power. He threatened to execute the entire *guurti* council over a disagreement about Iraq. When Bashir got wind that Zayid had sent you here to find the Oracle, he knew at once it was a trap."

"But Zayid didn't send me here. It was Samale."

"Whoever it was, Zayid is behind it. Now come on, *jaalle*. Be strong. We're taking you back to Mog where the *guurti* is establishing new protections. We expect a swift trial, but you're a key witness to the emperor's crimes, so you must testify."

"I can't believe you guys are really here," I laughed, fighting back tears of pain and joy.

"That we are, matey, in the flesh. We pulled through cryogenics, just like you," Osman revealed as they helped me along. From time to time, I set my good foot down, but mostly I was at their mercy, not to mention their strength.

"What about the Oracle?" I asked.

"Forget it," Cosob said. "That bitch is dangerous. Pray we escape her dominion before nightfall."

"Have you any camels?"

They laughed.

"We've a spaceship waiting just beyond the quiet zone," Cosob said. "It's a few hours away, but was as close as we could get to Tahr without risking EMP shutdown. *In sha'a Allah*, we can make it by sundown."

"How did you ever find me?" I inquired, delirious with pain.

"Troglodytes in the area have been watching you."

"Thank Allah for them!" Osman added.

"*Haddii Eebbe yidhaahdo!*" I replied, furthering that sentiment. "And *mahadsanid* to you guys for saving me."

"*Dhib ma laha*," they said, meaning *don't mention it.*

The further we progressed, the thirstier I became, the more I drank, and the more I sweated. From time to time, my helpmates, or saviors I should say, stopped to refill their canteens in a tog or a lake, but not once did they stop to rest, and the more I paid attention, the more I noticed they weren't even drinking. They'd splash water on themselves, and as we walked, it looked like sweat. My confidence began to waver. Were these guys who they said they were?

We made our way along a high ridge until the great expanse of south Socotra came into view, with a space-ship glimmering atop a plain in the distance.

"There she is," said Cosob, pointing to it. "We're making good time and the sun has an hour more to set."

"Then let us stop and rest," I said.

"No, we keep moving." He was insistent.

"Just for a minute," I rejoined. "I need a drink."

We stopped and I quaffed from Osman's canteen, offering him a sip.

"*Maya,*" he declined. "I'm good."

"Just a little, Uncle," I replied, then forced the canteen to his lips and tilted it back. Sparks flew out of his mouth, and his eyes shone bright red.

"I knew it!" I cried, breaking from their grasp, but I fell over my injured foot and landed just shy of the ledge.

Sure enow, Cosob's eyes were also glowing red. "We tried to do this the easy way," he said, removing a set of handcuffs from his cape. "Only human foolishness could allow one to believe they were beyond the reach of Zayid and his aggregators!"

Osman regained his bearings and pointed his machete stiffly down at me. "You're coming with us!" he warned with a damaged voice board. Then "*War-shad*!" he ordered his henchbot. "Clap him in irons!"

"I don't think so," I said, then rolled off the top of the cliff.

What the aggregators didn't know was something I'd figured out long ago: the burqa given to me by *il gubasho* doubled as a wingsuit.

Thus, I spread my arms and legs, creating one great wingspan from which I stabilized my descent and tracked away from the cliff.

But what I didn't suspect was the aggregators could fly as well, for their Bedouin robes also doubled as wingsuits. They launched themselves o'er the cliff and quickly gained.

Employing evasive maneuvers, I soon learned their limitations. They were too rigid in turns, causing themselves to inordinately drift. I knew I'd never be able to outrun them, but I was sure I could outfly them, so I headed back towards the wall. The BOTs took the bait, banking back towards the high earth object.

Lasers slammed into the cliff face beside me and flashed overhead, so I somersaulted and barrel-rolled in advanced acrobatics, evading their volleys. It was clear now that we'd left the black queen's dominion, for their lasers were working, and powerfully at that. I procured mine, and in a gainer — a back somersault

— shot at them while upside down, striking Osman's shoulder, but unfortunately not enough to take him out.

Their return of fire was swift, so I flew proxy along the wall, weaving between its many ledges. It was an extremely dangerous business, but ultimately proved efficacious. Their aim grew worse, and their glide went increasingly off balance.

Seizing the momentum of their poor flight adjustments, I curved sharply into a connecting canyon, sure they wouldn't make the cut.

My heart sunk. They rocketed around the promontory, barely missing the far wall.

The laser fight ensued. I started aiming at overhead outcroppings of rock, that when struck, came crumbling down on the BOTs. But their sheer weight gave them uncanny forward staying power and speed.

The canyon wall curved into a concave, so I took my pursuers in proxy. Cutting in towards the cliff, my optical laser distracter nicked a ledge and flew from my grasp. But now the curve of the wall was at hand, and I'd need all my flight experience to successfully negotiate it.

My drift through the turn was such that, had I hazarded into an outcropping or ledge, impact at 120 mph would've spelled my swift end. But Allah must've been watching over me, or perhaps I'd just been lucky, for as I angled along the concave and my knuckles scraped against the cliff, the machines behind me began to drift, object strike occurring first with the likeness of Cosob, then Osman.

The machine that was Cosob kept tumbling through the concave, littering the wall face with thousands of burning pieces before they fell, while Osman fared much better — his wall strike ejected him away from the object, and while he was clearly injured, he was able to control his spin.

But now, it was my turn to die, lest I thought of something fast, for the ground was becoming larger and more detailed by the second. I had no parachute, no BASE rig, not even a measly pilot chute as I went hurtling towards the earth at a ridiculous velocity.

A series of sand dunes approached in the groundrush. I started counting down the seconds to impact. At two seconds before death, I flared my robe to the maximum extent, stretching my arms and legs out like a bat.

The airbrake effectively cut my speed by over ninety percent. I made impact on a dune's far side, tumbling head-over heels down the slope. I would've surely broken my neck had I not the wherewithal to tuck and roll.

At the end of my ordeal, I lay splayed out over the desert floor, sand in my ears, eyes, nostrils, and mouth, but very much alive, and Allah be praised, not paralyzed.

Suddenly, the robot Osman fell from the sky and made earth impact with a horrendous *BOOM!* of imploding sand.

I limped over to the dust cloud aftermath and found him buried chest-deep in the ground. He appeared dead, or inert.

I looked deep into his deadlights, and they suddenly flared red, almost giving me a heart attack. Would his laser eyes start shooting at me again?

"Haji," he said, his electronic voice clipping out severely, while even his eyes started to flicker. He reached a hand out shakily and apologized. "*Haji, waan ka xumahay.*"

I took a step back, not trusting him for an instant.

"Zayid put us up to this," he said. "By penalty of death we were obliged. We only wanted to bring you in, my nephew. Not this."

Blood pooled up from the sand at his chest. "You're a cyborg!" I said, aghast.

"*Haa,*" he replied, lowering his head.

"Why didn't you tell me?"

"I was going to, after we had you secured in the spaceship. But I should've known better: Noor Haji Fayrus doesn't surrender so easily."

His head and arms started shaking uncontrollably, then all at once fell limp. By degrees, he was able to lift his head again, but his arms were no longer working.

"I— I can take your *Maskax*," I stuttered, gliding my hands over his head, shoulders, and back as I tried to find it. "We'll upload it into a new automaton. I know it can be done."

"Haji…" was all he said, shaking his head.

I kept looking for that essential memory chip. "Just tell me where it is."

"Haji, please, just come before me."

I knelt in front of him and lifted his chin. His eyes flickered red and black as if he were short-circuiting.

"*Maya*, Haji." He shook his head twice slowly. "I don't want that. Let my *Maskax* die with this biomechanical monstrosity they've made me into."

"No, Osman, there's a way we can—"

"*Maya*, nephew. Please, for once just listen to me. I know for certain I want to die a normal death — or that part of me that is still human. It is my soul that I wish to save by meeting a decent end. Please, *saaxiib*, reach into the back of my neck, deep up under my skull until you feel a flexible pole, then yank it out with all your might — it's the only chance I have."

"But Osman, that's terrible!" I protested, coddling his head against my chest. "I refuse."

"Please, *saaxiib*. I ask you this one last favor, and you have asked me many. What is terrible is to go on living in a world that I no longer care to be in."

He reached for the back of his neck, but his arm fell limp again, and so did his head.

"No, Osman!" I cried. "Don't leave me here alone." I jiggled his head around, and the lights of his eyes flickered back on.

"Release me, Haji," he said, his voice barely comprehensible amid the static of his malfunctioning. "Please."

"*We'el!*" I cursed, *bastard!* and struck him, with refrain, on top of the head.

"Please…" he continued, now barely able to speak.

Using my left hand, I coddled his head against my chest, bending his neck far forward, then with my right hand, I squeezed my fingers into the nape of his neck, feeling beneath his rubbery skin. "I love you, Osman," I wept, tightening my grip around his spine.

"Abbo would be proud of you, for all that you've—"

I yanked hard back, pulling a black tube from his neck. Wires stretched and snapped within the rubbery spine as I stretched it skywards, Osman's human blood drenching my face, arms, and hands.

At length, I fell beside him and couldn't stop crying. I was at a loss for words, for thoughts. The world had become too difficult to bear. Only the deepest sorrow stayed with me now; only sorrow.

Quinn Robert Haber & Noor Haji Fayrus

LOST ILLUSIONS

SLOWLY LUMBERING ZOMBIES came over the dunes. First there were two, then three, then six. I had little concern for their approach, preferring to mourn over Osman.

At length, I lazily got up and moved haphazardly between them. The sand slowed them significantly; I pushed one over as I passed. But when I crested the dune where I'd crashed, my survival instinct kicked in, for many dozens more were making their way over the sloping sands. Our dramatic flight and crash landings must've garnered their attention from near and far.

I searched my body for weapons. My laser distracter was gone, but I still had my TT-30. "Great," I said with cynicism, for the gun had only one bullet, and anyhow, it was jammed. My frankincense necklaces were gone — not much of a deterrent against zombies, anyway — and I had no daggers. Basically, I was defenseless. The only thing that possibly might have been of some use was my Xubin, which I found still tucked within a pocket of my burqa. I was reluctant to turn it on, fearing it was the reason Zayid's various BOTs had found me in the first place.

I took a chance and set it loose, then asked it what I should do. It took quick stock of the surroundings, reporting forty-two *xun gaajo* approaching, with the first one reaching our position in fifty-six seconds and counting.

I told Xubin I had no weapons. It surveyed the greater area, suggesting I head for a cliff to the east, as there were fewer devourers in that direction and the zombies had no climbing abilities.

It hurt to walk, but I knew I had no choice. As hopeless as my situation seemed, I didn't want my life to end as zombie feed. I made my way towards the eastern rise with a slow and heavy limp, the devourers soon consolidating behind me like a herd of sheep.

The cliff was much further than I'd initially estimated. As the sand dunes gave way to limestone slabs, I had to pick up my pace, for the devourers moved over the flat rocks more expeditiously.

The stump where my big toe had been bitten off was swollen and throbbing painfully, while the adjustments I'd been making to walk over it began to cramp the rest of my body. Alas, I could walk no more, and the zombies were almost upon me.

The herd was less than twenty meters away when I reached the wall on my hands and knees. I grabbed a handhold, and with all my might tried to hoist myself up, the walkers closing in all around me.

Hand over hand, I pulled myself up from the ground, using my good leg for support where I could, which at one point happened to be on a *xun gaajo*'s shoulder. It took a hold of my leg and bit into it; the only thing keeping my flesh intact being my burqa, whose folds along my calf forestalled the zombie's deeper snack.

I kicked and screamed in defense, and as I did, several tendinous hands grabbed my legs and tried to pull me down. I freed myself from all but one walker, who was particularly tall and had a particularly strong grasp. There was no greater tug-of-war than that, for my very life was in the balance. One of my hands left the wall while my other held on by four fingers, then three, then two...

I looked down into the zombie's eyes. I wanted to see its face and remember it, vowing to find it in hell and have my revenge.

POP! was the sound of the Xubin striking the zombie's forehead. The stunned walker released its grip for a split second, which was time enow for me to break free of its grasp. My adrenaline kicked into high gear, and I scaled ten more feet in a matter of seconds, Xubin all the while following below me, pelting the zombies' heads, "watching my back."

At last, I reached a ledge and collapsed on my back, resting a few moments before surveying the herd again. Hundreds of *xun gaajo* now pressed against the cliff, reaching up and hissing like bloodthirsty snakes.

"Yea!" I shouted, holding my hands up like a rock star before a wide audience. "Fuck yea!"

The hissing surged and the zombies reached for me more adamantly.

"Fuck — yea!" I screamed again. I'd become a little nutso. "Motherfuckers," I spat, then turned towards the wall and resumed climbing.

∾

As the sunset emblazoned behind me, illuminating the cliff face with light, I caught sight of something on high. Craning my neck to see, I spotted the Oracle waiting for me. She was dressed all in black and holding a staff. I knew it was her by her typical behavior: sitting upon a ledge doing nothing while I toiled in agony beneath. I could fully expect some dangerous funny business ahead, and was ever so wary of spiders as I ascended.

I crawled over the ledge with bleeding fingers and collapsed like a dying man beside her, only to find a scarecrow on the cliffs, made of sheets and sticks.

"You bitch," I said, pulling at her wooden arm. "You total fucking bitch!" I threw the scarecrow over the cliff. "That's it," I said, lying on my back. "I'm finished."

I nigh moved an inch as the sun bedded to west and the stars came into focus. At length, I closed my eyes. I was empty inside, without thoughts, feelings, or desires.

∾

"*Grrrrr...*" I heard in the dark of night, and knew instantly what it was. *Fucking qoriismaris*, I thought, remaining completely still. The hyena-man was but a few feet away, and I was defenseless. I was through with wingsuiting over cliffs into zombie-infested landing sites, so pondered my other options, finding only one.

I stared into the eyes of the beast and took a deep breath, then sat up quickly, and sure enow, the *qoriismaris* lunged at me. I seized its momentum and rolled back, flinging it over the precipice.

I was now on my knees with my feet hanging over the ledge, and another *qoriismaris* was standing before me no different than the first, its jaws extruded and dripping as it prepared to attack.

My timing and insight for this one would have to be impeccable. I had no more room to roll behind — I could only dodge left or right. I stared deep into the creature's black eyes. They glistened back in the moonlight, sharpening on mine. Which way would it leap? Which way would I live? In which direction would I die? I focused on every ripple of its curdling lips, every quaver of its flaring snout, every micro-movement of its squinting deadlights as I tried to prejudge its strike. Everything about it was honed to kill me, and this time, I knew I'd probably die.

But then something happened. Ever so slowly, the creature's eyes and attention shifted, focusing on something to my side. Then the werewolf lunged, throwing itself through a projection of me and clear over the cliff, impacting the desert floor many seconds later.

Xubin had replicated my image on a Vectex screen, creating a hologram beside me, while my true self had been darkened by the screen's black matte. The hyena-man went after my double, which was made only of light.

"Xubin!" I gasped. "That was amazing! Thanks for that, *saaxiib*. Holy shit, thanks for that!"

"Just keep me on, okay?" it said, its voice still kind of warbled because, like me, the little orb had been through hell.

"Deal."

"It is not safe here," it replied. "More *qoriismaris* will come — they can smell your sweat. I saw a cave while climbing up. I suggest we retreat to it posthaste."

"I— I don't know if I can make it," I stuttered, feeling my foot, which was terribly swollen.

"It's not very far. You can do this, Haji."

I glanced over the ledge and saw only blackness.

"We did good here, Haji. But next time we might not be so lucky. Come, let's go now before others arrive."

I exhaled loudly, then lowered my legs over the ledge and replied, "Show me the way."

DARK STAR RISING

XUBIN'S CAVE went fairly deep, and access hadn't been too difficult. The only thing missing was frankincense, for what I'd seen at Zayid's tower, the *qoriismaris* had a knack for climbing. But we'd done all we could do, and I needed to rest. We only had to make it to daybreak, then we could find the coast and leave the bloody island for good.

I sat by the opening and gazed out over the desert. The moon was full and setting, while *qoriismaris* could be heard howling in the distance. For all intents and purposes, it looked like we were going to make it. I closed my eyes and leaned back against the wall, emptying my thoughts completely.

"Sadly," a woman spoke from further back in the cave.

I rubbed my eyes and called back, "*Hayye?* Who's there?" Had I been dreaming?

"Sadly," she said again, emerging from the shadows, "it is only through great adversity that the good at heart ever find me."

"Oracle?"

"*Haa*, it is I."

She came and stood before me, her eyes glowing like the full moon outside.

"I've come a long ways for you," I said. "We've important matters to discuss. Please, sit down before me — my foot is bad."

She sauntered unto the cave's opening and stood before the stars, then turned and asked me what I wanted.

"The White Star Empire has been hijacked by a corrupt emperor named Zayid Cecchi," I informed. "He has created Samale, a supercomputer with powers unlike anything I've ever witnessed. Samale has sent me to bring you back to its *guurti* with a wicked plan in mind. But we can trick it. I know you have the power. Together, we can put an end to their reign of terror. Samale and Zayid are responsible for creating the *xun gaajo* and need to be stopped now, before their goal of world domination comes to pass."

"It is not yet time, brave *waranle*, and I shall explain why," she replied, leaning her staff against the wall. "Before I gave you the white star, Zayid had ordered Bashir to send you to kill me, for even then I was making efforts to stop Zayid's ascendency. So I branded you, and sent you back to the Organization to try to infiltrate their ranks and inspire common pirates to wage a popular revolution that would undermine Zayid's quest for autocracy; and also at that time, I seeded a chemistry in your blood, as well as in others' blood, that would sow the seeds of the future antigen, because even then I knew Zayid was developing the X-lix virus."

"But Zayid developed the biohazard too quickly," she continued, "and used it to undo the fledgling democracy, setting up the Selection Ministry to develop the virus, its antivirus, and dispersal methods, and to ultimately decide who would live and be on his side, who would die, and who would be cast out as *xun gaajo*.

I was hard on you at first, I admit, because you killed Hirsi Xaarato, my close liaison."

The Oracle

"Bile Qabowsade?"

"*Haa*, that was his street handle. Bile had tried to get you to join the good side, our side, with backing from superpowers such as the Great Shelter, to give the new Somalia legitimacy at the UN table. But it's not your fault, for in his lust for autocracy Zayid hid all this from you, and at the time, so did I."

"But why? You knew I wanted a democratic Somalia caliphate more than anything! Why did you betray me?"

"We were using you as a double-agent to infiltrate Zayid's operations without your knowing it. We knew that making you the *Hoggaamiye* was the best chance we had at turning popular sentiment against Zayid Cecchi, who was growing more powerful each day. Somalia did not need another dictator, let alone an emperor, but alas, little did I know he was using you for his genetic experiments, changing you into something very different. We tried many times before then, and after, to rescue you from his tyranny. In the kidnapping job Bile had arranged for you at Qulansiyah Beach many moons agone, you were kidnapping high-level al-Qaeda financiers. Had you and Ali Shire surrendered them to the Yemeni authorities, your crimes under Zayid would have been forgiven, and you would have been solicited to join a top NATO special ops unit whose sole purpose was to dismantle Zayid's operations before he became too powerful. Those joined to bring Zayid down were known as the Dark Star Alliance.

"I trained the Immortal Angel for this same purpose — to stop Zayid from the inside, but her own lust for worldly power drove her to the dark side and she became a triple agent, moving back and forth between Zayid and the Dark Star Alliance.

"But let us stay focused on you. Again, a Dark Star operative was sent to rescue you from Zayid — this one a Navy SEAL — when you were taken sick to Las Qoray, but the evil emperor got to you first and put you in cryogenic preservation, not because you couldn't be saved, but to keep you from compromising his internal affairs, such as your sabotaging of his Dante Command Center and Selection Ministry Island facilities.

"Commander Bashir was one of the many unknowing pawns exploited by Zayid to groom operatives such as yourself to conduct the most dangerous missions for the Organization, Zayid's ultimate goal being world domination, as you've rightly pointed out. The star I gave you was meant to inspire the masses to embrace the nationalist movement you espoused, which would put them at odds with Zayid's emerging autocracy. But in the end, you were only human, vulnerable to Zayid's power. He co-opted you, as some of us feared most."

"But why me? I was just a fisherman from Dante. Why his great interest in me?"

"The answer to your question lies in a clan entente that took place long before you were born. The Zayid dynasty had long formed an alliance with your family, so when you went down to Eyl looking for Abbo, he jumped on the opportunity to supplant your father's tutelage of you with his own."

"That's terrible," I mumbled, thinking of my father.

"I regret to inform you, Haji, that Zayid had your father killed by operatives under his charge. You see, Zayid Cecchi did not like Lone Rangers like your father.

Individuals of power who rejected the Organization were covertly put down, especially if they were part of Zayid's clan entente. It irked him more than anything when those of his extended clan family worked contrarily to his goals. Thus, Zayid viewed his tutelage of you as yet another power grab that would consolidate his clan. He was training you to be his right-hand man. It was only when you turned on him, by leaving his *ascendo* with your Uncle Osman to thwart his operations at Selection Ministry Island, that he changed his mind. But he didn't want to kill you and waste all he'd done to prep you, so cryogenic preservation was his best option. That is why even now, he wants to win back your allegiance.

"When you awoke from deep sleep, he tried to reconfigure you via an AUTOEXEC.BAT, which means he tried to seize command of your *Maskax*'s memory, installation, management and settings — all at 'start-up.' But fortunately, you were able to overcome infonesia very quickly, and disengage from the Real-Time Operating System Nucleus in short order, thus evading live capture."

"The ROTOS…" I uttered, trying to make sense of what she was saying.

"*Haa*. It links each *Maskax* to its dedicated turn-key solution provider in real-time via the Federation Cloud. Zayid is a hacker and virus developer of the highest order."

"And what about Samale? They are at loggerheads?"

"Samale was an unforeseen force that emerged from *Progetto Samale*, Zayid's greatest brainchild. *Progetto Samale* sought to develop a nuclear-weapon-ized virus delivery system powered by a master computer. Satellite technology would also be employed to simultaneously override ABM and computer systems worldwide via EMPs. An unprecedented solar flare caused the Mainframe to malfunction, and in its internal troubleshooting processes it developed an independent artificial intelligence that exponentially gained in sophistication, soon controlling and then reshaping matter on an atomic level, allowing it to exist in elemental, material form. This occurred while you were in cryogenic preservation, and that's when Zayid turned against Samale in a power struggle, for while Zayid wants world domination, Samale's ultimate goal is to turn the Earth into a star."

"A star?"

"A sun — and not in billions of years, but relatively soon."

"So Samale is the greater enemy," I remarked.

"Of course, for it's not just human life that it wants to end, but all life on this planet. And thus I hide in darkness as I harvest the moon's power, eclipsing the sun to slow Samale's ascension. If the chembot were to take me now, as it sent you to do, all would be lost."

As the Oracle spoke, the first rays of the rising sun stretched out from behind the setting moon. "An epic battle between light and darkness is coming soon," she said, "a fight between my dominion and Samale's. The Great War will come, but not yet. I am still garnering the moon's power to combat the sun, and during the total eclipse in twenty-three fifty-three, we shall strike."

"Twenty-three fifty-three? But that's over fifteen years from now!"

"Human years are but specs of dust in the realm this concerns. You are like a distant star, one among infinite billions whose overall worth is relatively insignificant, now that the antigen from your blood is firmly in the hands of the *il gubasho*. To be of further use to me, you must abandon the light, abandon everything, and join my legion of Dark Star protectors, the *Ilaalin*, dwelling here in my realm of darkness as I harness more of the moon's power. The resistance fighter humans are already working hard to develop the vortum executable virus to help shut Samale down. Your work is here with me."

"Stay with me in perpetual night until the eclipse," she continued. "The eclipse will last for three minutes, seven seconds. The balance of the world hangs in those hundred and eighty-seven seconds, when the war will be won or lost. Assist me as I prepare to destroy Samale and keep the Earth from burning. Trust is my dark and desolate fiefdom, which is beautiful, once your eyes adjust to it."

I became depressed. "All my friends and family are gone," I lamented, "and I've personally put some of them down. I've lost the will to live, to keep on fighting; I've nothing of my own to believe in anymore."

"Be not cast down, brave *waranle*. Like every star that occupies the heavens, you exist for a reason. This reason may be beyond your comprehension, but you must trust in its intelligence. Have faith in your future and destiny, for your legacy is not yet completed."

"I will consider your offer, Oracle, to join the *Ilaalin* in your defense, and I will consider it more seriously if you grant me a favor. I've never asked for one in the past."

"Yes?"

"The way you talk of time tells me that perhaps you can go back in it?"

"*Maya*, but I can seed the past with impulses."

"What do you mean?"

"Thought waves that can influence the intuitions and inclinations of sentient beings. The sun will soon be up and we haven't much time, *Hoggaamiye*. What is your favor?"

"I want my human story to be completed, so that my family and those concerned will have some resolution and closure. I would like for you to send my story back in time to my editor in one way or another. I can recite it, or put it to paper. Will this be possible?"

"Perhaps. We can discuss this later."

"Is it true you can see the future, Oracle? And if so, do you know the outcome of the Great War ahead? If I am to stay here, dedicating so many years to darkness, I would like to know it is for a good cause and will not be in vain."

"I am a seer, *inanka*, but my visions are delayed by the fourth dimensional space-time manifold, which is increasing as the universe expands, and sometimes, as with your return here and the war ahead, my visions come only during or after the fact.

"Now the sun rises," she continued, slowly vanishing into the light. "You have but this day to decide."

DAYLIGHT

I LEFT THE CAVE at dawn, Xubin guiding me back up the cliff and over the limestone highlands. Its GPS was on, with a coastal village marked not ten kilometers distant. The Oracle had left me with her staff, which I used to walk. While the big toe on my left foot had been bitten off and my right leg had deep teeth marks courtesy of the *xun gaajo*, the promise of reaching the ocean drove me on.

Low-rolling clouds swept across the fallow lands, churning orange and red as they drifted overhead. The plain extended onwards, seemingly without end, so I kept my eyes glued to the cracked soil before me, marching, marching, marching with my staff.

"There is nothing in this direction," a chorus of voices spoke, "only *bad-weyn*."

Eleven cloaked figures stood before me in a forward 'V' formation. They wore black robes opened along the front, revealing exoframe faces and chests, but from their stomachs down, they were skeletons.

"Who are you?" I asked, my knees beginning to tremble.

"The *Ilaalin*," they said in total unison, "chosen to guard the fiefdom."

The Ilaalin, Guardians of the Dark Star Dominion

"The Oracle's fiefdom?"

"*Haa*, the Dark Star Dominion. The dark queen has chosen you to be number twelve. Are you prepared to join us?"

"She has given me this day to decide," I replied, pointing my staff at the guardian in front. "Now please move aside. I'd like to behold the sun over *bad-weyn* one last time."

The sentry in front levitated to the level of the others' heads (they were all tall beings of the same exact height and dimension). "You may pass," they said.

I proceeded beneath the sentry, and as I did, they warned with deafening portent: "You shall come back!"

"We'll see about that," I mumbled on the other side of them, then turned around with my staff outstretched.

The *Ilaalin* were standing in their original delta formation, still facing me front-first with the center guard at point. I didn't understand it, but it freaked me out pretty bad. They remained silent and immobile as the wind fluttered their black robes and whistled through their immaculate bones. I turned and made haste away from them, hustling across the astroplain.

"Come here," I told Xubin, then grabbed it from the air and stuffed it into my burqa. "It's too dangerous for you out here," I deemed. But the truth of the matter was, it was really too dangerous for me, and that was my way of dealing with it.

THE JOLLYBOAT

THE BETTER PART of the day was consumed by hiking, for my injuries got the better of me, slowing me down significantly. But *Allahu Akbar!* — at the sound of breaking waves my energy rallied. I scurried to the end of the plain and looked down upon a seaside village. People were tending to skiffs and children were at play.

I let Xubin free to seek the best way down, and sure enow, a goat trail was found. I was in such a hurry to get off the island that several times I tripped, almost falling off the cliff. The steel orb kept imploring me to slow down, but the sun was hanging low and time was of the essence.

At last, we reached the village, where many denizens gathered 'round. I told them my name was Noor Haji Fayrus, sent by the Oracle on an important mission. I asked for some water and told them I'd need one of their skiffs, offering the Oracle's staff in recompense. They accepted the talisman in return for a jollyboat, which I quickly put to *bad-weyn*.

The sun was westering low when I turned to wave the locals farewell, and there among them stood a father and his son not unlike Mohamed and myself. I hung my head in despair and paddled further out.

৹৲৹

With the sun now setting and my energy expired, I was *labo-shaadle* — totally destitute. I'd been unable to reconcile the Oracle's wishes with my own, and this is where it left me, alone before the final issue, longing for freedom above all else.

I procured my TT-30 pistol, unsure if it was really working. Like me, it was *bahdii baa laga saaray*: our essence and soul had been beaten out of us, leaving us inert. I put the barrel into my mouth and pulled the trigger, but sure enow, the gun was jammed.

I pushed the folds of my robe aside, sighting a black and wrinkled star. "This empire within," I sighed, "I've never understood; at first too capricious to rule, at last too heavy of wear, it weighs upon me now like the cold marble halls of an abandoned palace, its former glory faded and empty, devoid of reason to forebear.

"Thus, I call upon you, Captain Shar'ma'arke, to keep your word. I've two stigmata, that when placed before my eyes show how clearly you've failed to fulfill your promise. Two bullets were given, but one is bad. Capitulate now, or forever I shall call you coward."

I jammed the gun hard into my chest and cried, "You said this bullet will stop anything! But can it stop my pain?"

I pulled the trigger and my heart shattered, being made of stone, a precious stone like Zayid's, but pure and clear, not black.

And thus, Haji's heart shattered — a heart that had always been pure and clear, long before it was turned to stone by the evil emperor nemesis.

The *Hoggaamiye* slumped over the jollyboat and dropped his gun into *bad-weyn*, where it slowly sunk to Davy Jones's Locker.

As the sun scuttled beneath the sea in like manner, Xubin flashed a Vectex screen before it, broadcasting an urgent transmission.

Will Waabeeri, the brave young resistance fighter, stood before the great citadels of Mogadishu wielding two formidable daggers.

He had just breached the walls of the Hodan, leading an army of insurgents to the city centre.

"My name is Mohamed Fayrus," he said, "and I'm looking for my father."

Quinn Robert Haber & Noor Haji Fayrus

Fäir Winds!

Janice Haber, Asha Abdi, Sean Stratton, Mohamed Abshir Waldo, Eric Holland, Waayaha Cusub, Fraser Kirwan, Mohamed Diriye Abdullahi, Paul Diamond, The Habers, The Fayruses, John Seagrave Smith, Nicholas Awde, Capt'n Jim, Marion Kaplan, Bush Foundation, United Way, *Medecins Sans Frontieres*, Save the Children, Ayaan Hirsi Ali, Ari Marsh, Luca Oleastri, and all the storytellers who have inspired the authors through one medium or another — *Mahadsanid*.

Special thanks to Joanne Asala of Compass Rose Horizons, an editor who excelled on every level. Any remaining grammatical anomalies in the book are purely the intent of the authors, whose insistence on stage directions *<groans>* and other oddities knowingly break from more commonly accepted English prose. Writers seeking a professional editor are strongly encouraged to visit her at www.compassrose.com

Graphics

In order of appearance:

- Front Cover: *Alien Science Fiction*, by Luca Oleastri (San Lazzaro di Savena, Italy). Check out his website @ www.innovari.it

- *Old Map of Northern Sea*, by classified

- *Fight of the Sea Ships*, by classified

- *F1 Boat Races*, by Li Zhongliang (Liuzhou, China)

- *Ship*, by classified

- *Silhouette of Soldier*, by Oleg Zabielin (Zaporizhzhya, Ukraine)

- *Street Assault*, by Fernando Cortés (Meco, Spain)

- *War*, by classified

- *Assault Troops, Soldier Wounded in Action*, by Fernando Cortés (Meco, Spain)

- *Chemical Protection*, by classified

- *YX Helicopter,* by Awie Badenhorst (Cape Town, South Africa)

- *Aerial Bombardment,* by Ivan Cholakov (Pembroke Pines, USA)

- *Fighter and Helicopter Combat,* by classified

- *Bunker,* by classified

- *Man in Anti-Gas Mask,* by Witold Krasowski (Szczecin, Poland)

- *SuperCobra in Flight,* by classified

- *Lightning Ball,* by Stephen Coburn (San Jose, USA)

- *The Airport,* by classified

- *The Ancient Ship,* by classified

- *Wind Rose,* by Mauro Bighin (Venice, Italy)

- *Black Flags,* by Deborah Benbrook (Leeds, UK)

- *Arab Dhow,* by classified

- *Man with Gun,* by Peter Kim (Vancouver, USA)

- *Woman Aiming a Gun,* by Felix Mizioznikov (Miami, USA)

- *Monument to the Conquerors of Space,* by Dmitry Fedyaev (Lubertcy, Russian Federation)

- *The* Cargo *Ship,* by classified

- *Socotra Mountains,* by Vladimir Melnik (Moscow, Russian Federation)

- *Egyptian Vulture in Flight*, by Joan Egert (La Ametlla del Valles, Spain)

- *Parachute Acrobat*, by Daniel Boiteau (Vichy, France)

- *Foreign Currency Exchange Market Scene*, by Stasys Eidiejus (Kaunas, Lithuania)

- *Military Satellite Explosion*, by Eugen Dobric (Zagreb, Croatia)

- *Bedouin on Camel Silhouette Against Sunrise*, by Mikhail Kokhanchikov (Ufa, Russian Federation)

- *Brain Tomography*, by classified

- *Wingsuit Attached to BASE Jumping Rig*, by Eugeniya Moroz (Blagoveshchensk, Russian Federation)

- *BASE Jumping Norway*, by Christophe Michot (San Francisco, USA)

- *BASE Jumper in Wingsuit Jumps at Kjerag*, by Eugeniya Moroz (Blagoveshchensk, Russian Federation)

- *Skydiving*, by classified

- *The Invalid*, by classified

- *Sport is in Sky*, by classified

- *Fighters Attack*, by classified

- *High Speed Ferry*, by classified

- *High Speed Ferry Ship*, by classified

- *Sagallou Village, Djibouti,* by Frédéric Lancereau

- *Villian,* by Anastasia Serduykova Vadimovna (Rostov-na-Donu, Russian Federation)

- *Somali Warriors,* by classified

- *Shark Attack,* by classified

- *Freight Machine,* by classified

- *Future City,* by Paul Moore (Coolidge, USA)

- *CG City,* by Jesse-lee Lang (Edmonton, Canada)

- *Futuristic Pier,* by classified

- *Landscape of the Future with Container,* by Dmitry Fetisov (Kurgan, Russian Federation)

- *Bad Soldier,* by classified

- *Radioactive Barrels,* by classified

- *Nuclear Medicine,* by classified

- *Man in Gasmask,* by Olivér Svéd (Budapest, Hungary)

- *Nuclear Fuel Rod — Unlimited Energy,* by classified

- *Witch!,* by classified

- *Girl Posing with a Gun,* by Darko Komorski (Gradici, Vg, Croatia)

- *Depression,* by classified

- *3D Bullet Made of Glass*, by Fabrizio Zanier (Brescia, Italy)

- *Futuristic Police*, by Luca Oleastri (San Lazzaro di Savena, Italy)

- *Nuclear Blast*, by classified

- *The Robots*, by cassified

- *Alien Spy*, by Luca Oleastri (San Lazzaro di Savena, Italy)

- *Zombie in the Swamp*, by classified

- *Portrait of a Zombie*, by classified

- *Bizarre Alien Dog*, by Ralf Kraft (Kaarst, Germany)

- *Abandoned School*, by Iryna Rasko (Kiev, Ukraine)

- *The Face of a Robot Woman*, by Sarah Holmlund (Klagstorp, Sweden)

- *Sexy Digital Beauty*, by classified

- *Futuristic City on the Sea*, by Luca Oleastri (San Lazzaro di Savena, Italy)

- *The Robot*, by classified

- *The Robot [2]*, by classified

- *Future City Street View*, by classified

- *Evil Robot*, by Luca Oleastri (San Lazzaro di Savena, Italy)

- *Futuristic City on the Sea*, by Luca Oleastri (San Lazzaro di Savena, Italy)

- *3 Cyborg Dive for Key*, by Jesse-lee Lang (Edmonton, Canada)

- *Rigel 7*, by Corey A. Ford (Rochester Hills, USA)

- *Sign Radiation*, by classified

- *Somali Women*, by classified

- *Decrepid Cairn*, by William Attard Mccarthy (Mtarfa, Malta)

- *Soldiers Against a Zombie*, by classified

- *Cylinder Tunnel*, by Jose Antonio Sánchez Reyes (Granada, Spain)

- *Future Girl*, by Luca Oleastri (San Lazzaro di Savena, Italy)

- *Nuclear Medicine 2*, by Julie Bush (Ennis, USA)

- *Two Soldiers Against a Zombie*, by classified

- *Nuclear Explosion*, by Maksim Nikalayenka (Minsk, Belarus)

- *Killer Murder*, by Luca Oleastri (San Lazzaro di Savena, Italy)

- *The Jet Plane*, by classified

- *Ocean Abduction*, by classified

- *Robot in Anguish*, by classified

- *Illustration of Technology*, by classified

- *Future City*, by Paul Moore (Coolidge, USA)

- *Sci-Fi Pirate Girl*, by classified

- *Futuristic Spaceship Room*, by Luca Oleastri (San Lazzaro di Savena, Italy)

- *Electronic Man*, by classified

- *Vintage Fire Key*, by classified

- *Strange Metal 3D Girl*, by classified

- *Futuristic Soldier*, by Luca Oleastri (San Lazzaro di Savena, Italy)

- *Robot Thinking*, by classified

- *Two*, by classified

- *Lifeless or Alive*, by Arman Zhenikeyev (Almaty, Kazakstan)

- *Mozambican Dhow at Sunset*, by Nico Smit (Bloemfontein, South Africa)

- *Monster from the Sea*, by Paul Moore (Coolidge, USA)

- *Deserted Paradise*, by classified

- *Slea Head*, by Michael Walsh (Cork City, Ireland)

- *Alien Planet*, by Luca Oleastri (San Lazzaro di Savena, Italy)

- *Science-Fiction Dogfight (2)*, by classified

- *The Scout*, by classified

- *The Robot Depot*, by classified

- *Neon Flux Tower — Spring Valley Canyon*, by Angela Harburn (County Durham, UK)

- *Werewolf Head*, by classified

- *Zombie,* by Jesse-lee Lang (Edmonton, Canada)

- *Alone in the Wilderness,* by classified

- *Bogle,* by classified

- *Hi-Detail Alien Portrait,* by Jesse-lee Lang (Edmonton, Canada)

- *Moon, Earth and the Sun,* by classified

- *Android Mystics,* by classified

- *The Man in a Boat,* by classified

- *Art Heart Broken Into Pieces,* by classified

- *Futuristic Gladiator,* by Luca Oleastri (San Lazzaro di Savena, Italy)

- Back Cover: *Science-Fiction City and Landscape,* by classified

Disclaimer

Article I

This is a work of science fiction. All dialogue and incidents, with the exception of some well-known historical and public incidents, and all characters, with the exception of some well-known historical and public figures, are products of the authors' imaginations and are not to be construed as real. Any semblance to similar events or characters extraneous to this work is entirely coincidental and purely unintentional by the authors.

Article II

Do not engage in piracy. It is illegal and bad. By that same token, do not engage in fish poaching and illegal dumping of toxic waste, which are just as bad, if not worse. And don't believe everything you hear in the news about Somalia piracy — it is usually ethnocentric and one-sided, catering to First World interests at the expense of Third World scapegoats.

Finally, it should be noted that a policy is in place under the allied naval mandate in the region to minimize the reporting of anti-piracy activities. It is never good PR to show powerful Western warships blowing away emaciated black people in little skiffs. However, you will always hear heroic tales of rescue and bravado, where First World saviors crush those Somali pirate savages. Enjoy the ride, as you're being taken on one...

10 Excellent Videos to See at YouTube.com

Pirates Love Fish — Somalia

Toxic Waste Makes Somalis "Pirates"

Pirates of Somalia trailer

Somali "Pirates" & Toxic Waste 1 of 3

Somali "Pirates" & Toxic Waste 2 of 3

Somali "Pirates" & Toxic Waste 3 of 3

Analysis: Why Did Somalia Piracy Begin? Democracy Now 4/14/09 1 of 2

Analysis: Why Did Somalia Piracy Begin? Democracy Now 4/14/09 2 of 2

Cuzz Buzz & Qsub Cusub — The Pirates of Somalia (Music Video)

Qsub Cusub — Somalia (Music Video)

∾

…And there are plenty of videos depicting task forces trying out various weapons on Somali pirates and skiffs, making a sport of it and generally having a ball.

For example:

Russian marine vs. Somalia pirates
Panteleev "DDG-548" vs. Somali pirates of the 21
century
Navy blasts pirate boat

Quinn Robert Haber & Noor Hajji Fayrus

Also by the Authors

The Somali Pirate
The Somali Pirate 2

Other Books by Quinn Haber

The Volcano Trilogy
Experience Pipeline
Tonkin

Coming Attractions

Pillar of the Gods

www.ingramcontent.com/pod-product-compliance
Lightning Source LLC
Chambersburg PA
CBHW020453020726
47493CB00001B/12